holiday HIRE

A BILLIONAIRE SINGLE DAD NANNY ROMANCE

MAGGIE COLE

PULSE PRESS INC

This one's dedicated to my dad, who would be so proud that I wrote book #50.

RIP, Daddy.

I wish we could have one more hobo dinner on the lake, bonfire with you singing songs at the top of your lungs, and to hear you say "Pink stinks" while making your funny face.
Love you always.

XOXO, Maggie

Alexander Cartwright

"Wilder! Ace! Go get cleaned up!" I shout across the ranch, wiping the beads of sweat off my forehead.

It's abnormally hot for the start of November. My sons have been riding horses all morning while my three brothers, Sebastian, Mason, and Jagger, break in six new racehorses we purchased.

Wilder and Ace run their horses harder away from the barn.

Sebastian chuckles. "Doesn't look like they heard you, Alexander."

"Like hell they didn't," I mutter, then put my fingers to my lips and whistle.

Ace, my youngest son, shoots me a mischievous smirk, then refocuses on Wilder and kicks his horse to catch up.

I cross my arms over my chest. "I swear Wilder is teaching him bad habits."

"No different from when we were boys," Sebastian claims.

I ignore his comment, whistle again, then shout, "Don't make me get on a horse to come get you two!"

My other brothers step next to Sebastian and me. They all find humor in my sons not listening to my orders, but I'm not amused.

I snap, "You're happy your nephews are turning into disrespectful boys?"

Mason grunts. "That's a bit harsh, don't you think?"

"Yeah, they just want to keep riding. We were the same when we were kids," Jagger insists.

"We didn't ignore Dad when he called us in," I state.

"Your memory is fading," Dad bellows.

I turn my head. "Did Mom keep you in town all morning?"

"No. We've been back for a bit."

"You've been sitting inside?"

"Yep." A look passes over his expression. I can't tell what it is, and he whistles before I can question him. It's as shrill as mine.

My boys circle a tree and race toward us.

"Little shits," I mutter.

Sebastian chuckles again and pats me on the back.

It irritates me even more. My boys are good kids and have always listened to me. Yet Wilder's been pushing boundaries lately, and Ace is too happy to try anything his older brother does.

A cloud of dust trails them, and they stop several feet in front of us and then jump off their horses.

Mason opens the gate, and the horses trot past the fence.

"You need to lean into those turns," Dad instructs Ace.

"I told him," Wilder interjects.

I warn, "The next time you two want to ignore me, you'll skip lunch and spend the rest of the day doing chores. Understand?"

Wilder and Ace don't say anything.

"Well?" I push.

Dad interjects, "Boys, answer your father."

"We were finishing our ride," Wilder states.

"Yeah," Ace follows.

I point at them. "Don't push me right now."

My sons sigh and reply, "Yes, sir."

Before I can say anything else, Dad steps between them. "Let's go wash up." He turns them toward the house and guides them away.

"Unbelievable," I grumble.

"Chill out. They're just being kids. We were like that," Jagger reminds me.

"We wouldn't have ignored Dad," I repeat.

He grunts. "Sure we did. Stop insisting we didn't. We were hellions."

"You're wrong," I insist, stomping toward the house. The last thing I'm going to put up with are my sons turning into little disrespectful brats.

"Georgia! I did it!" Ace shrieks, breaking away from my father and running toward the porch.

All day, the women in my family have been taking down Halloween decorations and putting up Thanksgiving ones. Orange and gold lights wrap around the posts and hang from the awnings along with pumpkins and turkeys. A huge autumn wreath with burlap, acorns, pine cones, reddish-orange berries, and multicolored fall leaves hangs on the front door.

"Yay!" Georgia praises Ace, then ruffles his hair.

I can't help but smile. Our family fell in love with Sebastian's wife, and my sons weren't immune to her beaming personality.

She shouts, "Hurry up, guys. Lunch is ready."

"We're coming," Sebastian yells back.

Ace and Wilder disappear inside with Georgia, and the rest of us follow. We remove our boots, then take turns washing our hands in the kitchen.

I'm the last to enter the huge dining room.

Years ago, my parents had a custom-made table so the entire family could fit around it. It has several extra leaves, so it expands. My parents were smart and anticipated needing room for future spouses and grandkids. But even now, there are times we have to pull out kiddie tables. Today, we don't need one, since only my sister Evelyn and her three kids are here. Her husband and my other sisters, Ava, Willow, and Paisley, aren't home.

Before I step inside the room, an animated voice declares, "This looks amazing, Mrs. Cartwright!"

"Please, dear. I told you to call me Ruby," my mom insists.

I freeze outside the doorway, peek inside, then groan internally. My mother has an annoying habit of bringing home women and trying to set me up with them. She did the same thing with Sebastian, then once he married Georgia, she pinned her unwelcome matchmaking skills on me.

I've told her countless times to stop and to not bring them around my boys. The last time it happened, she claimed any woman I would get serious about needed to be great with my sons.

It only infuriated me. We got into a heated conversation, which rarely happens. I reiterated that the last thing I want is to replace the boys' mother.

She reminded me that my wife passed away eight years ago and that I didn't need to be alone forever.

Every statement cut deeper into my still-raw wounds. So I fired back harsher than ever.

That was about eight months ago. I thought she learned her lesson, but she's at it again.

The stranger with long, magenta hair, a diamond stud nose ring, and tattoos peeking out above her pink tube top says, "Sorry, Ruby. So I assume this is Ace and Wilder?"

Oh no you don't.

I take three long strides and step in front of my chair. I glare at my mother, stating, "We're not doing this."

5

Mom smiles at me. "Sit down, Alexander. We have some things to discuss."

"Like hell we do."

Dad orders, "Sit down, son."

I ignore him and pin my gaze on the stranger. She's wearing enough jewelry to stock a store. She rises, and I can faintly make out hearts and the letters D and A before her tattoo disappears.

I wonder, *does she already regret inking some dude's name on her chest?*

What's his name? David? Daryl? Dannie boy?

Doesn't matter, I tell myself.

My gaze drifts to her perky tits, the tanned inch of her skin between the top of her skinny jeans, and on to the rip on her thigh, exposing another tattoo I can't make out.

Where does that lead?

I raise my gaze back to hers, finding she hasn't flinched under my staredown.

Mom really got it wrong this time. This woman is definitely not my type.

She pins blue fuck-me eyes to my sneer, and smiles. "It's nice to meet you. I'm Phoebe."

Great. She thinks she has a chance.

"I'm sorry my mother wasted your time. She's delusional some-times. I think it's best if you go now," I state.

"Alexander!" Evelyn, my bossy older sister, scolds.

"Stay out of this," I say to her in warning.

"Jacob," Mom says, imploring Dad to intervene.

Dad's stern voice cuts through the air. "Alexander, sit down!"

I take a deep breath, my insides shaking with anger. I'm tired of my family interfering in my life. Nothing says I need a wife to raise my children. They're surrounded by grandparents, aunts and uncles, and their cousins. I assume there are only a few moments in their lives when they don't feel love.

Dad repeats, "Sit. We have things to discuss."

I cave and take my seat, then refocus on Phoebe. "Appreciate your time, but my mother once again overstepped. I'm not trying to be rude to you. I'm sure you're a lovely girl, but it really is best if you leave."

Her eyes widen. She glances at Mom and says, "Maybe this isn't a good fit?"

"Nonsense." Mom pats her hand. She pins her glare on me. "Alexander, I just hired Phoebe to be the boys' nanny."

I jerk my head back. "Nanny? They don't need a nanny."

"Just for two months while your father and I are gone."

Wilder asks, "Where are you going? Can I come with you?"

"I want to come too!" Ace exclaims.

Dad answers, "Sorry, not this time, boys. Your grandmother and I are taking a mission trip to South America for a few months."

"Mission trip? What's that?" Ace asks.

"It's where you help people who are less fortunate than you," Mom responds.

"You're going over the holidays?" Georgia asks with surprise and disappointment in her voice.

7

Mom smiles. "We're flying home for part of Thanksgiving week and also December 23rd through January 2nd."

"But you'll miss a lot of the fun stuff," Wilder says.

"Agreed. Why would you go over the holidays?" Sebastian asks.

Mom's eyes brighten. "They needed more help. Not many people want to go at this time of year, and your father and I have always wanted to help. Now that he's retired—"

"Semiretired," Dad interjects, as he still doesn't like the thought of being retired.

"They don't want to go because it's the best time of year!" Isabella, Evelyn's oldest daughter, chimes in.

Mom slides her arm around Isabella and tugs her closer. She replies, "Yes, but we'll be here for the main events."

I rise and focus on Phoebe. "Sorry, I misunderstood why you're here."

She asks, "Why did you think I was here?"

Evelyn answers before I can speak. "He thought our mom was trying to hook you up."

A flush crawls up Phoebe's cheeks.

To my surprise, my dick hardens. It makes no sense. This barely-out-of-college woman isn't my type.

Get her out of here.

I ignore my cock, hoping no one can see it, and explain, "I'm sorry my mom wasted your time. We don't need a nanny."

"You do," Mom insists.

"No, we don't," I hurl back.

"Alexander, sit down. You're making a fool of yourself and being rude to our guest," Dad scolds.

"We don't need a nanny," I reiterate.

"Sit down," he orders, pointing to my chair.

I release a frustrated breath and plop down, objecting, "I can manage the boys alone."

"Really? Who's going to help when you're working?" Mom asks.

I point out, "They spend all their free time outside where we can see them."

"Who's going to help with their homework?"

"I can."

Mom snorts. "You're working past dark almost every night."

Guilt hits me. I haven't been the best at helping the boys with homework. I hated school when I was their age. And my sons take after me. They'd rather be out in the pasture riding horses or playing Cops and Robbers. So they whine as much as I did. It frustrates me. But my mom is great with homework, so I've been happy to let her take on those duties.

I insist, "I'll do it."

Evelyn snickers. "Sure you will."

"Stay out of it," I snap.

She adds, "They have to do their homework. Plus, you're horrible when it comes to school stuff."

"I said to keep your nose where it belongs."

"She's right. The boys' schoolwork can't suffer," Dad declares.

9

"I'm good not doing homework while you're gone. No offense, Phoebe," Wilder states, then gives her his dazzling smile.

"Not funny," I warn.

"I don't need to do homework either," Ace proclaims.

Phoebe laughs and replies, "You're both doing your homework. But don't worry. We'll make it fun."

"Homework is never fun," Wilder mutters.

"It will be with me," Phoebe claims.

I clench my jaw, breathing through my nose, my heart racing faster. I assess Phoebe again, wondering how my mother could be so off base with her judgment. This woman is wild; I can tell. Surely, she won't be a good influence on my boys. They'll run right over her.

"She's very qualified," Mom says, as if she can read my mind.

"How?" I question, truly curious how this stranger could handle my sons, who are starting to push the boundaries any chance they get.

Phoebe's voice is confident when she smiles and states, "I've taught art for the last three years."

"Three years! And art! That's a lifetime of lessons there," I sarcastically declare.

"Alexander!" Mom reprimands.

"What? It's a fair assessment."

Phoebe straightens her back, narrowing her eyes on me, divulging, "Not really. I started babysitting when I was twelve. I nannied through college for a family with five children, and the parents were absent."

"I'm not an absent father," I snap.

She tilts her head. "I didn't claim you were."

I stare at her, and tension builds around the table, but mostly between the two of us.

Sebastian clears his throat. "Why don't you give her a chance?"

I jerk my head toward him. "Since when do you stick your nose in my business?"

He holds his hands up. "Mom and Dad interviewed her, so she must be overqualified."

Surprise hits me. I turn toward Dad. "You interviewed her?"

"Of course."

I ask Sebastian, "How did you know? You were outside with us."

Guilt fills his expression.

I glance around the table. More anger fills me. I realize I'm the only one who was kept in the dark besides the kids. "You all knew?"

Evelyn answers, "We didn't realize they were leaving over the holidays. Mom told us it was supposed to be in February."

Mom interrupts. "Your father and I didn't know how desperate they were for extra help. We couldn't turn them down."

Evelyn continues, "We assumed you'd try to claim you can handle everything on your own."

"I can. They're my children, after all," I remind her.

Georgia puts her hand on mine. She softly says, "Hey."

I glance at her.

She smiles, and I calm a tad. It's hard to be mad at her. Maybe it's because she's not blood but has always treated my kids like her own since the moment she met them. So while she's just as much a part of us now, she has a different perspective on things without the years of history of annoying me at times like the rest of my family.

She suggests, "Why don't you just have Phoebe nanny this next week and then you can decide if you need her?"

I take a deep breath, happy Georgia's on my side. It's not what I want, but she just gave me the green light to teach my family that I'm more than capable of handling everything on my own. I'll agree, then Phoebe can pack up and be on her way once everyone sees the boys and I don't need her.

I reluctantly turn toward Phoebe. "Fine. You can stay for the week. On Friday, we'll reassess."

"I need to go home and get my things first. My lease is up in three days," she claims.

"Where's home?"

"California."

Of course she's from California. That explains the piercings, tattoos, magenta hair, and tan.

I wonder what other tattoos she has hiding under those jeans.

What am I saying?

I scoff. "Let me guess. L.A.? Or is it San Francisco?"

She shakes her head. "Pismo Beach."

"You should take us to the beach!" Ace exclaims.

Phoebe smiles at him. "I saw you have a lake on your property."

"We do!"

"Why don't we have a beach party after you've earned your stars this week?"

He wrinkles his forehead. "Stars?"

She nods. "Yeah. You can earn all kinds of cool stuff with my stars."

"Like what?" Wilder asks.

"I want stars!" Isabella pipes up.

Phoebe laughs. "You can earn them too."

"It's going to be cold soon," I state.

Phoebe shrugs, then turns her gaze back to the kids. "So? We can still have a beach party, right?"

"Yeah!" Wilder pumps his arm in the air, and the other kids follow, chanting, "Beach party!"

My siblings and parents seem to find it funny, but it irritates me. The last thing I need is this woman putting ideas into my kids' heads when she won't be here to follow through. So I mutter, "Better do it this week, then."

The room goes quiet, and she says, "I can be back by Tuesday if that works?"

"It does," Dad answers.

Phoebe's lips twist. She arches her eyebrows as she asks me, "And for you? Tuesday through Monday will give you enough time to make your assessment?"

I wonder why she finds this funny. Come next week, she'll be hightailing it back to California, homeless. But I answer, "Yep."

"Great. Can we eat now? I'm hungry," Jagger states.

Trays full of lunch meat, cheese, and bread are passed around the table. Bowls with potato salad, Caesar salad, and fruit follow.

"Did you make all this, Georgia?" Phoebe asks.

"Evelyn and the girls helped. Didn't you?" she asks Emma, Evelyn's middle child, who seems attached to Georgia's hip lately.

"I washed the lettuce and broke it apart!" Emma exclaims, beaming.

"You did a great job too," Georgia says, and they fist-bump.

"Mmm, this lettuce is amazing," Phoebe declares, taking a huge bite and grinning at Emma.

Emma eats up her praise, and I internally groan.

Maybe this idea of Georgia's isn't so good after all. These kids are going to get attached to Phoebe and then I'll be the bad guy.

The conversation continues, but I barely hear it. I hardly taste my food either. Everyone around the table is eating and praising Phoebe like she's the most amazing person to ever stay at our home. It only convinces me further that this is going to be a disaster. Of all the things my mother has done, this is going to top the cake. Phoebe won't be needed, and these kids will be heartbroken once she leaves.

Better in a week than two months.

Two months.

What the heck were my parents thinking? My kids don't need to get attached to any woman who isn't family.

Warm apple pie crumble topped with vanilla ice cream gets passed around the table. It's another dessert hit by Georgia. She has a thriving cupcake business, but she can make anything. She even figured out how to make low-sugar stuff taste good for my brother, who's terrified of getting diabetes. Today is no different. She made the same dish but with reduced sugar for him.

"Who will do holiday stuff with us while you're gone?" Isabella asks my mom.

Mom points around the table. "Everyone here, plus your other aunties and Phoebe."

"Phoebe's only here for a week," I remind everyone.

"Alexander, you will give Phoebe a fair chance," Dad commands.

I grind my molars. I love my family, but this is one of those situations where I wished they'd stay out of my business.

This is what I get for still living on the ranch.

Maybe I should move out?

What am I saying? This is our home, and my sons would be devastated.

Phoebe pipes up. "It's okay. I'll prove to Alexander that I can add value while you're gone." She grins at me.

I stare back at her, my mouth turning dry. I'm not sure who this woman thinks she is, but if she thinks she can win me over, she's got another thing coming.

2

Phoebe Love

"*T*hank you again. I can't wait to start," I tell Ruby.

She hugs me and says, "We're excited to have you on the ranch."

"Beach party!" Isabella shrieks, and the other kids start to chant again. I laugh. They've done it several times throughout the night.

Alexander shakes his head, just as annoyed as the other times.

His parents warned me he would resist the idea of a nanny, and they weren't joking. At this point, I can't tell if it's the nanny issue or if he just doesn't like me.

"See you soon, kid," Jacob states, giving me a fatherly hug and then pulling away. He turns toward Alexander. "What are you waiting for, son? Get Phoebe off to the airport before you mess up the flight schedule. We don't need another fine."

Alexander wrinkles his forehead, narrowing his blue eyes until they darken. "What are you talking about? I'm not going to the airport."

"Of course you are. And remember your manners. Now, move," Jacob commands in a no-nonsense tone.

Alexander clenches his jaw, glares daggers at Jacob, then slowly releases a breath. The sun-kissed wrinkles around his eyes fade, and he puts on his cowboy hat, then yanks open the front door. He forces a smile, leers at me, and gripes, "Guess I'm taking you to the airport. Ready?"

Butterflies flutter in my stomach and heat crawls up my cheeks, and I scold myself for feeling like a schoolgirl caught staring at her crush. It makes zero sense. He's rude, doesn't want me near his family, and has made it clear he's on a mission to get me fired before I even begin. Yet my body reacts the same way every time Alexander Cartwright's disdainful, angry, frustrated gaze locks on mine. It's almost as if I'm a glutton for his disapproval.

"I want to come!" Ace interjects.

"No, you're on barn duty for the rest of the afternoon," Jacob announces.

Wilder snickers. "Have fun with that."

Amusement fills Jacob's expression. He declares, "Not sure why you think you're not on it with him."

"What? Why?" Wilder whines.

Jacob wags his finger between the boys. "You didn't think you'd get away with not riding your horses in when your father called you earlier? Or did you?"

Ace's face falls. He gripes, "We came back."

"Yeah. You whistled and we came back."

"Don't act like you didn't hear your father, or barn duty will be for the rest of the weekend," Jacob warns.

The boys glance at each other, then both sigh.

"Go," Jacob says, pointing.

Wilder grumbles, "Come on, Ace. Bye, Phoebe."

"Yeah, bye," Ace follows.

"See you," I reply, fist-bumping them and biting on my smile as they pass me and scoot through the door.

"Time to go," Alexander orders and motions for me to exit.

We walk quietly to his truck. He opens the passenger door for me, and it takes me by surprise.

He grunts. "Let me guess. You're one of those females who thinks it's insulting for a man to open a woman's door?"

I grab the bar, hoist my bottom onto the seat, and shake my head. "No. Why would you assume that?"

"You just froze and pinned your eyebrows together."

"So?"

"So you looked upset."

"No, just surprised. Is that a sin?" I question.

He pauses, then nods. "Ah. I get it. You only hang out with those California boys who don't know how to be a gentleman."

"Ummm..." I close my mouth, thinking about his statement.

Alexander shakes his head. "Pinned that one correctly."

"No, you didn't." *But is he right?*

"Really?" he challenges, shooting his disapproval deeper into me.

I have the same reaction as before, and I curse myself.

Why does he make me feel so flustered? He's an asshole.

And who cares if my boyfriend Lance and other men I'm around don't hold my door open?

Well, it's kind of nice.

Why do I even care? I can open my own door.

He tears his gaze off mine and shuts the door. Within seconds, he's inside the truck next to me. His scent of musk, sweat, and the outdoors fills the cab, and it's like an aphrodisiac. I inhale it deeply, my heart racing faster.

He starts the truck and maneuvers us down the ranch's long driveway, pulling through the magnificent wrought iron gates.

"Your ranch is really beautiful," I tell him.

He glances across the cab, dryly replying, "Thanks. It's been in my family for several generations. I assume you've never lived on a ranch before?"

My defenses rise. "No, but that doesn't mean I don't love the outdoors or animals."

He tightens his lips. "Sure." He refocuses on the road.

What a smug asshole.

I lower my gaze and freeze, my pulse quickening.

Alexander's jeans stretch taut over his thighs. The bulge between them is just as enticing.

The truck bounces, and he mutters, "Sorry. This dirt road's a bit rough right now."

I tear my eyes off his lower body and stare out the window. "No worries."

The cab goes quiet for several minutes. The unusually sunny day intensifies, warming the inside of the truck. Alexander's intoxicating scent grows stronger until my head spins and my heart pounds so hard I wonder if he can hear it.

What is wrong with me?

I have a boyfriend.

Not for long.

What am I saying? Lance and I only need some space. Then we'll be good again.

He's going to flip when he finds out I'm moving to Texas for two months.

Guilt eats at me. I didn't tell Lance I was coming here for a job interview. He thinks I'm here visiting a friend from college.

Then my guilt turns to anger.

Lance never asked my friend's name, where I knew her from, or anything about my trip. He barely listened when I said I'd be gone for two days.

In some ways, it didn't surprise me. He hasn't been super attentive since the first year we started dating, and even less this past year. If it doesn't have to do with his friends, career, or tennis matches at the country club, he's not interested.

My friends don't care for him either. They stayed quiet at first, keeping their opinions to themselves, but lately they've been voicing their disdain. He's never been overly friendly, so they stopped trying. It's a constant conversation of them telling me I can do better and me trying to convince them they don't know him.

The same debate erupts in my head.

When Lance and I are alone, it's different.

Well, it used to be. For the last year, everything has felt different.

I guess I shouldn't have been surprised when Lance didn't ask many questions about my trip. Maybe part of me was relieved. I didn't have to create a lie since my friend Alicia moved to Texas, and I did get to see her last night. All I did was leave out some details.

Now that the Cartwrights hired me, I'm going to have to fess up. I'm unsure how Lance will react when I tell him, but I believe with my whole being that we need some space. He'll miss me, realize all I do for him, and things can return to how they were when we first got together.

Or he won't miss me at all, and that will give me the courage to break up with him.

My heart sinks at that thought. We've been together since we met at my college graduation four years ago. His brother was in my class. We'd never met, but I literally ran into Lance coming out of the auditorium. He didn't waste any time getting my number, and the next night, we went out. The last four years have good and bad memories, but I remind myself that every relationship has both. And I hate thinking about not making any more good ones with him.

"You know my boys are going to push every boundary they can, right?" Alexander warns, pulling me out of my thoughts.

And we're back to a job interview.

I take a deep inhale of his scent, smile, and turn toward him. "Of course. As I stated, I know kids very well."

He snorts. "Doesn't mean you know my two boys."

"I didn't claim to," I chirp, turn, and put my knee on the seat.

His eyes drift down. He stares at my leg a moment, then stabs me with disdain. "Didn't you?"

I ignore the blood rushing through my veins, growing hotter with every second he continues to challenge me. "Yes, I know children. Wilder and Ace both have their own personalities, and of course I don't know them yet. However, I know how kids try to push the limits, especially boys their age."

He grinds his molars, focusing on the road.

Even though I don't feel overly confident he won't fire me after the trial period, I fake it, adding, "When I return, you'll see that I'm more than capable of taking care of your boys."

"I don't need anyone to take care of them."

"Your family seems to think you need some help," I retort.

"I don't. You'll see."

"Okay. Why don't we make a bet, then?"

Alexander's head snaps toward me. "So you're a gambler?"

"No!"

"You just said you want to make a bet."

My cheeks heat, and I stutter, "Uh...y-yeah. It's a phrase."

"A phrase gamblers use."

"I'm not a gambler," I insist.

He drills his gaze so hard into me that I try not to shrink back in the seat. But I also have to squeeze my thighs together.

Jesus. What is up with me? This guy is a complete jerk.

He hurls out, "I don't want my boys learning about gambling."

I put my hands over my face, groaning. I sigh, then lower my hands and force myself to look at him, insisting, "I can assure you I won't be teaching them to gamble. Because I. Don't. Gamble."

His expression hardens and he grips the wheel tighter. His shoulders tense, and the fabric of his T-shirt stretches across his biceps. He claims, "Irresponsible gambling ruins people's lives."

I stare at him.

He continues, "I'm raising my boys to be good human beings and future responsible adults."

Is this guy for real?

What a hypocrite.

Unable to stop myself, I point out, "Don't you train racehorses?"

He flinches, but it's so fast, I wonder if I actually saw it. He replies, "Yes. But that doesn't mean I agree with irresponsible gambling."

"What exactly is responsible gambling?" I tilt my head, narrowing my gaze.

His knuckles turn white. He answers, "Having limits. Knowing when to quit and walk away. Not being an addict."

I smirk. "But you train horses for both responsible and irresponsible gamblers to bet on?"

The color fades in his face. He snarls, "If you have a problem with how my family makes our money, you don't need to return."

I hold my hands in the air. "Whoa! I don't have any issues with it. I'm simply responding to your attack."

He scrunches his face. "My attack?"

"Your assumption that I'm going to teach your kids how to gamble; something I've never done, by the way," I admit.

"You've never gambled?" he asks.

I cross my arms over my chest. "No. I'm a teacher, remember?"

"So?"

I roll my eyes. "We don't exactly make a lot of money. It would be crazy for me to risk losing anything I earn."

He stays silent for about a mile, then questions, "So what bet did you want to make?"

Seriously?

"Go on. Tell me."

I debate whether to tell him I forgot or to answer him.

"Well, don't leave me hanging," he urges.

I finally reveal, "Fine. If at the end of my trial period, you realize you're wrong and need a nanny, then you owe me a favor."

"A favor?"

"Yep."

"What kind of favor?"

I shrug. "I don't know, just something in the future if I need it."

Mistrust fills his expression again.

"Fine. If you're scared of what I might ask you to do, then we don't have to bet," I mutter, then roll my eyes and turn away.

He blurts out, "What do I get when I'm right?"

I think for a moment, then reply, "Same thing. A favor."

He scoffs. "But you won't be here to make good on that favor."

Anger hits me. His assumption I won't make it through the trial period is insulting. "Just forget I said anything."

He veers to the right and pulls into the private airport. He parks close to the jet's staircase and gets out.

By the time he gets to my door, I've already jumped out of the cab, unsure why I'm agreeing to return here.

Because I need a job.

Because Lance and I need a break.

Because I'm running out of money.

"See you in a few days," I say, stepping toward the plane.

He moves in front of me. "Wait."

I freeze, hating the heat rising in my cheeks, and slowly glance up.

He towers over me. A gust of wind blows by us, and his scent flares around me, accelerating my flutters. His cowboy hat creates a dark shadow on his face, but I swear he's looking at the tattoo peeking out of my tank top.

Maybe he's a pervert and staring at my chest.

He declares, "Bet's on."

I put my hand on my hip. "I thought you were worried about collecting your win."

His lips twist. "Nah. I only take bets I can win, but I'll figure it out."

I sarcastically laugh. "So you train racehorses and gamble but you're worried about me influencing your boys?"

A hint of amusement fills his expression. He nods, agreeing, "Yep. Like I said, I understand responsible gambling. And apparently, you do not."

I huff, then straighten my shoulders. I hold my hand out. "Okay, Alexander. You're on."

His large, tanned hand reaches toward me. His fingers wrap around mine.

Electricity runs down my back. I take a shaky breath, surprised by the intensity.

The darkness in his gaze deepens. He locks eyes with me until I feel like I'll melt into a puddle at his feet. His gruff voice declares, "Looking forward to my win."

Everything about his statement and what it does to me, confuses me. It deepens an ache I haven't felt since I first started dating Lance. It gives a new spark to the anger burning within me. And it makes me more determined than ever to pass his test and win this bet.

I force myself to reply, "Likewise," then step around him and make my way up the steps to the jet.

Don't turn around.

He's looking at me.

Don't give him the satisfaction.

I get safely inside the Cartwright's jet, barely hearing the attendant greet me, and sit in the luxurious, soft leather seat, peeking out the window.

Alexander wastes no time, jumping in his truck and taking off.

"Champagne? Something else?" the attendant asks.

I shake my head. "No, I'm okay. Thank you."

She disappears, and I'm in the air before I know it. My thoughts regarding Alexander, whether I should even return to the ranch, and my situation with Lance, are all over the place.

The pilot announces we're ten minutes from landing, tearing me out of my musings. I stare out the window until we land and then I exit the plane.

I walk across the runway, into the small building, and out the front door, expecting to see Lance and his car.

The road is empty. I pull my phone out of my purse, turn it on, and call him.

After two rings, his voicemail picks up.

I hang up and text him.

> Me: Hey, I landed. Are you close by?

Several minutes pass.

I try to call again, but his voicemail comes on after three rings.

I hang up and return to text.

> Me: Are you still picking me up?

I wait five minutes, call again, and get tossed into voicemail. Rage and hurt fill me.

I finally give up and order an Uber. I text him again.

> Me: Can you at least confirm you're okay?

The car arrives, I get inside, and my phone dings.

> Lance: Sorry. I forgot you were coming back tonight. It's best if you order a ride.

My insides shake. The journey back to my apartment is a blur as my emotions continue to spiral.

When I enter my place, I'm determined to be done with Lance. I open the closet door, pull out all the cardboard I stored over the last few weeks, and find my tape gun. I put the boxes together and spend hours packing my apartment.

I finish around three in the morning. Only my toiletries, several outfits to get me by over the next few days, and my bedding aren't boxed up. I text Lance.

> Me: I took a temporary job in Texas. I'll be back in a few months. I think it's best if we take a break while I'm gone.

My phone rings. Lance's name and face pop up on the screen. I angrily answer, "Now you're going to call me?"

Voices and music blare in the background. I can barely hear him slur, "What do you mean you're going to Texas?"

"Just what I wrote. And thanks for picking me up," I hurl out, crawling under my covers, angry he chose to party instead of picking me up at the airport. I've been gone several days. It's clear he didn't miss me. Plus, we agreed before I left he would pick me up.

"I told you I forgot. It's not a big deal," he whines, right as a girl's voice cuts through the line saying, "Lance, your turn. Spin it."

My heart pounds harder. I demand, "Spin what?"

He ignores my question, then states, "I have to go. We'll discuss this later, but don't be dramatic, Phoebe. Your place is here, with me, not Texas."

I scoff. "Here with you? You can't even pick me up at the airport!"

He groans. "Jesus, woman. The drama needs to end. It's not a big deal. Besides, you're the one who wanted to run off to Texas and leave me all weekend. What did you want me to do? Sit at home by myself, missing you? That's not fair, now is it?"

So he did miss me?

Not much if he didn't show up.

Am I really not being fair to him?

He adds, "You don't know what it was like all weekend with you gone."

A feeling of pissed-off guilt floods me. Lance always has a way of initiating mixed emotions within me, and tonight is no different.

Before I can say another word, he adds, "I'll make it up to you that I wasn't at the airport. Go to sleep, and I'll see you tomorrow." He hangs up before I can reply.

Upset, I attempt to call him back, but he sends me to voicemail, which only enrages me further. I scream into my pillow, feeling a bit crazy, and toss my phone on the nightstand.

It's never been clearer that Lance and I need a break. Texas seems like a better idea with every minute that drags by. Any debate I had about dealing with Alexander and the headaches he's sure to create, disappears.

3

Alexander

Three Days Later

$\mathcal{M}$om shouts, "Alexander, it's time to pick up Phoebe!"

Anger resurfaces, and I groan. I point to Calypso, the horse I've been training the last few weeks, and order Jagger, "Run him again."

"Have fun on your excursion," he mocks.

"Have your fun while you can, little brother. Mom's going to focus on you next."

He grunts. "No way."

"She will. Your day is coming," I caution, knowing that my single brothers will be on the chopping block next. If my mother had her way, each of her eight children would be married with a dozen kids.

Plus, Mason's thirty and Jagger's twenty-eight. Knowing my mother, she'll soon turn her sights on them, relentlessly trying to fix them up with any single girl around. So soon enough, she'll give up on me and realize I'm telling the truth—I can handle the boys on my own. I don't need a wife or a nanny.

Clara's face pops into my mind, and I internally cringe. It's been eight years, and it still hurts. The sting has faded, but the memories of cancer treatments and watching the only woman I've ever loved—the mother of my children—shrink away to barely anything but skin and bones, still haunt me.

Images of my young boys fill my mind, especially Wilder, who was only two years old and watched his mother deteriorate. He was young, but he still remembers it.

Ace was only an infant. All the fears and grief I had while rocking him to sleep on nights my mother and sisters didn't, reappear.

I reiterate to myself, *I'm never getting married again.*

Jagger snickers. "You better get moving."

I swallow the lump in my throat, hating how the bad memories sneak up on me at strange times. I mutter, "I'm remembering this when Mom sets her focus on you." I spin and stomp toward the truck.

"Wait for me!" My twenty-five-year-old sister Willow screeches, darting out the front door and jumping into the passenger side of the truck.

I approach the driver's seat, yank open the door, and state, "You aren't coming. Get out."

She smirks. "Mom said to go with you. Ask me why."

"Don't care. Get out," I order again.

"Nope." Willow buckles her seat belt.

I groan and start the truck. "I'm tired of no one ever listening to me."

"Sorry," she chirps.

I ignore her for a few minutes, then ask, "Shouldn't you be running after a bull rider or something?"

She laughs. "Is that what you think I do all day? Run after them?"

I shrug and grin. "Yep."

"I'll have you know, *they* line up to see *me*. There's no running to do on my part." She beams at me.

"I'm sure they do," I reply with disdain.

Willow got her law degree and decided to become an agent for bull riders. She's always been obsessed with them. No matter how much my father, brothers, and I warned her to stay away from them, she never listened. Over the years, she's dated several local guys. Now, she's representing whatever rider she thinks has the talent to win, and the floodgates of rowdy, cocky men are open even wider.

In my eyes, it's a nightmare brewing. Several of her clients are past flings of hers. Whenever I watch them interact, it's clear Willow's moved on, but they still hold a sweet spot in their hearts for her. And I can't blame them.

Willow's beautiful, has a bubbly personality, and can run circles around most people. She's business oriented like Sebastian, and just as intelligent as him, if not more so, and she's fearless.

It's a recipe for drama, and I want nothing to do with it. At some point, her naive bubble is going to burst. She's going to have to deal with jealous men who thrive on testosterone and winning.

And when it happens, my brothers and I will have a hard time not saying, "We told you so."

Willow leans closer, stating, "I hope you'll be nice to Phoebe. I heard you were nasty last time she was here."

"I wasn't nasty," I claim, although some guilt hits me.

It's not Phoebe's fault my family set her up to fail. They should know I can handle my sons on my own. But this is what happens when they stick their noses into my business. Innocent people, like Phoebe, get hurt.

"Not what I heard," Willow declares.

"Why are you here?" I ask again, annoyed she's butting into this situation.

She grins. "Someone has to be friends with this poor girl so she learns how to navigate around you. Mom said we'd get along really well too."

I snort. "You seem to be delusional, along with the rest of our family. Phoebe's only here for the week. Then she'll be on her way."

"Sure. Whatever you say, brother." Willow pats me on the shoulder.

I jerk away from her, wishing I wasn't annoyed.

We all have great sibling relationships. Even Evelyn, who intrudes way too much, I normally don't mind. So, on a typical day, Willow and I wouldn't have any issues.

But I'm tired of my family insisting on the boys having a nanny. This Phoebe woman isn't capable of keeping them on track anyway, and I doubt she'll be able to instill any sense of discipline in them.

I know my sons better than anyone, and they're going to run all over her. She'll soon regret ever accepting this position. Once she leaves, my family needs to accept that I'm the boys' father and I know what's best for them.

I pull into the airport and follow the signs for the tarmac. I park next to the jet, and the door opens. The staircase gets stabilized, and Phoebe appears at the top.

"She's gorgeous!" Willow exclaims.

I stay quiet. Phoebe's not my type, but I wish I could deny Willow's statement. Phoebe's magenta hair blows in the breeze. Her sun-kissed legs, displayed from her cut-off jean shorts, are as perfect as I imagined. A purple, oversized sweater hits the top of the frayed hems. The right side of her thigh has a streak of hearts and flowers running up it. I can barely make out the letters M-A-R.

My mouth turns dry. My dick strains against my zipper, and I curse myself.

She tattooed another man's name on her body.

What's his name? Mark? Martin? Marcello?

Willow opens the door and bounces out of the truck, rushing toward the steps and calling, "Phoebe!"

I tear my eyes off them and stroll toward the back of the jet. Dale, the runway employee, has boxes loaded onto a cart. He wheels them to the truck and I help put them into the bed.

"And you've met my ornery brother, correct?" Willow chirps.

I shoot her daggers with my glare.

"Sure have. How are you, Alexander?" Phoebe asks, meeting my gaze.

I force myself to be polite. "Fine. Let me help unload the rest of your boxes, and we'll be on our way."

"That's everything in the jet," Dale states.

I glance at the handful of boxes, questioning, "Did you put things in storage?"

Phoebe shakes her head. "No. That's all my stuff."

I arch my eyebrows. Since when don't women have way too many things?

Phoebe proclaims, "I'm a minimalist. Don't like a lot of clutter."

"Very California of you," I tease, but it comes out sounding rude.

"Alexander! Behave!" Willow reprimands.

Guilt fills me, but I'm not admitting anything to my sister. "It was a joke. Phoebe knows that, right?"

I'm unsure why I expect her to have my back, and for a moment, I'm sure she'll call me out. Yet she doesn't.

She straightens her shoulders, lifts her chin, and smiles. Her blues beam brighter. She replies, "Of course."

"See?" I tell Willow, then open the passenger door. "Let's get out of here."

"You can have the front," Willow says to Phoebe, and climbs into the back.

Phoebe grasps the grab bar, hoists herself onto the seat, and asks, "Any chance we can stop in town first?" She crosses her legs, and the letter I is revealed next to the M-A-R.

I stare at it, a lump forming in my throat.

Not Mark. What guy's name is M-A-R-I?

"Is that okay?" Phoebe asks.

I snap out of my trance, look up, and realize she caught me gaping at her thigh.

Her lips twitch and pink crawls around her cheeks.

I quickly answer, "Fine," shut her door, and go around the truck, scolding myself. The last thing I need is to have the nanny thinking I'm interested in her.

I start the truck, pull out of the airport, then ask, "Where in town do you need to go?"

"Any art store will do. I want to get watercolors for the kids."

"Oh! Let's go to Lilac on Main! They have art stuff but also other crafty things," Willow declares.

I snap, "Willow, this isn't a shopping spree. I don't mind stopping, but I need to get back to work."

"Oh, shush. Jagger and Mason have it under control," Willow states.

"Because I do nothing all day?" I blurt out.

My sister laughs. "You know they can handle it when you're gone."

"Willow, I have a lot going on. I don't have all day to wait for you to spend money."

"I like it better when you're fun, Alexander," she says.

I groan.

Phoebe pipes up, "Actually, if we can run in and run out, I think that's best. I want to unpack before the boys get home from school. We can go shopping another day if that's okay?"

Once again, I'm surprised she seems to have my back, but I remind myself not to let her fool me. She wants to stay for two months, and I don't need her.

"If that's what you want," Willow replies.

Phoebe nods. "It is. But I definitely want a rain check on the shopping trip."

"Deal," my sister agrees.

I focus on driving, trying to keep my eyes off Phoebe's sun-kissed, toned legs, but it's hard. A few times, she catches me. I know because of her blush.

I grip the steering wheel harder and pull up to the store. I shift the gear to park and beg, "Please don't take all day."

Willow snorts.

Phoebe meets my gaze. "I'll be quick."

"Thank you."

"Sure," she softly says. She opens her mouth, as if she wants to say more, then shuts it.

I want to ask her what she wants to say, but she leaps out of the truck. I stay in the cab, staring at the back of her killer calves and thigh tattoo.

Maybe his name is Mario.

Is she still with him? Or is she with the D guy?

Maybe she dumped both of them.

I'm stumped, trying to think of more M-A-R-I male names, when she pops out of the store. She's carrying a big shopping bag, and Willow's in tow.

"That was fast," I praise.

"I'm known to have laser focus at times," she claims.

"That's a good trait to have," I admit.

Willow shuts her door, declaring, "Why don't we return on the weekend?"

Phoebe turns and replies, "Let's play it by ear if you don't mind. I want to make sure the boys have my full attention."

"Alexander isn't a total tyrant. You don't have to work 24/7," Willow informs her.

I shoot my sister a dirty look in the mirror. No matter how much Phoebe doesn't need to be here, she is here for a job. At least her priorities seem to be in the right place—on my sons.

Phoebe chirps, "I think it's important the boys know they can rely on me. Why don't we talk about going a few weeks from now?"

Good answer.

But you won't be here in a few weeks.

Willow huffs. "Alright. But you have to keep Saturday night open. There's a huge rodeo. I can introduce you to all the bull riders."

My pulse quickens. I can imagine all the riders swarming around Phoebe like she's fresh meat. I glare daggers at my sister through the rearview mirror and grip the wheel so tight I see stars.

Phoebe says, "I've never been to a rodeo."

"Really? Oh my gosh, you're going to love it! Just get ready to have lots of prospective dates!" Willow gushes.

Why can't my sister shut up?

Phoebe shifts in her seat. She announces, "I'm kind of in a relationship."

"Kind of?" I ask, unable to stop myself. I glance at her, wondering if she's like Willow, running through guys like they're water.

Phoebe's blush reappears. She slowly licks her lips, and my dick tries to burst through my zipper. My heart pounds faster, and she answers, "My boyfriend and I are taking a break."

"What does that mean?" I blurt out.

"It's a break. Don't you know what that is?" Willow chides.

More annoyance fills me.

Phoebe talks fast, stating, "We've been together four years, and I just think we need a break."

"So you broke up?" I ask.

She shakes her head. "Not exactly."

"Sorry. I'm still confused. What does that mean?"

Willow interjects, "It means she still has feelings for him but she knows it's over. She isn't ready to give him up. Oh, and she's ready to see what else is out there without dumping him completely."

"So it's a way to string him along," I say with distaste.

Phoebe's face turns fire-engine red. She opens her mouth, shuts it, then shakes her head.

"Jeez. You're so out of touch, Alexander," Willow adds.

"Or maybe you treat guys like they're disposable and aren't worth some basic respect?" I challenge.

Willow scoffs. "You're delusional."

"Spoken from the queen of delusion herself," I retort.

"Whatever. So, Phoebe, you're free to come with me on Saturday night, correct?" Willow asks, leaning toward us.

"Umm..." Phoebe shifts in her seat.

My sister pushes. "Just say yes."

"Won't the boys need me Saturday night?"

I almost tell her yes so the riders can keep their drool in their mouths.

Willow orders, "Tell her she's free to have some fun, Alexander!"

She's only here for a week.

"Alexander!"

I cave and wave my hand in the air. "Nah. Go have fun with Willow."

"Yes!" my sister exclaims.

"Okay, but I'm not on the market," Phoebe says.

Relief hits me, but it's short-lived.

She still has a boyfriend.

Why am I thinking like this? This woman isn't here to date, nor is she my type.

I refocus on the road, barely hearing the rest of the conversation, trying not to imagine Phoebe with some smug Californian or one of the riders. Both situations irritate me.

I don't care who she's with unless it affects my kids. Since she's staying only a week, her dating life will never intrude on them, I remind myself, pulling through the ranch's gates.

"Do you ever get used to those?" Phoebe asks.

"The gates?"

She stares at the side mirror. "Yes. They're so grand and beautiful. Are you still awestruck, or has it worn off?"

"They've always been here, so I don't think any of us have ever been awestruck," I admit.

"That's a shame," she states.

Curious, I glance at her. "Why is that?"

She softly smiles. "Beauty should be appreciated, shouldn't it?"

I ponder her statement, then shrug. "I guess."

Her smile widens. "I know my first project with the boys."

I arch my eyebrows. "Oh? What's that?"

Her gaze darts across the ranch, and she declares, "We're going to find beauty in the places they take for granted. That way, they'll have a different perspective about the ranch."

"How are you going to do that?" Willow questions.

Phoebe's expression lights further. She confidently answers, "Not sure yet, but I'll find a way."

I park the truck and turn off the engine, wondering if maybe there's value in Phoebe nannying the boys, but then I shake that thought off.

My family underestimates me. I'm more than capable of taking care of my children on my own. If I don't prove them wrong, they'll never stop interfering in my life. Before I know it, Mom will be inviting all the single women to the house again, trying to marry me off.

I get out of the truck and go around to open Phoebe's door, but she jumps out before I get to it. A strange feeling hits me, and I realize it's disappointment.

What the heck is happening to me with this woman?

It's just her door.

She should let me open it for her.

Doesn't matter, I remind myself.

My family magically appears, and I ignore all the banter. I lift a box and move toward the main house.

Dad stops me, asking, "What are you doing?"

"Taking Phoebe's things to the guest room. What does it look like?"

He shakes his head. "Her room isn't here. It's in your house."

My chest tightens. "Why would it be there?"

"The boys are there."

"So?"

"Did you miss the memo that she's their nanny?"

I shake my head. "She doesn't need to stay at my place. She can stay here and still do her job."

"Not necessarily. Now, move her things to your guest room."

I stare at him, not moving.

"Did you not hear me?" he questions.

"You're overstepping," I state.

He crosses his arms. "Maybe so, but this is still my ranch. I'm the head of this family. So whoever's on it lives by my rules. Now, take her boxes to your place."

I still don't move. It's rare my father throws that card out, especially since I'm thirty-five and a parent.

Mason grabs the box from my hands and offers, "I'll take it."

"Stay out—" I spin and freeze.

Jagger and some ranch hands have already unloaded the truck, and boxes sit neatly stacked on my porch.

I glance at Phoebe, surrounded by my family, already fitting in like she belongs here. Her magenta hair flutters in the wind, and I wonder how I'm going to get through this. Not only is this young, carefree, surely wild woman taking care of my kids, she's now living in the room next to mine.

I have no way to get out of it except to suck it up for the week.

4

Phoebe

*a*lexander shifts nervously. He opens a door and cautiously states, "This is your room." He waves for me to go in first.

I step past him, inhaling the same intoxicating scent as the first day I met him, wondering how a man can smell so good after working on a ranch for hours. I place my purse on the bed and then glance around the neutrally decorated space that matches what I've seen of the rest of the house.

This place needs some color.

"This up to your standards?" Alexander inquires.

I smile, offering, "This is a big room."

He points to the wall. "I'm glad you approve. The bathroom is next door, and the linen closet is in the hallway. I'll grab you a set of towels, but if you need fresh ones this week, help yourself."

"Okay."

He vanishes momentarily, only to reappear with a set of brown towels. He places them on the desk, spins back to face my direction, and fixes his gaze on me.

My butterflies erupt. I open my mouth and then shut it.

"Is there something you want to say?" he asks.

"No. I'm good."

"You sure? Because you opened your mouth, then shut it. So my instincts tell me you have something on your mind. Best if you spit it out, then I can answer any question you have," he gruffly informs.

I blurt out, "Did I hear you say you thought I was staying in your parents' house?"

He clenches his jaw, sighs, then admits, "Yes."

"Oh, sorry."

His eyes turn to slits. "You weren't surprised you'd be staying here instead of there?"

I shake my head. "No. Your mom showed me your house when I was here before."

He closes his eyes and shakes his head. "Figures."

For some reason, I feel bad for Alexander. I know he doesn't want me here, but it appears his family is calling the shots. Yet the vibe I get from him is that he's usually in full control. "I'm sorry you didn't know. I'll make sure I inform you about things that they might not tell you. Not that there will be more things...but if there are..."

He tenses.

His expression makes me nervous. It's as if he's debating whether to believe me or not.

"I will," I vow.

He slowly nods. "Thank you. That would be nice—especially about things concerning my sons or home."

"Understood. Ummm..." My pulse quickens.

"What is it?"

"Can I be blunt?"

"Haven't you been?"

"Have I?" I question, wondering if I've overstepped.

"Yeah."

"Sorry."

His stare intensifies until I feel like my cells are on fire. He asks, "Why are you sorry? I'm not a magician who can read minds. I prefer bluntness over games any day."

"That's good. I only play games with kids, or maybe on family game night." I nervously laugh.

He stays quiet, his leer pressing down on me.

I add, "So I won't play any games with you."

He grinds his molars, inhaling a deep breath of air.

"Unless you want me to?" I laugh again, tapping my fingers on my thigh.

Why did I say that?

His eyes dart to my legs. It's not the first time I've caught him staring at them today. I'm unsure what to make of it. His parents told me to dress casually on the ranch, including when I came for the interview. Since the weather is still abnormally hot for this time of year, I put on my shorts. I wonder if he disapproves.

He dryly asks, "How many tattoos do you have?"

Anxiety creeps into my gut. "Several."

"That's not a clear answer."

I tease, "Isn't the mystery part of my stunning magnetism?"

"Since I won't be undressing you, an answer would be appreciated."

I reprimand myself, realizing my statement sounds flirty.

I'm not flirting with him.

I did.

Nope!

Heat crawls up my cheeks. "Sorry. I didn't mean to sound like that."

"Like what?"

"Like I was suggesting anything," I admit, a blush exploding on my face. I bite my lip, still under his darkening gaze.

He blinks twice, his face hardening, and he stands taller, looming over me. He says, "Good to know."

My pulse pounds between my ears. I glance at his bulging bicep, taut against the sleeve, as if it might break the material.

Stop staring!

My eyes dart down the V of his waist, and his belt buckle with a C on it.

He pulls me out of my trance, asking, "So, how many?"

For some reason, I don't want to tell him. "Why do you want to know? Are you a tattoo hater?"

"No. I have a few."

Surprised, I arch my eyebrows. I assumed Alexander was too straitlaced to ink his body. Now, I'm curious. "Really? Where? And what are they?"

His lips twitch. "Ladies first."

"Nope! I'll follow your lead," I state, pretending to lock my mouth and throw away the key.

He crosses his arms in disapproval.

Something tells me not to cave and tell him. But maybe I should since he's my boss and determines whether I keep my job or not. Yet I decide to change the subject, asking, "What time do the boys get home from school?"

He doesn't flinch. "In about an hour."

I smile. "Great. I'm going to unpack, if that's okay?" I open my purse, rifle through it, and pull out a pair of nail clippers. I select the closest box and try to tear the tape.

Alexander scoffs, then steps up next to me. He opens a pocket knife, stating, "Let me help."

"That's chivalrous of you," I tease.

"You don't know what chivalry is, remember?" he replies, and it's the first time I've witnessed him smile. He slides the sharp edge of his knife over the tape.

"What's with you and chivalry?"

He moves to the next box, slicing through it just as seamlessly. He turns, challenging, "Is there something wrong with treating a woman like a woman?"

"Did I say that?"

He assesses me a moment, then answers, "No, but I'm trying to decide if you're just used to boys who will always be boys or if you're one of those feminists who refuse to let a man step into his role."

"His role?"

Alexander nods. "Yes, his role in life."

Confused, I question, "Which is?"

He grunts. "A man's role is to care for his woman and family."

"And that's achieved by opening doors?"

"It's a sign of respect for a woman."

"Is it?" I ask, not because I feel one way or the other but because I'm unaware of these viewpoints. Lance has never held a door open for me, nor had any guy I dated before him.

Very adamantly, he declares, "Yes, it is."

I shift on my feet, feeling naive. It's rare I do, but right now, I feel ignorant. I open the box, pull a handful of clothes out, and say, "Okay, good to know."

He stares at my hand, and I glance at the black lace lingerie. My mouth turns dry. I quickly go to the dresser, open a drawer, toss them inside, and shut it. I spin and chirp, "I really should get unpacked."

He nods, finishes cutting the tape off the boxes, and steps outside the room. Then he turns back and says, "There's one thing you should know about me, Phoebe."

My chest tightens. I tease, "You have tattoos of unicorns on your ass?"

He stills, then breaks out in a smile. "No. Why would you even suggest something so ridiculous?"

I shrug. "You train horses. Maybe you think they're magical or something. I don't know."

His smile grows. "Well, horses are magical, but without a fake horn on their head."

"Good to know. I'll remember that if I ever decide to take up riding."

He pretends to be in shock, his mouth hanging open.

I ask, "What?"

As if I committed a crime, he questions, "You've never ridden a horse?"

"No."

"And my family hired you?"

My nerves reappear at full throttle. I admit, "It didn't come up in the job interview."

"How is that possible?"

"I… I don't know." I furrow my eyebrows.

Great. I'm going to get fired before the week is over because of my lack of riding skills.

"My boys ride," he says.

"Yes, I know."

"Guess you're going to need a crash course in riding if you're going to do your job this week," he declares.

I open my mouth and shake my head. "No. Umm...that's okay. I'll do my job from the ground."

He steps back into the room and crosses his arms, making his biceps strain harder against the T-shirt. In a teasing yet stern tone, he questions, "Phoebe Love, are you scared to ride a horse?"

I debate if I should confess my fear.

Amusement fills his expression. "You are, aren't you?"

I stay quiet.

He purses his lips and spins, walking out of the room and calling out, "Get unpacked. Lessons will start once the boys are home."

I rush toward the door. "Alexander, it's okay. I can do my job and not get on a horse."

He turns. "My boys will be riding all over this ranch. If you're going to be in charge of them, you'll have to ride with them. But we can end the week now if you're not up for the challenge."

My heart pounds within my chest cavity.

Alexander waits me out a few moments, then declares, "Okay. Decision made. I'll get some tape for your boxes."

"No! I'll..." My stomach flips.

He arches his eyebrows.

I release an anxious breath. "I'll learn to ride."

What am I saying?

His expression shows both surprise and approval. "Great. I'll saddle Coco up."

"Don't you have to return to work?" I ask, trying to think of how to get out of this sudden requirement.

He shakes his head. "Nah. I've always got time to make sure my boys have the resources necessary to ensure their supervision."

I'm not getting out of this.

I'm going to get hurt, maybe paralyzed.

As if he can read my mind, he adds, "You can stop freaking out. There's no one better to teach you how to ride than me."

"Can't I ride something else?" I ask.

Amused, he questions, "Like what?"

"I don't know. Anyone or anything other than a horse?"

"Anyone?" He arches his eyebrows.

Mortified at the realization of what I just said, I gape at him.

He chuckles, then says, "Let's stick with Coco."

"Coco?" I mumble, still embarrassed.

"Yeah. She's our fastest horse."

"What?" I shriek.

He chuckles. "I'm kidding. Don't worry. Coco won't hurt you. She's our tamest horse, and is perfect for a beginning rider."

It should make me feel better, but it doesn't calm my fears.

Alexander points to my legs. "I suggest you put on a pair of jeans."

I meekly reply, "Okay."

"See you outside," he cheerfully proclaims and then disappears.

I do nothing for a moment, then force myself to unpack, unable to stop thinking about how I'll get out of riding. I'm breaking down the last box when the kids come home.

"Phoebe!" Ace sings.

I step out of the room, and he flings himself at me.

"Whoa!" I laugh, hugging him.

"Hey, Phoebe," Wilder calls out, waving from near the door.

"Hi!" I reply.

Ace pulls away, gushing, "Dad said we get to teach you how to ride?"

My gut dives. "That's what I hear."

"He says you're scared," Wilder adds.

"Well, that was nice of him to say," I reply.

Ace insists, "You don't have to be scared. Horses won't be mean to you unless you're mean to them."

"Is that so?"

"Yep! Plus, Dad taught us all the tricks to get them to do what we want. We'll show you!" Ace exclaims.

I put on a false smile. "Great. Did you two want a snack?"

"Yes! I'm starving," Wilder replies.

"Okay. Let's see what's in the kitchen."

"We don't keep a ton here. Most of the good food is in the main house," Ace informs me.

"I'll be the judge of that," I state, and go into the kitchen with the boys in tow. I open the refrigerator, but the only things in it are fresh milk, jelly, cheese, orange juice, and three bottles of beer.

"We eat almost all our meals at Grandma and Grandpa's. Everyone there cooks better than Dad anyway," Wilder declares.

"I see. But what's in here?" I open the pantry. There are a few boxes of cereal, a jar of peanut butter, half a loaf of bread, and some crackers.

"See, we told you so," Wilder chirps.

I shut the pantry, making a mental note to get some food in the house. I tell the boys, "Guess we're going to the main house. Lead the way."

Ace and Wilder guide me to their grandparents' place. Alexander's with his brothers, running horses in a circle inside the corral. He's shouting orders, and sweat soaks the back of his T-shirt.

"I was wondering when I'd see all of you," Ruby's voice interjects, tearing my gaze off her son.

I admit, "There isn't a lot of food in the house."

"Yes, I know, dear," she says with a smile. Then she pats my shoulder and suggests, "Maybe you can help get some basics in their pantry and fridge?"

I nod. "Sure."

We all go into the kitchen. A bowl of mixed fruit, cheese chunks, and nuts sits on the table. The boys grab handfuls of food.

"Did you wash your hands?" I ask.

They freeze.

I point to the sink. "Go on."

They obey, and Ruby gives me a satisfied look. She says, "Help yourself to anything in our home, Phoebe. Our things are yours, so don't hesitate to eat or use what you need. Okay?"

"Thank you," I reply, grateful. The moment I met her, I liked her. She's nice, and clearly a very strong woman. I know she cares a lot about her family.

The boys finish washing their hands, and I take their spot at the sink. I scrub up, dry off, then grab a few raspberries and almonds.

We eat in silence until Ruby says, "I heard you're going to learn to ride today?"

My apprehension reappears. "Is this really a requirement for the job?"

Her lips form a tight smile. She stares at me.

"It is?"

She shakes her head. "No, not a requirement. At least not for me."

"But it is for Alexander?"

Ace chimes in, "You don't have to be scared."

"Yeah, riding is awesome!" Wilder states.

Ruby stares at me, then says, "Boys, go see what your father and uncles are doing. Phoebe will be out soon."

They don't argue, running out of the house.

When the door slams shut, Ruby says, "You know how I told you Alexander will push you to see what you're made of?"

My stomach flips. "Yes."

"This is one of those times."

Silence fills the air.

She continues, "And you remember how I told you that it's always your choice to get pushed or push back?"

"Yes."

"Well, you always have that choice, dear."

I stare at her, finally admitting, "I don't understand how I can push back on this one. He's adamant that I ride in order to take care of the boys."

"Why is he so adamant about it? Answer that, and the solution will come."

I rack my brain, but nothing comes to me.

Ruby steps in front of the window and says, "Come here, Phoebe."

I do as she asks.

"Why did he say you had to learn to ride?"

"To watch the kids since they'll be all over the ranch."

"Okay, so what is the problem, and what is the solution? That is, if you're not ready to learn to ride?"

I think for a moment, then snap my fingers, answering, "I need to find a way to keep up with the boys, but not on a horse."

She nods, smiling. "That's right. So, figure that out, but I suggest you do it before you step outside. Because once you do, you'll have all those men and my grandsons trying everything they can to get you on Coco." She points to the horse Alexander leads across the yard and toward the corral.

My pulse skyrockets. The magnificent white horse moves with confidence and beauty. It doesn't calm my nerves. If anything, it makes me more anxious.

Ruby leans into my ear and says, "It's all in front of you. I have faith you'll figure it out." She pats me on the shoulder and then leaves the room.

I scan the ranch, trying to calm down. No solutions come to me. Then Alexander catches me staring at him and curls his finger in a "come here" gesture.

"Oh crap," I murmur, clenching my thighs.

What the hell is wrong with me?

That man wants me to get on a horse, knowing I'm petrified.

He's sexy.

No, he's not!

I step away from the window.

What am I going to do?

I peek out the other window, fretting, and then my solution comes to me. But I need to ensure I'm interpreting what Ruby said correctly.

I leave the kitchen, move through the house, and call, "Ruby!"

She replies, "In the living room."

I step inside and ask, "When you said I can help myself to anything, did that include everything on the ranch, or is anything off-limits?"

She grins. "Ah, you've found your solution."

"Yep!"

"Great! You can use whatever you want as long as no one's safety is at risk."

"Funny you say that when they all want me to get on a horse," I comment.

She laughs. "Phoebe, I'm confident you'll learn to ride at some point while on our ranch."

"No, I won't."

"We'll see."

"Okay, but I can use anything as long as it's safe, correct?"

"It's a free-for-all," she sings, wiggling her eyebrows.

"Perfect." I exit the room and go back into the kitchen. I step outside the side door and stroll over to an ATV. As I suspected, the keys are in it. So I get on it, turn it on, and put it in gear.

When I turn the corner, everyone stops and stares at me. I pull up to the corral and park the ATV.

"What are you doing on that?" Alexander asks.

I beam at him. "Your mom said I can utilize anything on the ranch. So, there's no need to learn to ride. I can watch the boys on this."

Alexander's expression reveals a mix of competing emotions. If I'm not mistaken, it's disappointment but also approval. Yet the longer he stares, the more his approval fades. His eyes darken, narrowing under the shade of his cowboy hat.

Feeling like it's time to make my escape, I turn toward the boys. "Why don't you show me around the ranch?"

Alexander

I glance at my watch and mumble, "Great." Then I race back to the house. I yank open the door and run toward the bedrooms.

Phoebe steps out of the bathroom at just that moment. A towel covers her hair, and another one wraps around her body. Her dewy skin seems to glow brighter in the dull light.

"Whoops! Sorry," I offer.

She smiles. "Where's the fire?"

My heart pounds harder. "I have to wake the boys up."

"I already did. They're in the kitchen, eating cereal," she states.

Disappointment hits me. I blurt out, "I'm the one who wakes them up in the morning."

She arches her eyebrows. "Oh, I'm sorry. I didn't mean to over-step. You said they had to get up at six thirty, and I saw you outside. I figured you would want me to wake them up so you could work."

"You were watching me?"

Pink crawls up her neck and into her cheeks. She shakes her head. "I... I wouldn't say watching."

I laugh, but it comes out awkwardly. "I was just kidding."

"Right," she says, smiling.

I'm seriously an idiot.

A moment of silence fills the air between us.

She tilts her head and states," It's five after seven right now."

"Yes, I'm aware," I respond, gruffer than I intend.

Hurt briefly appears in her expression, but she quickly asks in a confused tone, "Going forward, you don't want me to wake the boys up if you're not here?"

"No... Yes... No. It's my job," I ramble.

Why do I sound like I can't form a coherent sentence this morning?

She puts her hands in the air and offers, "I'm sorry. I didn't mean to overstep."

I take three deep breaths, realizing I sound like a moron. I add, "I should have looked at my watch."

Her lips turn to a small curve, and the extra room below my belt vanishes. She says, "Stuff happens when you're busy working. And that's why you have me here, right?"

I groan internally. The last thing I want to do is admit to Phoebe I need her here.

I don't need her here.

I declare, "I forgot to set my alarm on my watch. It won't happen again."

"Okay..." She stares at me, and I can tell she wants to say something else.

"Don't leave me hanging. Spit out whatever you're dying to say," I order, once again sounding rough when I intend it to be funny.

She replies, "If by any chance you are late, do you want me to wake them up?"

"I won't be late again."

"But if you are—"

"I won't be," I vow to her and myself.

Disbelief fills her expression, but I'll prove her wrong. She slowly nods. "Okay. You're the only one on wake-up duty, then." She smiles and lightly scratches her collarbone.

My eyes drift to the top of her towel. Her cleavage and part of that damn tattoo are on display, making my lower body ache. And I hate myself for reacting.

This woman is too young, not my type, and not here past Monday, I remind myself. Then I order myself to stop staring at her, but I can't.

The D and the A of her tattoo are clear as day.

She claims, "I had to shower because Wilder ran into the bathroom around six o'clock and didn't come out until twenty minutes later. Then he crawled back into bed, and it was a nightmare getting him back up. I'll have to get up earlier to shower so I'm better prepared."

I shift on my feet, but I can't think about her words. There's only one thing going through my mind, and it's driving me nuts. I ask, "What dude's name did you tattoo on your chest? Danny Boy? David? Damon?"

Amusement fills her expression. She teases, "Didn't we go over how I can't tell you?"

I should let it be, but once again, I can't control my mouth. "Is it your current boyfriend or ex?"

She bites on her smile. "Why do you assume it's a boyfriend?"

A new thought hits me. I assess her, wondering how I could have gotten it so wrong, and a new wave of disappointment floods me.

She has a boyfriend, but she must be into men and women.

Embarrassed, I apologize. "Oh crap! I'm sorry to assume things. It's your girlfriend's name?"

Shock fills her expression and then she starts laughing.

"What's so funny?" I question.

She wipes at some tears running down her cheek, then takes control of her outburst and declares, "I don't date women."

"Well, that's good," I blurt out as relief replaces my disappointment.

"Why is that?"

"Oh, I didn't mean anything would be wrong with it if you were into women. I just meant—" I stop, tongue-tied, realizing I'm sounding like an idiot talking about who she does or doesn't date.

Her blush reappears, darker than before, and my cock aches.

What is this woman doing to me?

She's the enemy.

Get her off the ranch and move on with life.

"I should get my clothes on," she declares.

"Oh...right." I step aside, and she disappears inside her bedroom.

I close my eyes and shake my head, wondering why I'm acting like a schoolboy with a crush, especially toward a woman who is anything but good for me. After I beat myself up a bit, I take a deep breath and go into the kitchen, just in time to hear Wilder and Ace arguing.

"Good morning," I boom out, then kiss both of them on the head.

"Dad, tell Wilder I can run my horse as fast as he can run his," Ace whines.

I groan. "Doesn't this same breakfast argument get old after a while?"

Wilder sits back in the chair, a cocky grin on his expression. It always reminds me of Jagger. They have a lot of the same features. And Wilder loves getting under Ace's skin and always knows how to do it. He states, "It's okay to admit I'm a better rider than you."

"You aren't!" Ace claims.

"Isn't that an easily solvable question?" Phoebe interjects, stepping into the kitchen, wearing skinny jeans, a tank top, and a flannel.

"How?" Ace asks.

"We can have a race after school," she answers.

"That's a good idea. Then we can put this argument to rest so I don't have to hear it every morning," I grumble.

Wilder crosses his arms. "I've already proven it."

"No, you haven't!" Ace shrieks.

"Sure I have," Wilder claims.

Phoebe softly laughs.

We all stare at her.

"What's so funny?" I question.

She assesses Wilder and then questions, "Are you scared to race your brother?"

"No!"

"You are! Scaredy cat!" Ace accuses.

"Am not!"

Phoebe calmly says, "Then we'll have one more race. We'll do it after school so we can solve this argument about who's faster. But after today, you're not allowed to debate this. The loser of the race can rechallenge the winner only once a month, and it's the only time you're allowed to discuss this topic. The winner can't brag either. Understand?"

"Fine. I'll beat him," Wilder declares.

"No, you won't," Ace retorts.

Phoebe continues, "Shake hands on the deal. No more discussing this topic unless it's once a month to rechallenge. And if anyone breaks the rule, your dad will hand out the punishment, which will be..." She glances at me.

Shocked I never thought of this, and happy I won't have to keep hearing them argue every morning, I answer, "Barn duty for a week."

"A week?" Wilder spouts.

"Would two be better?" I ask.

He huffs. "Fine. A week."

"Great. Problem solved. Go brush your teeth so you can get to school on time," Phoebe commands.

The boys obey.

"That was a good idea," I praise her, impressed with her quick thinking.

She beams. "I figured a once-a-month debate was better than daily."

I grunt. "That's the truth."

She scrunches her forehead and glances around the room. "There's not a lot in the kitchen to make the boys' lunches."

Guilt hits me. I rely too much on my parents, but I don't have time for grocery shopping, so I admit, "My mom makes it for them."

"Ah. I see."

I try to explain. "I'm working all day, and when I get to town, it's typically for work stuff, so the grocery isn't a priority since my kids won't starve when my parents' place is right next door."

Phoebe nods. "Gotcha."

I continue to babble. "They get all the food they need. Promise I'm not starving my kids."

"Nope! They definitely aren't malnourished."

"My mom's a way better cook anyway. I'm good with horses, not stoves and such. Well, unless you want to see my microwave skills. I have mad microwave skills."

What the heck is wrong with me?

Shut up!

I take my cowboy hat off and scratch my head.

Humor fills Phoebe's expression. "I'll remember that the next time I need popcorn. But, since your mom won't be here over the next few months, is it okay if I grab some groceries when I drop them off today?"

"Well, you're only here for a week," I remind her.

Her face falls.

I'm hit with a stab of guilt. I don't usually try to be a dick when it comes to anyone. And it's not Phoebe's fault that my family has it all wrong about me.

She quickly recovers with a smile and chirps, "Still, I'd like to make a few things, and I can freeze some as well."

I stare at her.

She leans closer and lowers her voice. "I'll even show you the trick to reheating something in the oven."

I laugh. "I'm not that bad."

"Good to know. I've got the go-ahead on getting groceries, then?" she asks.

The stubborn part of me wants to say no, but having a kitchen full of food is nice. It's been several months since I could do a grocery run. So I cave. "If you want to. Let me get you a credit card."

"Perfect!" she exclaims.

I reach for my wallet and pull out my credit card. I hold it out, warning, "This is only for groceries. It's not for any shopping sprees with Willow."

It was supposed to be a joke, but it comes out sounding as awkward as everything else I say around her.

Her expression changes. In a stern tone, she replies, "That would be stealing. I've never been a thief and don't plan on starting anytime soon."

I sheepishly admit, "It was a joke since Willow wanted to go shopping. I didn't mean to offend you."

She stares at me, then releases a breath and smiles. "Okay. Sorry I took offense."

"It's okay. Sorry everything I say doesn't seem to come out right."

"It doesn't?" she questions.

Way to dig myself deeper in the hole!

I ignore her question and state, "I better get back to work. My mom will meet you near her truck." I exit the house before she can reply.

I rush toward the corral where Mason and Jagger are running two horses. A small dust cloud fills the area.

71

Jagger gives me the same cocky grin Wilder had on his face earlier. "How's it going with your lady friend?"

I smack the back of his head.

"Watch it!" he warns.

I spout, "She's not my lady friend."

"I'd make her mine if Mom handed her to me on a silver platter," Mason adds.

My hand automatically flies toward his head, but he ducks, laughing.

Jagger whistles. "She even looks good with wet hair."

I spin and watch her and the boys walk toward the truck. Mom's waiting near it with two lunch sacks.

Guilt eats me again.

I should be making those lunches.

I have to step up these next two months.

Once Phoebe gets groceries in the house, it'll be easier to restock, I lie to myself, knowing my work habits won't allow me to stick with my intentions.

Mason adds, "I wonder if she needs any help with the soap."

I turn and smack him a good one. His cowboy hat goes flying.

"Jesus!" he cries out.

I grab him by the shirt and yank him toward me, threatening, "Don't disrespect the boys' nanny."

"So you're keeping her?" Jagger asks.

I release Mason and answer, "No. She's here for the week. But regardless, she's the boys' nanny, not some floozy you'd pick up in town. You'll respect her, understand?"

Mason taunts, "You seem to have a soft spot for her now."

"No, I don't. You should know better than to disrespect a care-giver for your nephews," I reprimand.

The truck engine revs, and I turn toward it.

The boys and Phoebe wave as they drive away from the house.

I wave back and watch it disappear through the gates.

Jagger mocks, "You've got the hots for your nanny."

"Shut up, you idiots," I order and then stomp away from them. I step into the barn, and the scent of hay flares in my nostrils. I grip a wooden pole and inhale deeply, trying to calm myself.

"Immature idiots," I mumble, then open the gate.

"Hey, buddy," I coo, grabbing Calypso's bridle. He nuzzles my shoulder, relaxing me.

I spend a few minutes with him, then lead him out of the barn, taking him to the other corral so I don't need to deal with my brothers.

Like always, I lose myself in my work. At one point during the day, I spot Phoebe carrying in groceries. At other times, she's with Mom. I'm careful not to give her any attention.

When the boys arrive home, they race to the barn and saddle up their horses.

Phoebe appears and stands between two stakes with red T-shirts wrapped around them. She has a big stick and drags it through the sand.

The boys ride over on their horses, and I join Phoebe.

She points to a thirty-foot-tall river birch. "Race to the tree, steer your horse around it, then rush back here. The first to cross this line is the winner. Understood?"

"Easy-peasy," Wilder claims with the same cocky grin on his face he wore at breakfast.

Ace's expression turns serious. He leans forward on his horse and mutters, "Eat my dust, Wilder."

Phoebe arches her eyebrows at me, biting her smile. Then she asks, "Do you know how to whistle?"

I grin. "Can you be a cowboy if you can't whistle?"

She laughs. "Is that a rule?"

"Yep."

Her smile expands. "Good to know. Boys, you can start when your dad whistles on the count of three. Ready?"

"I was born ready!" Wilder exclaims, positioning his horse next to Phoebe.

"Count down!" Ace orders, and moves his horse right to the line, then focuses on the tree.

Phoebe catches my eye, steps back, and counts. "Three. Two. One."

I whistle as loud as possible, and it cuts through the air.

The boys take off, their horses neck and neck.

Phoebe asks, "Who's going to win?"

"Not sure," I admit, not taking my eyes off the boys.

They get to the tree, and Wilder leans into his turn. Ace doesn't lean enough and loses ground.

"Damn it! I've been working with Ace on that turn," I state.

"What did he do wrong?" she asks as Wilder comes charging at us, Ace four feet behind him.

"He needs to lean farther when he turns," I answer.

Wilder pounds past us, and within a second, Ace follows.

Wilder turns his horse and stops next to us. He pumps his fist in the air. "I win!"

A disappointed Ace trots over to us.

"You didn't lean enough into your turn," I point out.

"Ha ha! I told you I'd win!" Wilder exclaims.

Phoebe interjects, "You did well, but no bragging, remember? Ace, you can challenge him again in a month, okay?"

"We need to keep working on your turn. You could have had him," I tell Ace.

"But he didn't!" Wilder points out.

Ace groans. "You're so annoying."

"Okay, boys. Time for a snack and homework," Phoebe orders.

"Aww, come on. We just got on our horses," Wilder whines.

She points across the yard. "Sorry. But no more riding until you finish your homework. Now, go wash your hands. I have your snacks on the picnic table. We can do homework there while it's still nice out."

Wilder huffs and takes off on his horse toward the barn.

Ace slowly follows.

"Poor Ace," Phoebe mumbles once they're out of earshot.

"He has to lean into his turns," I repeat.

"I still feel bad for him."

"Don't. Once he gets it, he'll ride better than Wilder," I declare.

"How do you know that?"

I chuckle. "I know my boys. Ace is further ahead than Wilder was at his age."

"Really?"

"Yep."

"Okay. Good to know."

I stare at her for a moment.

She takes a deep breath and nods. "Okay. Off to homework."

"I should help them," I say.

She stares back at me. "Is that what you want to do?"

No way. Homework sucks.

But I need to step up and prove she doesn't have to be here.

She suggests, "Why don't I get them started, and you can come over when you're free?"

"I'm free now," I insist.

"Great. Let's go do homework," she challenges.

I instantly regret my words as I follow her to the picnic table.

The boys join us, and she takes the lid off a bowl in the shape of a turkey, revealing cut-up apples and a side of dip.

Ace asks, "Is that Georgia's caramel cream cheese dip?"

"Yep. Your grandma said you love it," Phoebe replies.

"Yes!" Wilder exclaims, then picks up an apple and dips it.

Ace grabs one too.

Phoebe opens a binder and pulls out two worksheets. "Math first."

Wilder groans. "I hate math."

"I like it better than reading stupid books," Ace claims.

"Books aren't stupid," Phoebe states.

Wilder whines, "My teacher makes it too complicated. Two plus two equals four. I don't need to break it down into multiple steps. It's stupid."

"Agreed," I state, unable to keep quiet.

"Then I don't have to do it?" Wilder asks with hope in his eyes.

Once again, I regret my words. "No, of course you have to do it."

Wilder pushes, "But you just said—"

"Your father meant he agrees two plus two equals four, correct?" Phoebe firmly declares, locking her gaze with mine.

"Ummm...yeah," I agree, feeling like a kid caught with his hand in the cookie jar but also happy she covered for my mistake.

Phoebe taps the pages, saying, "The sooner we get through this, the sooner we can have fun. Plus, if you work hard, I'll give you a star for our beach party."

The boys take a few moments to settle, but they eventually do. Phoebe begins instructing them, and I know I should step in, but I don't.

I can't.

I don't understand Texas Essential Knowledge and Skills or TEKS, which is their new math standards. I've been told it's similar to Common Core math. Not that I would understand that either. So I think the same as Wilder. Two plus two equals four. It's straightforward. I don't need to have it broken down.

Phoebe breezes through it, explaining things so the boys understand, yet I'm still lost.

I hate it. I run numbers for my business all the time, yet I can't wrap my brain around my kids' homework. It makes me feel stupid and useless.

The more I watch Phoebe in action, the more panic hits me.

I have a week to learn everything I can about how to help my boys do their homework.

And I have zero clue how I'm going to figure it out.

6

Phoebe

Several Days Later

"Where are you, Phoebe?" Lance demands for the fifth time.

"Now you want to know?" I question, pissed off. I've not heard from him since the night I returned to California.

As if it's normal to disappear for days, he claims, "I told you I was busy."

Enraged and hurt, I snap, "Busy! For how many days? Let's be real. You haven't thought about me once. Now that you've sobered up and I'm not there, you want to know where I'm at?"

He groans. "Stop being dramatic. I went out and had things to do. Now, stop playing games. Tell me where you're hiding out."

I shake my head, pacing my room. "I told you I'm in Texas. I accepted a new job."

"Yeah, right."

Infuriated, I snarl, "What do you mean, 'yeah, right'?"

He scoffs. "Why the hell would you go to Texas and leave California? That's the most ridiculous thing I've ever heard."

A wave of anger crashes in my stomach. "There's nothing wrong with Texas."

He snorts, claiming, "There's nowhere better than California. Anyone even considering leaving is a fool."

I run my hand through my hair, glancing out the window. It's a nice, sunny day. The air turned crisp a few days ago, but it's still decent weather. And I'd rather be outside than having this conversation that is going nowhere. So I state, "I have to go, Lance."

"Wait," he cries out.

I pause, my heart pounding hard.

He lowers his voice, and it tugs at my heart, just like it always does when he uses that tone. He says, "Phoebe, where are you? Come on, don't play games. I miss you."

I close my eyes, sighing. He always does this. He messes up and then professes his feelings for me. Whenever he does, I cave and let whatever he's done get buried in a grave of disappointment.

He's not going to manipulate me this time.

He disappeared for days!

He repeats, "Phoebe, where are you?"

"I told you, I'm in Texas," I say, softer, hating how he can make my tone lose its edge.

"Where?"

"At the Cartwright Ranch."

A moment of silence falls between us. Lance finally mutters, "The Cartwrights?"

"Yes," I confirm.

"Why are you at the Cartwrights' Ranch?" he questions, adding, "You know nothing about country living."

I don't know why his comment offends me. It's true; I know more about oceans and mountain life than this one. But Lance's way of saying it makes me think I can't figure this out, but I can. I know I can. I've been on the ranch for the past few days, and there isn't anything I don't like about it.

So I reply, "I told you I have a job."

"What kind of job?" he pushes.

"I'm nannying for them."

"Nannying? You have a degree, for God's sake," he says, as if nannying is beneath me.

"Yeah, I do. So what? It doesn't make me unqualified."

"You're supposed to be teaching art. Why aren't you doing that, Phoebe?"

I cringe inside. It's the same accusation he always makes.

Lance has never understood the dynamics I faced working for the school system. I did it for a few years, but I couldn't handle it anymore.

Several kids threatened to punch me in class. They'd call me names and not do their work, and I could do nothing about it. The administration wasn't supportive of their teachers. Parents were an even bigger joke, mostly absent whenever I tried to contact them.

So, I spent the last year trying to get into a better school district, but no one was giving up their jobs—especially art teachers, which is a dying subject in many districts.

Lance knows everything I've gone through while teaching. I've hidden nothing from him, yet he can't seem to show me any sympathy or realize how much the environment I worked in affected me.

The last thing I want to do is rehash things with him. He's never going to try to understand where I'm coming from. He'll always think I need to be an art teacher in a school, and nothing else.

He adds, "Or we can get married, then you don't have to work. It's silly that you even thought you had to get another job. You know you'll be my wife someday, and I have money."

I swallow the lump forming in my throat. When I first met Lance, I saw our future together. And it's what I wanted. Now, I'm not so sure.

He always talks about marriage, yet he's never actually proposed. I'm unsure what I'd say if he got down on a knee and offered me a ring.

He lowers his voice, whining, "Phoebe, come on, babe. It's time to stop these childish antics and return to California. I'll take care of you. You don't have to worry about this nanny nonsense or getting a job. I think it's time we start our life anyway."

My pulse shoots to the sky, and I should be happy that he wants to finally commit. But I don't trust him. Right now, I don't really trust myself to make the right decision either. So, I muster up all my courage and tell him what I wanted to tell him in person before I left California but couldn't because he was nowhere to be found. "Lance, we've been together a long time."

"We sure have. So stop being dramatic. You know I love you. No one will ever love you the way I do either," he adamantly states.

Fear hits me. It always does when he says that, and I usually tell myself to be thankful he loves me. I could be alone, but Lance usually treats me well.

What if it's true, and no one will ever love me better than him?

What if I give him up and end up alone in life?

My insides quiver. An older version of me, alone and unloved, fills my mind.

"Admit I'm right," he insists.

He's not.

Is he?

I muster my courage and state, "If we're going to survive this, we need to take some time and figure out what's important to both of us. Then we can make a decision to continue forward or not."

"Make it through what?" he questions.

I sigh, explaining, "I love you, Lance. But things haven't been good between us for a while. I think it's best if we take a time-out. Then, we have some space to think. We don't want to make a bad decision and stay together just because we've been together so long."

"Don't be silly. There's no reason to take a time-out. Stop playing games, Phoebe," he demands.

"I'm not playing games. I've tried talking to you, but you don't listen. I wanted to talk to you about this before I left—"

"So you just run off to Texas and throw this on me over the phone," he spouts.

"Well, I wanted to talk to you face-to-face, but where were you? Huh? And I'm still waiting for you to tell me where you've been the last few days!"

He ignores my question and replies, "I'm not playing this game, Phoebe."

"It is not a game! We're taking a break. Some space between us will be good, and when my job's over, we can talk and decide what we want to do going forward," I adamantly repeat.

"And when exactly is this job over?" he fires back.

"Two months."

"Two months? Are you serious, Phoebe? You think I'm going to just let my life sit on hold for two months while you do whatever you're doing on that ranch?" he fumes.

I squeeze my eyes shut again, holding on to the window sill. His voice is taking on the tone that I hate. It tends to turn ugly and makes me want to crawl into a hole and never come out. So I gently order, "Calm down, Lance."

"Don't you tell me to calm down," he hurls.

I cringe, then lift my chin, square my shoulders, and stare out at the ranch.

It's Saturday. The boys are running around the yard. Alexander and his brothers are in the corral, working their horses. The posts and fences all have lights, burlap, and pine cones wrapped around them.

The sight normally makes me feel happy, but right now, nothing is calming the shaking in my gut. And I realize I want to be outside, not arguing with Lance. So I say, "I'm hanging up now. We can talk about this later. Maybe in a few days?"

He booms, "A few days?"

Anger hits me at a new high. It slaps me, pushing past all the heartache and disappointment I was starting to feel again. I seethe, "Yeah, Lance, in a few days. That should be fine since you know how to disappear and not tell me where you are. Correct?"

"Don't you—"

"I'm hanging up now," I inform him, then hit the button and toss my phone on my bed.

"Ugh!" I exclaim, leaning against the wall and staring at the ceiling, taking deep breaths, trying to slow my racing heart. I don't know how long I stand there until I'm finally calm enough to leave my bedroom.

I'm halfway through the house when I run into Willow.

She chirps, "Hey, I was coming to get you."

I smile. I really like Willow. Ever since the first day, she's made a point every night to come talk to me and try to hang out. We're becoming friends, which I didn't expect when I took this job.

We're only a year apart in age. We have a lot in common, but she's also a breath of fresh air, as her world is so different from mine.

"Okay, so you're still going to come with me tonight, right?" she asks, her eyes burning with excitement.

I laugh. "I'd love to. But are you sure it's okay for me not to be on kid duty?" I ask, still worried that the boys might need me.

She scoffs. "Yeah, of course. Alexander and the boys will be there anyway. Actually, so will our entire family."

I arch my eyebrows. "They will?"

She nods. "Yes. Tonight's a charity event for the Thanksgiving holiday. All the money raised goes to the food bank to feed needy families over the holidays."

"That's great," I declare.

She nods. "There are a lot of different events over the next few months since we're getting into the holidays. But the rodeo is one of the biggest events. The food bank really depends on the money that'll be raised tonight."

"We had a lot of different programs in the school where the food bank was involved."

"I bet. But we should talk about the most important part."

"What's that?"

She wiggles her eyebrows. "I get to introduce you to all the bull riders."

I groan but can't help smiling. "Willow! I thought we went over this."

She laughs. "We did, but you're on a break with your boyfriend, right?"

The conversation with Lance fills my mind. My insides quiver once more.

She puts her hand on my forearm. "Hey, what's wrong? Did I upset you?"

I shake my head. "No. I just had a conversation with Lance. That's all."

Concern fills her expression. "I'm sorry. Do you want to talk about it?"

I force a smile, answering, "No. I'd rather not if that's okay?"

She studies me and then nods. "Okay. But I'm always here to talk if you need someone."

"Thank you," I gratefully tell her, then admit, "And thank you for being so kind to me. I didn't expect to meet anyone so soon I thought I could call my friend."

She grins, babbling, "Well, good. My mom said we were going to be good friends. She's usually right about these things. She's horrible about picking women for my brothers or men for me and my sisters. But she's good at friendships."

"Your mom's a great woman."

"She is. And I still can't believe they're leaving for a mission trip over the holidays. It's the best time of year, and our family celebrates like nobody else."

Happiness envelops me. I've always loved the holidays but never spent them anywhere except in California. I'm excited to see how the Cartwrights spend Thanksgiving, Christmas, and New Year's. Even being on the ranch with everything decorated shows they love celebrating. I can't imagine what it's going to look like for Christmas and New Year's.

They also seem to be a very close family, but they don't hide it when they don't like something someone does. I respect how they interact with each other. They put it all out on the table, but in a way where they still love each other.

87

Plus, I've never been around a big family. I have a sister who got into a car accident. She lives in a home because she can't support herself and is incapacitated both mentally and physically. I try to visit her as often as possible, but she no longer knows who I am.

It's been eight years since that accident, and it still hurts. My sister and I were close before it happened. My mother and father divorced long ago, and we were each other's rock. When the accident happened, it changed everything in my family.

My mother suffers from depression. She was driving the car, and the guilt over that finally got to be too much for her to take. Several years ago, I had to admit her into a facility because she isn't able to take care of herself. I try to visit her as well, but it's hard. Both my sister and mother are in state-funded places, and they're several hours away in opposite directions.

My father disappeared shortly after the accident. I have no clue where he lives or what happened to him.

There was one holiday I spent alone. The next year, I met Lance and have been with his family since.

It could be another reason I feel tied to him and keep trying to make it work. It may be why it's harder for me to break up with him for good, even though I'm relieved I don't have to see his family over the holidays this year.

Strangely, I feel more at home with the Cartwrights after a few days with them than I ever have with Lance's family. But I never would've complained about them. I was always grateful I had somewhere to go during this time of year.

Willow tilts her head. "Sorry. Did I say something else that upset you?"

I shake it off. "No. Everything's fine. I'm just really happy to be here."

"We're happy you're here too."

"I just hope your brother decides to keep me on," I say, trying to make a joke, but the fear in my voice comes out.

The truth is, if Alexander doesn't let me stay, I don't know what I'll do. I don't want to have to go back and live with Lance. We really do need space to figure things out between us. If we live together in the future, I want it to be our choice, not a necessity because I'm broke and have nowhere else to go.

Yet, every day, Alexander makes it clear my time here is limited. Monday is coming soon, and no matter how much I try to show him I can help out with the boys, he's determined not to let me stay.

Willow groans and rolls her eyes, declaring, "My brother's a moron. Don't worry. You're staying."

"How do you know that? He seems determined to make sure I leave on Monday."

She waves her hand in front of us. "Nah, he'll let you stay. Don't worry."

"He doesn't seem to be the type who changes his mind very easily. I'm trying my best, but…"

She scoffs. "Oh, we know you're trying. But don't worry. Every-body sees how good you are for the boys and him."

"Him?" I question, the heat rising in my cheeks, which I hate.

"Yeah, he needs help too. You're good for him. But anyway, let's talk about important stuff." She leans closer, lowers her voice, and states, "There are two bull riders I think you're going to be into tonight."

I sigh, asserting, "Willow, I don't want to get into a relationship right now. I need time to consider whether I want Lance in my life or not."

She shrugs. "Yes, but you're taking space. You're on a break. That means you get to see what's out there. Right?" Her eyes dazzle brighter.

I don't know how to answer her question. The thought of Lance seeing what else is out there, hurts. And I don't think it's fair to do that to him because I wouldn't want him to see anyone else.

A new flash of panic hits me.

Will he do that?

No, he wouldn't.

How do I know?

He might've done it before, I remind myself, the sick feeling in my gut reappearing over all the nights I've spent wondering if he's been faithful.

Willow's eyes turn to slits. "Why do you look sad again?"

"No reason. I just don't think I'm ready to date anyone," I confess.

She puts her arm around mine and leads me through the house. "That's okay. You don't have to date them. You can just have some fun."

I stay quiet.

"Hint, hint," she nudges.

I laugh, stating, "While that sounds really appealing, I don't know."

We step out onto the porch. A gust of wind hits me, and I cross my arms over my chest, wondering if I should grab a jacket.

Willow adds, "Tell you what, why don't I just introduce you to them and then whatever happens from there is your call?"

I stare at her. "You won't push me to do anything?"

She puts her hands in the air. "Nope. Scout's honor."

"You promise?"

"Promise," she sing-songs.

I cave. "Okay, fine. You can introduce me to them."

She claps her hands and beams at me. "Great. Now, let's talk about what you're going to wear tonight. I have a few gifts for you."

7

Alexander

"Where are they?" I question the boys, annoyed. But it figures. Anytime Willow's involved with anyone, we're late.

Standing near the truck, I put my hand on my hip and stare at the front door. It opens, and my sister and Phoebe step out.

My heart almost stops. Phoebe's wearing skinny jeans and a turquoise midriff-baring, long-sleeve top with hints of yellow and orange. She has a tan jacket over it, brown and turquoise suede cowboy boots, and a matching hat. Her long magenta hair is in curls, and her lips are painted red.

They walk toward me, and my blood buzzes. The same floral scent I've been smelling all week flares in my nostrils. I hold in a groan. It's the most intoxicating thing I've ever smelled, and it's been driving me nuts.

My sister chirps, "She cleans up well, doesn't she?"

I keep an annoyed look on my face, wishing Willow wasn't coming with us. The rest of my family's already left for the rodeo, but Willow seems to have made it a mission to become besties with Phoebe. I normally wouldn't care, but Willow is intent on parading Phoebe around all the bull riders.

I don't care.

I do.

No, I don't.

She's only here until Monday anyway, I remind myself.

"Those cowboys aren't going to know what hit them when they see you," Willow says to Phoebe, beaming at her and continuing to annoy me.

I go to the passenger door and open it. "Let's move," I order. It comes out sounding a tad nasty.

Phoebe meets my eyes and offers, "Sorry we took so long."

"It's fine. Let's go before we miss the whole rodeo," I reply.

She gets in the front, and Willow climbs in the back next to her nephews. I shut the door, go around, and slide into the driver's seat. I start the engine and then pull through the gate, barely listening to my sister babble with my sons and Phoebe. I concentrate on the road, wishing her scent wouldn't stay so pungent in the cab.

I don't say anything the entire ride to town. And before I know it, Willow's pulling Phoebe through the crowd, and my uneasiness grows.

"Dad, can we go with Aunt Willow?" Wilder asks.

"No," I say, knowing she's taking Phoebe where the bull riders hang out. It's a VIP lounge, and it's not far from our VIP area, but I don't like it. I steer my kids into the room where my family already is, and sidle up next to my brothers.

"Where's Sebastian?" I ask.

"He just called. He and Georgia are running late. They should be here any minute though," Mason answers.

I nod. I have some things I need to talk to Sebastian about, and I've always preferred to do things in person. I wish he'd come back to live on the ranch, but I also know someone has to stay in Dallas. Plus, it's where he and Georgia thrive. Their careers are there. My brother is brilliant at running the corporate end of our businesses and doing all the things in Dallas I would never want to do. And Georgia's cupcake franchise is taking off.

As if on cue, my brother bellows out, "What are you all waiting for? Where's my drink?"

I spin toward his voice.

Georgia laughs, shaking her head. Everyone greets them with hugs and kisses.

Georgia embraces me.

I ask, "How are the plans for the new bakery coming along?"

Her face lights up. "Great. I love our new franchise owners. They're going to do well."

I grin. "That's great news. I'm really proud of you," I tell her, excited that her dreams are coming true.

"Thanks. I couldn't have done it without Sebastian though."

I grunt. "Eh. Not true. You would've gotten there on your own."

Sebastian joins us, declaring, "I keep telling her that. She doesn't listen though." He hands Georgia a can of seltzer and then takes a long sip of his beer.

She takes a sip and asks, "So, how are things going with Phoebe?"

Phoebe. I forgot about her for a brief minute.

I shrug. "Fine. She'll be gone on Monday though."

Amusement fills Georgia's expression. Her lips twitch. She tilts her head, questioning, "Really? You haven't found any value in her?"

The question makes me feel guilty, especially with Georgia looking at me like that, but I answer, "No."

Georgia's voice turns stern. "Alexander, you've found zero value in Phoebe? There's nothing she's done that's been helpful?"

"No, I didn't say that."

She keeps pushing. "I figured. So tell me the things she's done that you see as valuable."

The hairs on my arms rise. I stepped into a trap. I didn't think Georgia would do that to me, but she has. I ignore her question and ask, "So you're on their side too?"

She shakes her head. "I'm not on anyone's side. Well, I'm on all of your sides. So tell me what value she's added."

"You can't be on everyone's side," I state, ignoring her demand again.

"Well, I am. I love all of you and want what's best for you. But I'd love to know what value you see in Phoebe. Because I know she's worth a lot more than you're giving her credit for."

I sigh. "I didn't say she wasn't worth anything. I admit she has done some valuable things."

"Okay. Like?" She arches her eyebrows, waiting.

I confess, "She was helpful with the boys' homework, especially with that TEKS math crap. You know I hate that stuff."

Georgia nods. "Yeah, I hear most parents don't like it."

I grunt. "It's the most useless thing I've ever seen. Why can't they teach kids the normal way?"

Georgia shrugs. "No idea. But it's good that Phoebe understands it, especially since your kids have to learn it. Is there anything else?"

I rack my brain, not wanting to answer, but a list of things scrolls through it.

"Come on. Phoebe's had to have done more good stuff than just homework."

Sighing, I cave, and answer, "She put groceries in my house. I'll admit it's nice for the kids or me to grab a snack. And the other night, she cooked. It was a nice change to eat at home instead of at Mom and Dad's.

"Is she a good cook?" Georgia questions.

I hesitate but admit, "She made some pretty mean tacos."

Amusement fills Georgia's expression. She teases, "Well, Alexander, I do believe that a girl from California who can make tacos in Texas is a winner."

I reply with a "Hmm," not wanting to admit much more.

"Is there any other way she's added value?"

I can think of all the things Phoebe has done in the last few days, but I still don't want to reveal them all to Georgia.

I'm saved by Mason, who teasingly shouts, "Get away from her! You're not worthy!"

I turn and squeeze my fists at my side.

One of the bull riders, Jericho, who I've never liked and tries to date Willow all the time, is talking to Phoebe. Before I can think about it, I charge toward them.

Right as I get there, I hear him say, "Come on, just give me your number. It's not that hard. Plus, I'm not a psycho."

"Yeah, he is," I interject, glaring at him.

He jerks his head back. "Man, why are you interfering in my business?"

"Phoebe's business is my business," I claim.

"Oh?" she says in surprise.

Jericho scoffs. "Yeah? How's that?" He glances at Phoebe, then adds, "She doesn't look like she agrees with your statement, man."

I meet Phoebe's eyes.

A blush crawls up her neck and into her cheeks.

Directing my disapproval back on Jericho, I declare, "She doesn't date. She's got a boyfriend, so back off."

Surprise fills his expression. He asks Phoebe, "Is that true? You're taken? Willow said you weren't."

She gapes between me and Jericho.

I ignore her expression and affirm, "She is. She's on a break with her boyfriend, but it's just a break. They're just taking some space from each other," I say, as if I actually understand their stupid arrangement.

Jericho puts his hands up. "All right, man. Phoebe, let me know when you're done with that dude, and we'll exchange numbers." He walks away.

Phoebe stares at me.

I can't tell if she's unhappy or glad I stepped in, but I suddenly feel foolish. I blurt out, "He's the biggest moron here. You can do better than that."

She studies me for a moment, then bites out, "Do you think you can keep my business to yourself?"

I freeze, my heart beating faster.

She continues, "I can decide who I want to know my business, but it's my decision, not yours. And I already told him I didn't want his number. There wasn't any reason for you to step in and shout my personal problems all over the place."

"He wasn't taking no for an answer. I know that slimeball."

She puts her hand on her hip. "We're in a public place. He asked for my number. I'm more than capable of replying and deciding whether I want to give it to him or not."

"Well, what's the point? You're only here until Monday," I remind her, then instantly regret it.

Anger flares on her cheeks and she glares at me.

All the times I've said that to her this week, I've never seen her angry, but I realize she is, and maybe I've said it too many times and pushed her too far.

She releases a deep breath. In a calm tone and through gritted teeth, she asks, "Why don't you remind me one more time?"

I instantly feel bad. In reality, my life would be much easier if I kept Phoebe here. She is valuable, and I recognize that. My life's been easy this week because she's helped out so much, and the boys love her. So do the other kids. Hell, my entire family loves her.

I need to prove to them that I can care for my children, with or without my parents here.

Before I can apologize for being such a dick, she spins and stomps toward Willow. For the rest of the night, she doesn't talk to me.

I try to think of what to say to get her back on my side or at least not be angry with me, but nothing comes to mind. The whole night, I watch her, barely taking in any of the rodeo or hearing the conversations around me.

Even when Sebastian tries to talk to me about several business ventures we need to discuss, I can't keep my mind on it. There's only one thing it's on, and it's how to get back into her good graces.

It all confuses me. I don't even understand why I care about her feelings, but every time she roams into our VIP area, I feel guilty. She interacts with the kids, chasing them when they're running around between the bull rides. My family fusses over her, and to everyone, it looks like we're fine.

I know we're not though.

She's still upset with me, and every time Willow tugs her across the rodeo to the riders' area, my gut churns.

At the end of the night, we get into the truck. She sits in the back with the boys, and Willow sits in the passenger seat. My mind races the entire drive home. We pull up to the ranch, and there's a sports car sitting outside the gate with its lights on.

I roll down the window, and ask the guard, "Who's in the sports car?"

He replies, "Guy says he's Phoebe's boyfriend from California. Name's Lance."

My insides tighten. I glance at Phoebe. "Are you expecting company?"

She shakes her head, answering, "No. I don't know what he's doing here."

I want to tell her to get rid of him, but she jumps out of the truck and goes to his vehicle before I can say more.

He gets out of his car, and I cringe. He looks as California as they come with blond, disheveled surfer hair. But it also has a preppy style to it. I figure he's a country club boy.

He towers over her, but he isn't as tall as me. He grabs her, hugging her so tight he lifts her off her feet.

I grip the steering wheel until my knuckles turn white.

She protests, "Lance, put me down."

I get out of the truck just as my parents pull up.

Dad rolls down his window. "What's going on here?"

"Um... I... Uh..." Phoebe stammers, trying to find her words.

Lance strolls over to my dad's car and sticks his hand out. "I'm Phoebe's boyfriend, Lance. I hope it's okay that I flew out here to surprise her."

"Well, of course it is," Dad states, and I scowl at him, hating everything about this situation. The only thing I like is that Phoebe looks shocked and not entirely happy he's here.

Mom says, "Well, you'll have to stay the weekend. You can take the guesthouse so you two have your privacy."

I tense.

No. That isn't happening. She cannot stay with this douchebag.

I blurt out, "I'm sure he'd be more comfortable in a hotel."

Lance turns and studies me. "Sorry, who are you?"

I hate everything about this guy.

Who does he think he is, questioning me on my property?

Phoebe quickly interjects. "This is my boss, Alexander. His boys, Wilder and Ace, are the ones I take care of."

"Oh, nice to meet you." Lance offers me his hand, but he doesn't like me any more than I like him. I take it and squeeze as hard as I can.

His eyes widen. I hang on longer than I should, until I finally release it.

He pulls his hand back, scowling.

"Well, don't sit out here all night. Let's all get through the gates," Mom directs.

Phoebe grabs the truck door, and Lance questions, "You're not coming with me?"

She freezes, catches my eye, then turns toward him. She sighs. "Okay, I'll ride with you."

I want to protest but don't. Adding to my disdain is his incompetence on how to be a gentleman and open the door for her.

She gets into his car, and everyone pulls through the gates. I stare after them, trying to calm my skyrocketing pulse.

"Dad, let's go," Wilder commands.

"Yeah, what are you doing?" Willow questions.

I begrudgingly get into the truck and pull up to the house.

Mom's already hugging Lance, which only irritates me further.

I step beside Phoebe, stating, "Didn't realize we were going to have company."

She shakes her head. "I didn't invite him."

"You want me to get rid of him?" I say quietly.

The corners of her lips turn up, and I almost think she'll say yes until my mom steps between us.

"Phoebe, darling, do you want the butterfly or stallion guesthouse?"

Phoebe doesn't answer.

Mom continues, "Do you remember which is which?"

I groan, wishing my mom would shut her mouth and not interfere.

Phoebe replies, "Either is fine, but honestly, he can stay in a hotel. I don't want to put you out, especially with no notice."

"Nonsense. You pick which guesthouse you want, then go get your stuff from your room," Mom orders.

"Stuff from my room?"

"Yes. You'll want some things so you won't have to run back and forth all weekend, right?" Mom answers.

My gut churns. *She cannot stay with this idiot all weekend.*

"Won't the boys need me?" Phoebe asks.

Mom waves her hand, answering, "Nah."

At the same time, I say, "Yes."

Both my mom and Phoebe stare at me in surprise.

Oh shit. What did I say?

Mom's expression looks disapproving. In a stern voice, she states, "I think you can handle them for a night, Alexander. Can't you?" She shoots me a challenging stare.

My insides tremble. I'm caught between a rock and a hard place, so I admit, "Yeah, of course I can."

"I thought so," Mom replies, then pats Phoebe on the arm. "So, dear, do you want the butterfly or stallion guesthouse?"

My chest tightens, and I don't move. I try to figure out how to make sure Phoebe stays in my house and not with her moron boyfriend.

He needs to leave Texas quickly. If he doesn't, I'm going to have to toss him out.

8

Phoebe

It shouldn't surprise me Lance disregarded my need for space and showed up, but it does. He always does what he wants, yet I'm shocked he came all this way to see me.

Why is he here?

He's going to sabotage my chances of keeping my job.

I pace my room, then grab my overnight bag out of the closet. I toss some random stuff in it, freaking out.

I have two days. Well, maybe two full days. Who knows when Alexander's going to throw me off the ranch. Any remaining time is crucial for me to prove he needs to keep me as the boys' nanny. Now Lance is going to steal it.

He can't have it.

I need to get him to leave tomorrow morning first thing.

This is so like Lance. Disappear, take no responsibility for it, and disregard all my wishes. Then, when I least expect it, make some grand gesture that's supposed to make me forget everything that's happened.

I'm not falling for it this time.

More determined than ever to take the space we need, I exit the bedroom.

Alexander and Lance stand in the family room. In an arrogant tone, Lance asks, "So you guys do real cowboy stuff out here, huh?"

Alexander answers with disapproval, "Yeah, something like that. I assume you know nothing about it though."

Lance grunts. "No need to."

I've got to get him out of here before he ruins everything I've been working so hard for.

"And what exactly do you do?" Alexander prods.

Lance shrugs. "I dabble in my family's business dealings."

Alexander's eyes turn to slits. "You 'dabble'?"

Oh no! This is going to get ugly fast!

From what I've witnessed this week, the Cartwrights value hard work and getting your hands dirty. It doesn't matter how much money they have. Every day, they get up and work. Lance doesn't have the same values or work ethic. So I avoid looking at Alexander and hightail it to the door, asking, "Ready, Lance?"

"Have a good night. I appreciate your family giving Phoebe and me our private space," Lance says.

"Space. That's an interesting word lately." Alexander scowls.

My insides quiver. He thinks I'm leading Lance on, but I'm not. All I want to do is give us the time we need to realize what we both want so we can move forward. And I still intend to be with Lance after we've taken our space.

At least, I think that's what I still want.

Regardless of what happens between Lance and me, it's another checkmark for Alexander to toss me off the ranch come Monday.

I don't reply, and step through the front doorway. The door slams behind me, and I turn my head, glaring at Lance. I snap, "You don't have to disrespect their property."

"Disrespect their property? What are you talking about?"

"Slamming their doors."

"I didn't," he claims.

"You did."

He goes to his side of the car, and it hits me how I've become accustomed to Alexander opening the passenger door for me. It strikes me as odd, as it never used to bother me. Yet it's a blinking red light, reminding me of another thing Lance doesn't do for me.

Why am I with him?

We have too much history to toss us aside without taking time to think.

Who cares if he opens my door? I never did before.

We just need space, I tell myself.

Lance starts the car, then leans over. He puts his hand behind my head and tugs me close to him, giving me a kiss, but I pull back.

"No kiss for me? You're not excited to see me when I flew all this way?" he accuses.

"I told you we needed space. This is my work environment. I only have until Monday to prove that I can make a positive difference here, and I need to focus on earning my place."

His eyes widen. "Monday? I thought you said you would be here for two months."

I reprimand myself for admitting my situation to him. It's just another thing I have to explain, and he won't understand it.

"Well, which is it?" he pushes.

I confidently assure him, "I'll be here for two months."

His eyes narrow. "Then why did you say Monday?"

I swallow the lump in my throat. This is all going in the wrong direction. I don't need this right now.

"Phoebe, answer my question," he demands.

My chest tightens. I admit, "I'm on a trial run. The family wants to make sure I'm the best person for the job. I came out here for a few days to show them how I'd interact with the kids and that I knew what I was doing."

He grunts. "So you're wasting your time?"

"No!" I protest, wishing I hadn't spilled the beans. I want to stay on the ranch more than anything. I want to prove to everyone that I belong here and that I'm qualified to take care of Wilder and Ace. Plus, I really like everyone—the kids and the entire family.

"The thought of you living as a country bumpkin is amusing," Lance says insultingly.

"The Cartwrights aren't country bumpkins! Plus, they've been very welcoming, and it's been a nice change from California."

Lance snorts. "You must have inhaled too much cow manure. You'll be back home on Monday, and I came all this way for no reason. You should have been honest with me, Phoebe."

Insulted, I glare at him, seething, "How dare you say that to me."

He chuckles. "Jesus. When did you get so uptight?" He takes off down the driveway.

I don't answer him, more irritated with him than I was when I left California. I shake my head, twist my fingers in my lap, and try to calm down.

He turns down another driveway. The orange glow from the lights on the fences looks beautiful, but I can't even appreciate it right now. He mutters, "Where is this place? How does anyone live somewhere this desolate?"

The guesthouse comes into view, the windows bright from the inside lights, and the front porch as decorated as the main house. Yet I'm so angry, I can't remember what guesthouse they put us in. I inform him, "It's right there."

He pulls up to the house, and *Stallion House* is lit up and displayed above the porch.

Lance mockingly says, "Jesus, it's straight out of *Little House on the Prairie*."

"Why are you here, Lance?" I demand, offended he's being rude about the Cartwrights and their property. There's nothing out of date or simple about the ranch or guesthouse.

"I told you, to come get you. This is absolutely ridiculous. I know you want some attention, so I'm giving it to you."

I gape at him.

He adds, "Time to end this game."

My rage boils. I hurl out, "What are you talking about? I don't need attention. I need space. We need to work on things. We need to think about what we both want and need. Then, we can decide what we want to do."

"Meaning?"

"If we still really want to be together!"

Tension builds as Lance leers at me. My insides quiver harder. I finally said what I'm afraid might happen.

He asserts, "I don't need time and space, Phoebe. We're meant to be together, and you know it. So tomorrow, you're going to get your shit, then we're going to get on a plane, and we're going to go back to Pismo. We'll get married. You don't need to worry about working. Everything will be fine." He parks the car and gets out, going directly to the house.

Once again, I'm reminded how he's never opened my door. Not that I can't do it myself, but I didn't realize how nice it was that a man actually thought about you enough to do it—even when I'm just the nanny.

I open my door and get out, taking my bag with barely anything in it inside the guesthouse.

Knotty pine walls, brown leather furniture, a vase of fresh fall flowers, and a huge set of bull horns adorn the space.

He snickers. "Man, this is as country as country gets, isn't it?"

"What is wrong with you?" I scold.

"Nothing's wrong with me. What's wrong with you? You've been here a few days, and you've forgotten your roots," he replies scornfully.

Every ounce of hurt and anger erupts within me. I roar, "I haven't forgotten anything! I haven't forgotten how you disappear for days at a time! And I haven't forgotten how you used to want to spend time with me, and you no longer do!"

"I flew across the country to come get you."

I scoff. "You didn't fly across the country. You flew across several states. Let's be honest."

"You're an ungrateful person, Phoebe. You give me no credit for making things right between us and then you act like you're perfect."

"Don't you dare blame me for this! I didn't stay out for countless days and ghost you!"

"Oh, go cry a bit more. And for God's sake, grow up!" he roars.

I take several large breaths, trying to stop trembling.

He claims, "You're overreacting, just like you always do."

I ponder his statement. *Am I overreacting?* Shouldn't I give him some credit for coming all this way?

Lance looks at me with puppy-dog eyes and lowers his voice. "Are you trying to tell me you don't want to be with me at all?"

His question and expression tug at my heart.

He adds, "Are you going to throw away our love and all the years we've been together?"

I blink hard. I'm so confused. If Lance could be the Lance he used to be, I'd say no in an instant. But I remind myself that I don't know who he is anymore.

His voice sounds scared and full of hurt when he asks, "You don't want to be together anymore?"

"No, that's not it," I reply, unsure of what I want but also fearful of making any big changes.

He arches his eyebrows. "Really? Seems to me that that's the message you're trying to give me right now."

"It's not."

"How is it not?" He crosses his arms, leering at me, and it's almost as if I can see fumes coming out of his ears.

I try not to wither beneath the weight of his stare. I normally do. The moment he gives me that look, I normally back down. But maybe I'm changing.

I close my eyes and try to slow my rapidly beating heart. He steps closer to me, puts one hand on my cheek, and his other hand around my waist. He tugs me into him.

His expensive cologne flares in my nostrils. It hits me how different it is from Alexander's scent. I don't know why I'm thinking of him or how he smells, but something about Lance's cologne is suddenly too sweet...too preppy...too clean.

What is wrong with me?

Why am I thinking these things?

"Come on, Phoebe, you know we're meant to be together. Stop playing this game."

"I'm not playing a game."

He presses his lips to mine, but I push him away.

"You still aren't going to kiss me?" he asks incredulously.

I cry out, "You're not listening to me."

He angrily shakes his head. "What am I not listening to, Phoebe? It's clear that you'd rather be here, hundreds of miles away from me, with strangers."

"It's not about that. I'm working," I declare.

He snorts. "You're nannying, and that's ridiculous."

I glare at him. "Why is that?"

"Nannies are for second-class citizens."

I jerk my head back. "Excuse me?"

He points at me. "You heard me. And you don't need to work. You'll have your own nanny when we're married and have kids. You don't need to *be* the nanny."

"What exactly is wrong with nannying?" I question.

He makes a frustrated noise. "Oh, Phoebe. You've always been so innocent and naive. You're willing to do things that you don't have to do, which is comical."

His statements infuriate me further. "I am not, and there's nothing wrong with me nannying. Plus, I like these children. They're nice and sweet, and I like the Cartwrights. They treat me really well."

"Before they toss you on your ass on Monday?" he throws out.

I freeze. I hate how his question might be the truth.

I'm barely able to breathe, and I curl my fists at my sides. Somehow, I find the courage to hold firm to what I want, ordering, "Lance, you need to go tomorrow morning."

"Yeah, we'll go. I have our tickets already bought. We're definitely not staying in this place all weekend," he replies.

My voice shakes when I say, "*You* are leaving. *I'm* staying."

He scoffs. "Stop being dramatic. This game is over, Phoebe." He steps closer, puts his hand under my chin, and roughly pushes my face back so I'm looking up at him. His other arm tightens around me, and I can't move. For the first time in a while, I'm scared.

"Ow, you're hurting me!" I whine, flashbacks of the last time I was scared he might get violent on me, darting in my head.

He seethes, "You listen to me. Tomorrow morning, you're getting on that plane with me. We're going back to Pismo. We're going to get married, and you'll be my wife. You're going to bear my children, and you're going to do what I say. You understand me?"

"You're hurting me," I repeat, tears filling my eyes and my neck throbbing.

He stares at me for a minute, then releases me. "This game is over." He steps into the kitchen, opens the fridge, and mutters, "Thank God they're hospitable enough to have drinks here." He cracks open a beer and downs half of it.

My mind races, wondering again why I'm with him. But then all the memories of the first year we were together pop up. It was the happiest I had ever been, and at a time I needed love in my life after everything happened with my family.

I know that man is still in there somewhere.

Isn't he?

Maybe it was all just a show.

No, that's who he really is, I tell myself, trying to give him the benefit of the doubt.

He spins on his heel, paces, then opens a door. "Not that big of a room, but it'll do for the night."

My irritation grows.

He continues, "Now, we haven't seen each other in a while, and you've been a bad girl, so get over here. I missed that pretty little mouth of yours." He unbuckles his belt and drops his pants.

My stomach turns. I shake my head. "You're disgusting."

"Now I'm disgusting. So you don't want to be with me?"

"I didn't say that, but you're acting disgusting. I'm not your whore."

"I didn't say you were. Although, a whore would give me less trouble than you."

His comment is the final straw. I glare at him one last time and announce, "I'm not going to tell you again. I need space, and this is my place of work. You have no right to be here unless you're invited. Tomorrow morning, you're leaving, and I'm not staying here tonight. I'm going back to do the job that I was hired to do. A job I love. And I'm going to stay here for two months."

He proclaims, "No, you're not. You're going to get fired on Monday. You just told me."

My anger toward him flares. "Why don't you have a little faith in me?"

He grunts. "You're not meant to be a nanny, Phoebe. You're meant to have a nanny. Now, squash your ridiculous ideas, and let's move on with our lives."

I blink hard, remaining silent, and flee toward the door.

"Phoebe," he shouts.

"Bye, Lance." I open the door and step out.

"Phoebe, get your ass back in here," he barks.

I don't obey him. It's dark, but I already know my way around the ranch. The orange lights help guide me as I maneuver myself down the road and back to Alexander's house.

When it comes into view, I hurry toward it, hoping Alexander has left the door unlocked, which he normally does. It took me a day or so to get used to the fact that they don't have to lock the doors here. The ranch is one of the safest places I've ever stayed. But still, I'm hoping I can get inside without waking him up.

The closer I get, the more I realize I won't have to. He's sitting on the porch, gripping a beer bottle. The six-pack is on the table next to him.

I climb the steps.

He asks, "What are you doing here?"

I can't tell if he's angry at me. I blurt out, "I'm sorry. I didn't invite him. I take my job seriously. Please don't hold it against me."

He studies me momentarily, and I try not to quiver, but my lips and insides won't stop. I might break down and cry.

His face softens. He grabs a bottle, asking, "You want a beer?"

Surprised, I meekly reply, "Sure."

He opens it, then orders, "Here, take it."

I cautiously step forward and grab the bottle, then I sit in the seat next to him.

In a disapproving tone, he asks, "So that's your boyfriend?"

"Yes. No. Yes. I don't know," I admit.

"Why aren't you with him now?"

I shrug. "It's complicated."

"What's so complicated about it?"

A million thoughts go through my mind. When nothing forms a coherent sentence, I finally reply, "Can we not talk about it? Can we just... I don't know. Can we talk about something else?"

He pins his intense gaze on me.

"Please," I beg.

He hesitates, then says, "Okay. Then tell me why you want to be here so badly. It seems like you've got a life back in California. Texas is pretty different from there."

I take a long swig of beer, then answer, "I told you I want to continue being your nanny. The boys are great, and your family is too. Plus, I like it here."

He doesn't say anything.

We drink our beer in silence.

After a few moments, he asks, "Don't you miss California?"

I briefly consider his question and then shake my head. "No."

"Why not?"

"I don't know."

"You don't know?"

For some reason, I start to laugh. "Yeah, I don't know. I can't give you any reason. All I know is I don't miss it, and I like it here."

My answer seems to appease him. We don't say much more. I finish my beer and get up.

"Where are you going?"

It's my turn to stare at him, and all I can think about is how different he is from Lance. "I'm going inside to go to bed. I'm your kids' nanny. And even if you kick me off the ranch come Monday, I will do my job while I'm here."

Disdain swirls in his tone when he says, "What about your boyfriend?"

I lift my chin and square my shoulders, replying, "He'll be leaving tomorrow morning. If he doesn't, just kick him off the ranch." I step inside the house, leaving a shocked Alexander on the porch.

As I try to sleep, a mix of guilt, relief, and more confusion than ever about where Lance and I stand, haunts me.

9

Alexander

"Breakfast!" Paisley yells, banging on a cowbell.

I look toward the main house, and my gut drops.

Lance struts inside, shooting me a haughty look over his shoulder.

What's he doing now?

I need to get him off this ranch.

Phoebe told me I could kick him off.

That's what I'll do. I'll let him eat his last meal, then drag him out of here.

"Shut the gate," Mason orders, snapping me out of my thoughts.

I secure the latch and then follow my brothers into my parents' house. Phoebe, Wilder, and Ace are several feet in front of us.

The uneasiness I can't seem to escape reappears. I take my turn and wash up, then step into the dining room.

"Sit down, Phoebe," Mom says brightly, pointing to the chair beside Lance.

He grins. "Yeah, sit down, babe."

Phoebe's lips pull into a tight smile. She obeys Mom's orders, and Lance puts his arm around her shoulders.

I take several large steps toward the empty chair on the other side of Phoebe, but Wilder slides into it. I almost tell him to get up, but then realize how that would look. So I quickly assess the situation and then sit in the chair directly across from Lance.

He smirks. "Did you finish rodeoing up those horses this morning?"

I snarl, "Rodeoing them up?"

He grins and shrugs. "I don't know what you call it. Sorry. I don't know much about living in the country," he offers, nodding at my dad.

Normally, my father wouldn't fall for Lance's act, but he lets the comment slide and states, "That's understandable. So, you're from Pismo Beach as well?"

Lance nods. "Born and bred. You can kind of say I'm royalty around there. Right, Phoebe?" He grins and puts his hand on her thigh.

My insides churn. I make a fist under the table until my knuckles turn white.

Phoebe's cheeks turn pink. "That sounds arrogant," she reprimands.

He whines, "I'm just joking, Phoebe. Lighten up. Come on."

An uncomfortable silence follows, but it doesn't last very long. There are too many kids and other family members around.

It's how things always are. Normally, I embrace it all, but this douchebag needs to get the hell off my ranch.

Mom chirps, "Was the guesthouse okay for you two?"

"It was good for me. How was it for you, Phoebe?" Lance asks, arching his eyebrows.

I bite my tongue, wanting to tell everyone she didn't stay there, but it's not my business.

Phoebe doesn't lie and instead answers, "It was nice of you to put Lance up when he didn't give me any notice he was coming."

"Of course. Your boyfriend's always welcome here," Mom states, further infuriating me.

My chest tightens. How can Mom be so naive? This guy's a total loser. On the outside, he looks like a well-put-together guy, but he's definitely a loser.

I interject, asking, "Lance, what time is your flight today?"

He stares at me momentarily, as if to intimidate me, but this boy doesn't have what it takes to achieve that.

My scowl deepens.

Phoebe answers, "He's leaving after breakfast. I saw there's a noon flight with plenty of seats left."

Lance's eyes narrow. He demands, "You mean *we're* leaving."

"No," she says.

Ace cries out, "You can't take Phoebe! She's our nanny. Dad, tell him!"

"Yeah. We haven't had our beach party yet," Isabella pipes up, her eyes widening.

Arrogance fills Lance's expression. He adds, "It doesn't seem to make sense for her to fly back on her own tomorrow."

"Tomorrow? Dad, tell him he can't take Phoebe!" Wilder demands.

I squeeze my fist tighter. I always knew this was coming. I had prepared all sorts of things to tell the kids when it was time for Phoebe to leave, but I can't think of one of them right now. I glance at her, and my heart thumps harder.

She stares at her plate, biting her lip. Her anxiety adds more fuel for my hatred of the man sitting next to her.

Lance announces, "Your dad's firing her tomorrow. And I don't see any point in letting her go through that. If she comes with me, she won't be alone and upset on the plane."

Before I can think about the repercussions, I blurt out, "Who said I'm firing Phoebe?"

Lance arches his eyebrows, challenging me. "She said come Monday, she won't have a job."

"No, that's not what I said," Phoebe interjects, glaring at him, then refocusing on me. She takes a deep breath, lifts her chin, and squares her shoulders, claiming, "I'm staying until tomorrow, until you make your decision."

Willow says, "Decision? What decision? That's a ridiculous statement. There is no decision to be made here. You're perfect for the boys, and you're a great nanny. There's no reason that you would leave. Alexander, reassure her."

I don't say anything. A lump forms in my throat, and I swallow hard.

"Dad, Phoebe can't leave. Tell her she's staying," Ace whines.

"Yeah, Dad. Besides the beach party we haven't had yet, who's going to make sure we have food at our house? I'm getting used to it now," Wilder chimes in.

Lance puts his hands in the air, stating, "It's okay, kids. Phoebe doesn't need to work anyway. We're getting married. I've got plenty of money. Once she pops out a baby, she'll have her own nanny, won't you, babe?"

A wave of heat floods my veins until nausea pummels me. An image of Phoebe in a wedding dress saying "I do" to the idiot in front of me and then with a big belly, bearing his children, taunts me.

Paisley chirps, "You're getting married?"

"Yeah, you're getting married?" Willow follows with a doubtful tone, then glances at Phoebe's hand.

Phoebe shakes her head. "No, we're not getting married. Lance has never asked me to marry him."

He claims, "I've talked about it quite a bit."

Dad narrows his eyes, questioning, "Have you asked her father for permission, son?"

Lance straightens up in his chair. His expression turns solemn. He reveals, "Phoebe's father isn't in the picture."

Phoebe's cheeks turn bright red. Shame and embarrassment cross her expression, and it makes me want to kill Lance. I don't know what the story is, but it's apparent she's upset about it.

Mom coos, "Oh dear. I'm sorry to hear that."

I want to ask her what happened to her father, but now isn't the time.

Willow tilts her head, her eyes in slits. She hurls out, "So you've gotten down on one knee? You've given her a ring?"

For once, I'm happy my sister is in the same room as Phoebe and me. She doesn't like Lance any more than I do. It's clear as day.

Lance clears his throat. "No, not yet. I wanted to give Phoebe some time to live a little while we're young. Isn't that right, babe?" He slings his arm around her, tugging her closer.

She doesn't say anything, gaping at her plate, and takes deep breaths.

I glower, seething, "You wanted to give her or yourself time to live a little?"

Lance answers, "Her," then grinds his molars, meeting my stare.

"Looks to me like she doesn't want to marry you."

Lance crosses his arms. He snarls, "That's a strange thing for a man to say who has nothing to do with our relationship. Or do you?"

My stomach flips. It's my own fault for speaking up. There's nothing going on between Phoebe and me, but I can't blame a man for asking me when I'm butting into their business. Still, I step further into hot water, fuming, "Meaning?"

He tries to intimidate me again with a glare, then takes a sip of coffee and nonchalantly shrugs. "Just asking. You seem to be fond of her for a guy who's going to fire her."

"I'm not firing her," I repeat before I think about the consequences.

"Woo-hoo! Yes," Wilder says, pumping his arm in the air.

"Beach party here we come," Isabella cries out.

"Good. Phoebe's way better at homework than Grandma or Dad. No offense, Grandma," Ace declares.

A smile forms on Phoebe's face. Then she pins her blues on me and quietly questions, "You're not firing me tomorrow?"

Now I'm between a rock and a hard place. My mouth turns dry. A few minutes ago, I couldn't think of one reason not to keep Phoebe. Now, all I can think about is how I need to prove to my family that I can handle the boys on my own.

"Of course he's not firing you. He'd be a fool to let you leave. Well, sometimes he's a moron, but he's not that big of an idiot," Willow teases.

I glance over at her, my pulse skyrocketing, once again wishing she knew how to mind her own business.

Phoebe clears her throat, then asks, "Alexander? Are you letting me stay?"

Lance grunts, then insists, "He already said he's firing you, so he's firing you. After we eat this delicious breakfast, we're getting on a plane and going home."

Dad speaks up. This time, he's not on Lance's side. "Now, hold on a minute, young man. Phoebe took a job with our family, and I'm pretty sure she can make her own decisions. And my son clearly stated he's not firing her."

Lance glances over at Dad. "Why should she stay in an environment where she's constantly being threatened to lose her job?"

"She's not," I claim.

He arches his eyebrows. "That's an interesting statement. She told me on the phone the other day, and again last night, she was getting fired on Monday."

"Stop saying that! You didn't listen to what I said. I told you I was on a trial run and Monday would be the deciding day," Phoebe corrects.

"Sounds like threats to me," Lance adds.

"My son doesn't threaten women," Dad declares.

Lance sits back in his seat and sighs. "Sir, I'm not trying to get on your bad side. I'm only trying to protect my woman."

His woman.

It's another statement that makes me want to hurl. He doesn't deserve Phoebe. I've only known him a few hours, and it's clear he doesn't deserve one ounce of her time or attention.

I meet Phoebe's eyes. "I think she can make up her own mind and decide if she wants to stay or go. Can't you?"

She confidently states, "Yes. Of course I can."

Good girl.

I toss Lance a smug look and then turn back to Phoebe. I ask, "Are you still interested in staying on the ranch as my kids' nanny? Or are you ready to go back to Pismo?" My chest tightens as I wait for her answer.

What if she says she wants to go back to Pismo with Mr. Douchebag?

Why do I care?

My kids love her. It's only about my kids.

Plus, I want to put Lance in his place.

Not that Phoebe's not a great nanny or hasn't shown her value, but sending this idiot back to Pismo and keeping Phoebe away from him is suddenly way more important than proving to my family that I don't need help.

She beams at me. "Of course I want to stay. I love it here. And I really enjoy helping the boys."

She loves it here.

I grin, directing it at Lance, and boast, "See, she's not going anywhere with you."

He grabs her hand. "Phoebe, don't be ridiculous."

Dad warns, "Now, hold on, son. She came here to do a job. She's clearly stated she wants to continue working. And I'll add that I believe she has a great situation here. My son pays her well. She has a roof over her head and food in her belly. Plus, she's great at what she does. So I believe she's made her decision and you should respect it."

He snaps, "Her commitment that was held over her head until I showed up?"

"Not true," I state, even though he's got a point.

Would I really have let her go? I think, then push the question away. I convince myself that some things are more important than proving your point, and this is one of them.

"Excuse me, but that's not how I see it," Lance argues.

Phoebe begs, "Lance, please. Let it go."

He can't. He shakes his head, insisting, "That's not a situation for her to be in. She shouldn't always be worried about losing her job."

I nod. "No, I agree. And that's why she doesn't have to worry about losing it. I just told you I'm keeping her on. Actually, Phoebe, you passed with flying colors. Congratulations. We're happy to have you here for the next few months. In fact, maybe when my mom and dad get back, we'll extend your employment into a permanent position."

Lance's eyes turn to slits.

Jagger chuckles, then declares, "I'm hungry. And this conversation is boring me. Can we talk about something else and eat?"

I reply, "I'm okay with it if Phoebe is good with her position here and moving forward?"

She nods, smiling bigger. "Yes, I'm happy. Thank you for keeping me on."

"Thank you for doing such a good job," I respond, then pick up my fork and dig into my potatoes.

Lance lowers his voice, commanding, "Phoebe, I need to talk to you. Alone."

She releases a frustrated breath. "Lance."

"Phoebe."

She sighs. "Can you all excuse us for just a moment?" She slides her chair back and gets up.

Mom offers, "Of course, dear. You and Lance take all the time you need."

I press my fingers so hard into my thigh they hurt. "Lance, let me know when you want a ride to the airport."

He shoots me daggers with his glare.

Wilder interjects, "He drove a car here, remember, Dad?"

"Ah, that's right, son."

Lance spends another moment trying to stare me down, then rises.

Phoebe follows, and they disappear from the room.

"He's leaving as soon as breakfast is over," I mutter, then shove potatoes into my mouth.

Mom scolds, "That's not your decision. It's Phoebe's. He's her boyfriend."

"So what? Besides, they're on a break. He should be giving her the space she needs," I declare, still not sure what that phrase means, but it's what she said she wanted. So he should give it to her. If he's any sort of man, he should respect her wishes.

The room erupts in lively conversation about Thanksgiving and all the holiday plans over the next few months, but I don't engage. I barely taste my eggs or bacon. I swirl my toast through the yolk until the picture of the turkey on the plate appears, then I toss it down.

Phoebe and Lance seem to be taking forever.

What if Mr. Douchebag is convincing her to leave with him?

She won't go.

But what if she does?

The door opens and Phoebe steps into the room. She sits back down in her seat.

Willow questions, "Where's Lance?"

Phoebe clears her throat and smiles. She puts her napkin on her lap and replies, "Lance decided to go to the airport now. He said to say thank you for all your hospitality."

Sure he did.

Mom frets, "Is everything okay, dear?"

"Hopefully, you dumped him," I mumble under my breath.

Phoebe's blues meet mine in surprise.

I don't flinch.

"Phoebe?" Mom softly questions.

Phoebe tears her gaze off mine and refocuses on Mom. She answers, "Everything's fine, Ruby. I'm happy to stay on the ranch and nanny for the boys. It's best if Lance returns to Pismo. But don't worry, I'm one hundred percent focused on my job."

It's a statement she doesn't have to make. She's proven she's good at what she does. I already trust her with my boys. And the realization hits me like a slap in the face.

My insides shake. All I can do is wonder how a woman got me to trust her with my kids so quickly.

She's a nanny. It's normal, I tell myself.

Is it though?

I can't be sure. I've never had a nanny before. My family has always stepped up to help me after my wife got sick and died.

Mom doesn't want to let Phoebe's relationship issues go. She replies, "Of course you're here to do your job. And you're excellent at it. But are you sure... Is Lance okay too?"

Who gives a shit? I almost blurt it out but manage to keep it to myself.

In a cheerful voice, Phoebe answers, "Yes, he's fine. We'll be fine."

"We'll be fine." As if they're still together.

Panic sets in, causing my heart to race. I shift on my seat.

Phoebe smiles and asks, "Can we change the subject now?"

"Of course, dear," Mom answers.

Isabella pipes up, "Phoebe, can we make those turkeys and other decorations today?"

"Sure!" she answers.

The rest of the meal is spent in cheerful conversation with more holiday talk. By the time we finish breakfast, Lance is nowhere to be found, and there's no further mention of him.

Dad walks back to the corral with me, pats me on the back, and declares, "About time you admitted you needed a nanny."

I groan, realizing for the first time since breakfast, what just happened.

10

Phoebe

The Next Day

The Cartwright kitchen buzzes with excitement. Ruby, her daughters, and Georgia help prepare vegetables and meat for the beach party.

After Lance left, I felt a weight had been lifted from my chest. Shortly after breakfast, Ace earned the final star for the beach party, so I suggested we have it today.

The kids were nearly jumping out of their skins with excitement. It must have been contagious because Alexander surprised me and suggested the entire family participate, especially since Ruby and Jacob leave for their mission trip tomorrow morning.

My little beach party soon became a big event. Within hours, a tent with tables, chairs, and a sound system was put up next to the lake. Alexander and Sebastian dug the leftover ashes out of the fire pit and reconstructed it for the hobo dinner I suggested we make. Georgia and Paisley went to the store and bought all the ingredients I requested. And Willow, Evelyn, and I spent hours with the kids, finding or creating everything we needed for games and making decorations for the tent.

Georgia asks, "Phoebe, how does this work? Do we toss everything in the can, or is there a specific order?"

I answer, "Meat first, then vegetables. Then we pour the beer and water over it. The corn on the cob will go in the basket insert."

"Gotcha." She picks up the smoked sausage and tosses it in. The rest of us add the green and purple cabbage, parsnips, turnips, radishes, red potatoes, and rainbow carrots.

Paisley positions the steamer basket filled with corn inside the can, and states, "I still can't believe we've never heard of this."

Evelyn declares, "I just don't know how it's possible Georgia's never heard of it! She always knows everything about cooking."

Georgia laughs. "Not everything!"

"Yeah, right," Ava adds.

Georgia shrugs. "I never went camping, but I'm excited to see how this turns out."

"You're going to love it," I claim, feeling nostalgic. When I was a kid, my family used to camp in the mountains. My dad would always take a metal garbage can, and we'd fill it with all the food, cooking it for hours over the bonfire. I haven't done it since I was ten, but the idea came to me this week when I was thinking about what we could do for the beach party. When I told the Cartwrights about it, the kids thought it was cool to cook and eat out of a garbage can, and the adults all rallied around the idea.

Ruby says, "Let me get someone to come get this can." She opens the back door and shouts, "Alexander! Mason! Can you come help?"

Within minutes, they step into the kitchen. Alexander grasps a handle, glances into the can, and says, "Never thought we'd be eating out of a garbage can."

"It's going to be delicious!" I declare.

"I guess we'll find out." He shoots me a smile.

My butterflies take off. Since yesterday morning, he's been more relaxed. It's a nice change from his usual scowl, but every time he grins, my flutters have a party in my stomach.

"This is heavy," Mason says with a grunt.

Alexander mocks, "Need me to carry it myself so you don't hurt your muscles?"

"Ha ha," Mason replies, then steps toward the door.

They exit, and all of us follow.

They put the can on the trailer that is hooked up to a double-seated ATV.

"Where are the kids?" I question, gazing across the ranch.

"Jagger, Sebastian, and Dad took them down to the lake on the horses," Alexander informs me.

"Ah." I glance at the horses several feet away, tied to the fence post. Each one has a saddle and bridle, ready to ride.

Since the first day I arrived, Alexander hasn't pushed me to ride a horse again, but I always feel like it's coming.

He teases, "Don't worry. I'll let you ride in the ATV with me."

I arch my eyebrows. "You're not riding your horse?"

He shrugs. "Nah, there's a lot on this trailer, and it can be hard to maneuver through the woods. It's best if I don't make you attempt it. Unless you have previous experience hauling a trailer?" His lips twitch.

I shake my head. "Nope."

He points to the passenger seat. "Then I'll drive. Get in."

I don't argue. I slide onto the seat, and he goes around the vehicle. Mason, Ruby, and Willow leap onto their horses. Paisley, Ava, and Evelyn get into the other ATV.

We make our way through the wooded area to the lake. Alexander's scent flares between us, and I wonder if there will ever come a day when it doesn't intoxicate me.

We whiz past trees. Then he slows, ordering, "Hold on, Phoebe, there's a bumpy patch."

I reach for the side rail, and he guides us over the pitted dirt road. He speeds up again and steers the ATV around the final bend.

The lake appears. The sun glistens over the sparkling water, and the sound of country music grows louder. The kids run along the shore, chasing each other and playing tag.

"Your family really knows how to step up for a little party," I comment, amazed at how the Cartwrights put all this together in such a short amount of time.

He shoots me his dazzling grin and chuckles as he parks the ATV. "One thing we know how to do is represent on the party front."

"Looks like it," I agree, then get out of the vehicle.

Alexander adds, "Also, this is Texas. Go big or go home is our motto."

I laugh. "I don't think Texas would be disappointed with this setup."

The others arrive behind us. Alexander and Mason haul the trash can to the bonfire site. Then Alexander grabs the lighter fluid and douses the kindling and wood. He hands me a box of matches. "Your party, your fire."

I take the matches, open the box, and pick a stick. I strike it along the side of the box and then toss it in the pit.

A flame erupts, and he grabs the side of the can. Mason grabs the other, and they put it on top of the metal grill.

Alexander asks, "What now?"

"Now we have fun," I say, then shout, "Who wants to play Pumpkin Ring Toss?"

"I do! I do!" Jacob Jr., Evelyn's five-year-old, yells.

The others echo his excitement, jumping up and down.

I walk over to the first area I set up earlier this morning. Pumpkins sit staggered on the sand. Signs reading 10, 25, 50, 75, and 100 are in front of them. Cones and plastic rings are behind the line drawn on the ground.

The kids run over, and I instruct, "Everyone gets ten rings. You can toss your rings on whatever pumpkin you want. The number in front of the pumpkin is how many points you earn. At the end, you have to add up your points. Whoever has the most points, wins."

Isabella asks, "What do we win?"

I point to the picnic table. "You get to pick whatever you want from the prize box."

She beams. "Okay, I'm going to win."

"You wish," Wilder says. Determination fills his expression, and he picks up the red rings.

She rolls her eyes. "You'll see."

I laugh. "Let's be nice to each other."

"Good luck with that," Alexander states, stepping next to me and crossing his arms. The shadow from his cowboy hat shades most of his features, but I don't miss his lips twitching.

"I want to be pink!" Emma declares, stepping next to the rings and picking one up.

"I'm orange!" Ace claims.

"Red!" Wilder decides.

Jacob Jr. picks up a green ring, and Isabella selects the purple.

Alexander leans closer, lowering his voice. "You have yellow and blue left, but we don't have another two kids."

I nod, replying, "Better to let everyone have a choice than someone whining they didn't get to choose."

"Ah. That's good thinking," he praises.

"Yep!" I step forward and ask the kids, "Are you ready?"

They all shout, "Yes!"

"One, two, three, toss!" I call out.

Rings fly across the beach. Some hit the sand while others go around the pumpkins. Every time one does, excited shouts fill the air.

When all the rings have been tossed, the kids count their points, shouting them out.

Isabella jumps up and down. "I did it! I won! Told you, Wilder!"

He shrugs. "Big deal."

I laugh and point to the prize box. "Great job. Go ahead and pick something out."

"Yay!" She runs over to the table and pulls out a sheet of stickers.

I ask, "Okay, who's ready for pine cone bowling?"

"I was born ready," Ace states, stepping in front of the other line and picking up the plastic bowling balls I bought in town the day before.

"I'm ready!" Jacob Jr. says, taking the space next to Ace.

Alexander asks, "Where do you come up with these games?"

"You've never played these before?"

He shakes his head. "No."

"That's shocking to me."

"Why is it shocking?"

I point out, "Your family seems really into holidays."

"We are into holidays."

"Then how have you never played these games?" I ask in a teasing tone, a little bit shocked.

He shrugs. "Not sure."

Willow yells, "Mark, get set, go!"

I turn my attention back to the kids. They aim the balls at the pine cones.

Wilder's the first to knock his pine cones down. He pumps his fist in the air, shouting, "Yes."

I instruct, "Okay, go set your pine cones back up. We're going to do it for ten minutes and see how many times you can knock them down."

He furrows his brows. "What? I don't win?"

I shake my head. "Not unless you're the only one to knock the most sets down. Now, go set yours back up."

"Ugh!" he grumbles and then runs over to set up his pine cones.

Alexander chuckles next to me. "You crushed his dreams."

I laugh. "Sorry, but not sorry?"

He chuckles again and refocuses on the kids.

By the time the pine cone bowling's over, Ace has the most wins. He taunts his brother. "See! I beat you!"

Wilder spouts, "Whatever. I can still ride a horse better."

"Uh-uh-uh. Not allowed to say that," I remind him.

"It's true!"

"Did you want barn duty for a week?" Alexander warns.

Wilder quickly shuts his mouth.

"He should do barn duty. He went against the rules," Ace claims.

Alexander suggests, "I could have you do it with him so you two can learn to stop harassing each other."

Ace protests, "No!"

I interject, "Let's focus on beach day. Ace, go get your prize."

He runs over and pulls a slinky out of the box.

I step over to the white plastic sheet. We spent hours painting a huge turkey on it, along with red, blue, yellow, and green dots. I ask, "Who wants to play Turkey Twister?"

The kids all run to the edge of the sheet, and the adults follow.

Alexander states, "I was the master at Twister."

I arch my eyebrows. "Were you?"

He nods. "Yep! I could beat all my siblings."

"Why don't you play, then?"

"You want me to play?"

"Yeah."

"The games are for the kids."

"Who said adults can't play?"

"Let's have the kids play first and then adults," Evelyn suggests.

We agree. After several games and tons of laughs, the kids finally have enough. At one point, all of them win, and all get prizes.

Alexander looks at me. "Ready to see how this is done?"

I smirk. "Who says you'll beat me?"

"Guess we'll find out," he says in challenge.

I tease, "Should I be scared?"

He grins. "We'll see." He takes his cowboy hat off and sets it on the picnic table. He grabs my hand and pulls me in front of the game, adding, "Don't chicken out now, Miss Nanny."

I hold in my laugh. He's never called me that before. I realize how much I like the relaxed side of Alexander. He hasn't shown me it until now.

Paisley grabs the spinning wheel that we made. She flicks it, calling out, "Blue."

Alexander puts his left foot on a blue dot. I put my right foot on one.

Isabella takes a turn and spins. She chirps, "Red." We both put a hand on red.

The kids all take turns spinning and calling out colors until our bodies are twisted, and I end up underneath Alexander.

"You're going down, nanny," he taunts, reaching over me and moving his hand to the green.

"You wish!"

"Yellow!" Jacob Jr. yells.

I move my hand, and Alexander moves his leg over my torso so his body is in a V over me. His T-shirt falls toward his neck, revealing his six-pack...and another surprise.

My pulse pounds between my ears. I stare at the ink trailing over the right side of the V of his torso. A rope twists between the letters s, t, a, l, l, i, and o.

What word is that?

"Red!" Isabella orders.

He moves his leg, and I adjust my foot over a row. I stare at his tattoo, then blurt out, "Stallion!"

His body tenses, which makes his abs even more appealing.

"Yellow!" Ace says.

We try to adjust our bodies, but we end up falling. He lands over me, catching his body weight so he doesn't crush me. His face and hot breath come inches from mine. Heat flares in his expression and his gaze darts to my lips.

I inhale sharply.

He slowly redirects his eyes to mine.

Snap out of it.

"You tattooed the word stallion on your V?"

His heated look morphs to one of mortification, and he once again tenses up.

Willow teases, "He didn't tell you about his tattoo?"

Ava smirks, adding, "It's his pride and joy!"

He groans, then snaps, "Quiet, Willow," before he carefully rolls off me.

I get off the ground and repeat, "You tattooed the word stallion on your stomach? Is that your favorite horse?"

The Cartwright siblings erupt into laughter.

"What am I missing here?" I question.

Alexander's face reddens. He declares, "It was a long time ago. I was young."

Evelyn interjects, "Phoebe, did you see the arrow at the end of the rope?"

He turns his head, and says in warning, "Evelyn!"

I bite my lip, not taking my eyes off a humiliated Alexander.

Willow laughs, announcing, "He claims the bull riders are cocky, but he has no room to talk."

"Too bad he's not as big of a stallion as I am," Jagger claims.

"Shut up," Alexander mutters, clenching his jaw.

I try not to laugh, but I can't help it. I put my hand over my mouth.

"You should tell her how you got it," Evelyn adds.

Sebastian chimes in, "Yep. That was a brilliant day in decision-making."

Alexander puts his hand over his face and groans. "All of you need to stop."

Ace tries to protect him, claiming, "He loves horses that are winners! Don't you, Dad?"

Alexander quickly looks at him. "Yeah, that's right."

The adults snicker.

Mason urges, "Why don't you tell Phoebe the story?"

"Seriously, you all need to stop," Alexander orders.

"Oh no. I think I have to know this story now," I claim, glancing again at his torso even though his shirt is over it. My butterflies flutter harder.

He says, "It was just something stupid I did."

Mason announces, "He was drunk. Well, we were all drunk. Might not have been our best moment."

Amused, I question, "Oh? Do you have a stallion tattoo with a rope and arrows?"

"Ugh, it sounds so bad," Alexander mumbles.

Mason squares his shoulders and shakes his head. "Nah, my tattoos are legit."

Alexander moans. "Please, shut up."

"Kids, go play another round of pine cone bowling," Ruby orders, and points toward the game.

"We already played that," Emma whines.

"Yeah, play it again. The winner gets another prize."

It does the trick, and the kids run over to it.

Sebastian urges, "You might as well just tell her. It's probably better coming from you than us."

Alexander's face turns redder. He shakes his head at his family. "You all don't know when to stop."

"Aw, come on now, brother. You're inked for life. Be proud of it," Sebastian taunts, his grin widening more.

A new wave of embarrassment fills Alexander's expression. He claims, "There's nothing to tell. We were out. We were young. We were drinking. It was a bad mistake."

Jagger mocks, "Oh? So you're admitting you're not a stallion."

"You wish you had my skills," Alexander retorts.

My blood heats further.

Mason teases, "You sure about that? There's probably a lot of women who would claim differently."

Alexander shakes his head. "Time to change the subject."

Jagger continues, "So, are you or are you not a stallion?"

"Jagger," Ruby reprimands.

He puts his hands in the air. "What? It's fair to ask him to clarify that."

Jacob chuckles hard, chiming in, "If a man's going to tattoo that on himself, he might as well be positive that that's what he is."

Alexander's mortification amplifies as the taunting continues.

I finally decide to help him out. I say, "I'm glad we cleared that up. I think it's time to check on the hobo dinner. Alexander, can you help me get the can off the fire?"

"Please," he says, as if relieved to be let off the hook.

When we get to the fire pit, he puts on gloves, takes the can off the fire, and opens the lid.

"Can you take the corn out for a moment?" I ask.

"Sure." He removes it.

I pull a few pieces of food out and study them, then announce, "It still needs about another hour."

"Okay." He covers it and puts it back on the fire.

I can't help myself, so I quietly ask, "So stallion is your big secret tattoo?"

He puts his hand over his face and groans again.

I laugh.

He recovers and says, "Now that you know mine, you have to tell me what yours say."

"No way," I reply, pretending to zip my lips and throw away the key.

"It's only fair."

I laugh even harder. "Nope. Just because you accidentally showed me yours doesn't mean I'm going to show you mine. Sorry."

"Are you embarrassed by them?"

My face falls. "No. Not at all."

He studies me. "Then why won't you tell me?"

Before I can think about what I'm saying, I blurt out, "Only the lucky ones get to see them. Maybe someday your luck will change."

He pins his heated look on me.

I realize what I said and how it sounds. My cheeks turn as hot as the fire.

"That so?" he asks, giving me a challenging stare.

I open my mouth but then shut it, quickly walking away and putting distance between us. I pretend to check on the kids' bowling game, but I can't stop beating myself up about why I said something so inappropriate to my boss.

And there's another question plaguing me.

Did he look at me how he did because he liked my suggestion, or was that all in my mind?

11

Alexander

*P*hoebe sits far away from me at dinner, barely looking at me. Whenever I catch her eye, she looks away and starts a new conversation with one of the kids or my siblings.

I can't stop thinking about how to get her to show me her tattoos.

What names did she ink on her body, and why?

Does she think about those guys every day when she's naked and in front of the mirror?

My cock aches, thinking what she'd look like naked.

Jesus. I need to get my head out of the gutter.

We finish eating, and it's turning darker. The kids run around, playing Ghost in the Graveyard. I add more logs to the fire while Phoebe pulls cans of fruit filling, bread, graham crackers, chocolate, and a huge bag of marshmallows out of a canvas tote.

I go to the ATV, grab the roasting sticks and metal pie makers, and set them on the table. "Dinner was good. That was a great idea," I compliment.

She glances at me. "You liked it?"

I nod. "I did. It was really creative. We should make it an annual event."

She smiles, but then it falls. "Maybe you can invite me every year."

The thought of Phoebe not being on the ranch shouldn't feel odd, but it does. My chest tightens. All I can say is, "Sure."

She beams again. "Okay, then I'll pencil it into my busy calendar."

I chuckle.

She adds, "Actually, I haven't done this in a long time. That last time my family went camping, I was only ten." She stops, as if remembering something, and her expression turns a little sad.

"Is everything okay?"

She forces a smile and picks up a can opener. She presses it against the lid of cherry pie filling and turns it. "Yeah, every-thing's fine."

"Was it a memory or something?"

She hesitates. "Why'd you ask that?"

"You looked sad for a moment. Was it about your father?"

As much as I know it's not right to pry into her life, I want to know what Lance meant about her father not being around.

Why isn't he?

She's a good person. Why wouldn't he want to be part of her life?

Did something horrible happen to him?

She doesn't answer at first, concentrating on opening the can.

I add, "Sorry, I didn't mean to pry. I'm just curious about your family."

"You are?"

I shrug. "Sure. You know about mine. It seems like I should know about yours."

She sets the open can down, releasing an anxious breath. Then she says, "My family situation is a little complicated."

"Oh?" I say, hoping she'll tell me more. I don't know why, but all of a sudden I want to know everything about her. I tell myself it's because she's watching my kids and is an interesting person. She's so different from us or anyone I've encountered, and I find it refreshing.

Her voice is sad when she reveals, "My mom and sister were in a car accident."

Goose bumps break out on my skin. "I'm sorry to hear that. Are they okay now?"

She shakes her head. "No, my sister's in a home because she can't care for herself. She doesn't know who I am. And my mom... Well..." She looks away.

I put my hand on her arm. "I'm sorry."

She takes a deep breath and looks back at me. "It's okay. It's been a while. It took a long time for me to process things and get used to it."

"I'm sure it's hard for you."

She nods, continuing, "My mom lives in a mental institution. After the accident, she couldn't handle the guilt. She was driving the car. Within a year of my sister not recovering, my mom had such severe depression, I couldn't take care of her anymore. The last time she..." Phoebe glances down and blinks quickly.

I step even closer, lowering my voice. "I'm sorry."

Her eyes glisten, and she puts on a brave face. She speaks quickly, stating, "That's my family's story."

"That's a lot for a young woman to deal with," I offer.

She picks up another can and secures the opener on it. "You don't really get a choice when someone you love is sick or injured."

"No, you don't. And it really sucks." I swallow down the lump in my throat.

She freezes, then turns toward me. "I'm sorry. Your parents told me what happened to your wife. I'm sure that was hard on you."

My heart beats harder. "Let's say it was a super-shitty time."

Her expression turns, but it isn't like everyone else's. It's sympathetic, but I don't see pity, which is what I normally experience when people hear my wife died. Instead, there's an element of understanding in her silence.

After a moment, I add, "I'm really sorry to hear about your mom and sister. But where's your dad in all this?"

She returns to her can, cutting the lid, answering, "My parents divorced when I was eleven. That's why my last camping trip was when I was ten. But after the accident, he just took off. It's like he disappeared into thin air."

It's an unfathomable reality for her. I can't imagine ever leaving my sons, especially after their mother died. Phoebe basically lost her mom and sister, so her dad disappearing is inhumane to me.

Shocked, I blurt out, "So you don't have any idea where he went?"

She schools her features, chirping, "Yep. So that's my story. Anyway, do you like cherry or apple pie?"

I glance down at the cans. "Either."

She tilts her head and peers at me closer, teasing, "Why, Alexander Cartwright, are you telling me that you don't have a favorite between cherry and apple?"

I laugh. "Busted. Cherry."

She beams. "Good choice. It's my favorite too."

"Really?"

She nods. "Yeah, but there's nothing like a homemade one, right?"

"Agreed. But you haven't had pie until you taste Georgia's. Just wait until Thanksgiving. And it's too bad you weren't here this past summer. She made the best pies ever. She even took the kids to pick the cherries."

Phoebe pushes her hair behind her ear and says, "I bet they were good. She's really talented."

"Yeah, she is. You're pretty talented too."

Her lips curve. "I am?"

"Yes. You're great with the kids, and you're super creative. Way more creative than I am."

"Well, you were pretty creative when you picked out your tattoo," she teases.

I groan and put my hand over my face. "I'm never going to live that down, am I?"

She laughs. "It's okay. Sometimes, we do things we wish we wouldn't have, don't we?"

"Are we talking about your tattoos again?"

She shakes her head. "No, I'm okay with what I inked on my body."

"And what would that be, again?"

She wags her finger. "Uh-uh-uh. Not telling you."

"What if we make a bet?"

She dramatically gapes at me.

"What did I say?" I question.

"A bet? I think you're becoming an irresponsible gambler, Alexander Cartwright."

"Why is that?"

She turns more toward me, answering, "Because you lost our last bet. Actually, you owe me a favor."

I freeze. I had forgotten about that bet, and it was a stupid mistake. I don't lose very often when I gamble. I always take calculated risks. But I have to hand it to her. She's right. I do owe her a favor. So I cross my arms, suggesting, "Why don't we make another bet?"

She taunts, "Are you becoming an irresponsible gambler?"

"No, I can assure you I'm a very responsible gambler," I assert.

She scoffs. "I'm not sure how anyone can claim that."

"Trust me, I am."

She doesn't say anything, just stares at me.

"So here's what I propose. You can ask for anything you want, but if I win, I get two things."

"Like?"

My blood heats, rushing through my veins. I declare, "I get to see your tattoos."

Red creeps from her neck and sprawls across her cheeks.

My dick hardens. The image of her and what I think she might look like naked appears in my mind. And I should stop all this before it goes any further, but I can't seem to. She's quickly become the most intriguing person I know.

She inquires, "What's the second thing?"

"You let me teach you how to ride a horse."

Her eyes widen. "We're back to this horse craziness now?"

I chuckle. "Yep. You're on the Cartwright ranch. It's a sin not to know how to ride a horse."

"Is that so?"

"Yep. God's honest truth."

She sighs. "I don't want to ride a horse. It's scary."

"Why are you so scared? Tons of people ride horses every day," I point out.

"And people fall and die or become paralyzed."

I scoff. "Everyone around you on this ranch is riding horses. You'll never have a better teacher than me. I promise."

"Oh, I don't doubt you're a good teacher. It's the horse I don't trust."

I grin. "So you trust me, then?"

She stills, peering at me closer.

My pulse pounds between my ears. I've only known her a week, but I'm dying to hear her admit she trusts me. I know she doesn't trust that douchebag, Lance.

She has a boyfriend.

No, she's done with him.

She's not. They're only taking space, whatever that means, I remind myself.

"I guess I trust you," she confesses.

Even though she has a boyfriend, my ego soars. "Good. And I would never put you in danger. So I would never put you on a horse that I didn't trust with my kids."

"Your kids know how to ride though," she points out.

"Yes, because I taught them, and I can teach you too," I declare.

She nervously laughs. "You really want me to ride, don't you?"

I nod. "I do."

"Why?" she questions.

I shrug. "Because I love it and think you will too."

She stares at me.

My chest tightens. I want to know what she's thinking but can't figure it out. I finally question, "So what do you want if you win the bet?"

She tilts her head. "I thought you only make bets you can win."

I grin. "I do. But humor me."

She shrugs. "I don't know. I haven't had time to think about it."

"There must be something you want."

She ponders it for a moment, then snaps her fingers. "Okay, I got it."

"What do you want?"

"You can't be upset with me."

"Why would I be upset with you?"

She bites her lip, hesitating.

"Go on. Whatever it is, you can say it."

"You're not going to be mad at me?" she questions.

"No."

"I'm not going to insult you?"

"I don't know, are you?" I tease.

She arches her eyebrows, biting her lip harder.

"I was kidding. You're not going to insult me. I'm pretty tough," I declare.

Another moment passes.

I add, "Come on, Miss Nanny. You can tell me."

She slowly caves and says, "If I win, we get to paint your house."

I jerk my head back. "Paint my house?"

"Yeah, add some color to it."

"You don't like my house?"

"I didn't say that. I promise you that's not what I meant. I love your house. It's really nice."

I chuckle. "Okay, but you want to paint it?"

"Yes. Some color would be nice."

"So you think it's boring."

She cringes and wrinkles her nose. "It sounds bad, doesn't it?"

I chuckle. "It's okay. I don't have a problem painting the house."

Surprised, she questions, "You don't?"

I shake my head. "Nope. I'm not much of a decorator, and I'm horrible at picking out paint colors. If you want to redecorate, do what you want. Just no pink walls, okay?"

She pretends to be offended. "What do you have against pink?"

I groan. "Pink stinks."

"No, it doesn't."

"Yes, it does. Ask my nieces. I tell them that all the time," I admit.

She laughs. "Okay. No pink."

"Okay, so what else do you want?"

"You seriously want me to pick two things?"

"Yes."

She ponders a few moments, then shakes her head. "I really can't think of anything else, Alexander. Painting your house is a big project, so I'm okay with only that."

"Really?"

"Yeah."

"It doesn't seem fair to me."

"No?"

I continue, "Nope. So I'll let you think about the second thing and tell me later, okay?"

"Is that fair?" she questions.

"I'm a man. I can handle it."

Amusement fills her expression. She finally asks, "Alright. So, what are we going to bet on?"

I don't hesitate. It rolls out of my mouth before I can even think about it. And it's strange because I didn't have it in my mind going in. I blurt out, "Next Saturday, there's a race at the track. We'll go and each place a bet on the horse we think will win."

She stares at me as if I'm crazy, then states, "I don't know anything about horses or betting. And I don't have money to risk losing."

"Don't worry about the cash. I'll give it to you," I say.

She huffs. "That's not fair."

"It's fine. You pick your horse, and I'll pick mine. If you win, you keep the winnings too."

"What if neither of our horses win?"

"Don't worry, my horse will win," I cockily state.

She laughs. "And there you are again, so sure of your bets."

"Yep."

She tilts her head, asking, "So this is your version of responsible gambling?"

"Yep. So, are you in?"

She takes a few deep breaths, then asks, "Are you sure I don't have to put money down?"

"Nope. Don't worry about it. I'll give you $1,000 for your bet."

"$1,000 dollars! That's a lot of money!"

Amused, I try not to laugh. I realize she's in a different financial position than I am. Maybe I should have said $100, but I normally toss $10,000 down. So I decide it's best to keep that detail to myself.

Her eyes are wide with shock as she looks up at me.

"Are you in?"

She finally holds out her hand. "Okay. It's a bet." We shake on it right as the kids run over to us. Wilder screams, "Pie time!"

Within minutes, my entire family circles us. We spend the next hour making s'mores and pies over the fire.

Mom states, "Jacob, we should get going. We have to leave tomorrow morning."

He nods. "Agreed."

We clean up, and everyone slowly disappears. Evelyn and her husband, and Sebastian and Georgia, take the kids back to the house.

Willow announces, "I'm taking off. I need to get ready for my date."

I groan. "Which idiot are you going out with tonight?"

"None of your business." She smirks, then turns to Phoebe, wiggling her eyebrows. "Are you sure you don't want to come? I can have my date bring one of his friends."

My gut churns.

Don't go.

Don't go.

Don't go.

Phoebe shakes her head. "No, I'm good. But thanks. Have a good night."

Relief hits me.

Willow whines, "Aww, you're a party pooper!"

"Sorry!" Phoebe chirps.

"Fine. But one of these days, you have to come out with me and tear up the town!"

"Okay. Rain check, then," Phoebe agrees.

My stomach flips at the thought.

"I'll go with you," Paisley offers to Willow.

"Okay! I'll have Chase bring Tyler."

Paisley lights up. "Awesome!"

I groan. "They're both idiots."

"No, they aren't," Willow insists.

Jagger asks, "Mason, are you ready to go too?"

"Yep. What bar are you girls going to?" Mason inquires.

Paisley scoffs. "Like we're telling you."

Willow orders, "Stop trying to interfere with our personal lives."

"Then don't give us a reason," Mason states.

I chuckle. "Have fun."

"We mean it," Paisley warns.

"Then behave. See you all later," Jagger says, and he and Mason hop on their horses.

Willow, Ava, and Paisley get into an ATV, and they disappear.

"Ready?" I ask Phoebe.

"Sure."

I unhook the trailer before I get into the driver's side.

She asks, "You're not taking that back?"

"No, I can get it tomorrow. I want to show you something, if you're up for it?"

"What is it?"

"I'm not telling you. You just have to see it."

"Okay," she says nervously.

"I'm sure you'll love it," I state, starting the ATV and leaning close to her. "Don't worry, you won't end up found at the bottom of the lake or anything."

She giggles. "Well, I didn't think of that scenario."

"No?"

She squints, asking, "Do I need to worry about those situations?"

I grin. "No. Hold on."

She grabs the side rail, and we take off. There's a full moon, and the lake glistens. We go into the woods, winding around trees and several rough patches.

"Where are you taking me?" Phoebe asks after several minutes.

"Here," I answer, steering the ATV out of the woods and parking it. I put my fingers over Phoebe's lips and whisper, "Stay quiet."

Her hot breath hits my fingers, and tingles race down my spine. She looks up at me and nods.

Bullfrogs croak all around the lake, and an owl hoots loudly in the sky.

I reach for the gun in the side compartment.

Phoebe's blues widen.

I put my finger on her lips again to remind her to stay quiet.

We sit there for a few moments until the faint yips and howls of the coyotes turn louder.

Phoebe scoots closer to me.

I hold in my chuckle, put my arm around her, and murmur, "Don't worry. Just watch."

She takes an anxious breath. Then her gaze darts across the field and back to me.

I tug her tighter to me, reassuring, "It's okay. I won't let anything happen to you."

She sinks farther into me and rests her head on my shoulder.

A pack of coyotes charge from the other side of the woods into the field. They circle each other in the open area.

I keep my gun in my hand, my eyes alert for any threats, and watch Phoebe's awe as closely as I can. I take deep breaths of her floral scent, wishing my dick would stop taunting me.

The coyotes' sounds get louder, and the head of the pack breaks from the circle. He leads the rest of the animals along the lake, and they all disappear into the woods near the beach.

"Wow," Phoebe utters when their sounds can barely be heard.

"Thought you'd like that," I state.

She looks up. "I did." Her eyes drift to my mouth.

I drop my gaze to her lips, my heart pounding harder, replying, "Glad I could amuse you." I lean closer, and the ringing of my phone suddenly blares through the air.

She jerks away out of my grasp. Her blush appears, and she looks more beautiful than ever in the moon's light.

I remain frozen.

The phone continues to ring.

She says, "You should get that."

What the heck am I doing?

"Right." I pull my phone out of my pocket, then answer, "Hello."

Sebastian booms from the other end of the line, "Ace has a fever. Are you coming back soon?"

My gut drops. "On my way." I put my gun in the side compartment and then shift the ATV into gear with a wave of disappointment soaring through me.

12

Phoebe

*T*he full moon illuminates the path through the trees. Alexander races home, winding around the trail with ease, occasionally warning, "Hold on," while we fly over bumps.

My pulse never calms, and the disappointment won't fade as an argument plays out in my head.

I wanted him to kiss me.

No, I didn't. I'm still with Lance.

Am I?

Alexander's my boss.

So what?

It's wrong.

Alexander drives out of the woods, through the yard, and parks the ATV next to the porch.

We jump out and hurry inside.

Sebastian grimaces. His shirt's wet. He sloughs something gross-looking off his chest and into the wastebasket.

"Is that what I think it is?" Alexander asks.

Sebastian wrinkles his nose. "Kid's got a mean projectile."

Alexander groans. "Yeah, he always has." He rushes past Sebastian toward the bathroom.

Georgia stands near the door, declaring, "He wouldn't let me in after he threw up. He's in the bathtub, but he says I can't see him naked." A tiny look of amusement lights her face.

"Thanks, Georgia," Alexander says and opens the door. "Hey, buddy. What's going on?"

Sebastian whines, "Georgia, can you come here and try to get this off of me before I get sick?"

She glances at me, bites on her smile, and stifles a giggle. She moves toward him.

I fret, "Why did he get sick? He seemed fine all day."

Sebastian shrugs. "Your guess is as good as mine. Maybe he ate too much. But I'm the one you should worry about. Georgia, please!" He holds out the towel, turns his face away, and makes a disgusted noise.

She rolls her eyes and shakes her head. "Geez, Sebastian. When did you become the drama queen? You're not going to die from this."

I can't help myself and put my hand over my mouth to stop myself from snickering.

He arches his eyebrows at me. "You find this funny, Phoebe?"

"Sorry. It's not funny that Ace is sick, but, well..."

"There's nothing funny about this." He scrunches his face again.

Georgia orders, "Spin."

He turns.

She rolls the bottom of his shirt and commands, "Duck down a bit."

He obeys, complaining, "This is nasty. Please don't get it on my face."

She tugs the back of his shirt over his head and moves in front of him. She bunches the front and carefully slides it over his arms.

"Thank God! Let's go. I need a shower," he says, moving toward the door.

"Good thing we don't have a baby yet. I'd be on my own," Georgia points out, rolling her eyes at me.

He claims, "You can be on sick duty and I'll do everything else."

She snorts. "Sure you will." She smacks his butt and orders, "Go on. Bye, Phoebe." She smiles at me.

"See you, Phoebe," he says.

I wave. "Bye! See you later."

They step out the door. I go to Wilder's bedroom. The door is halfway open, so I peek my head past it.

He lies on his bed with his hands under his head, staring at the ceiling.

I knock.

He looks over.

I tease, "You're missing all the action out there."

He scrunches his face and asserts, "I don't want anything to do with that. That was disgusting. Did you see Uncle Sebastian?"

I keep a straight face, answering, "Yes. He'll be okay though. He's going to take a shower. Are you feeling sick at all?" I sit down on the edge of the bed next to him, studying his semi-flushed face.

He claims, "Nope! I'm fine. Why did Ace get sick? He was fine all day."

I shrug. "Not sure. I take it he doesn't get sick very often?"

Wilder shakes his head. "Nah, none of us get sick, especially Dad. Everybody else on the ranch can get sick, but Dad never does. He's got the immune system of a vulture."

Amused, I question, "A vulture?"

A serious expression appears on Wilder's face. "Yeah. They never get sick and eat all the rotting animal carcasses."

"Eww." It's my turn to wrinkle my nose.

Wilder laughs. "It's true."

I reach for his forehead. It feels normal, but I still ask, "And you're sure you're feeling okay?"

"Yep. I'm staying away from Ace though."

"Good idea. At least until he's better," I add.

Wilder sits up. "That was a fun party today."

I beam. "It was, wasn't it?"

"Yeah. Can we have more beach parties?"

"Sure. But it sounds like we have lots of holiday parties coming up."

The excitement leaves his voice. "True."

"Why don't you sound excited about them?"

He ponders my question, then blurts out, "I just like doing new stuff. Everything we do is tradition."

"You don't like traditions?"

He thinks another moment. "I wouldn't say I don't like them, but I think new stuff is more fun. So can we do different things?"

"Like what?"

"I don't know. You're the creative one, and today was really fun!" he claims.

My heart soars. "I'm glad you had a good time. I did too."

His eyes light up. "Okay, then can we do something else that's special for the holidays? Something we wouldn't do normally?"

"I'll have to think of something."

"You will. You're creative," he states again.

I point out, "You're creative too."

"Nope. Not like you. I'm more like my dad."

The vision of Alexander's face inching toward mine and his arm pulling me closer flashes before me. His scent flares in my nostrils, as if he's standing right next to me.

Wilder pushes, "So we can do something different?"

I snap out of my thoughts. "I'll try to think of a new project for us."

"A fun one?"

I dramatically answer, "Duh!"

Wilder grins and pumps his arm in the air. "Awesome!"

"Phoebe," Alexander calls.

I rise. "Duty calls. Get some rest."

Wilder grunts. "Okay." He slides down in bed.

I pull the covers over him, then bend over him and tussle his hair. "Night."

"Night, Phoebe."

I get to the door.

He calls out, "Phoebe!"

I turn back to him. "Yes?"

"I'm really glad you're here."

My heart swells. "Thanks. I'm really glad I am too."

"Night."

"Night, sweetie." I turn off the light, step outside, and shut the door.

Alexander steps out of the bathroom.

"Is everything okay?" I fret.

Worry fills his expression. "Ace is sick again. Can you go in my bedroom and into the bathroom cabinet? There's a first aid kit with a thermometer. I'm worried about how hot he feels."

A new fear fills me. "Sure." I do as he's asked and go into his bedroom.

It's the first time I've been in his room. It's like the rest of the house—neutral walls with no color anywhere. It strikes me as sad.

The Cartwrights are such a fun family, and the main house isn't boring, but something about Alexander's house not having any color, especially when he has two awesome boys living in it, seems depressing.

I make my way into his bathroom and find the first aid kit. I bring it out and set it on the table. I grab the thermometer and take it back to Alexander.

I knock on the bathroom door, and a moment later, Alexander opens it. Ace has a towel wrapped around him. His face is flushed.

I rush inside and squat down so I'm eye level with Ace. I coo, "Oh, you're not feeling well, sweetie?"

He shakes his head, then throws his arms around me, snuggling into the curve of my neck. He mumbles, "I feel bad."

I wrap my arms around him. "I'm sorry."

Alexander warns, "Ace, be careful. We don't want Phoebe getting sick."

"I'll be okay."

"Not if you get sick," he argues.

"I won't."

He grunts. "How do you know that?"

"I rarely get sick."

He arches his eyebrows. "Really? I never do either."

"Wilder said that. But don't worry about me. I've taught a lot of kids. My immune system is strong."

"Hmmm," he says, then grabs the thermometer from me. "Here, Ace, open up and keep this under your tongue."

Ace stays close to me, turning his head toward his dad.

Alexander turns on the thermometer and slides it into his mouth. It doesn't take long before it beeps. He pulls it out, announcing, "101.5."

"That's not too horrible," I state.

Alexander nods. "I'll keep an eye on it tonight. Ace, let's get you in bed."

"Can Phoebe put me to bed too?" Ace asks, his blue eyes glistening.

"Sure. I can come in."

"Good." He hugs me harder, and my heart almost breaks.

"Oh, sweetie, I'm so sorry you're sick," I offer, rubbing his back. "Come on, let's get you to bed."

We get him in his bedroom, then I step outside so Alexander can help him get dressed in his pajamas, and when they're done, I go back inside. I bring a cup of water, directing, "Take a little sip if you want."

Ace shakes his head. "I don't think I can keep it down."

"Okay, I'll leave it here in case you wake up in the middle of the night and need it." I set the glass down on the nightstand.

Ace curls up in bed.

Alexander states, "Why don't you try to get some sleep? I'll be back in to check on you in a little while." He leans down and kisses Ace's forehead. Then he rises and glances at me with a worried expression.

I ruffle Ace's hair just like I did Wilder's. "Get some rest."

He closes his eyes and we leave the room.

We keep the door halfway open, and Alexander goes to the kitchen. He grabs the soap and orders, "Hold your hands out."

I do as I'm told, and he pumps some foam in it. We wash our hands at the sink and then he goes to the fridge. He grabs two waters and hands me one, stating, "Well, that was an unexpected turn of events."

I add, "Hopefully it's just a twenty-four-hour bug."

"I'm sure that's all it is. My kids usually bounce back pretty quickly," he claims.

"Wilder told me you never get sick."

Alexander nods. "That's true. I haven't been sick since I was a kid."

"Really? Wow."

"Hopefully you don't get sick," he says with genuine concern in his voice.

"Don't worry, I won't," I insist and then sit down on a barstool.

He pulls the one out next to me and sits. He studies me for a moment.

Butterflies go crazy in my stomach, and heat crawls up my neck and into my cheeks.

He slowly states, "It was a fun day." His gaze drifts to my lips, then quickly returns to my eyes.

My flutters make me dizzy.

I imagined that.

No, I didn't.

I did.

He clears his throat and starts, "So anyway—"

A shrill ring cuts him off.

I jump and realize it's my phone. So I reach into my pocket and answer it without looking. "Hello?"

Lance's booming voice asks, "Are you ready to come home yet?"

I can tell he's been drinking. I close my eyes and release a frustrated breath.

"Well?"

I rise, put the phone to my chest, and state, "I'll be right back."

Alexander's eyes darken.

I go into my bedroom and shut the door. "Lance—" I start.

"Why don't you want me anymore, Phoebe?" he whines, cutting me off.

Guilt fills me. I reply, "Lance—"

He cuts me off again, accusing, "Admit it! You're playing games—"

"Lance, call me when you're sober. I don't need to be harassed!" I interject.

He scoffs. "Harassed? Calling you is harassing you now?"

"Calling me when you're drunk and making insinuations is harassing me."

"Making insinuations? What am I insinuating?" he hurls out.

I sit on the bed and close my eyes. My heart pounds harder, but it's not with anticipation or excitement anymore. It's with annoyance.

He continues with more disdain in his tone. "So what have you been doing with the Cartwrights?"

I answer, "I'm not having this conversation with you right now."

"No? Then when are you going to talk to me? You don't want me there. You say we're still together, but it sure as hell doesn't feel that way, and then I call you and you don't even want to talk," he accuses.

I cringe. Everything he said is true. I can't deny it, but it sounds worse than it feels in my head.

Lance lowers his voice to a softer tone. "You don't miss me at all?"

There's another tug on my heart, mixing with my anger. I haven't thought about him since he left. And we didn't exactly part on good terms.

He asks, "What's the point of us taking a break if you don't even miss me?"

"I do," I claim, but deep down it's a lie. I know I haven't missed him.

It's because I'm so busy.

No, it's not.

Yes, it is.

"Do you, Phoebe?" he asks softer, piling on the guilt.

So I reassure him. "Yeah, of course I do."

"Then talk to me. If you've ever loved me, talk to me. Please."

I take a deep breath. The desperation in his voice is something new. I'm not sure how to take it.

He continues, "Tell me what you've been doing all night."

"We had the beach party."

"Isn't it too cold to go swimming?" he asks.

"Yeah, but we didn't swim. We cooked over the campfire and the kids played games."

"And you had fun?"

"Yes, I did."

"That's good," he says, and for a brief moment, I'm reminded of the Lance I first met.

"What have you—"

"Lance," a woman's voice shouts just as loud music fills the line.

He quickly states in a normal, everyday voice, "Okay, Phoebe, got to go. Just wanted to check in."

"You miss me so much that you only called me to talk until your party started?" I accuse.

He groans. "And there you go being dramatic again. Talk later. Bye." He hangs up.

I stare at the phone and then pace around the room, trying to calm myself. But I can't. I put my hand on the doorknob, then stop.

I'm too angry to leave the room. I have to cool off first. So I go sit on my bed and attempt the techniques my instructor taught me in meditation class.

After a minute, it's not working. So I reposition myself on the bed and then close my eyes, breathing deeply. Before I know it, I fall asleep.

When I open my eyes, the alarm clock's illuminated numbers shine at me, telling me it's 5:00 A.M.

I sit up quickly. I've left Alexander all night on his own while Ace is sick. I leave my room to go check on him, but I hear a groaning in Alexander's room. I cautiously step inside, calling out, "Alexander?"

The light in the bathroom's on. A retching sound fills the air.

I hurry toward the doorway and freeze at the entrance.

Alexander's face is over the toilet. He gets sick, then leans back against the wall. He wipes his mouth.

I rush over to him and crouch down. "Oh my gosh! You're sick."

His bloodshot eyes stare into mine. He weakly declares, "I'll be fine."

I put my hand on his forehead. "You're burning up."

"I'll be fine," he insists.

I turn on the shower. "Get in the shower. Try to cool off." I leave the bathroom to go find the thermometer. Then I go back to the bedroom and stop at the doorway.

The outline of his backside is just barely visible through the frosted glass.

My heart beats harder.

He leans against the wall with his forearms, his head pressing against them.

Stop staring!

I call out, "I have the thermometer. I'll be back when you're done with your shower."

177

He doesn't reply.

I check on Ace, but he seems fine, sleeping peacefully. I feel his forehead, and I'm pretty sure his fever's broken. The flush he had earlier is no longer on his cheeks.

Then I check on Wilder. He seems okay too.

I find a bottle of fever reducer, wait for ten minutes, then reenter Alexander's bedroom. He sits on the side of the mattress in his boxer shorts.

My pulse skyrockets. I force myself to tear my eyes off his tattoo, and say, "You're green."

"I'll be fine," he reiterates.

"You're not," I insist, and hold the thermometer in front of him. I push the button, ordering, "Open up."

He obeys, and I slide the thermometer into his mouth.

As soon as it beeps, I take it out, read it, and fret, "It's 102.5!"

"I'll be fine," he weakly repeats.

"Maybe I should take you to the hospital."

He looks at me like I'm crazy. "No, I'll be fine."

"But you're sick. That fever is dangerous."

"Phoebe, I'll be fine," he sternly states.

I stare at him a moment, unsure what to do.

He softens his tone. "I just need to rest."

"Okay. But if it gets any worse, I'm taking you to the hospital."

He grumbles, "Fine."

I pull the covers back, and he slides into bed. I pull a sheet over him, stating, "I'm not going to put the rest of the blankets on until your fever goes down."

"Good. I'm too hot."

I go into the bathroom, find a washcloth, and run freezing-cold water over it. I fold it as I return to his bedside. I place it on the back of his neck.

"Shouldn't it be on my forehead?" he questions.

I shake my head. "No. You want the fever to pull *away* from your brain, not *through* it."

He arches his eyebrows.

"It's true," I state.

A tiny curve appears on his lips. "Okay, if that's what you say."

I shake a bottle of pills, ordering, "You should take this to lower your fever. I'm going to grab some water for you."

He doesn't argue.

I go into the kitchen, fill the glass, and take it to him. I hand him a pill and hold the water to his lips.

He swallows it and closes his eyes. "Thank you."

I hesitate, then say, "You're welcome. I'm going to come back in a little while and see if your fever's down, okay?"

He mumbles, "I'll be fine."

"I know. But I'll be back in a little while," I repeat, leaving the room and pacing for a half hour until it's time to check on him and the boys.

13

Alexander

A Week Later

Whatever Ace had stuck with me like the plague. I don't remember ever being so ill, even as a child. It's been a week. Yesterday, I hoped I could get back to working and sweat the remaining bug out of me, but I only lasted two hours. Then, I felt like death was upon me. I could barely stand, so I finally caved and returned to my bedroom to rest.

Phoebe's been beyond amazing, taking care of the kids and me. Every day, they surprise me with get-well cards or pictures they've drawn, paper flowers, and other crafts. She's taken on more than her nanny duties, like our laundry and all the cooking. I feel bad that she's having to carry the load, and I keep apologizing, but she always just waves me off.

I'm not used to feeling helpless like this. When I woke up today feeling energetic, relief hit me. Plus, it's race day. I haven't forgotten about our bet or the time we spent alone on the ATV.

The scent of pancakes and bacon wafts through the air. My stomach growls. It's the first time I've been hungry all week.

I get out of bed, quickly get dressed, and join the others in the kitchen.

Ace exclaims, "Dad, you're up!"

"Are you better now?" Wilder asks.

Phoebe flips a pancake and turns her head. Her beautiful smile forms on her lips. "You look a lot better."

"I feel a lot better." I pour myself a cup of coffee and ask, "You need a refill?"

She glances at her mug and then says, "I'm good. But I still don't know how you drink that black."

I grunt. "Real men drink black coffee."

Amusement fills her expression. "Men all have the same taste buds?"

I chuckle. "Real men do." I take another sip, and the hot liquid slides into my stomach.

She asks, "You want some breakfast?"

I nod. "Yeah, I'm starving."

"Good. You must be feeling better, then?" She picks up a plate and adds bacon, eggs, and pancakes. She hands it to me.

"Thanks. And I do feel normal again." I set the plate on the table and point, adding, "Please, sit down and eat. You've been doing everything all week."

She fills another plate and hands it to me, smiling. "Okay."

I pull the chair out, and she sits. I take the one next to her.

Wilder questions, "Dad, are we going to do anything cool tonight?"

"Aunt Evelyn is coming over with the girls. You're going to stay in the main house tonight."

"Why are we staying there?" Ace questions.

"Phoebe and I are going to the races," I tell them.

She asks, "We're still going?"

"Yeah, I feel great. Why not? Unless you're not up for it," I challenge.

She smirks. "Don't worry, I won't disappoint. But don't cry when I win."

"What are you winning, Phoebe?" Ace asks.

She glances at me.

I tell the boys, "We both have different ideas on what horse is going to win."

"Ooh, who are you going to bet on?" Wilder asks, turning to Phoebe.

"Um...uh..."

I interject, realizing that she doesn't know any of the horses' names. "Boys, which one do you think Phoebe will bet on?"

Wilder and Ace cry out at the same time, "Sweetie Pie!"

I jerk my head back. "Sweetie Pie? Why would you think Sweetie Pie will win?"

"Duh. She's going to take it all tonight!" Ace proclaims.

Wilder agrees. "Yeah, she's been running really well. She's beaten Tycoon all week."

"No way," I state, not believing it. I always bet on Tycoon. He's our golden goose, winning more races than I can count. I've trained Sweetie Pie the same way I trained Tycoon, but she's still young and never beat him before.

"Dad, Sweetie Pie is going to win," Ace confidently asserts.

"You think so, huh?" I ask, taking a bite of the pancakes. The buttery syrup bursts on my tongue, and I groan. "This tastes so good."

"That's because you've barely eaten this last week," Phoebe acknowledges.

"Maybe you're just a good cook," I offer and then wink.

She laughs. "Maybe I've picked up some talent from Georgia."

"Ah. Now, that would be every man's dream. A woman who could cook like Georgia and do art like you," I tease.

Red sprawls up her neck and into her cheeks, and I realize what I just said. I quickly add, "Figuratively speaking."

"Right." She takes a sip of coffee and turns toward the boys. "So, Sweetie Pie gets my bet!"

"Yes!" Wilder shouts, pumping his fist in the air.

"Tycoon's going down tonight!" Ace exclaims.

I chuckle. "Easy there. You've always loved Tycoon."

"But Sweetie Pie's going to win," Ace insists.

"Yep. No doubt," Wilder claims, and shoves another forkful of food in his mouth.

"Well, I think Tycoon will prove all of you wrong," I declare, confident in his abilities. I dip bacon in my egg yolk, then bite half the strip.

The boys get up, take their plates to the sink, and wash them.

I lean closer to Phoebe. "What have you done to my sons?"

Her lips twitch. She whispers, "They earn gold stars."

"Ah. And what are they earning now?"

She shrugs, confessing, "I told them it's a surprise." She glances at the boys, then murmurs, "I have to figure it out." Her hot breath hits my ear, and zings fly down my spine.

She sits back, puts her finger over her lips, and smiles.

The room lights up. My heart pounds harder in my chest. I don't know what's happening to me, but anytime she's come into my bedroom this week, I've felt something in my gut. I don't know what it is. I'm trying to push it away. After all, she is my kids' nanny and way younger than me.

My deceased wife and I were the same age. But Phoebe's ten years younger than me.

I'm sure she thinks I'm too old for her.

We probably have nothing in common.

Why am I even thinking these thoughts?

Jesus, I need to get a grip.

I rise, put my plate in the soapy water, then grab my cowboy hat off the hook. I put it on, announcing, "Time for work."

"Are you sure you're going to be okay today?" Phoebe asks, her face filled with concern.

"Yep. Just be ready to leave around five tonight. Okay?"

She gives me a tiny salute. "Aye, aye, sir."

I chuckle and go outside. I take a deep breath, breathing in the fresh air.

It's a true November day. The air's crisp, but the sun's out. The wind has picked up, but I welcome it. I spent so much time in my bedroom this week I thought the walls would close in around me.

Within minutes, I throw myself into my duties, trying to catch up on things I got behind on. Then, I spend several hours at the corral, running the horses with my brothers.

Mason states, "You bounced back quickly compared to yesterday."

"I feel a lot better."

"Well, it looks like you were in good hands." His lips twist.

My gut flips. Phoebe's face appears in my mind, and my blood heats. I reprimand, "Don't get any ideas."

He chuckles and then starts shouting at one of the trainers. "You're not leaning in! Come on, you know better than this!"

The day goes by quickly but also slowly. I'm excited to go to the races tonight. I tell myself it's only because of the thrill of seeing my horses compete, but it's a lie. I can't wait to spend more time alone with Phoebe. It's nice when it's just us.

Us.

The thought of Phoebe and I together shocks me. I don't know why I'm thinking any of these thoughts. I continue to remind myself that she's my kids' nanny and it's just a friendly bet.

I chuckle, thinking about how badly I want to paint the house. As I lay in bed all week, I couldn't help but stare at the tan walls, wishing they had some color. I kept telling myself it was because I was stuck inside, but everything looked as blah as I felt.

When four thirty arrives, I grab a handful of a dozen flowers from the garden and then go into the house. I put them in a vase and make my way down the hall.

Phoebe steps out of the bathroom with a towel wrapped around her body. The D and A inked on her chest appear shiny on her damp skin.

My pulse beats between my ears.

She glances at the flowers. "Those are beautiful."

"They're for you."

Her eyes widen. "Oh?"

My anxiety tightens in my chest, and I'm suddenly speechless. My gaze darts back to her tattoo.

She cautiously asks, "They're really for me?"

Why didn't I think about what to say to her?

I tear my gaze off her chest.

She stares at me in question.

I nod. "Yes. I thought you might want some color in your room."

She grins and takes them from me. "Thank you. They're beautiful."

187

I glance back at her tattoo, blurting out, "Are you ever going to tell me what that says?"

She stifles a laugh. "Nope. I told you there wouldn't be any mystery, then."

I shake my head but smile, half annoyed, half amused. I add, "Okay, I have to shower. We can leave a little early, if you're going to be ready?"

"Sure. I only need another five minutes. I just have to put my clothes on."

Or you can take that towel off.

Ugh! Why am I thinking these things?

"Sounds good. I won't take too long." I scoot past her and go into my bedroom. I take a shower, put on a spray of cologne, which I normally don't do when I'm working, and then freeze.

Why am I acting like I'm going on a date?

This is a date.

No, it's not.

I go into my closet and put on a pair of jeans I only wear when I go to nicer places. I tuck my T-shirt in and secure my belt buckle. When I finish, I step out into the family room and stop short.

Phoebe's on the phone. She states, "I'm not talking about this anymore."

I quietly step back into the hallway and press my back against the wall. I shouldn't eavesdrop on her conversation, but I can't help myself.

Her voice grows more frustrated. "I've gone over this with you. You're just not listening to me."

Mr. Douchebag.

What's it going to take for her to realize that boy isn't worth a second of her time? She's way out of his league.

My gut flips. I hate she's still talking to him.

Why is she still talking to him?

I cautiously peek past the wall.

She puts her hand on her neck as she stares out the window. She declares, "I'm busy. I'll talk to you later." She hangs up and sighs.

I pull my head back, my heart beating faster. I wait ten seconds, then call out, "All set?" as I step into the family room.

She spins to face me and forces a smile. "Yep."

"Is something wrong?" I ask, moving closer.

She smiles bigger and shakes her head. "No, everything's great. I can't wait to go, and I can't wait to beat you."

I chuckle. "Alrighty, then. Let's get out of here." I go to the door and open it. I motion for her to go through, stating, "Ladies first."

Her smile stays on her face as she walks outside. I put my hand on her lower back and lead her to the car, opening her door.

She gets in, and I close the door.

I round the hood and then slide into the driver's seat. I start the truck. Country music blares from the speakers.

"Whoa." I turn the volume down. "Sorry about that."

189

She giggles. "It's okay."

"Do you know who was in my truck last?" I question.

She hesitates, then cringes. "I think Jagger. He had to move it for some reason."

"Huh," I say. I make a mental note to talk to my brother. Jagger likes to take my truck out for no reason, and I always yell at him whenever he does.

During the entire ride, nerves dance in my belly. We make small talk until we get to the track. I get out of the truck, go around to open her door, and grab her hand as soon as she steps out. I steer her toward the betting area and tease, "Are you sure you want Sweetie Pie? I feel kind of bad that I'm going to beat you and demolish all your dreams in an instant."

"Oh no you're not. That's my horse, and I'm sticking with her."

"Fair enough."

I release her hand and pull out my billfold. I already know there's two grand in it. I slap it down in front of the bookie, saying, "One thousand on Tycoon and one thousand on Sweetie Pie."

Phoebe shifts next to me. She looks uncomfortable.

I murmur in her ear, "Stop worrying about the money. It's fine."

She releases an anxious breath. She slowly tilts her head up, her mouth only inches from mine. She breathes, "Okay."

"Let's have fun," I order, locking eyes with her.

She lifts her chin and straightens her shoulders. "You're right."

"Of course I'm right. You'll learn that someday." I wink.

She laughs. The bookie gives us our tickets, and I hand her the one for Sweetie Pie, instructing, "Hold on to this. If you lose it and a miracle happens and you win—which you won't because Tycoon's going to—you'll need this to cash in."

She rolls her eyes. "You're so overly confident, but cockiness won't make your horse go faster."

"We'll see about that. I know my horses. Although, I am intrigued that both my boys think Sweetie Pie will win," I admit.

Tycoon doesn't always put everything out during practices, but I'm okay with it. He saves it for race days. I'm sure he's an adrenaline junkie. And I taught him to know his role, so I'm not worried about it.

Phoebe asks, "Do you have a color in mind?"

"Color?" I question.

"Yeah. For your room."

"Nope. I'm not good with colors. I told you you're the creative one. That'll be up to you."

"Really? So I have free rein when I win?"

"Yeah, you would have free rein." I lean closer to her. "But remember, my horse is winning, not yours."

"We'll see about that." She beams up at me.

I grab her hand again and lead her through the racetrack to the box my family owns. Inside, there's a full spread of food, including appetizers, main courses, desserts, and a full bar.

I question, "What do you want to drink?"

"A beer's fine," she says.

"You always drink beer? Nothing else?" I ask.

She ponders the question and then admits, "No. I normally get martinis or cosmos or margaritas. Lance doesn't like me to drink beer."

I tense. "Seriously?"

She cringes. "Did I just admit that out loud? I don't think I've ever thought about that."

"So you realize that's really messed up?" I ask.

She waits a minute, then confesses, "Yeah, it is."

"So what does Phoebe want?"

She glances at the full bar, then back at me. "I just want a beer."

I chuckle. "Okay, then beer it is."

I get us two bottles, then lead her to the large window that looks out over the track. I hold my bottle out. "May the best horse win."

"That'll be Sweetie Pie," she chimes, clinking my beer with hers.

"Don't be so sure of yourself."

"Oh, don't worry, I'm not. But this is fun. Especially since it's not my money I'm losing, although I still feel bad about it."

"Don't."

"Still... It feels a bit wrong to risk your hard-earned cash. Not that I'm going to lose," she corrects herself.

I grunt, take a mouthful of my beer, swallow, then say, "No more talk about the money. Okay?"

She exhales deeply. "Okay."

I start pointing things out to her since she's never been to the track. I explain how things work and then the announcer says it's time for the race.

The horses line up.

"Oh, this is so exciting," Phoebe says, leaning closer and tapping her hand on her thigh.

I grab it, taunting, "You aren't a little nervous that you made the wrong bet, are you?"

She smirks. "No. Eat Sweetie Pie's dust, Alexander."

I chuckle, then release her hand, and the buzzer sounds. The horses take off.

We step closer to the glass. The horses fly around the track. The crowd's shouts grow louder.

I'm used to these races, but tonight, everything is different. Tycoon's running well, but Sweetie Pie's just behind him. Since they're both Cartright horses, that makes me happy, but I'm not used to being surprised at races. Like I said, I usually only take calculated risks when I'm gambling. Plus, I know my horses well.

But as fast as the race is, it becomes clear Ace and Wilder have a great eye for assessing the horses. Sweetie Pie and Tycoon suddenly are neck and neck.

Phoebe shouts, "Come on, Sweetie Pie! Let's go!"

I tear my eyes off the track, watching her excitement and joy, and it makes me happy.

"Come on, come on, come on! There you go! A little bit farther!" she urges.

I glance back and blurt out, "Tycoon, move it," all of a sudden worried he might not win.

Sweetie Pie and Tycoon take the last turn, continuing the pace, leaving other horses eating their dust. About five feet in front of the finish line, Sweetie Pie makes a tiny break, crossing the line a horsehead before Tycoon.

"Yes! Oh my gosh! Yes! Yes! Yes!" Phoebe shouts, clapping. Then she surprises me by jumping up and throwing her arms around me, squealing, "She won!"

I slide my arm around her, grip her ass cheek, and plant my other palm on the back of her head. Before she can get out of the way or I can think better about it, I press my lips to hers.

14

Phoebe

The world tilts on its axis, and my knees buckle. Alexander keeps me pinned to his warm, hard flesh. His tongue takes control of mine, stealing my breath.

My blood ignites into a fiery rush of intoxication. I run my fingers over his neck and through the soft strands of hair that escape from under his cowboy hat.

His entire palm spans the back of my head. His thumb strokes behind my ear, creating a wave of tingles that burst under his touch.

A violent tremble consumes me until I'm shaking so hard I'm sure if he wasn't holding me up, I'd fall to the ground. Instead of letting me go, he holds me tighter against him.

His erection hardens against my stomach to the point my pussy's throbbing. He gently squeezes my ass.

I whimper, closing my eyes, submitting to whatever rhythm he decides to play with my tongue.

He deepens our kiss, then murmurs against my lips, "Good girl," besieging me with another round of desire.

I drown out the crowd around us, lost in him, devoured by his dominance, pressed against him, and aching for more.

He retreats an inch. I try to move closer, but he holds me in place. I open my eyes to find his dark, heated blues studying me, as if searching for something, but I'm unsure what.

I swallow, attempting to catch my breath.

He gives me a quick peck on the lips. "Let's go collect your winnings." He turns me, grips the curve of my waist, keeping me close to him, and steers me toward the door.

The crowd outside the suite grows. Alexander weaves us through it, offering thanks to those who congratulate him on Sweetie Pie winning, never stopping to converse further.

We get to the bookie's station, and he instructs, "Give them your ticket, Pheebs."

Pheebs.

My flutters intensify so much I get dizzy again.

"Ticket?" Alexander nudges, pulling me out of my daze.

Flustered, I reach into my pocket and pull it out, sliding the paper under the glass.

The man reads it and states, "Congratulations. Good bet."

"Beginners luck," Alexander teases, then winks.

"Seven to two," the man says, picking up a stack of hundred-dollar bills. He slaps them on the counter counting out loud.

I look at Alexander in question.

He explains, "For every two bets on Sweetie Pie, you get seven times that amount. So $4.50 for every $1 wagered."

I calculate it in my head, then burst out, "That's $4,500!"

Amusement fills his expression. "Yep."

I gape at him.

He adds, "Too bad it wasn't 10-1. You would have gotten eleven times instead of four and a half."

The man interjects, "$4,500. Do you want an envelope?"

Still shocked, I answer, "Umm... Yes, please."

He slides the wad of cash into an envelope and then hands it to me. "Well done."

I stare at it.

Alexander chuckles. "You're supposed to take your winnings and run, Pheebs."

I grab the cash and hold it out to him. "It's your money."

He grunts. "No way. A bet's, a bet. Put it in your purse where it's safe."

I open my mouth, but he puts his finger on it. Tingles resurge, racing down my spine.

He nods to the crowd, adding, "There's a line behind us. There's no point in arguing. Put it away, and we can get out of here."

"Oh. Sorry." I put the envelope in my crossbody.

He takes control again, protectively weaving me through the frenzy of people and out the door.

197

Tonight's the coldest it's been all year, and the wind howls around us. I breathe deeply, welcoming the fresh air, my hair blowing in my face.

Alexander steps to the other side of me and puts his arm around my shoulder, shielding me from the harsh elements. He quickly leads me to his VIP parking spot and opens the passenger door.

I reach for the bar, grip it, and hoist myself into the truck.

He shuts the door and hurries around the front, then slides inside. He turns on the engine and asks, "You ready to go home, or do you want to hit the town?"

I smirk. "Why, Alexander Cartwright, do you actually go out and have fun?"

"Now and then," he answers, grinning, but then his face falls. In a serious tone, he asks, "Did I give you the impression I'm a stick-in-the-mud?"

"Ummm...no. I wouldn't call you that..."

"But you'd call me...?" He arches his eyebrows.

I bite on my lip, cringing.

He groans. "Yep, you think I'm a stick-in-the-mud."

I softly laugh. "No! You're just serious. But you have a lot of responsibilities," I quickly add.

He stares at me for a moment.

"I didn't mean it in a bad way," I offer, putting my hand on his.

He picks it up, kisses the back of it, then releases it. "That settles it. We're hitting the town." He shifts the truck into drive.

I clap. "Yay! Where are we going?"

He glances at me as he drives through the gates. "Well, Pheebs, that would depend on you."

"Me?"

"Yep. Are you looking for a good old-fashioned Texan bar or one of the fancy, new nightclubs?"

I question, "Are nightclubs your thing?"

He keeps his expression neutral. "I can hang."

"But you don't prefer them, right?"

"Not my first choice, but I can represent," he claims, then puts his hand on my thigh.

I put my arm on the console and lean closer. "Are you a closet dancer?"

"What is that?"

"You know, someone who surprises everyone and goes nuts to techno?"

He scoffs. "Techno gives me a headache."

"Me too."

"Good. We'll cross techno off the list."

"Deal. So you're a closet hip-hop lover?"

His lips twitch. "I'm more of a country or hard-rock guy, but I can handle hip-hop."

"Really?"

"I'll have you know I'm a very versatile human being."

I slap him lightly on the shoulder. "Duh. I already knew that."

His voice turns serious again. "You did?" He locks his gaze with mine.

My face falls. I match his tone. "Yes. Of course."

Something passes in his expression. I think it's relief, but I can't be sure. He returns his focus to the road.

I sit back in my seat.

He asserts, "Pick your poison, Pheebs. Do you want to live it up Texan style or hang like in L.A.?"

I tilt my head. "L.A.?"

He shrugs, grinning. "Yeah. L.A. has tons of clubs."

I groan. "I'm not a huge fan of L.A."

"No?"

I shake my head. "Nope! Want to know another secret?"

"Please. Spill it."

I hesitate, then admit, "Clubs aren't really my thing."

He dramatically gasps. "How very un-Californian of you!"

I put my hand over my face and groan. "Don't tell anyone."

He chuckles. "Your secret is safe with me. But thank God you said that, because I'd go represent at a club if you wanted to, but I'd much rather go out in Texan style."

I tilt my head, peering at him closer, challenging, "You'd go if I wanted, even though you don't want to be there?"

He catches my eye, then affirms, "Yes."

All the times I wanted to go to an art gallery or try a new restaurant, flash in my mind. Lance never went anywhere *he* didn't want to go. I always had to go on my own or with friends.

"Did I say something wrong?" Alexander asks.

I take a deep breath and shake my head. "No."

He squeezes my thigh and then releases it. He grabs the steering wheel and pulls into a full lot. "Then let's go tear it up Texan style." He shifts the truck into park, turns off the engine, and jumps out of the truck. He makes his way around the front.

I glance at the pink neon sign that reads Boots. Country music blares from the building. A line weaves around the brick walls.

Alexander opens my door. He holds out his hand. "Ready to have the night of your life?"

I chirp, "Are you able to guarantee that?"

"Yep. I'm no stick-in-the-mud," he claims.

I take his hand and step down to the ground. "I told you that isn't what I think."

He chuckles. "Come on, Pheebs." He returns to his protective stance, guiding me toward the building. Instead of going to the back of the line, he steps in front of the bouncer.

"Alexander. Been a while," a huge man with tattoos all over his neck greets, holding his hand out.

Alexander slaps it, replying, "Yeah. Things have been busy on the ranch. Good to see you, Matt."

Matt glances at me, then back to Alexander, "And who's this?"

Alexander tugs me closer to him. "This is Phoebe. Phoebe, Matt."

"Nice to meet you, Phoebe," Matt offers.

"You too," I say.

Matt unhooks the black rope and steps back. "Have fun."

"Thanks, man," Alexander offers, and Matt pats him on the back as we walk past the line and into the bar.

The noise grows louder. Energy buzzes around us. There's a live band, and they end the current song by going straight into a rock one. Bodies fill the dance floor, and there isn't an empty seat in the house.

Alexander weaves us through the crowd and shouts, "Carter!"

A twenty-ish man with a tattoo sleeve, big gauge earrings, and a gold chain looks over. He grins and leans across the bar. He takes both hands, pushes them between two people, and shouts, "Step aside."

The line of people obeys.

Alexander moves us forward, keeping me in front of him. He yells, "Beer or something else?"

"Beer," I reply.

He holds up two fingers and slaps down cash.

Carter fills two pints and sets them down. He slaps hands with Alexander, nods at me, then picks up the cash.

Alexander hands me a beer and takes the other one. Then he guides me to a round high table where a petite brunette and a stocky man stand. He sets his drink down.

Their eyes light up. The man states, "Where've you been hiding out?"

Alexander replies, "Work's been crazy. Katie, good to see you."

"You too!" She beams.

"Katie, Dean, this is Phoebe," Alexander says. His fingers stroke my back.

Katie puts her hand on my arm. "Nice to meet you."

"You too."

"Phoebe." Dean nods.

I smile at him and take a sip of beer.

Alexander takes a mouthful of his own beer, then tells me, "The three of us went to school together."

Katie leans close to me. Her brown eyes twinkle, and she teases, "Yep. I know everything about Alexander—all the dirty gossip."

I laugh. "Well, do tell!"

"And on that note, I think we'll rest our drinks for a minute," Alexander states, takes another large mouthful, then grabs my hand. He maneuvers us through the crowd until we're on the dance floor.

The band switches to a well-known classic 70s rock song, and the bar erupts in cheers and singing.

Alexander swings me around the dance floor, surprising me further.

He's not a good dancer—he's a great dancer. He guides me through several songs, leading me so well that I don't even feel like my usual clumsy self. I usually avoid dance floors at all costs, but we dance to several songs, and I don't feel any self-consciousness.

The band's lead singer declares, "We're going to slow it down now."

Alexander doesn't skip a beat, pulling me close to him. The atmosphere turns quieter, and the lights darken. My body molds into his, and I lean my cheek on his chest. His heart thumps against my ear, and butterflies fill my stomach.

The aphrodisiac scent of musk, sweat, and everything Alexander, flares around us, mixing with the smell of beer and thickening from the heat. I dive deeper into it, closing my eyes, melting into the opposite of everything I've ever experienced.

Another song comes on, and Alexander keeps me in his arms, swaying in time with the music. When the music turns fast again, he asks, "Should we get a cold one?"

I nod, and before I know it, we have two cold drinks in our hands. He steers me through the bar, out the back door, and into a tiny patio area.

String lights glow above us, and heated lamps flicker in the corners. There are only two tables—one with seats and one for standing. Three people are in the chairs, chatting.

We set our beers down on the other table.

Alexander states, "It feels good out here."

"Agreed." I take a big sip.

The wind picks up, and my hair flies over my face.

"Whoa!" He steps on my other side, shielding me from the gust.

"Thanks! That wind is fierce!"

"You're welcome," he replies, then slides his finger over my cheek, tucking a lock of hair behind my ear. He pins his blues on mine before dropping them to my lips.

My heart thumps harder. I'm pretty sure there's a pool soaking my panties.

"Excuse me," a man says.

I tear my gaze away as Alexander moves me closer to the wall.

The people at the table get up, and I tear my eyes off him. They open the door to return inside, and music vibrates around us.

The three people disappear, and the door slams. I turn, and Alexander's intense gaze is back on me.

This time, I break the stare and glance at his lips. Adrenaline races through my veins. I deeply inhale, then slowly meet his stare.

He spins me so my back is against the brick wall, slides his hand through my hair, and lowers his face to mine. He stops inches from my mouth, and his hot breath tickles my chin.

My chest rises and falls faster. I open my mouth, but nothing comes out.

His jaw tightens. He presses his body against mine, places his palm on my cheek, and strokes my chin with his thumb. Blue flames flicker in his eyes, growing hotter every second he peers at me.

Music blares around us. Voices fill the patio.

Alexander turns his head. A drunk crowd fills the tiny patio.

"Excuse me," a woman shouts.

Annoyance fills his expression. He presses closer to me so she can get by, then asks, "Do you want to go back inside, or are you ready to head home?"

"Home sounds good," I reply, disappointed we got interrupted and wanting nothing more than to be alone with Alexander.

He doesn't waste time, leading me into the bar, parting the crowd, and getting me safely to the truck. He opens the door, I get in, and he hurries to the driver's side.

We don't say anything on the way home. He keeps his palm on my thigh. Country music plays on a low volume, and my butterflies flutter harder every second that brings us closer to the ranch.

15

Alexander

 hanksgiving lights create a glow around the ranch, welcoming us home. I pull through the gate, my cock hard and aching like never before. The country music playing on the truck's radio barely registers. Phoebe's floral scent teases me, creating havoc in my veins to the point I feel semi-delirious.

I park in front of the house, get out, and walk around the truck. I open the door, and my heart hammers harder against my chest.

Phoebe's eyes swirl with a wildness I saw the first day I met her. Mixed in is something else.

I help her step down and then shut the door. I study her closer and realize she's a bit nervous.

I don't think, I just react. I push her against the truck and lift her chin. "Hey."

"Hey," she softly replies, her eyes shining under the moonlight.

"I think I forgot something at the bar."

She arches her eyebrows. "Oh? Do we have to go back?"

"No." I run my thumb over her lips, stating, "It's right here."

Her lips twitch. She inhales deeply.

I lower my head and slide my tongue into her mouth as a gust of wind howls around us. I cage myself farther around her, and my blood turns so hot I barely feel the brisk onslaught of air.

Her tongue dives deeper against mine. She slides her hands around my neck, caressing it like before. A whimper vibrates from her.

Tonight, with her, I feel alive. It's as if I've somehow been dead, and she's unearthed me from the grave.

I retreat, breaking our kiss, remaining an inch from her face, murmuring, "Glad I got that back."

She smiles, her blues more luminous, her skin glowing, and wisps of her magenta hair blowing around her angelic face.

I peck her on the forehead and then step on the side of the wind. I slide my arm around her and lead her into the house.

The fireplace creates a tranquil illumination. Someone on the ranch must have come in and turned it on, which isn't abnormal when I'm not home. I leave the lights off and ask, "Do you want a beer?"

"Sure. But I really want to kick these boots off," Phoebe chirps.

"Do your feet hurt?" I ask.

She glances at them, then admits, "I think they're half a size too small."

"Then why are you wearing them?"

She cringes, then admits, "They're beautiful, and it was so sweet of Willow to give them to me."

I stare at her.

She nervously says, "I shouldn't have said anything. Please don't tell Willow."

"Pheebs, you don't have to suffer instead of telling my sister your boots are too small."

"I'm okay. I'm not suffering. Forget I said anything," she frets.

I sigh, then grab her hand and take her to the couch. I order, "Sit down."

She obeys but blurts out, "I don't want to hurt her feelings. I love them. I think I just have to stretch them out or something."

I kneel and tug off each boot. I point at the sofa. "Put your feet on the couch."

"Why?"

"Go on."

She repositions her body, and I lift her feet and slide under them. I pick up one foot and rub it.

She moans. "Oh my gosh, that feels good."

I chuckle, boasting, "I'm a man of many talents."

"Never thought you weren't," she states.

I keep my focus on her expression, pressing on her foot, hoping I still have my skills.

"Wha—" She takes a ragged breath, and her mouth turns into an O.

I roll my thumb over the same spot, fighting a grin, taunting, "What's wrong, Pheebs?"

"I...uh..." She locks eyes with me.

Jesus, I want to hear her beg me.

I keep the same hand on her foot, then pick up her other one. It takes two seconds for me to find the same erogenous zone.

"Oh my... Oh my gosh," she breathes, her lips quivering.

I still got it. I give myself mental high fives.

"Everything okay?" I tease, clenching my jaw, my cock straining against my zipper.

She doesn't answer, swallowing hard and closing her eyes for a brief moment.

I release her first foot and slide my hand up her calf, then knead the back of her knee.

Her breathing shallows further, her cheeks heating. She mumbles, "What are you doing to me?"

"You want me to stop?" I challenge.

She opens her mouth, but nothing comes out.

I slide both hands to her thighs and tug her so her head's on the cushion. She yelps.

I chuckle and press on her inner thighs.

"Holy..." Her cheeks blaze red. A shudder runs through her. The fire crackles, flickering across her features.

"Why have you been taunting me all night, Pheebs?" I ask.

"Wh-what?" She scrunches her face, then closes her eyes and exhales slowly.

I continue, "You heard me." I graze my fingers over her thighs, inching toward her pussy, then back down.

She blinks several times.

I question, "Is there something you want from me?" I slide my fingers up again, stopping an inch from what I'm dying to taste. Heat penetrates through her jeans.

She stutters, "I-I... I don't know what you mean," she claims, licks her lips, and swallows hard again.

I chuckle. "Sure you do. You've been torturing me all night."

She furrows her eyebrows, glancing at my hands, then pinning her blues on me.

I take my index finger and slide it over her denim-covered slit.

She gasps.

Adrenaline rushes into all my cells. I force myself to bring my hand back to her lower thigh, stating, "I think you've been such a bad girl tonight that you owe me a favor."

Her eyes widen. She whispers, "Like what?"

I grab her hips and tug her closer.

"Alexander!" she shrieks.

"Pheebs!" I whine, pulling her shirt out of her jeans and then dragging my fingers around her navel.

She whimpers.

I lock my gaze on hers. "You want me to stop?"

She doesn't answer. She shakes her head in tiny movements.

I clench my jaw and unbutton her jeans. I slowly lower the zipper, revealing her hot-pink panties. "Oops."

She glances at her lower body and then back at me.

I slide my fingers over the wet material.

She whimpers.

My pulse skyrockets. I hold in my groan, demanding, "I want my favor, Pheebs."

"Wh-what do you want?" she questions, her skin turning a dewy red.

I put my hands on her jeans and tug, asserting, "I want you to tell me you want me to eat your pussy."

She gapes at me.

I yank the denim to her ankles and pull them over her feet. I question, "What's wrong? You've never had a man devour you?"

"I...um..." She bites on her lip.

"What's wrong? You don't like it?"

"No."

"No, as in you do or don't like it?"

"I..." She looks away, then back at me, blurting out, "It doesn't feel very good."

I jerk my head back, appalled. "What?"

Her expression turns embarrassed. She shrugs.

"Wait. So you're serious?" I ask, unable to fathom her statement.

She nods.

I jump off the couch, lean down, and slide my arms under her body.

"What are you doing?" she blurts.

I kiss her, sliding my tongue into her mouth so fast she takes a second to return my affection. I carry her into the bedroom and lie her on the bed. I cage my body over her and declare, "It's clear to me you've never been with a man."

She takes a deep breath.

I kiss her again, then move my lips to her ear, murmuring, "I'm going to lick every inch of your sweet pussy. If you want me to stop, tell me, but I guarantee you, you'll never utter that statement."

"Really?" she whispers.

I smile against her skin, then lick her lobe, and slowly make my way down her neck. I tug her shirt, stating, "This needs to go," and pull it over her head. I slide my hand under her and unclasp her bra, then easily slide it over her arms until she's in nothing but panties.

I trail my mouth over her chest, rolling my tongue around her nipple, then pause, staring at her tattoo.

Day at a time.

"Not a guy's name," I blurt out.

She laughs. "Nope!"

I add, "We'll talk about this later," then I bury my face in her chest, sucking on her tits until she's arching her back and gripping my hair.

I slide over her, kissing her stomach, then pausing with my head between her thighs. I glance at her. "Want me to stop?"

She shakes her head.

"Say it, Pheebs." I slide my finger under her panties, teasing her clit.

She breathes, "Don't stop, Alexander."

Thank God!

I kiss her skin above the top of her panties, praising, "Good girl," then slide my finger out and grip her hips. I inhale her scent, closing my eyes momentarily, my mouth watering. I move my lips over the thin material but don't break the barrier yet.

Another whimper comes out of her. She squirms, her fingers lock over my head, and her panties become more drenched.

"Fuck, you're perfect," I mutter, then move the wet satin to the side of her thigh, displaying her glistening pink pussy, mumbling, "Jesus fucking Christ." I slowly drag my tongue from her hole to her clit.

"Oh my gosh!" she exclaims.

I chuckle, then pin my gaze on her. "Thought you didn't like this."

She gapes at me.

"Should I stop?" I tease, circling her clit once with my tongue, never taking my eyes off her.

"No!"

I slide my finger inside her, torture her clit some more, then add another finger.

"Alexander," she whimpers.

I work my fingers inside her and suck her clit.

"Oh...oh...oh!"

My ears have never heard anything sweeter. The ache in my body intensifies. I grunt. "Fuck, I love how you taste, baby girl." I flick her clit, suck, and flick some more.

She tugs on my hair, writhing on the bed.

I freeze, glancing up, taunting, "Should I stop?"

"Don't you dare!"

I gently nibble her clit, then challenge, "I thought you didn't like this."

"I do!"

"You sure?"

"Yes!"

I flick my tongue ten times.

"Oh...my...oh...my!"

"Are you sure you want me to keep going?" I tease, my mouth against her pussy.

"Please! Don't stop!" she cries out, digging her fingertips into my head.

I suck her so hard her hips jerk up. I hold them down, and incoherent sounds fly out of her.

I groan, loving every minute of her pleasure. And as much as I want to be inside her, I know she has more to give me.

I wait for her to come down, slide my hands under the thin straps of her panties, and tug. They rip with ease.

She gasps.

I lunge over her, slide my tongue in her mouth, and kiss her until she's unbuttoning my belt.

I assert, "Now you're going to ride my face."

She freezes. "What?"

"You heard me, Pheebs. You're going to take your sweet, dripping-wet pussy and ride my face until you have nothing left."

She stares at me, speechless.

I tug my shirt off, roll onto my back, and pat my shoulders, ordering, "Get up here."

"Ummm..."

"Don't make me tell you twice, baby girl."

She caves, grabbing the top of the headboard and putting her knees next to my ears.

The scent of her arousal flares around me, more potent than when I was over her. I groan, wanting to suck every ounce of it out of her.

She doesn't move.

I squeeze her ass and order, "Now, move those gorgeous hips and show me how much you love riding my face."

She releases an anxious breath.

I press my thumb to her clit and slide my tongue around her hole.

She moans.

I grip her hip, rotating her over me until she's grinding without my help. I praise, "That's it, Pheebs. Ride me like a good little girl. Get nice and wet for your stallion."

She freezes, looking down at me, her eyes wide in question.

"You didn't think I'd tattoo something on me that wasn't true, did you?" I question.

She opens her mouth but nothing comes out.

I slap her ass.

She inhales sharply.

I warn, "This is an appetizer, baby girl. My stallion's going to make you come so hard all night, you're going to hurt in the morning." I push my tongue in and out of her while circling her clit with my thumb. I reach up and palm her breast, then tweak her nipple.

She breathes, "Alexander..."

My body's on fire, the sweat on my torso merging with hers. I lose my patience and latch my mouth onto her, not letting up.

Sounds I can't comprehend make my blood boil. Pre-cum seeps out of me. An earthquake shatters her, erupting over me, and she drowns me in her juice.

I'm sure I've died and gone to heaven. She's perfect, and if I could spend every moment making her react like this, I would.

She claims, "I-I can't take anymore!"

I grip her hip and argue, "You can." I don't let up.

She orgasms again, and when she comes down, I release her. Her breath's ragged, face scarlet, and her body glistens. She carefully moves off me and lies down.

I tug her into my arms and kiss the top of her head.

We don't say anything for a few moments. She looks up, then lifts her head. She sweetly kisses me, then intensifies it. She reaches for my belt buckle, but I grab her wrist.

Her eyes widen. She looks at me in question.

I grin. "If you want my stallion, you have to tell me you're going to let me lick your pussy for breakfast tomorrow."

16

Phoebe

*G*iddiness rolls through me. I giggle, then press my lips against his, offering, "If that's what you want."

He grunts, kisses me, then retreats, asking, "Is it fair to say I've changed your mind about getting your pussy licked?"

Another wave of heat burns my cheeks. I've only had a few lovers. Not once did I enjoy them going down on me. It always felt awkward, and I always wanted it to be over.

"Phoebe?" he questions, dragging his fingers over my ass.

I lock eyes with him, admitting, "I like it with you."

Approval fills his expression. He flips me onto my back.

I shriek, laughing.

He shimmies out of his jeans, then cages his body over me. He kisses me with a new intensity but suddenly stops, pulling his head back and studying me.

"Why are you staring at me like that?" I ask.

His hand slides over my thigh tattoo. He furrows his eyebrows and asks, "Are you a runner? I haven't seen you go for any jogs or anything."

Amused, I answer, "Nope!"

Confusion washes over his features. "Then why does your tattoo say 'Marathon'?"

My amusement fades. Emotions swell in my chest. I confess, "It's to remind me that life's a marathon and not to give up."

Worry replaces his confusion.

I quickly add, "I did it after my mom went into a mental home. She tried to hurt herself. I just thought..." I swallow the lump in my throat and take a deep breath. "I didn't know if I would ever feel that hopeless. So, I thought my tattoo could serve as a reminder that sometimes you have to remember that life is a marathon and there are good and bad parts. Then, if I ever felt like my mom did, I could look at it and not give up." I blink hard, wishing what my mom tried to do wouldn't hurt so badly.

Sympathy fills Alexander's blues. He strokes my cheek and gently says, "I'm sorry about your mom."

I nod, choking up. Tears form in my eyes, and I try to push them away.

He sweetly kisses me, then shoots me a stern look.

I nervously ask, "What's wrong?"

His lips twitch. "Nothing. I was just thinking about how you have better tattoo decision-making skills than me."

I burst out laughing, and my tears fall down my cheeks.

He chuckles with me and swipes them away.

When we calm, I tug his face toward me and slide my tongue against his. He moves his mouth to my neck, and I blurt out, "I think your tattoo's hot."

He arches his eyebrows.

My cheeks heat again.

He arrogantly grins, leans into my ear, and murmurs, "Guess you'll have to tell me if I overstated my skills or if I'm worthy of it." He flicks his tongue over my lobe and glides his erection over my clit.

A loud whimper rolls out of me. I'm still sensitive from all the attention he gave me, and a new ache spurs to life.

He chuckles and puts his forearms next to my head. More cockiness flashes across his face, and butterflies attack my belly. His hot breath merges with mine. He continues teasing me, gliding slowly, then speeding up.

Adrenaline creeps into my cells. I close my eyes.

"Look at me, Pheebs," he demands, and returns to a slower pace.

I obey, my chest rising and falling faster. My lips tremble. Uncontrollable moans fly out of me, and I can't take my gaze off his until a slow wave of endorphins turns into a violent act, hitting me with an intense high that makes my eyes roll.

"There you go, baby girl," he praises, as if I've accomplished something at the magnitude of a historical level.

My fingertips dig into his shoulders. He doesn't let up, keeping me dizzy. I slide my fingers over his head and pull him toward me, meeting his tongue with desperate need.

"You're beautiful when you come," he mumbles against my lips.

I clasp my arms tighter around him, rolling my tongue deeper against his, inhaling the aphrodisiac of his scent.

He retreats from our kisses, puts both hands on my cheeks, and shifts his hips back. He pins his heated blues back on mine and slowly slides all the way inside me.

"Oh!" I cry out, catching my breath and seeing stars.

He groans, then slowly thrusts in and out, mumbling, "What are you doing to me, Pheebs?"

I shift my hips, effortlessly falling into rhythm with him, barely getting out, "Alexander..."

He strokes my cheek, then lowers his face, submerging me in an onslaught of passion I didn't know could exist.

I grip his ass cheek with one hand and his hair with my other, pushing him back toward me every time he thrusts away.

"Greedy girl, squeezing that pussy all over my stallion," he teases against my lips, then grabs my hand off his ass and pins it above my head. He taunts me further, sliding in and out even slower.

Tingles race down my spine, erupting in flames at my core. "Oh...my...oh..."

Alexander's gaze doesn't waver. He keeps his full attention on me, as if he's concentrating on something important. He thrusts several more times. The approval in his eyes grows with every uncontrollable sound that flies out of my mouth.

I lean up and flick my tongue over his lips. He purses them, not allowing me to kiss him.

He increases his pace and returns to studying me, stating in a low voice, "You're beautiful, Pheebs."

My heart soars. No one's ever made me feel so special or wanted. I don't recall ever enjoying sex like this either. I try to catch my breath, but I can't. A new orgasm rips through me, and my eyes roll back in my head.

Alexander grunts. "That's it, baby girl. Give your stallion everything you have."

"I am," I claim, my back arching, pushing me closer to him.

He groans, thrusting deeper.

I quiver harder, moaning louder. I try to reach for something, but he still has my wrist pinned.

He slides his fingers between mine. I squeeze hard, digging my nails into the back of his hand. He finally lowers his lips to mine.

Our kisses turn sloppy, our tongues frantic, our eyes locked on one another's in a trance. Every thrust he makes, I meet with more enthusiasm, desperate for every inch of his body.

Sweat erupts on our skin, merging together. The air turns thick with the scent of our arousal. The twinkling orange Thanksgiving lights and the radiant moon shine through the window, creating a soft glow around us.

"Alexander!" I cry out, a wave of heat and endorphins hitting me so hard I almost black out.

"Shh, let go. Your stallion has you," he murmurs in my ear, gripping my hip. He thrusts faster, moving me since I can't do anything besides shake and moan with vigorous euphoria.

My high recedes, only to begin again. He releases my hand and pushes my thigh higher, somehow thrusting even deeper into me.

My voice turns hoarse, and broken sounds crackle through the air. My eyelids flutter over and over, with flames burning into my soul.

His groans intensify. His cock hardens further, stretching my walls and creating a frenzy within me. He lowers his mouth to my shoulder, his teeth pressing into my skin. A deep groan vibrates against me. His body violently convulses, and his cock pumps hard, spewing his hot cum inside me.

My adrenaline spikes to a new high. I dig my nails into his shoulders and cry out, my body trembling against his with no mercy.

His orgasm seems to last forever as he continues to fill me. The air between us thickens, and his tongue returns to mine.

As our bodies slow from the exertion, so do our kisses. He finally rolls onto his back, cradling me in his arms, kissing the top of my head, and stroking my spine.

We both try to catch our breath, the scent of our arousal flaring around us. A while passes before his beating heart slows to a normal pace.

He slides his palm over my ass, holding me close, and caresses the top of it with his thumb. He asks, "Should we get under the covers?"

I tease, "This isn't where you kick me out?"

"Kick you out?" he says with a mix of confusion and disdain in his tone.

I look up. "It was a joke."

"Oh."

"Sorry."

He kisses me on the forehead. "Bad joke." He pats my ass and says, "Let me get the covers sorted." He slides off the bed, then pulls them down as I lift my ass off the mattress. He tucks them around one side of me, then slides under them. He leans on his shoulder and pulls me into him.

I gasp, teasing, "Alexander Cartwright, are you a spooner?"

He slides his palm over my thigh and kisses the back of my ear. His lips tickle my skin as he says, "Only with the right woman."

My butterflies reignite. I turn my head, smirking. "So you do kick some women out of your bed?"

He grunts. "No, but I also don't bring women home and into my kids' space."

My pulse picks up again. I blurt out, "So the stallion is celibate?"

He chuckles so hard he swipes at his eyes. When his laughter fades, he says, "I'm never living this tattoo down."

"Nope," I agree.

He murmurs in my ear, "But you don't have any complaints, right?"

Heat rushes to my cheeks. It's silly to feel shy after all we just did, yet I do. I thought I knew what good sex was, but now I realize I was clueless.

Sounding vulnerable, he asks, "Do I need to try harder?"

I kiss him on the lips and shake my head. "No. I have zero complaints."

He grins. "Good. We'll see if you feel the same way tomorrow morning."

I bite on my smile, the fire blazing hotter on my face.

He grunts and pecks me on the lips. "You're cute when you're embarrassed."

"Am I?"

"Yeah." He tugs me closer and lays his head on the pillow next to mine. "I think I'm going to sleep well tonight."

"Me too," I agree, and sink farther into him.

"I had a lot of fun tonight. Thanks for letting me take you out."

My heart soars. I confess, "I had the best night ever."

"You did?"

"Yep!"

He kisses my shoulder. It's tender from his teeth, but it's a sweet ache. He says, "Good. Me too."

His statement makes me happy.

Silence fills the air for a few moments.

He sleepily asks, "What do you plan on doing with your winnings?"

Guilt hits me again. "I'm going to give you the cash back."

He grunts. "Like hell you are. A bet is a bet. Besides, I'm not a man who can't handle losing, even if I prefer to win."

"It doesn't seem right."

"I'm telling you there's no way I'm keeping your money. Now, what do you want to do with it?"

I ponder his question, but nothing comes to mind. I admit, "I have zero clue."

"Try to do something fun with it. Don't do something responsible."

"Why not?"

He slides his thumb on my shoulder, declaring, "Gambling winnings are for fun. If you use them to pay your bills, you shouldn't be risking your money. That's how you know you have a problem."

"Well, it wasn't my money," I point out.

"True, but it's still winnings. Do something fun with it. Be young and carefree. Tell me when you decide what you're spending it on," he orders.

I laugh. "Okay. I'll let you know."

"Good." He kisses my cheek and then relaxes his head on the pillow. "Sleep well, baby girl."

"Night," I reply, feeling safe, content, and borderline giddy with joy. I close my eyes and fall asleep within seconds, melting into Alexander's arms.

17

Alexander

𝒫 hoebe's floral scent flares in my nose. I open my eyes and blink a few times, inhaling deeper. I'm still spooning her, and she's curled into me, peacefully sleeping, her magenta hair all over the place.

Last night was real.

Weak morning light seeps through the darkness. The rooster crows, signaling it's time to wake up, but I'm always awake at this time of the morning. I can never sleep in and normally love getting up to start my day, but not today.

I would stay in bed all day with Phoebe if I could. But there are things to do, and if I don't go soon, my brothers will barge through my front door, wondering why I'm not outside.

I glance at her, debating whether to wake her up or let her sleep.

I'm hungry.

She can sleep later.

I slide out from underneath her and roll her onto her back. Her eyelids flutter. She smiles and shyly says, "Hey. Good morning." She bites on her lip.

"Morning," I reply, then give her a chaste kiss.

She asks, "What time is it?"

"It's about four thirty. Time for me to work."

"Four thirty! Is that the time you get up every day?"

I chuckle. "That sounds about right." I kiss her again, only this time slipping my tongue in her mouth.

She slides her arms around me, pulling me close, and it's a nice feeling I haven't felt in a long time.

I'm no saint. There's a woman in town named Cheyenne. We have a friends-with-benefits arrangement, and it's purely about sex.

So is this.

Is it though?

I glance at Phoebe, wondering what this is between us. It's different from my arrangement with Cheyenne; I've never brought her to the ranch. My kids are here, and I'm not about to confuse them by mixing my personal adult life into the equation. And I'm always back before they wake up and it's time to start work.

Yet everything feels different with Phoebe.

She interacts with my kids.

That's even more dangerous.

"Alexander? Is everything okay?" she asks, snapping me out of my thoughts.

"Yeah, baby girl. I'm hungry," I state, unable to get up and leave the room.

Her eyes widen. "Do you want me to make you something before you go outside?"

I grin. "It's not food I'm after."

She opens her mouth, then shuts it, her juicy lips curving.

"I warned you," I tease, and slide down the bed.

She giggles, and I bury my head in her pussy, eating her out quickly.

"Oh my... Oh my gosh," she blurts out, gripping my hair.

I don't take my time like I did the night before. I consume her over and over until we're both drenched.

I rub my finger over her clit and shove my tongue inside her, wanting to devour every ounce of her.

"Alexander!" she cries out, her body convulsing.

All I smell and taste is her. And I want to spend the day drowning in it.

She comes down from an orgasm, and I lunge my body over her, ordering, "Taste what's making your stallion hard as a rock."

She desperately meets my mouth, urgently rolling her tongue around mine.

There's a bang on the front door, and I groan.

She freezes, her expression reminding me of a kid caught with her hand in the cookie jar.

I retreat from our kiss, stating, "Thank God I locked the door last night."

She glances out the window. We can see Mason and Jagger striding toward the corral, which already has two horses trotting around it.

"I have to go. I'm already late."

"No," she whines, pouting.

I chuckle. "Get some rest. I'll see you at breakfast in the main house?"

"Sure," she says, then opens her mouth. She snaps it shut and stares at me in question.

I tuck a lock of her magenta hair behind her ear. "What's wrong, baby girl?"

"How does this work, Alexander?"

"Work?" I ask, and my stomach drops. She asked the one thing I don't have an answer to and don't want to decipher right now.

And what I've done dawns on me in the growing morning light.

I fucked my sons' nanny.

I close my eyes briefly, my heart sinking.

What have I done?

"Well, that wasn't exactly the expression I was expecting," she mutters.

I snap out of it. "Sorry, I didn't mean it like that."

"No?" she asks, tilting her head, hurt exploding over her features.

I shake my head. "No, I'm just worried about the boys. They've never seen me with a woman before."

Her eyes widen. "Never?"

"No. Not since their mom..." I pause.

Phoebe puts her hand on my arm.

I shake my head again, continuing, "Not since their mom passed, and they were both babies. They really don't remember her, to be honest."

Pity enters Phoebe's expression. She offers, "That must've been really hard for all of you."

I can't stare at her for too long. I hate pity. People shoot that look at me all the time when they find out I'm a widower. I'm never going to like others directing that look toward me. So I assert, "The boys and I are fine."

She adds, "Yes, but that doesn't mean it was easy."

I quickly agree. "No, it wasn't."

She studies me closer.

"The boys really like you, and I think they're already attached to you. I don't want them to think things if they see us together."

"Things?" She arches her eyebrows.

I ramble on. "Yeah. They're very impressionable. You're from California, and I'm from here. I know you have your life, and we have ours. I don't want them to expect anything and then they get let down."

Her face hardens, and she turns it toward the window, breathing faster.

"Shit. I'm not saying this right, Pheebs," I admit, tugging my hair.

She slides out of bed and pulls the sheet around her. "It's okay."

"No, Pheebs—"

"No, it's fine. Don't worry. It was fun. I won't attack you or anything in front of them." She tosses me a tight smile.

"Phoebe, I didn't mean it like that," I declare.

She forces a bigger smile and chirps, "It's okay. I'm going to take a shower. I'll see you later at the main house. Don't worry. Your secret's safe with me."

"Pheebs—"

"All good," she practically sings, disappearing through my bedroom door.

Shit, shit, shit!

I sit on the end of the bed, pissed at myself, wondering why I said what I did the way I said it.

What exactly was I trying to say anyway?

"Ugh," I mumble, putting my hands over my face.

This is new territory for me. I don't bring women I sleep with to the ranch, and I definitely don't sleep with women who have an important role in my kids' lives.

What have I done?

I need to fix this.

But I need to protect my sons.

I didn't expect this. It just happened.

Bullshit. I've been dying to get her in bed since I met her.

No, I haven't, I tell myself, knowing it's another lie.

Until I know what Phoebe and I are and what this means, I need to keep the boys in the dark.

I step into the hallway and knock on the bathroom door, but the shower's on. I turn the knob, finding it locked.

Great. Way to go, Alexander.

I step back into my room, shower, toss on clothes, and brush my teeth. I return to the bathroom, but Phoebe's hair dryer is blaring.

I decide it's best to give us both a little bit of space and figure out what exactly I'm trying to say or even what I want us to be to each other.

I remind myself this can't go anywhere. She's leaving in less than two months. And she still has a douchebag sort-of boyfriend in her life.

Not for long.

She can't be with him. She's with me.

Is she?

What is this between us?

My thoughts go around and around, adding to my frustration. So I leave the house, stepping into the crisp air. The pink morning glow lights up the ranch, creating a false hope that everything will be okay.

I meet my brothers at the corral.

Jagger grins, taunting, "Well, well, well. How did your date with Phoebe go?"

"Yeah. Was your bed rocking last night?" Mason asks.

I try to hit Jagger and Mason simultaneously, but they both duck. I advise, "Shut up. I won't tell you again not to disrespect Phoebe."

"You two looked pretty cozy coming back," Jagger declares.

I freeze, my heart thumping hard in my chest. "What are you talking about?"

He smirks. "I saw you two. It looks like there was a little kissy-kissy face going on."

I go to smack him again.

He jumps back, holding his hands in the air. "Calm down. I don't blame you. I'd bend Little Miss Nanny over my knee too if she were in my house."

I grab him by the collar and pull him close to me. I seethe, "Don't you ever talk about her again."

He pushes back, ordering, "Get off me."

I don't let go, warning, "Listen to me right now. You saw nothing. You understand?"

He gives me a sarcastic look. "Sure I didn't."

Mason shoves us apart. "Calm down, Alexander."

"I mean it. I don't need this," I spout.

Mason declares, "It's not a big deal, so chill out."

I turn to face him. "It is a big deal. I have two young boys who are already attached to her. I don't need them getting ideas in their heads. Do you understand?"

Jagger scoffs. "Ah. So you're admitting that you banged her?"

I spin in his direction and throw a punch. He leans back and it hits his shoulder.

"Jesus, Alexander, calm the fuck down," Mason commands.

"You two better watch it," I say, then go to the barn.

What the fuck have I done?

Visions of everything I did with Phoebe the night before fill my head. My dick hardens, and I groan. I've gotten myself into a mess. It's going to be hard not to want to get her back into my bed.

I open the stall, and Calypso takes a few steps forward. I pet him and coo, "Hey, buddy." Then I put on his harness and attach the leather lead. I take him out of the barn and over to the corral.

Mason and Jagger have three horses running in circles. They don't say anything else to me, but I know how they are. The whole time I'm working, I can't stop thinking about how to keep Phoebe's and my situation hidden from the boys so they don't get the wrong idea.

The bell at the main house rings, and Willow yells, "Breakfast."

I glance over.

Phoebe's magenta hair blows in the wind. She's bundled up in an oversized sweater and has on her skinny jeans and the too-small boots she shoved her feet into the night before.

She quickly moves toward the house, and I stare at her, wanting to run over and kiss her.

I have to control my urges.

Why did I dip my toe into Satan's well?

Jagger tears me out of my thoughts, jabbing, "Your nanny's looking smoking hot today."

"I swear to God, you're two minutes away from digging your own grave," I warn him.

He chuckles, adding, "Chill out. We're not going to say anything. Are we, Mason?"

Mason shakes his head. "No. We'll stay quiet."

"Are you sure?" I ask, not fully believing them.

"Promise," Mason affirms.

"I mean it. Nothing. No innuendos, no teasing, no saying anything to Phoebe or the kids or anyone else. Got it?"

Jagger nods. "You're good. Just chill out. Okay? Don't go in there acting all wound up."

I take a deep breath, warning, "Don't lie to me." I know how my brothers are, and my gut says not to trust them.

They can never keep a secret when my family is involved. They always reveal it at the most inopportune times.

Mason claims, "We have your back."

"You swear? Because if you do say anything, the boys are going to end up hurt. They're your nephews," I remind them.

My brothers' faces turn serious.

Mason repeats, "We understand, Alexander. We're just teasing you. Don't worry, we won't say anything."

I study them for a moment and realize they're telling the truth.

Jagger adds, "You know we wouldn't do anything to hurt the boys."

Relief washes over me. "Thanks."

"I said breakfast," Willow shouts, ringing the bell again.

"Let's go. I'm hungry," Jagger announces, then secures the gate shut.

The three of us make our way to the house. We go inside and wash up.

"Dad, guess what?" Ace calls out, running up to me.

"Hey, buddy." I tousle his hair. "What's going on?"

"We have a special project we're doing with Phoebe."

"You are? What is it?" I question.

"We're not telling you. It's going to be a surprise," Wilder claims, stepping next to his brother.

"Oh?" I say, glancing at Phoebe and wondering what she has up her sleeve.

She has her back to me, and she's talking to Willow in the kitchen. My heart beats faster the longer I stare at her.

"Yeah, you're going to love it," Ace claims.

"Okay, well I can't wait to find out your secret," I tell them, and we step into the dining room.

Everyone sits. I pull out a chair for Phoebe to sit next to me. She looks at it and then goes and sits down on the other side of Mason.

My chest tightens.

She's still upset with me.

Why did everything I said have to come out sounding so wrong?

My number one job is to protect my kids. If she can't understand that, then I'm not sure what to tell her, I say to myself, trying to justify our conversation earlier.

Paisley looks at Phoebe and asks, "How were the races last night?"

Phoebe doesn't look at me, answering, "It was fun."

"Who won the bet?" Willow asks.

"Pheebs won," I interject.

"Pheebs?" Mason mutters under his voice.

I kick him under the table. He chuckles, and I realize I shouldn't have let the nickname slip.

It's just a name. Lots of people give other people nicknames.

Yeah, when they like someone.

Stop worrying about this, I tell myself.

"Yes! Told you Sweetie Pie would win!" Wilder boasts.

"Yeah! We knew she'd beat all of them!" Ace adds.

"Phoebe had seven to two odds too. And that was a good eye you both had," I say, praising my sons.

"I called it first," Wilder claims.

"No, you didn't. I pointed out she was ready to win," Ace proclaims.

I groan. "Do you two ever stop fighting?"

"He always takes all the credit. But I said it first," Ace continues.

"Enough. Let's eat our breakfast in peace," I scold.

Wilder shoots Ace a funny face, and Ace gives him one back.

"Come on, knock it off," I order.

"So how much money did you win?" Paisley asks.

"$4,500," Phoebe answers.

"Awesome. What are you going to do with it?" Willow inquires.

Phoebe smiles. "I have some ideas, but I'll let you know when I figure it out."

"Secrets don't make friends," Willow chirps.

Phoebe laughs, and my heart aches. I hate not being able to sit next to her, hold her hand, and be as affectionate as I want.

She beams. "Sorry. I'll tell you as soon as I know for sure."

Willow groans. "That sucks, but okay."

"What did you do after the track?" Paisley asks.

"Yeah, Alexander, what did you do?" Jagger chimes in, arching his eyebrows.

I'm going to kill him.

I glance at Phoebe, but she picks at the food on her plate. I answer, "Went for some drinks at Boots."

Willow chirps, "I love that place! You should have called and told me to meet you there!"

I grunt. "Figured you were out with some bull rider."

She smirks. "I was, but I would have made him bring me over to the bar."

"Willow, pass the sausage," Jagger orders.

She picks up the platter and says, "Mom and Dad are home in two days. We've got a lot to do to get ready for Thursday."

The conversation changes about the upcoming Thanksgiving week. I spend the entire breakfast trying to get Phoebe to converse with me, but she barely does.

I curse myself. It's my own fault. I set the stage for this, and now I'll have to fix it. Yet I'm still determining exactly what it is I want to fix. The way I see it, whatever route I go, I'm screwed.

18

Phoebe

*R*egret continues to expand within me with every word Alexander utters.

How could I have been so stupid?

He keeps asking me questions, but I can barely look at him. I wish I could tell him to shut up, but that would make things worse. Plus, it wouldn't be right to say that in front of his sons or the rest of the family.

The entire breakfast, I replay everything we did. Alexander keeps trying to pull me into conversation, but I quickly answer things and then redirect questions to the others.

It feels like this meal will never end. I can barely eat, only playing with my food most of the time. Somehow, I make it through, ignoring Alexander as much as possible, and continuing to feel sick.

He just wanted to get laid.

While I didn't have any expectations, nor did I think I'd end up in bed with him, it's clear I'm just another notch on his belt. And did he think I would run and tell the boys I slept with him? I realize it's a touchy subject, but seriously!

His voice haunts me. All I hear is, *"You're from California, and I'm from here. I know you have your life, and we have ours."*

My gut twists every time it repeats in my head. And it's clear I'm nothing to him. Alexander doesn't see me as anything but someone to play with his stallion.

Disdain fills me. I slept with my boss. I wish I could go back in time. I wouldn't have gone to the races or bar with him. And there's no way I would've slept with him in his bed.

When everyone is finished eating, I take my plate into the kitchen. I need some fresh air, and I'm ready to leave the house.

Alexander follows me, stepping so close, my skin buzzes. And I hate myself even more. I shouldn't feel anything toward him now, but I can't easily turn my attraction off.

"Pheebs—"

"Don't," I warn, my voice shaking.

He pauses and glances behind me. He lowers his voice even further, claiming, "Everything I said came out wrong. You're not understanding what I meant."

I scoff. "I understand everything. You were perfectly clear about where you stand." I place my plate in the dishwasher and brush past him, exiting the kitchen and returning to the dining room.

I force a smile and say, "Ace. Wilder. Are you guys ready to go?"

They jump up.

I point at their plates. "You know the drill."

They pick up their dishes and disappear into the kitchen.

I move toward the entranceway. I snatch the keys off the hook; they're for the SUV Ruby told me I was allowed to drive whenever I wanted.

Alexander appears again. "Where are you going?"

I take a deep breath. I'm going to have to deal with him. He's still my boss. No matter what happened between us, I still love my job, and the kids mean a lot to me. Plus, I'm not ready to go back to California. I have nowhere to go, and I don't have enough money saved to even put a deposit down on an apartment.

I have my gambling winnings.

No, they're not mine, I remind myself.

I meet his eye. "I'm taking the kids to town. We're going shopping."

He arches his eyebrows. "Shopping?"

"Yeah, is that okay?" I question and then cringe. I sigh. "Sorry, I didn't mean to be snippy."

He steps closer. "Pheebs—"

"Where are you going, Phoebe?" Jagger asks, interrupting us.

Alexander's face fills with annoyance. He shoots his brother a glare.

"You two going together?" Jagger smirks.

My stomach churns so fast, I put my hand over it. The blood drains from my face to my toes. Then, heat burns my cheeks.

Jagger knows.

Goose bumps pop out on my skin. My lips tremble. I look at Alexander and mutter, "You told him?"

Alexander's eyes widen. He shakes his head. "No, of course not," he says.

I don't believe him.

He spins on his brother. "She's going to town. I'll meet you at the corral."

Jagger gives us an arrogant look, and I want to crawl into a hole.

As soon as the door shuts, I seethe, "You told your brothers? How could you?"

Alexander steps closer and grabs my arm. He pulls me into a side room and shuts the door, starting, "Pheebs—"

"Stop calling me that," I say through gritted teeth.

"Phoebe, I did not tell them anything. I promise you."

"Them? Who else knows?"

He cringes.

"Who?"

"Just Mason."

"You jerk! How could you?"

"I didn't tell them anything!"

"Then how do they know?"

He tilts his face to the ceiling, shakes his head, and closes his eyes.

"How?" I push, close to tears and trying to hold them back.

He opens his blues and informs me, "He saw us kissing outside when we got home last night."

I gape at him, feeling like a total failure and more embarrassed than ever. I'm sure his brothers think I screw my bosses all the time.

He tries to reassure me. "They aren't going to say anything."

"Sure they won't," I accuse.

He steps closer. Before I know it, his arms are around me and he holds my head to his chest. I try to push him away, but he holds me tightly. He murmurs in my ear. "Everything's fine. You're taking what I said the wrong way. And I know what I said didn't come out right, but don't let Jagger bother you. Everything's fine."

I melt into him for a moment, but then I push out of his grasp. "I'm ready to go."

"Phoebe..."

In a stern voice, I state, "Alexander, I'm not doing this right now. If you feel the need to talk about this, we'll do it at another time, okay?"

He studies me for a moment and then nods. "Okay. But I'm sorry I said things the way I did."

I don't respond. I just walk out the door and head toward the SUV.

The boys come running out after me.

Alexander follows, questioning, "Do you need money for your trip?"

"No," I answer.

"Do you have the credit card?"

"I don't need it."

"Dad, we're good," Ace says.

Alexander glances at us suspiciously.

"Come on, kids, let's go," I say, then get into the SUV.

Wilder jumps in the front and Ace in the back.

"Put your seat belts on," I tell them.

They buckle up, and we take off toward town.

Wilder asks, "So we can pick whatever color we want for our rooms?"

"Yep. Do you know what color you want?" I question.

"Hmm, maybe red."

"I'm going to do green," Ace proclaims.

I ask, "Light green or dark green?"

"I don't know. Maybe in the middle."

I smile at him through the rearview mirror. "Green's a good color. So is red. What about you, Wilder? Dark or light?"

"I don't know. I'll let you know when I see it," he says.

I smile. "Fair enough."

By the time I get to town, my insides have calmed. I push the issues between Alexander and me out of the way and focus on the kids. We go into a hardware store and find the paint samples.

"Have at it," I tell them, then pull several colors out to see how they coordinate next to each other.

Wilder asks, "What color will you do your room, Phoebe?"

"I don't know yet. It'll depend on what we do for the rest of the house."

Ace asks, "You're going to do the same color?"

"No," I say, as if it's a sin.

"Good. That would be boring," he declares.

I laugh and then pick up several bright colors and a few muted ones.

Ace picks out an apple green, and Wilder selects a cherry red. We go up to the man behind the paint counter, and I put all the swatches down, telling him which colors we want and how much of each.

He points to a chart. "Do you want flat, eggshell, or one of our other finishes?"

I study the sheens and decide, "Let's go with eggshell. Can you do it in the one that claims it doesn't scuff up?"

He nods. "Sure. It will take me about twenty minutes to mix all this."

"That's okay," I reply.

The boys and I stroll down different aisles, picking out a couple of new light fixtures.

We return to the counter and load the paint cans into the cart. Then we head to the checkout, and I pay with my racetrack winnings.

We leave, and the boys load all the paint into the back of the SUV. I chirp, "Ready to go find some more stuff?"

"Yeah, this is fun," Ace says.

"Dad's going to be so surprised," Wilder adds.

Alexander's face appears in my mind, and my heart aches. I push it out again, saying, "Okay, let's go."

We get back in the car and drive down the street. I pull into a lot for a home decor store. The boys and I pick out posters and art for their walls. I grab a handful of blank canvases so we can each create something for our rooms.

Then, we find some window treatments, sheets, and quilts for all the beds, and some throw blankets for the main room. By the time we're done, I've spent everything except $820.

"I don't think we can fit anything else in the SUV," Ace states.

"Nope. What do you guys say? Are you hungry? You want to go grab some lunch?"

"Can we go to Piggly's?" Wilder suggests.

Ace nods. "Yeah, they have the best food."

I haven't been to Piggly's, so I ask, "Where is it at?"

"We know where. We'll direct you while you drive," Wilder says.

"Shotgun!" Ace proclaims, running to the passenger door.

Wilder groans. "Younger kids should be in the back."

I tousle his hair. "Not a chance. Get in the back seat. It's your brother's turn to ride up front."

He grumbles but gets in the back. They direct me where to go, and we pull up to Piggly's. It's a cute little diner, and there are a lot of people inside. We have a five-minute wait and then they seat us in a booth. Ace sits next to me, and Wilder sits across from me.

He asks, "Can we start painting today?"

I glance at my watch. "I don't know. There's a lot going on because of Thanksgiving. We'll have to see what Willow and Paisley want us to do when we return," I reply.

Ace adds, "I'm so excited we don't have school this week."

"Yeah, I'm over school," Wilder agrees.

I claim, "School's not that bad, especially yours. It's a really nice place with great teachers. Besides, you need to learn. You'll be happy with your education when you're older."

Wilder shrugs. "I don't know what good it'll do when I'm running the ranch."

"Well—"

"Wilder. Ace. Fancy meeting you here," a blonde with curly hair chirps.

"Hey, Cheyenne," Wilder says.

"Hi! Have you met our nanny, Phoebe?" Ace asks her.

She peers at me, and my stomach flips. She holds her hand out, stating, "Oh, yes. I heard there was someone else staying on the ranch. You were at Boots last night, right?"

My heart beats hard. I take her hand and reply, "Yes."

"She went to the races with Dad. He lost a bet and she won big-time!" Ace boasts.

I glance over at him, wishing he wouldn't tell her anything. I'm unsure why, but she's making me uncomfortable.

I look back at her. "How do you all know each other?"

Her lips curve into a tight smile. She says, "I'm friends with Alexander. I've known him for a long time. We go way back."

Something about the way she says it makes me feel even more off.

Wilder offers, "They went to school together."

"Oh, that's nice. Well, nice to meet you," I reply.

Her gaze drifts over me and then locks back on my eyes. "Yes, very nice meeting you. I'm sure I'll see you around."

"Okay. Sounds good," I say, but everything inside of me tells me I don't want to see this woman again. She seems friendly enough, but the bad feeling I'm getting is telling me something isn't right.

She disappears just as the server steps up to the table.

"Welcome to Piggly's. I haven't met you before. I'm Martha," the older woman states.

"Martha, this is our nanny, Phoebe. She's awesome," Ace exclaims.

I laugh. "Well, thank you!"

Martha's warm smile makes me feel better. She declares, "It's nice to meet you. And I haven't seen you guys in a while. Has your dad been too busy to bring you to town?"

Wilder offers, "Yeah, and Grandma and Grandpa aren't back in town until Tuesday."

"I heard they went on that mission trip early. I was surprised they'd leave over the holidays," Martha admits.

"They're going to return for Thanksgiving and Christmas," I inform her.

Martha smiles in approval. "That's good. Holidays without Ruby and Jacob just wouldn't be the same. Now, what can I get you to drink?"

I order water, and the boys order sodas.

Martha asks, "Do you like Reubens? We have those on special today."

I admit, "I don't think I've ever had one."

She feigns shock, dramatically gasping. "What? Then you have to have one. It's absolutely delicious. I guarantee it."

I laugh. "Okay, a Reuben it is."

"I want the cheeseburger and fries, please," Ace tells her.

Wilder states, "I'll take the bacon grilled cheese with the tomato soup, please."

"Done and done. Let me get your drinks, and your food won't take that long. I'll put it in as a priority." Martha winks.

I grin. "Sounds good. Thank you."

She pats me on the shoulder. "It's nice meeting you, Phoebe. Glad someone's taking care of the boys."

"Thank you."

She leaves, and I glance around the restaurant. My chest tightens.

Cheyenne's staring at me through slitted eyes, tapping her fingers on the table. She's not faking anything now.

I look away and converse with the boys, but I can feel her glaring daggers at me. I look back and find I'm not wrong.

Why is she looking at me like that?

My insides quiver.

Our food comes out, and Martha sets it down just as Cheyenne gets up. She strolls over to us and waits for Martha to leave, then says, "Make sure you tell Alexander I said hi."

"Okay, I will," I reply, hoping she'll leave.

Her lips twist into a vicious smile. "Good. And let him know I'm ready to ride that stallion of his again."

19

Alexander

*A*ll I want to do is crawl back into bed and hit the reset button. What started off as an amazing day, quickly went from bad to worse. I hurt Phoebe, and she's embarrassed that my brothers know about last night. I wish I could somehow undo the damage I've done, but I don't know how.

The only thing I know how to do is throw myself into my work. So I run the horses hard, especially Calypso.

Mason shouts, "Enough! You're going to risk injuring him."

I assess the situation. He's right. I've already made Calypso run four more rounds than normal.

I sigh and step into the corral. I reach for his harness, snapping the leather lead in place and patting his wet face. I praise, "Good job, buddy."

He nuzzles his face into my chest, out of breath.

I take an apple from my pocket and hold it out to him. He takes it and chomps down on it. I direct him toward the water basin and let him drink for a few minutes before taking him back to the barn.

My phone buzzes as soon as I shut the gate to his stall. I take it out of my pocket and pull up my text messages.

> Cheyenne: Met your nanny today.

The hairs on my arms rise. It's a small town, and everyone knows everyone. As far as the boys know, Cheyenne is my former classmate, and that's it.

And she knows how I feel about my kids. She's always respected my boundaries regarding them, so I've never worried when we've happened to run into her in town or at events.

Before I can reply, another text pops up.

> Cheyenne: She's cute. A bit artsy for my taste, but she seems perky.

> Cheyenne: Her diamond nose stud is a nice touch.

I close my fist, staring at the screen, debating how to respond.

> Me: She's been great with the boys.

> Cheyenne: Can you get away tonight? I'm down for a bit of playtime.

> Me: Sorry, I can't leave the kids. There's too much going on.

> Cheyenne: Too much going on with the nanny?

The air in my lungs turns stale. The last thing I need is for Cheyenne to be jealous of Phoebe. She doesn't even know what happened between us. Even if she did, we're strictly friends with benefits, nothing more. She has no dibs on me. And whenever she goes out on dates, I don't interfere. I know our little arrangement can end at any time.

Cheyenne: Didn't think she was your type.

Me: Stop making accusations about things you know nothing about.

Cheyenne: Then come over and punish me for being bad.

A photo of Cheyenne touching her naked pussy comes across the screen.

Normally, it would heat my blood, and I'd figure out a way to go fuck her, even if I only had twenty minutes of free time. Right now, it's annoying me.

Me: I'm busy. Gotta go. Talk later.

Cheyenne: But I need the stallion. And you owe me.

My pulse skyrockets. The only place my stallion wants to be is inside Pheebs.

What's Cheyenne talking about anyway?

Me: Owe you?

Cheyenne: Yep. I fucked you a few weeks ago before I went out for the night. I had to redo my hair and makeup.

Me: I don't have time for this. Talk later.

She tries to call me.

I send her to voicemail.

She texts me crying emojis.

It annoys me further. I slide my phone into my pocket and leave the barn. I'm halfway across the yard when the SUV pulls through the gate.

Ace jumps out of the front seat and runs toward me. "Dad, you're going to love our surprise!"

I ask, "Are you going to tell me what it is now?"

"Nope! You have to go away so we can unload the trunk," he answers.

"I can't peek?"

"No! You'll ruin it!"

I chuckle. "All right. I'll go away in a minute. Did you boys behave?"

"They were perfect. Ace, go help your brother unload everything," Phoebe orders.

He obeys.

I glance at her. "Glad the boys didn't give you any trouble. I can't wait for this surprise to be revealed."

She smiles, but there's a hint of disapproval in her eyes. She adds, "Met your friend, Cheyenne."

"We went to school together."

"Yes, so I hear. She said to tell you she wants to ride your stallion again." Phoebe's smile hardens.

Oh shit.

Fucking Cheyenne.

I open my mouth, but nothing comes out.

Phoebe glares at me and spins on her heel. She joins the boys, unloading the SUV.

My gut continues to sink. I take a few deep breaths.

She'll understand once I explain to her my arrangement with Cheyenne.

Besides, Phoebe is still with Mr. Douchebag, for all I know. She doesn't have the right to be pissed at me for something I did before I slept with her.

I walk toward the vehicle, hoping to pull Phoebe aside.

Wilder shouts, "Dad, you can't come here! You'll ruin the surprise."

I freeze, unsure what to do.

Ace orders, "Go away! We want to surprise you!"

Wilder adds, "Don't come inside until it's dark out."

I say to Phoebe, "We need to talk later."

She tilts her head and pins her eyebrows together. "Do we?"

I sternly assert, "Yes, we do."

She chirps, "Sure. Whatever you say, boss. Come on, boys. Let's start our project." She leads them away, and I stomp over to the corral.

Jagger asks, "What's going on there?"

"Nothing."

He tilts his head. "Didn't look like nothing."

"Mind your own business," I fume, and head to the stable. I put a saddle on my riding horse, Trojan. I put my foot in the stirrup and pull myself up. I toss my leg over his back and sit.

I spend the rest of the afternoon riding around the lake. It's the one thing that's always been my saving grace, except for today. I can't shake the hole I've dug myself in.

I tell myself a dozen times I have nothing to apologize for regarding Cheyenne, but it still feels as if I do. And I curse myself for letting myself act so irresponsibly.

Phoebe is my sons' nanny. She's my employee and responsible for the two people I love more than anyone else. My job is to protect them and worry about my own needs last, and I didn't do that last night.

The sunshine fades, and darkness sets in. I should have cooled off but I'm still fuming over too many things, feeling a bit lost, and trying not to go down the rabbit hole I avoid at all costs.

It's the place where I lose all control and wallow in self-pity, and one thing I hate is being a victim. There are only a few times I've allowed myself to go there. Tonight, I'm struggling not to step into the shadows of the "what-ifs," "why me," and "life is unfair" talk.

Part of me wants to stay outside forever, but I know I need to face the music and try to clear the air between Phoebe and me.

I run Trojan hard until I get to the barn. I jump off him, take off his saddle, rub him down, put him in his stall, then head toward the house. The orange lights and the automatic outside lanterns turn on, guiding me to the porch.

When I open the front door, the smell of homemade cookies hits me. Laughter rings in my ears, and I pause, smiling.

Maybe I shouldn't go in there and ruin their fun.

"Dad's going to love this!" Ace exclaims, pulling me out of my debate.

I step into my bedroom, asking, "What do I need to see?" Then I freeze.

The laughter stops. My kids and Phoebe stare at me.

I glance around my bedroom. The walls are a tranquil blue. There's a new, multicolored bedspread on my mattress and a glass vase on the nightstand. Across from my bed, a huge canvas with a turkey and the boys' names painted on it hangs on the wall. A silver hammered-metal horse hangs above my bed. "Stallion" is written under it.

Wilder shouts, "Surprise!"

Ace asks, "Don't you love it, Dad?"

Phoebe takes a deep breath and offers a small smile.

Stunned, I take everything in again, admitting, "It's great."

"We're doing my room next; I drew the longest straw! I chose red paint," Wilder states.

"Then we're painting mine! My walls are going to be green!" Ace chimes in.

I lock eyes with Phoebe. "This is really nice."

"You like it?"

"Yes."

Her smile grows. She softly replies, "Good."

I glance at the metal horse over the bed, then at her. I arch my eyebrows, my heart beating faster.

She bites on her smile, her cheeks turning pink.

For some reason, a chuckle flies out of me. Maybe it's the stress of the day. Perhaps I'm so out of my element in my own house I don't know how to handle anything right now. It might be due to my undeniable attraction for Phoebe, even though I've spent the entire day trying to tell myself I can squash it.

Then again, maybe I just want to feel the happiness I felt twenty-four hours ago before I opened my mouth and ruined everything between us.

Whatever it is, I keep laughing. Phoebe suddenly joins in, and tears fall down my cheeks. I swipe at them but can't stop howling. My sides begin to hurt.

Ace asks, "What are you laughing about?"

I can't answer him. I glance at the horse again, and Phoebe giggles harder. She rubs tears off her cheeks as well.

"I don't get it," Wilder adds.

It takes another few minutes for us to calm. I kneel down and toss my arms around the boys. "Thanks. This is really nice."

Wilder declares, "It was all Phoebe's idea."

Ace offers, "She said we had to do your room first."

"Yeah. She said you deserved it since you work so hard for all of us," Wilder states.

I pin my gaze on her. "Thank you. It's really nice."

"You're welcome."

We don't say anything for a moment.

Ace's stomach growls. He announces, "I'm hungry. What's Aunt Willow cooking?"

Phoebe answers, "It's steak night."

"Yes! My favorite," Wilder exclaims, pumping his arm in the air.

"Why don't you two run to the house? Phoebe and I will meet you there. I need to talk to her for a minute."

"I'll race you," Ace says, running out of the room.

"No head starts allowed!" Wilder claims, following him.

The front door slams, and I step in front of Phoebe. Anxiety creeps back into my chest. I blurt out, "Where did you find the horse?"

Her lips twitch. "The home goods store in town."

I glance at it again, chuckling. "It's nice."

"I thought you'd appreciate it," she says, taking a deep breath. Her smile fades.

A million thoughts race around me. I start, "Look, I..."

She waits.

"I fucked up this morning. I said things the wrong way."

"I'm not looking to be another notch on your belt, Alexander."

I close the space between us and palm her cheek. "I never thought of you like that."

"No?"

"No. Not once."

Tension builds between us.

I swipe my thumb over her lips and add, "I like you—a lot. But I don't know what to make of us. I'm not used to...well, any of this. I just don't want to hurt my sons if... I don't even know if you're still with that dickhead."

Her lips curve, but she stays silent.

My pulse races faster. I push, "Are you with him?"

She slowly shrugs. "I don't know what's going on between us."

My heart sinks. I blurt out, "I don't go for women taken by other men."

Phoebe clears her throat. "What about Cheyenne? Sounds like you have a lot going on with her."

I admit, "It's a friends-with-benefits situation. That's it."

Phoebe cringes. "People really do that?"

I shrug. "I have a lot of responsibilities with the boys and the ranch, but I still have needs. What can I say?"

She pauses, then offers, "Fair enough."

"This is complicated all around, and I don't know what to make of it."

"Well, it doesn't help that I broke the golden rule."

Confused, I ask, "Be nice to others?"

She shakes her head. "No. Don't sleep with your boss."

"I'm not exactly innocent. It goes both ways," I declare.

We're quiet for a long moment.

She puts her hand over my palm that's on her cheek and closes her eyes. Then she opens them and says, "Maybe it's best if we're just friends. We both have things going on we need to deal with, so it's probably best if we don't cross the friend line again."

My stomach churns, but I can't argue with her. I slowly flip my hand over hers and kiss the back of it. "Okay."

She smiles.

"So you don't hate me?" I question.

She sighs. "No."

"Good. It was a pretty crappy day knowing I hurt you," I admit.

"I'll agree I've had better days than today."

I glance around the room. "This really was nice of you to do."

"Thanks. I had a good team to help me," she states.

"Should we go to dinner?" I ask.

"Sure."

I motion for her to go first, and almost put my hand on her back but stop myself.

Friends only.

It might be hard not to want more, but Phoebe's right. Neither of us is in a position to get involved with the other. All it will do is hurt someone, possibly my boys.

We leave the house, not saying anything, and cross the yard to the main house. When we get inside, dinner is ready. My family's in the dining room, ready to eat.

We grab chairs across from each other, and unlike breakfast, we fall back into our usual banter. It feels good, yet I can't help wishing things could be different, even though I know it's not our reality.

20

Phoebe

Thanksgiving Day

The aroma of fresh coffee and bacon flares in my nostrils. I slowly open my eyes, groaning, and shut them again. My pulse pounds against my skull. My mouth tastes dry, like something died in it.

I blink a few times, then slowly sit up and glance out the window. Frost covers the corners of the glass, and big snowflakes fall on the other side of the pane.

I force myself to get out of bed, put on a robe over my pajamas, and slide my feet into my slippers. I go into the bathroom, brush my teeth, and gurgle some mouthwash.

I leave the bathroom and slowly make my way into the kitchen.

Alexander leans against the counter with a cup of coffee in his hand. I can tell he's already been outside this morning—his boots and cowboy hat are on. The corners of his lips curve, and sympathy fills his expression.

Even though I feel like crap, my heart beats harder at the sight of him and that smile. I wish he weren't so sexy, but no matter what we agreed to, my attraction for him hasn't waned. We've done our best to return things to how they were, but it's hard. Several times this week, I've wanted to reach out and touch him and had to remind myself not to.

"How are you feeling, Pheebs?"

I groan. "How many beers did I have?"

He chuckles. "I didn't count. Especially after you made that bet with Sebastian."

What bet?

I try to remember the events of last night, recalling them step by step. A vision of the Cartwrights chanting my name pops into my mind. "Oh geez," I say, shaking my head and then wincing at the stab of pain.

"Easy there," Alexander warns. He turns and pours another cup of coffee. He sets it on the table. "Sit down."

I obey and wrap my hands around the warm mug.

He reaches into the cabinet, pulls out a bottle of headache tablets, and puts two in his palm. He holds them out, ordering, "Here, take these. They'll help your head."

I take them from him, and he moves a glass of water toward me.

I swallow the pills and ask, "What exactly did Sebastian bet me?"

"Oh, it wasn't Sebastian," Alexander reveals, trying to keep a straight face.

I furrow my brows, admitting, "I'm lost. Can you be more specific?"

Amusement appears on Alexander's expression. "You were the one who bet him you could chug a beer faster than him."

I put my hand over my face, moaning, "I did?"

Alexander's lips twitch. "You sure did."

I take a sip of coffee. The hot liquid flows into my belly but doesn't feel very good. I cringe, clutching my stomach.

He sits next to me, puts his hand on my back, and leans closer. "Pheebs, you look green."

"I'll be okay."

He takes a sip of coffee, then declares, "If it makes you feel any better, I've never seen anyone beat Sebastian. You've got some real beer chugging skills."

I faintly remember poking a hole in a can and then holding it to my mouth while everyone around us was cheering. I put my arms on the table and hide my face in them. I close my eyes and mumble, "It's your family's fault. There's too much peer pressure."

Alexander chuckles. "Is that the story you're sticking with?"

I force myself to meet his gaze. "Yeah."

He grins and then puts his hand on my thigh. He leans closer. "You know they'll want to party again tonight, right?"

I wince. "They will?"

He grins. "Yep. Do you want a beer now? You can get a head start by having some of the hair of the dog that bit you."

I whine, "That sounds disgusting."

"Your call." He sits back, amused, and takes another sip of coffee.

I force myself to pry my head off the table and glance out the window, then state, "It looks like the snow's coming down hard."

"Yeah. Started right before we got home."

"It did?" I pin my eyebrows together, trying to remember walking home from the main house, but nothing registers.

He asks, "You don't remember me carrying you, do you?"

My cheeks heat. I admit, "No. How bad was I?"

"I wouldn't say bad. You were just pretty animated," he teases.

"I'm sorry. Not very nanny-ish of me."

He laughs. "You're not really on nanny duty right now. It's Thanksgiving. Happy Thanksgiving, by the way."

"Happy Thanksgiving," I reply, and take another sip.

"Do you want anything to eat? Some toast might help," he offers.

My belly flips. "No. I might get sick if I do."

"Aww," he coos, scooting closer and slinging his arm around me. "I feel bad I let you drink so much."

I close my eyes, resting against his chest. I mumble, "It wasn't your fault."

"Still..."

"I'll be okay," I insist. Then I ask, "Why did you carry me?"

"You might have had some issues walking in the snow after your third round with Sebastian."

I gape at him.

He grins, then suggests, "Why don't you get some more sleep and let the headache tablets kick in? It's still early."

I force myself to move my head and look up. "What time is it?"

"A tad past eight."

"I need to help cook dinner."

He grunts. "You won't miss much for a few hours. Get some rest so you can enjoy the day. Besides, I'm cashing in on my winnings after we eat."

"Your winnings?"

He nods, studying me.

My gut drops. I'm scared to ask but have to. "What did we bet?"

"Something fun. You'll see." He rises and downs the rest of his coffee. "I need to get a few things done."

"You aren't going to tell me?"

He rinses his mug and puts it in the dishwasher. "Nope. Since you don't remember, I'll keep it a surprise. But you did tell me you were excited."

"I did?"

"Yep."

I rack my brain, but I can't remember anything about that conversation.

He asks, "You sure you don't want any toast?"

"No, I'm okay."

"Okay. Go rest."

I question, "Where are the boys?"

"All the kids are outside taking advantage of the freak Texan snowstorm."

"It never snows here?"

"It does on a rare occasion, but typically never this early. The kids built a few snowmen before they started a snowball fight. The others are at the main house, but feel free to go there when you're ready. You should go back to bed and rest a while longer."

I cave, agreeing. "Okay. If you're sure?"

"I'm sure. Besides, I think Paisley and Willow might still be asleep."

A flashback of the three of us laughing, then Paisley asking for a tarp from the barn, hits me. I ask, "Did we do something with a tarp last night?"

Alexander's eyes light up. "There might have been a few attempts at a slip 'n slide in the snow."

"A slip 'n slide?"

He nods. "Yep."

Another flashback rolls through my brain. Horrified, I ask, "Did I almost freeze to death, and you put me in a hot shower?"

"Sure did," he states.

The color drains from my face. I groan. "Ugh. I'm sorry."

He chuckles. "It's okay."

"Did the boys see me wasted?"

"No. All the kids stayed at the main house with my parents. It's a tradition."

Relief fills me. "Thank God!"

He chuckles again. "Get some rest, Pheebs."

He goes to the door, and I stare at his hard ass as too many questions run through my mind.

What happened in the shower?

Images of Alexander putting my pajamas on me, and me tossing my arms around him and slurring, "Bring out the stallion," assault me.

More embarrassment floods me. I put my hands over my face again, my heart racing and head banging.

I stay in the kitchen, trying to remember more, but nothing else comes to me. I finally force myself to get up and go back to bed. I set an alarm for two hours and then quickly fall asleep.

When the buzzer blares, I shut it off and slowly open my eyes. I wait for the headache, but it doesn't appear, seeming to be gone.

I slide off the bed and freeze.

A white box sits on my dresser. An orange and brown ribbon is wrapped around it, and an orange envelope is tucked under the extravagant bow.

My heart beats harder. I reach for the envelope and take the card out.

The front has a picture of a turkey and the words Gobble, gobble on it.

I smile and open the card. It says "Happy Thanksgiving." The left side has a handwritten note.

Pheebs,
Our secret.
Don't tell Willow.
Alexander

My butterflies go nuts. I lift the lid and pull out a pair of identical boots to those Willow gave me. I check the label, and they're half a size bigger.

My pulse pounds harder, but my heart also hurts a bit. It's such a sweet gift. For the millionth time this week, I wish things weren't so complicated, and I could be with Alexander.

I put the boots on my bed, then package the ones Willow gave me in the box. I tuck it in the back of my closet, then go shower, brush my teeth, and do my hair and makeup.

I get dressed and put on my new boots. They fit perfectly. Happiness fills me. Even though the boots Willow gave me were too small, I wore them daily. I love them. Plus, we're on the ranch. There's dirt everywhere. It'd be stupid to wear anything but boots.

I put on the winter coat, gloves, and a hat I bought earlier this week, then trudge through the thick blanket of snow to the main house. When I step into the warm parlor, I stomp my feet and take off my coat, hat, and gloves.

It still feels strange not taking my boots off, but Ruby told me she gave up years ago worrying about her floors. She said she finally realized farmhouses have wood floors for a reason.

I hang my coat up. I can hear all the women chatting in the kitchen, so I step inside.

It's chaos. The entire kitchen is full, and multiple conversations are going on at the same time.

Georgia turns, and her face lights up when she sees me. "How are you feeling, Phoebe?"

Everyone stops and turns toward me.

I answer, "A little better now. Alexander gave me some headache tablets."

She teases, "I don't think Sebastian's ego will ever recover."

I put my hand over my face, my cheeks heating. I mumble, "I don't even want to know."

Laughter fills the air.

"Don't worry. Paisley's hungover too," Ruby says.

Paisley's complexion is pale. Her cheek rests on her forearm as she slumps over the table. She mutters, "Don't talk to me about it."

"Aw, you'll be okay," Ruby says, patting her shoulder.

She winces. "Mom, bruise!"

"Oh. Sorry. Guess it'll teach you not to pull tarps out in the snow."

I ask, "You got hurt?"

"Just a little bruise."

Evelyn snorts. "Little, meaning her entire arm and part of her back."

"It's fine," Paisley says and shuts her eyes.

Willow interjects, "I'd trade you the bruise for the date Cyril took me on last night."

Georgia catches my eye, biting her smile.

I ask, "Why?"

Willow wrinkles her nose. "You'd think a man who can handle a bull would know how to take charge on a date."

"Oh?" I question.

"Maybe you should give him another chance. He might have been shy," Ruby states.

Georgia snickers.

"I thought he was nice," I offer. He came over before things got fuzzy for me. I add, "I didn't realize there were any issues."

"He doesn't like bars, so we came home early on the biggest bar night of the year," Willow complains.

"And this is a bad thing?" Ruby asks.

Willow scoffs. "Duh." She picks up a carrot and points it at me, stating, "Phoebe, this is a lesson in why you don't want to be the first person to date a bull rider when he first gets to town. You don't know what their issues are. If you let a couple of other women date them first, you'll find out their quirks and save yourself time and energy. So don't be stupid like me. Last night, I got to discover all of his issues." She rolls her eyes.

Georgia prods, "What were his issues?"

"Not over his ex-girlfriend."

"Ooh, that sucks," Georgia sympathizes.

"Doesn't like crowds."

"Not the one to take you out on the night before Thanksgiving," Paisley offers, then rises. "I need a glass of wine to help counter the effects of last night. Anyone else want one?"

I consider it, but I can't stomach it, so I decline.

Willow picks up a celery stalk and then runs it under the water to wash it. "I couldn't get him to leave fast enough. I was glad the rest of you were here so I didn't completely waste my night."

"I'm sure you'll find another date soon," Ruby chirps.

I offer, "Sorry he wasn't the one. What can I help with?"

"I've got to peel all these potatoes, if you want to jump in," Evelyn states.

"Sure." I step next to her and start peeling the boiled potatoes.

We spend the next few hours getting everything ready for the main meal. From time to time, the kids run into the kitchen, and around two o'clock, everything's finally ready.

Paisley declares, "I'll go ring the bell."

It takes another half hour until everyone's inside and washed up.

Alexander holds his chair out and motions for me to sit beside him. My butterflies take off like they always do around him. I sit down, and his aphrodisiac of musk, sweat, and outdoors flares around me. I cross my legs, squeezing them together.

He asks, "Feeling better?"

I nod. "Yeah. Thanks for the headache tablets."

"You're welcome."

I lean closer and whisper, "And for the boots."

"They fit okay?"

"Perfectly!"

"Great." He winks.

My butterflies go crazy.

Jacob says a prayer and then one by one, everyone states what they're thankful for.

It's my turn, and I declare, "I'm thankful you gave me a chance to be Ace and Wilder's nanny, and that I've been so graciously welcomed into your family. Thank you." A swell of emotion hits me and I tear up.

I realize I've never felt so welcome in anyone's home. The Cartwrights truly love each other, and they've always made me feel so comfortable. It feels like home, and sometimes it's hard because I know I'll have to head back to California in a little over a month or figure out another place to go.

The longer I go without hearing from Lance, the more I realize I don't want to be with him.

I want a man like Alexander. Someone who treats me as well as he does. And it sucks he's unavailable.

I've never felt chemistry with someone before. Now that I've had it with him, I know what it feels like. Yet I don't know if it exists beyond him, and it's becoming clearer and clearer I never had it with Lance and probably never will. What I thought were good times are different from how things should be.

Ruby beams. "That's so sweet. We're so happy to have you here, dear."

"Yeah. Everything is way better since you got here," Ace adds, making my heart soar.

"I agree," Wilder chimes in, then gives me a wink.

I laugh. It's cocky and looks just like Jagger's, who has a really big ego, but he seems to be able to get away with it.

Jacob says, "Your turn, Alexander."

He shifts in his seat and then locks eyes with me. He confidently states, "I'm grateful for Pheebs. The boys and I would have been lost the last few weeks. Mom, you were right to make me hire her."

My pulse skyrockets through the roof. My voice catches, but I manage to get out, "Th-thank you."

"It's true." He focuses on me for another few seconds, then turns back to the table.

Jagger states, "Well, I'm grateful for Pheebs too."

"Don't be a dick," Alexander mutters under his breath, and I bite on my smile.

Jagger chuckles and says, "I'm also thankful for all the women who have yet to meet me but are dying to." His grin erupts larger than life.

Georgia groans. "Didn't you say that last year?"

He shrugs. "Yeah. And there are still a lot of women out there who are dying to meet me and have me take them out."

"You're so full of yourself," Evelyn reprimands.

"That's what I'm thankful for, and I'm sticking with it," he claims, taking a large mouthful of beer.

The rest of the family says what they're thankful for, and the dinner remains jovial. Alexander and I converse with everyone, but I can't get what he said out of my head. I wish things could be different between us, and I also wish I didn't want him so badly.

A few times, he puts his hand on my thigh and then quickly removes it, as if he forgot what our deal was. Every time he does, I clench my thighs, wishing the throbbing inside of me would stop, but it won't.

We finish dinner and dessert. I help the women clean up and then I exit the kitchen.

Alexander states, "There's something we need to do, Phoebe."

"Oh?"

"Yep. Come on. Put on your coat, and get your gloves and hat on too."

"Okay," I state, unsure what's going on. I get bundled up, and he leads me outside.

The snow has stopped, and a blanket of white covers everything. The lights are on, except now they aren't just orange. Christmas colors light up the ranch.

I gasp in awe, declaring, "This is so pretty."

"Yep. Come on." He takes my hand and leads me toward the barn.

"This isn't what you wanted to show me?"

"Nope."

"Then what is it?"

"You'll see."

We step inside the barn, and he opens a stall door. He grabs the bridle of a big horse. "You've met Trojan, right?"

"Yes," I nervously say, glancing at the double saddle.

"Great. Let's go for a ride."

"What?"

"There's nothing better than a ride in the snow," he says.

"No way."

"You told me last night you wanted to after you lost the bet," he states.

I gape at him.

He chuckles. "I swear on my kids' lives you told me that."

"No way."

"You did," he insists.

I glance at the horse, my chest tightening.

"Come on, Phoebe. You might never get this chance again. The snow is perfect and there's no wind right now. Trust me. You won't regret it, and I promise I'll keep you safe," he asserts.

I glance at Trojan. He's a huge horse. He looks fierce. I shake my head. "No, thanks."

"You don't trust me?" Alexander asks with disappointment in his voice and expression.

"No, I trust you. I just..."

He steps forward and puts his hand on my cheek. "Then trust me. Come on. I'm going to be on the horse with you. Everything's fine. You're going to love this."

I glance back at the horse.

"You only live once, Pheebs. And I promise you I won't do anything crazy. We'll go slow."

I take a deep breath and then release it, agreeing. "Okay."

His face lights up. "Yeah? You'll go?"

"If you promise I'll be safe."

"Scout's honor," he says, putting three fingers in the air.

I laugh nervously, not believing I'm going to do this. "Okay. How do I get on this thing?"

21

Alexander

Trojan nuzzles into my chest, blowing air through his nose.

"Do horses get colds?" Phoebe asks.

I arch my eyebrows. "They can. Why do you ask?"

"They seem to sneeze a lot."

I chuckle. "Trojan's just happy to see you."

He nuzzles deeper into my chest, then snorts loudly.

She teases, "He looks like he's into you."

"You're stalling. Time to get on him." I reach for the stirrup and order, "Put your foot in here and swing your leg over the saddle."

Her eyes dart between Trojan and me. She says, "Why don't we let him rest in case he has a cold."

"He doesn't have a cold. Come on. The snow doesn't come often."

She takes an anxious breath and then puts her hand on my shoulder and left foot in the stirrup.

I say, "On three, boost yourself up. I'll help you."

"You're sure about this?" She bites on her lip.

"Yep. One, two, three." I grab her ass and push.

She shrieks and swings her leg over the saddle. She leans forward and hugs Trojan's neck. She squeezes her eyes shut and begs him, "Please be nice to me."

I put my foot in the stirrup and jump up behind her, then put my arm around her waist, pulling her into a sitting position and closer to me. I murmur in her ear, "Don't worry, Pheebs. I won't let anything happen to you." I grab the reins and make a clicking sound with my mouth twice.

Trojan moves.

"Whoa!" Phoebe exclaims.

I tug her closer to me. "Stay calm. Relax into me." I steer Trojan out of the barn and over the blanket of snow. I keep a slow pace, letting the horse get used to the cold, wet ground.

When we get near the woods, Phoebe's body finally relaxes.

"See, not so bad, is it?" I ask, surprised I finally got her on a horse with me.

She turns her head and smiles. She softly confesses, "No. It's...it's nice."

Happiness surges through me. I give her a quick peck on the lips.

She furrows her forehead.

My heart races faster. She might have been drunk last night, but she told me she doesn't want to be with Lance anymore. She claimed she wanted to be with me.

My intoxicated self didn't work too hard to keep my feelings secret either. I freely told her I wanted to be with her and hated our agreement to just be friends. Yet I don't think she remembers our conversation.

She begged to stay in my bed, but I forced myself to say no since she was so intoxicated. I didn't want her to wake up and regret me. So I kept my clothes on and stayed with her until morning, then crept out of her room.

I blurt out, "You made my day, admitting you aren't hating this ride."

She beams, then faces forward. "You were right. It's nice."

"Do you trust me enough to go a bit faster?" I question.

She takes a deep breath, lifts her shoulders, then affirms, "Yes, I trust you. A little faster will be okay."

I lightly kick Trojan and click twice.

He picks up his speed. A fog circles in the air from his breath.

I can tell he wants to run until he's sweating, but Phoebe's not there yet. The last thing I want to do is scare her or freak her out so badly she never wants to ride again.

I put the reins in front of Phoebe, asking, "Want to steer him?"

She shakes her head. "Nope!"

I chuckle. "Okay, then." I steer left on the trail, and we trot through the path of frozen trees.

"It's really beautiful," she claims.

"I thought you'd love it. We don't get to see this often. I assume you don't have many opportunities in California to see a frozen forest either?"

"No. Thanks for making me come with you," she says.

I tighten my arm around her, my heart beating faster. "You should let me take you out more often."

She turns, wiggling her eyebrows. She teases, "Like on a horse date?"

I stare at her, inhaling her floral scent, my dick hardening.

Her cheeks turn red. She refocuses on the path, offering, "Sorry. It was just a joke."

We need to talk.

"Hold on," I order, clicking twice and kicking Trojan.

He picks up speed, and I veer out of the woods and across a small field.

"What's that?" she asks, pointing to an old cabin.

"It's the old ranch hands' bunkhouse," I inform her, stopping Trojan several feet from the porch. "Want to go see the inside?"

"Sure."

I jump off Trojan and instruct, "Put your foot in the stirrup, then swing your leg over."

She masters the task perfectly, and I praise, "Look at you go!"

She beams. "I did okay, didn't I?"

"You did." I loop the reins over the post, then grab her hand. "Come on." I lead her up the steps and open the door.

"You don't lock it?" she questions.

I chuckle. "The ranch is secure at all times."

"I know, but still..."

Amusement fills me. I've never felt anything but safe on the ranch. It's fenced and has a gate. Plus, no one would ever attempt to mess with my family.

So I tease, "You aren't in California anymore."

"Guess not," she says.

I flip the light switch, and a lightbulb flickers a few times before staying on.

"It doesn't look or smell abandoned," Phoebe comments, glancing around the room.

I admit, "That's because I come here quite a bit."

She arches her eyebrows. "You do?"

"Yes."

"Why?"

My chest tightens. I take a few moments, then confess, "I love my family, but sometimes, I need to be alone."

She briefly studies me, then states, "That makes sense."

I put my hand on her cheek. "All I've wanted to do since the morning I woke up with you in my bed is bring you here."

She swallows hard and then opens her mouth. Nothing comes out.

My pulse pounds harder. I slide my thumb over her chin. "I think we need to talk."

She takes a deep breath, a flush growing on her cheeks. "Alexander..." She bites on her lip.

"I think we made the wrong decision and need to talk this through."

She blinks a few times, her chest rising and falling faster.

Fuck this.

I slide my hand through her hair, tug her against me, and lean down. Her hot breath hits mine, and I quickly slide my tongue against hers.

She gasps, then kisses me back until we're both breathless.

I retreat a few inches, murmuring, "We need a different arrangement."

She whispers, "Arrangement?"

"Yeah. You and me."

"You and me..." She looks away, furrowing her eyebrows.

My stomach flips. I turn her chin so she can't avoid looking at me. "I like you."

"I don't think it's about that," she states, then shivers.

I lead her to the couch. "Sit."

She obeys.

I place a blanket over her and declare, "I'm going to start a fire and then we're going to figure this out." Before she can object, I step in front of the fireplace, arrange the wood, and grab the box of matches off the mantel. I light several until the kindling catches. When I'm confident it'll continue to burn, I join her on the couch.

She blurts out, "I don't think we should discuss this."

The air in my lungs turns stale. "Why not?"

She tilts her head, her expression neutral. "I thought you didn't want to disappoint the boys."

"I don't."

She looks away and taps her fingers on her thigh.

I grab her hand. "Pheebs, you don't understand what I'm saying."

She turns toward me, her eyes in slits. "I understand perfectly, Alexander."

My heart pounds so hard against my chest I think it might explode. I demand, "Then tell me what you believe I'm trying to say."

"You think I should be your friend with benefits until my two months are up," she declares, her cheeks turning fire-engine red.

I jerk my head back. "Why would you ever think that?"

Her lip quivers.

This isn't going the way I wanted it to go.

I tug her across the couch and onto my lap. "Pheebs, tell me why you think that's what I want."

She blinks hard and turns away.

I softly state, "You have the wrong idea."

She turns back. "You slept with me. When I woke up, you pointed out I'm from California, and you're from here. You actually stated that you have your life, and I have mine. You made it clear you only wanted a fun night. Well, we had fun. Then it was over. Let's not rehash why you think I'm a bad idea."

"Bad idea? I never called you a bad idea."

She scoffs. "You might as well have." She pushes off me and goes to the window. She crosses her arms. Her voice shakes when she says, "Why are you even talking about this? I thought we learned our lesson. Everything has been back to normal between us."

I rise off the couch. "It wasn't last night."

She spins, scrunching her face in horror and confusion. "Last night?"

I close the distance between us. "You wanted to stay with me all night."

She gapes, the bright-red flush dancing once again on her cheeks.

I put my hand on her cheek and push her against the wall. I lean in an inch from her lips, searching her expression, wanting her to remember everything she admitted to me.

She takes a shaky breath. "What are you talking about?"

I glance at her lips, revealing, "We both agreed this was hard, and we shouldn't fight it anymore."

She freezes, holding her breath.

I graze my thumb over her mouth. "It's true. We're both miserable. Let's admit it."

She stays quiet, her lips quivering under my touch.

"I'm sorry I made you feel bad. I never meant to. And I thought we had gotten past that when we agreed to be friends."

"We did. But now..."

"I'm telling you that you mean more to me than a friend. And I know you still have feelings for me too. So let's stop fighting it," I state, locking my gaze on hers.

She narrows her eyes. "What about Cheyenne?"

"What about her?"

Anger fills Phoebe's expression. "I'm not going to be one of your girls, Alexander."

I scoff. "I don't have a bunch of girls. And I meant, what about her? I've not seen or thought about her since before you stepped foot on the ranch. And I'll add that I have no desire to either."

She stares at me.

I question, "You don't believe me?"

"Should I?"

"Have I ever lied to you?" I ask, feeling offended she thinks I would lie about such a thing. I'm not one of those guys who sleep with multiple women at a time and then lies about it.

She admits, "No, you haven't."

Hope fills me again. "Then I think you should give me the benefit of the doubt."

She sighs. "Okay. You're right."

I press closer. "If Cheyenne isn't an issue, what other objections do you have?"

She closes her eyes, breathing slowly.

I kiss her lightly, murmuring, "I've missed you. Now, be a good baby girl, and tell me how much you've missed me and my stallion."

She bursts out laughing.

"That's more like it. I hate seeing you upset," I admit.

Her laughter fades.

I kiss her again. This time, I wait for her to return my affection, then retreat. "We're more than friends, Pheebs."

"What about the boys? You just said you don't want to disappoint them."

"I don't."

"Then—"

I put my finger over her lips. "All I've done all day is think about this. And I don't want to hurt them. They already love you. I know they do, and I've never brought any woman around them before. So I don't know how to do that. But I also know no one gets together and thinks they won't stay together. So maybe we take it slow. We keep things between us until we're both sure about whatever this is."

She stays quiet.

My heart races. "Pheebs, I'm trying to be a responsible adult. Trust me, if I could be an irresponsible one, I would. But I can't. I'm their only parent."

Another moment passes. She reaches for the side of my head, softly replying, "I know you are. And I would never want to hurt them."

"So we can stop pretending about how we feel and see how this goes?"

"You mean in secret? Pretend to everyone else we're platonic but secretly we're not?" she cautiously asks.

I groan. "That sounds so bad."

"But that's what you're asking me to do, right?"

I grind my molars. It doesn't sound fair. I know it doesn't, but I'm unsure how else we can explore whatever this is between us and still protect my boys.

"I'm not saying I blame you for asking me to keep it between us for now," she offers.

"You don't?"

She shakes her head. "No. I wouldn't want to hurt the boys either."

"So..."

She licks her lips, then bites on the bottom one.

I ask, "Are you good with it, or do you want me to never make another move on you again?"

She giggles. "Make a move? Is this your move?"

I pull her toward my lips, answering, "No, this is." I slide my tongue into her mouth and grab her ass, holding her against my straining erection. I kiss her with everything I have, not remembering ever wanting someone so much and feeling like I might never get them.

Her knees buckle. She grips my head and shudders.

I retreat, staying close to her mouth, ordering, "Tell me we're on the same page, baby girl."

Her lips curve. "Okay."

"Yeah?" I say enthusiastically.

She laughs. "Yeah."

"Good—"

My phone rings, cutting me off.

I groan.

Amusement fills her expression. "Should we take a bet which one of your family members is calling?"

"No, I don't have good odds on that," I state, then answer, "Hello."

"Dad, where are you?" Ace inquires.

"I'm teaching Pheebs how to ride," I state.

Excitement fills his voice. "She got on a horse?"

I grin and peck her on the lips. "She sure did."

"Awesome!"

Evelyn's voice interjects, "Tell him why you're calling."

The hairs on my arms rise. I sternly ask, "Ace, why are you calling me?"

A moment of silence fills the line.

Disappointment overpowers my happiness. "Don't make me ask you twice."

He moans, confessing, "I'm kind of in trouble."

"In trouble?"

Phoebe's eyes widen.

I kiss her on the forehead, then ask, "Why are you in trouble?"

He hesitates.

"Tell him," Evelyn orders.

He answers, "I might have put something in Wilder's drink."

I freeze.

"What's wrong?" Phoebe whispers.

I put it on speakerphone and warn, "Ace, you have five seconds to tell me what you put in his drink."

"He dared me to do it to Uncle Jagger, but Wilder picked up the wrong glass," Ace states.

Phoebe's eyes widen.

My gut dives further. "Ace, what did you put in his drink? And I'm not asking again."

He admits, "It's Wilder's fault! He took the eyedrops from the medicine cabinet and double-dog dared me to put it in Uncle Jaggers's drink!"

Horror fills Phoebe's expression.

Anger fills me. "You could kill someone doing that!"

Ace's voice cracks. "I didn't kill Wilder! I swear! He's just pooping a lot!"

Phoebe's hand flies over her mouth.

I try to control my annoyance as I ask, "Why would either of you want to do that to Uncle Jagger?"

"He says he has a stomach of steel. Wilder bet him he was wrong," Ace claims.

I burst out, "You did this over a bet?"

Evelyn's voice comes across the line. "Are you coming back soon? The doctor said Wilder should be okay since Ace admitted it was only two drops, but he's been in the bathroom for a while."

I shake my head, mouthing "Sorry" to Phoebe.

She shrugs, smiling.

I tell my sister, "We're on our way." I hang up and say, "I'm sorry."

Phoebe lets out a giggle. "I'm sorry. I shouldn't laugh."

"They're both grounded." I kiss her on the forehead and put out the fire. I meet her near the door.

She opens it.

I slam my hand against it and shut it.

She jumps and spins to face me.

I eliminate the distance between us, fist her hair, and tilt her head.

Her eyes light on fire.

I stare at her lips and warn, "You better always be on the lookout when we're back at the house."

"The lookout?"

I nod, dragging a finger over her jawbone.

She shudders.

I warn, "The moment I find a dark corner, I'm dragging you into it."

22

Phoebe

A Week Later

My phone rings. I glance down at it, and my gut dives.

Lance's name glares at me on the screen. It's the fifth time he's called today. He left me drunk messages last night saying horrible things, then babbled about how much he loves me, before he returned to criticizing me.

I'm over his bad behavior. He's gone too far this time. I don't want to deal with him anymore. So, as far as I'm concerned, we're done.

I decide to send the same message I sent a few days ago.

> Me: Stop calling me. We're done.

> Lance: Don't be ridiculous.

> Me: If you keep contacting me, I'll block you.

> Lance: Why are you doing this to me, Phoebe?

> Me: I'm not talking about this today. Go sleep your alcohol off. I have to go to work. Don't call me again today, or I'm warning you, I will block you.

I put my phone on silent and slip it inside my purse. Then I pull on my jeans, oversized red sweater, and boots. I glance at myself in the mirror, add some gloss to my lips, brush my hair one last time, and exit the bedroom. I step into the hallway and go into the family room.

Wilder urges, "Come on, Phoebe. We're going to be late."

"Sorry," I say sheepishly.

"You take a long time to get ready," Ace says.

"Sorry," I repeat, making a mental note to get ready earlier. Since Alexander and I have gotten together, I'm spending more time getting ready.

"Stop harping on Phoebe. And she looks nice, doesn't she, boys?" Alexander says, stepping out of the kitchen, wearing his jeans and a green button-down shirt.

My butterflies take off. I glance at him, trying not to smile too much, remembering all the ways he made me orgasm with his hand over my mouth last night so the boys wouldn't hear.

But then I had to sneak back into my bedroom, which, like always, sucked.

Wilder gives me a cocky Jagger smile, stating, "You look great, Phoebe. Can we go now? It's party day."

I move toward the door, saying, "I'm ready."

"It's going to be awesome today," Ace adds, rushing to the front door and yanking it open.

A rush of cold air hits me.

He grins. "After you!"

"Why, thank you!" I say, then tousle his hair, step outside, and hurry to the truck.

Wilder slides in front of me and opens the passenger door.

"Thanks!" I beam, my heart swelling. Alexander is teaching the boys to be every bit of a gentleman like the rest of the Cartwright men.

The boys and Alexander get into the cab. He turns on the engine, pulls past the gates, and turns onto the road.

It's the last day of school before the new year, and the kids have been talking all week about their party. The school wanted volunteers to help, so I asked Alexander if he could take the day off. I didn't know if he would, but he surprised me and agreed to come. The boys were ecstatic when we told them.

Wilder and Ace babble with excitement the entire ride. Alexander and I fall into platonic mode. It's been hard hiding things between us, but we've managed to keep things under wraps. It's been a week since he took me to the cabin, and we take any chance we get for alone time. Yet the fear of someone catching us is always there and someone is always close by.

Alexander pulls into the school parking lot, and before he turns the truck off, the kids open the doors. He questions, "Can I park first?"

They don't answer and jump out.

Wilder opens my door.

I slide out of the cab. "Thank you!"

"Sure. Come on, Phoebe," he says, grabbing my hand and pulling me toward the entrance.

Ace and Alexander follow close behind. We get into the school and go directly to the gym.

"We don't even have to go to our classroom today. It's a free-for-all," Ace declares.

Alexander chuckles, and the boys run off. He puts his hand on my back and guides me through the school.

Tingles race down my spine the entire way. It's the same thing that happens every time he touches me. He leans close to my ear and murmurs. "If you see a janitor's closet, let me know."

I smirk. "Bad boy."

He winks, and my insides turn to jelly.

We enter the gym and both freeze.

It's organized chaos. The entire student body fills the space, along with teachers and volunteers. Tables and chairs are lined up in rows, creating different craft stations.

Alexander surveys the room, then says, "First stop is over there."

"Where?"

"To the survival area." He guides me over to the table, picking up two Styrofoam cups. "I assume you want some coffee?"

I laugh. "Good call."

He fills up a cup and hands it to me. He has his half filled when a school teacher approaches us.

She's an older woman with dark reddish-gray hair and thick purple glasses. She says, "Mr. Cartwright, it's great to see you here."

He turns to face her. "Thank you, Mrs. Linsley. And this is Phoebe, the boys' nanny."

My heart drops. I don't know why. I am the boys' nanny, but I'd love it if he could say I was his girlfriend.

Is that what I am?

Yes.

He hasn't called me it.

He can't.

He could behind closed doors.

Why am I questioning this?

Mrs. Linsley beams. "It's great to meet you. I've heard a lot about you." She holds her hand out.

I shake it, surprised. "You have?"

"Yes. Ace brags about you all the time."

"He does?" I question, unable to stop my grin from growing larger.

"He sure does. It sounds like you have a keeper here, Mr. Cartwright. Thanks for volunteering today," she states, then pats me on the shoulder and walks away.

"Definitely a keeper," Alexander utters, then guides me to where Wilder is sitting.

The tabletop has different-shaped ceramic ornaments, glue, glitter, stickers, and tiny charms sprawled across it. Kids fill the chairs, already decorating.

Alexander picks up a horse. "I think I'll make this one for you, Phoebe."

Wilder glances over. "Yeah. Phoebe needs a horse, Dad. You should buy her one."

"A horse?" I exclaim.

Wilder nods. "Yeah. Now that my dad taught you to ride, you need your own horse."

Alexander chuckles.

I declare, "I wouldn't claim I know how to ride."

"Sure you do. And I can teach you how to ride better. It's easy. You'll see. Now that you're not scared to get on one, the sky's the limit," Wilder insists.

I assert, "A horse is a pretty big responsibility. I'm not ready for that."

"Sure you are," Alexander claims, with mischief in his expression.

Wilder turns his head, shouting, "Ace, Dad's going to get Phoebe her own horse!"

"Yes!" Ace exclaims, pumping his arm in the air.

Several people look over at us.

I hold my hands in the air. "Whoa. He didn't say that. And I'm not ready for that," I repeat, unable to imagine anyone buying me a horse. I'm sure it's expensive, but it's also a huge responsibility.

Alexander teases, "It sounds like the boys have their hearts set on it. You know I don't like to disappoint them."

"Don't! There are plenty of horses on your ranch if I'm going to ride again."

"If?" He jerks his head back dramatically, as if I sinned.

"I don't need my own horse," I insist.

"Maybe we'll each get you one." He wiggles his eyebrows, lowers his gaze to my lips, then gives me a semi-lewd stare.

I've seen that look before. Heat rises to my cheeks. I squeeze my thighs together.

"Dad, come help me make a hat," Ace orders.

Alexander chuckles again and rises. He puts his hand on my back. "You take ornament duty, and I'll take hat duty."

I nod. "Sounds good."

Wilder and I make our ornaments. He grabs my hand, drags me across the gym, and exclaims, "Phoebe, let's go to the ginger-bread house station."

I laugh. "Okay!"

We go to the table and sit down. We spend the next hour making a gingerbread house. Wilder dips his toothpick in the frosting and adds his dad's, Ace's, and his initials near the front door.

"Looks good," I praise.

He adds my initials next to theirs and announces, "Now it's done."

"Aww, thanks for adding me."

"Duh! Where should we go now?"

Joy and love surge through me. The boys always want to include me. It makes me feel like I'm part of the family.

Maybe someday I will be.

I scold myself for the thought. I shouldn't get ahead of where Alexander and I are. Neither of us wants to hurt the boys if things don't work out.

Why wouldn't we work out?

It's like what Alexander pointed out. No one gets together thinking they'll break up.

Don't romanticize what's going on between us until we're solid.

Aren't we?

Only when we can come clean with everyone.

Will we get there?

Of course we will.

What if we don't?

Wilder interrupts my thoughts. "Phoebe, let's go to the sugar cookie table!"

I squash away my musings and focus on the task at hand.

The bell rings, and someone announces on the loudspeaker, "Lunchtime."

Everyone gets up, and Alexander shouts, "Wilder! Phoebe!" He motions for us to join Ace and him.

We meet them halfway.

Alexander asks, "Do you boys want to stay or hightail it home early?"

"Home!" Ace and Wilder both shout at the same time.

I laugh.

"Great. Let's go to Piggly's for lunch," he adds.

"I'll race you to the truck," Ace challenges and takes off.

Wilder runs after him.

Alexander and I stop at the office. He signs the sign-out sheet, and we meet the boys in the truck.

They're more excited now than they were this morning.

Wilder shouts, "Christmas break! No more homework!"

Ace chimes in, "A month off school!"

"Can't believe they made it a month this year! Put your seat belts on," Alexander reminds them before pulling out of the parking lot.

"Why did they add an extra week?" I question.

He shrugs. "Who knows."

Piggly's isn't far from the school, and we're soon sitting in a booth with Martha serving us.

Lunch takes about an hour and then we return to the ranch. We go inside Alexander's house. I put my purse in my bedroom and then join the others. Alexander stands in front of me with his hands behind his back. He orders, "Pick a hand."

"Oh, this is pressure," I tease.

His boyish grin graces his lips. I tap his right shoulder, and he reveals his right fist. He turns his hand and opens his palm.

I pout. "Oh, it's empty. Now I don't get anything."

He puts his arm back behind him again. "Go ahead and pick again."

I tap the left shoulder this time.

He opens his hand, and the horse ornament is in it. It has my name on the front in red and green. "Just for you," he teases with a wink.

Heat floods my cheeks. I study it and chirp, "Wow. You did a great job painting this. I'm shocked at your skills."

"I have lots of skills," he boasts.

My cheeks flare hotter, but he must have spent a lot of time painting the ornament. It's flawless. I agree, "Yes, you do."

"Turn it over," he orders.

I flip it and read out loud, "Always choose a stallion."

"You should get Phoebe a stallion!" Ace declares.

"Yeah! Get her a white stallion!" Wilder adds.

Alexander states, "White stallions are hard to come by, but we can try to find one."

"What? Don't be crazy!" I interject.

Alexander's grin widens. "You got on a horse. There's no going back now!"

I shake my head but can't stop my smile from hurting my face. Everything with Alexander seems too good to be true. We have mad chemistry. He treats me like gold. His kids love me, and I love them. He protects and takes care of me, but I'm scared it'll end. Things were great with Lance for the first year and then they weren't.

No, they weren't great. They were never like how things are between Alexander and me, I remind myself. So I shouldn't compare the two relationships.

We're a secret.

The nagging thought pops up again. I long for the day when we can be normal and not hide. The last week's been excruciating. Every secret look, touch, and rendezvous gave me an adrenaline high but also put me on edge. I remind myself I need to give it time, but it's hard. I'm not used to pretending, and our situation feels like a lie in some ways.

"Time to decorate our house," Alexander states, tearing me out of my thoughts. He goes to the closet and starts pulling out boxes.

Over the next hour, we put up the tree and decorate it. They put stockings on the mantel and Alexander stares at it.

"Looks great," I praise.

"Nope! It's missing something."

"What? It looks perfect," I gush, taking in the garland and bright red and white stockings with their names on them.

Alexander snaps his fingers. "I know what's missing! Hold on." He disappears and returns with his hand behind his back.

"What are you hiding?" I question.

He grins, then reveals a matching stocking with Pheebs written on it, and a matching reindeer holder.

I gape at him.

He chuckles. "Why do you look so strange right now?"

I swallow down emotions, blinking hard. Lance's family had matching stockings with their names. No one ever added a stocking for me, let alone one with my name on it.

"Let's hang it up," Wilder says, then grabs it from his dad. He moves Alexander's stocking away from Ace's, then places the silver reindeer between the two. Then he hangs my stocking on the hook.

I choke back my tears, managing to get out, "That's really nice of you."

Ace holds the star up, suggesting, "I think Phoebe should put it on the tree this year."

"Really?" I ask, touched once again.

"Yeah, of course," Wilder says in a serious voice.

Alexander taps the ladder. "Well, come on, then."

I take the star from Ace and climb three rungs of the ladder.

Alexander steps right behind me, putting his arms on each side of it.

I glance down at him.

The mischievous expression I've grown to love is all over him. He adds, "I'll make sure the ladder's secure."

I refocus on my task, and attach the star to the top branch and plug it in.

It lights up and Ace declares, "Now it's Christmas!"

Wilder informs, "Time to go to Grandma and Grandpa's. Sebastian and Georgia just arrived!" He points out the window.

"Go on, you two. We'll meet you over there," Alexander orders.

They race out the door.

I get off the ladder and turn to face Alexander.

He puts his arms on both sides of the ladder again, caging his body against mine. He murmurs, "Thank God. We're finally alone."

My butterflies take off. Before I know it, his lips are pressed against mine, his hand is in my hair, and his tongue urgently explores every part of my mouth. My knees buckle, and he holds me to him, his cock hard against my stomach.

He groans. "We better get going, or they'll be knocking on the door."

Disappointment fills me. I'd rather go into his bedroom right now, but I nod. "All right."

He helps me into my coat, and I put on my boots, gloves, and hat. He leads me across the yard to the main house.

When we get inside, a stocking with my name on it is already on the mantel next to Alexander's.

"Did you do this?" I question.

He shrugs, then disappears, returning with two boxes, followed by his brothers.

The Cartwrights decorate for hours, which is funny because there were already so many decorations up around the ranch.

I excuse myself to the bathroom. When I step out, Alexander's waiting for me.

"Hey," I say.

He doesn't reply. He moves me over into the cubby hole under the staircase. He shuts the door. It's dark, and there's only a small portion where he can stand up, or he'll hit his head.

"What—"

His lips press against mine, his hands sliding into my pants, his erection pushing into my stomach. He mumbles, "Fuck, I've missed you," then slides his tongue back into my mouth, spinning me against the wall. Before I know it, my pants are down, as are his. He steps on my jeans and orders, "Lift your foot."

I obey, and my foot frees itself from the denim.

He picks me up, and I wrap my legs around his waist. He enters me in one thrust, grunting, "Jesus, my stallion's been dying to get inside your tight pussy all day."

He thrusts in and out of me until I'm shaking so badly and moaning, I'm afraid others are going to hear us.

He keeps his lips pressed to my ear, his breath ragged, ordering, "Quiet, baby girl." He thrusts faster.

Every cell inside me rages with adrenaline until my bones feel it.

His erection pulses deeper and harder, then he groans, feral, in my ear, vibrating as hard as I'm convulsing against him.

He drenches me in his orgasm, muttering, "Fuck, baby girl. Fuuuuck."

He thrusts until there's nothing left, and we're left in the aftermath, covered in sweat, still trembling.

The knob turns, and we freeze.

Willow's voice calls out, "Is this door stuck?"

I gasp.

Alexander puts his hand over my mouth. He slowly lowers me to the ground, crouches down, and helps me into my pant leg. He rises and secures his pants, then murmurs in my ear. "You okay, Pheebs?"

I release an anxious breath and nod. He kisses me one more time and then tries to open the door. He turns on the light.

I blink a few times.

"This door is stuck," he lies.

"Alexander? You're in there?" Willow questions.

"Yeah. Phoebe and I came in to find more decorations, but it's stuck."

She tries to turn the knob again.

Alexander pretends the door is still stuck, rattling the locked knob.

Willow tries one more time, and Alexander flips the lock. The door flies open.

"Thank God. It's getting hot in here," Alexander declares and brushes past her.

She stares at me, glances back at him, then looks back at me. She narrows her eyes and slowly asks, "Are you okay?"

"Yeah. It's really hot in here. And we couldn't get the door open," I fib, feeling guilty. The one person I like most besides Alexander and the boys is Willow. We've become good friends. I hate keeping secrets from her, especially when it concerns her brother.

She tilts her head. "Are you getting sick? You look like you're about to sweat."

"Like I said, it's hot in here,"

She steps in next to me. "Doesn't feel hot."

"No? You must have low blood pressure, then," I tease, stepping out of the closet and continuing toward the main room, worried she might know something is up.

23

Alexander

A Week Later

"Jagger, take over," I shout, then walk over to Phoebe, who just stepped outside. "Hey."

"Hi. The boys wanted to go to town with Evelyn and the kids. Is that okay?"

I nod. "Sure. It'll give you time to sharpen your skills."

"Ummm…"

I keep a serious expression, relaying, "I have a bet to make with you."

She tilts her head, narrowing her eyes. "Oh? What are we betting?"

"It involves Christmas trivia."

"Christmas trivia?"

"Yeah, I need to see how sharp your Christmas trivia skills are."

She laughs. "Okay. When and where are we figuring this out?"

"Tonight."

"Tonight?"

"Yep. But I have a challenge for you."

"And that would be?" Her lips twitch.

I glance behind me and then put two fingers on her collarbone, sliding them back and forth.

She inhales sharply.

I step closer, adding, "The winnings are high stakes."

"Does this involve more money I don't have? I really don't like using your cash to bet," she frets.

I chuckle. "There's no money involved."

"Okay, good."

I glance behind me again, ensuring no one's around, then lock eyes with her. "When I win, I get to lick your pussy."

She bursts out laughing, then wipes tears from the corner of her eye. She asks, "And what do I get when I win?"

I lean closer, brushing my lips to her ear, stating, "I still get to lick your pussy." I retreat, trying to keep a serious face.

She muffles her laugh and asks, "So either way, I win?"

"No. Either way, *I* win," I declare.

She bites on her lip, her cheeks red.

"So, do I have a date, or are you scared to see how good my Christmas trivia skills are?"

She studies me, claiming, "I didn't know you were so serious about Christmas trivia."

"Oh, us Cartwrights take Christmas trivia extremely seriously."

She asks, "Is everyone else coming with us?"

I shake my head. "No. Guess who's taking care of the boys?"

She thinks for a moment, then says, "Evelyn."

"Nope."

"Willow and Paisley in the main house?"

"Nope."

"Who, then?" she questions.

I announce, "Ace is at Mason's and Wilder's at Jagger's."

She scrunches her face. "They're staying at Mason's and Jagger's?"

"Yep."

"They've never mentioned staying at their place. Do they do it often?"

I puff my chest out. "No, they don't. And it's because my brothers are usually out at night, but not tonight."

She studies me harder. "So... They just volunteered to each take one of the boys?" She arches her eyebrows.

My stomach flips. I lower my voice again. "Well, you know they know about us."

Her face falls.

I quickly add, "You know how they saw us kiss the first night?"

"Yeah, I know," she admits.

I continue, "Okay, so I made a bet with them, and they lost."

"You really do have a gambling problem," she teases.

"I won," I remind her.

"Yeah, but you seem to always be betting."

"Only on calculated risks...bets I'm sure I'll win," I confidently state.

She points out, "But you lost the race and your money to me."

I wave my hand in front of our faces. "Minor setback. Anyway, they lost. The boys will stay with them for the night, and we get to have a hot date."

Her face lights up. She asks, "How hot are we talking?"

"Superhot, and full of Christmas trivia."

She bursts out laughing again.

I wiggle my eyebrows. "It was pretty smart of me, huh?" I grin bigger.

She snickers. "Yeah. Pretty smart."

I glance around and then lean back into her ear. "So it's a date? And if I win, I'll take my prize. If an act of God happens and I lose, then I'll take my punishment like a good boy."

She turns her face, inches from my lips. "Sounds like a date."

I almost kiss her but stop myself. Anybody could be looking, so I remind myself to wait until we're out tonight. "I'll pick you up at seven." I wink and then strut across the yard, excited I get adult time with Phoebe.

Plus, we'll have the house to ourselves tonight. It's hard to constantly be sneaking around. Someone in my family is always around the corner, ready to interrupt us.

It's been two weeks, and I hate every moment I have to pretend like we're just platonic. We're not anywhere near just friends.

I go over to the corral. Mason and Jagger are inside it, running three horses. I lean against the fence, assessing things. A few minutes pass, and then Phoebe sidles up next to me.

"Pheebs, is there something I can do for you?"

"Yeah. Where are we going, so I know what to wear?"

"Wear whatever you want...or nothing," I suggest, feeling giddy.

She wags her finger in front of me, reprimanding, "Uh-uh-uh, that wouldn't be appropriate now, would it?"

I chuckle. "Only if we're at the house with no one else."

She questions, "So what is the attire?"

"Whatever you want. It'll be at a bar, so wear something similar to what you wore when we went to the racetrack, okay? Unless you're dying to slide into something besides jeans."

She winces, admitting, "I don't have anything besides jeans and casual stuff."

"Perfect. We're going somewhere casual, so no need to worry. Besides"—I glance around, then lower my voice—"you look hot in anything you wear. Or don't wear." I wink again.

She nudges me with her elbow. "I'll see you at seven."

"Sounds good."

I watch her walk away, staring at her ass and thinking about how much I want to bend her over tonight until she makes those noises I love so much.

The rest of the day seems to drag by. Every moment of it, I spend thinking of Phoebe, excited about our date but also pumped she'll be able to stay in my bed until morning.

And, I know it sounds corny, but I really like Christmas trivia. I love the holidays. You can't be a Cartwright and not love them. Yet, ever since my wife died years ago, things haven't been as happy as they used to be. This year, I feel happy for the first time since before she got cancer and passed away.

Since Phoebe has come into my life, the typical, normal stress hasn't felt so intense. She's always making me smile or laugh, even when we have to be platonic in front of the others. And true happiness isn't something I've felt in years.

When it's quitting time, I go into the house. She's in the bathroom, but the door's locked, and she won't let me in. So I go into my en suite and shower. When I come out, she's standing at the window, staring out.

I step behind her, put my arm around her body, and splay my hands across her thighs. I kiss her neck.

She shivers slightly and turns her head.

"You smell good and look good," I admit, my gaze darting to her lips.

Her beautiful face lights up. She teases, "Well, that's good. It'd be a crappy date if you thought I looked bad and smelled bad."

I chuckle. "Very true." I give her a quick kiss. "You ready to go?"

"Bring on the Christmas trivia," she chirps, pumping her fist in the air.

I chuckle, leading her to the car, careful not to get too close to her. I hate that I have to be conscious about our closeness, but I don't know who's watching.

We get to the truck and I open the passenger door. She gets in, and I go around, practically prancing, reminding myself not to look so jolly, but it's hard. I slide into the driver's seat, and we make our way into town.

She inquires, "So, is this Christmas trivia a serious thing? Like, is everyone in town involved, and the stakes are high?"

"Something like that."

"Are we on the same team?"

"No. Opposite teams. Remember, if I win, I lick your pussy. If I lose, I lick your pussy," I remind her.

She laughs. "Oh yeah, I forgot."

"You forgot? I guess I need to do a better job at licking your pussy."

Her face turns red and she slaps my bicep.

I chuckle.

She claims, "Okay, so it's me against you. But don't worry, I know my Christmas facts."

I grunt. "We'll see about that."

We flirt and tease each other the entire way to the bar. When we get to town, I parallel park, get out of the truck, stride around the hood, and open her door. I help her out and hold her hand, walking inside.

The Stomping Ground is full of lots of people I know. I introduce Phoebe to several of them and then we get into a booth in the back corner. She slides in and I sit next to her.

Carrie, one of the servers, approaches us. She chirps, "Hey, Alexander, I haven't seen you in a long time."

319

"Carrie, how's it going? This is Phoebe."

"Oh, I've heard about you. You're the nanny, right?" she asks.

Phoebe's body stiffens.

I put my hand on her thigh, answering, "Yes, she is. And she's great with the boys. Pheebs, you want a beer?"

"Yes, please."

I refocus on Carrie. "Can we get two cold ones?"

"Sure. It's nice to meet you, Phoebe," Carrie offers.

"You too," Phoebe replies, nodding.

Carrie smiles and turns to head to the bar.

Phoebe questions, "How does everybody in town know about us? Well, about me?"

"It's a small town, don't let it bother you. People love to gossip," I state.

"What if somebody says something to the boys?" she asks.

My gut flips. "They won't."

Worry fills her expression. "How do you know?"

"Everyone in town also knows how protective I am of my kids. They won't," I insist.

She looks at me like she's not so sure. I pick up her hand and kiss it. "Stop worrying. You need to start thinking about whether you're going to win or lose."

Her lips twitch. "Oh, I'm going to win. Remember, I win either way." She smirks.

I put my hand between her thighs and flick my middle finger against her slit.

She inhales sharply.

I challenge, "Really? Are you sure you're the one who wins? Or am *I* the winner either way?"

Her gaze darts past me.

I turn and then sit back.

Carrie's walking toward us with two beers on a tray. I remove my hand before she gets to the table. She sets them down and hands two trivia sheets to us. "I assume you two are playing tonight?"

"Of course," I say and then take a mouthful of beer.

"I'm going to show Alexander he doesn't really know anything about Christmas trivia," Phoebe declares.

Carrie smiles. "I'll leave you two to it, then. I'll be back later."

I nod. "Thanks, Carrie."

She leaves, and Peter, a guy I know from town, booms into the microphone, "It's that time of year again. Who's ready for Christmas trivia?"

The room erupts into cheers.

A Christmas song starts to play. He asks, "Which popular Christmas beverage is also called milk punch?"

"That's easy," Phoebe says, writing down her answer.

I write down mine, claiming, "Agreed. If you get that one wrong, you know nothing about Christmas."

"Totally," Phoebe agrees.

Peter asks, "What did the other reindeer not let Rudolph do because of his shiny red nose?"

Phoebe states, "I feel like the kids would do really well at this."

"Yeah. They usually ace it," I admit, and we write down our answers.

She frets, "Aww. I feel bad they're going to miss out this year."

I grunt. "Don't be. There's a family night we can bring them to."

She beams. "That's awesome."

I hold up my beer, feeling a surge of giddiness. I declare, "Tonight, I get you all to myself. To date night."

A tiny flush creeps into Phoebe's face. "To date night." She clinks her glass to mine, and we each take a drink of beer.

Peter's voice calls out, "How many ghosts show up in *A Christmas Carol*?"

I groan.

"Oh, do you not know the answer to this one?" Phoebe taunts, tapping the pencil against her jawbone.

"This one always stumps me," I confess. "I want to say four, but it's three. Past, present, and future."

"Oh, you know the tenses. Great job," she teases.

"I may not have liked school, but my English teacher in third grade was hard not to pay attention to."

Amusement fills her expression. "Oh? You had a crush in third grade?"

I shrug, revealing, "She was fresh out of college and smelled good."

Phoebe laughs.

I debate, then write down three, cross it off and write four, then return to three.

Peter's voice blares across the bar. "The movie *Miracle on 34th Street* is based on a real-life department store. What is it?"

"This is easy," Phoebe says, and we write down our answers.

Peter states, "Elvis isn't going to have a white Christmas. He's going to have a what?"

The crowd shouts, "Blue," and the song starts playing.

Phoebe arches her eyebrows. "Wow. Peter knows how to bring it home."

"Hey, I didn't say it wasn't going to be cheesy," I admit, but I still love it.

"That was a freebie for you all!" Peter exclaims, then asks, "What's the green thing you stand under if you're desperate for a kiss and can't get it any other way?"

Phoebe giggles, then writes down her answer.

Peter adds, "I'm going to take a song break, grab a beer, then I'll be back. Make sure you tip your servers. And no cheating! Remember, that's bad Christmas behavior."

Mariah Carey's voice singing "All I Want for Christmas is You" comes from the speakers.

"I love this song!" Phoebe declares, then belts out the next few lines.

I stare at her in awe.

"Sorry, I get a tad carried away with that song," she claims.

"Don't apologize. And don't let me stop you. Sing away."

She takes another sip of beer.

I ask, "You hungry?"

"I could eat something."

"You want me to order some appetizers, or do you want your own entrée?"

"Appetizers are good. I've got to run to the ladies' room though."

"Okay, no problem." I scoot out and rise. I help her exit the booth, and she disappears into the women's room.

I put my hand in the air to call Carrie over when Cheyenne slides into the booth across from me, cooing, "Well, well, well, stranger."

I groan inside. The last person I want to see is Cheyenne. I tell her, "Hey, I'm on a date, so..."

I motion for her to go away, not into her antics. What she did the last time she saw Phoebe wasn't cool. She texted me a week ago, and I told her our arrangement was over.

She pouts. "Aw, is that any way to treat an old friend? Especially a nice friend?" She bats her eyelashes.

"Cheyenne, you need to go," I repeat.

She leans over and puts her hand on mine. "What's gotten into you, Alexander? I know you're into this nanny, but come on, haven't you had your fun? Surely you're bored by now? I know damn well she can't do what I do to you."

I open my mouth, but Phoebe's voice pierces the air, "Cheyenne, fancy seeing you here."

Cheyenne keeps her hand on mine and slowly looks at Phoebe. Her lips form into a smirk.

I move my hand back. "Cheyenne was just leaving, weren't you?"

Her eyes widen into an innocent expression. "Oh? Was I? I thought you were about to tell me you were ready to leave with me."

I look at Phoebe and say, with no emotion in my voice, "She's lying." I get up and put my hand on Phoebe's back, motioning for her to take her seat.

She doesn't. She continues to glare daggers at Cheyenne.

I softly order, "Pheebs, have a seat."

She glances at me. I give her a quick kiss on the lips. "Sit down."

Phoebe quietly takes her seat, and Cheyenne stays planted across from us. I put my thumb in the air and motion toward the door. "Up, Cheyenne. Now."

Cheyenne doesn't obey. She sits back and looks at Phoebe. "So you're from California, huh?"

Phoebe doesn't answer.

Cheyenne questions, "Oh, are you mute all of a sudden?"

"Cheyenne, that's enough," I reprimand.

Phoebe leans across the table. "I think it's clear you're not welcome here. Alexander doesn't want you. And frankly, the only thing boring anyone around here is you. So before you go, is there anything else you need to say?"

Shock fills Cheyenne's face.

I reiterate, "Cheyenne, time to go."

She doesn't move, glaring at Phoebe.

I bark, "Cheyenne! Go!"

"Come on, Alexander, enough with the games. I know you want a real woman," she claims, and it may sound confident to others, but I know her. Her statement only sounds desperate to me, which is an even bigger turnoff.

How was I ever with her, even just in a friends-with-benefits arrangement?

I hadn't met Phoebe.

She pouts. "Stop playing games. I'm ready for the stallion." She slowly glances at Phoebe, her lips twisting.

My gut churns with anger.

Phoebe's face hardens.

Time to get out of here. Cheyenne's going to cause trouble all night if we stay.

I reach into my wallet and pull out a wad of cash. I take several twenties and drop them on the table. I put my wallet back in my pocket and then reach for Phoebe's hand. "Come on."

She glares with disgust at Cheyenne, not moving.

"Pheebs, let's go," I insist.

She slowly breaks her stare and takes my hand. She slides out of the booth, and I lead her out of the bar.

We take a few steps and I reach to open the door to The Corral, suggesting, "Let's try this bar."

"No, I've had enough. Let's go home," Phoebe states, marching ahead of me and hightailing it to the truck before I can stop her.

24

Phoebe

*A*nger, jealousy, and too many bad memories tear through me. I'd sit at home at all hours of the night, wondering if Lance was cheating on me, and everything about the encounter with Cheyenne makes me relive those old ghosts.

The worst part is Alexander is the total opposite of Lance. He's always made me feel safe and excited about what's growing between us.

Until now.

The thoughts running through my head right now dig the knife deeper.

Why would a woman try so hard to get a man if he told her he wasn't interested?

She wouldn't unless he left a door open.

Maybe I'm wrong.

Am I?

Don't be stupid like last time.

Alexander wouldn't do that to me.

I didn't think Lance would when we first got together either.

I stomp to the truck, yank open the door, and jump into the passenger seat. I slam the door hard, my rage growing.

How dare she?

Why was he even with her?

Does he really find her attractive when she's so bold and pushy?

The thought of them together makes me feel ill. More agonizing assumptions enter my mind.

If he was into her, how could he possibly be into me?

Why am I saying was *into her?*

Maybe he's still into Cheyenne and only pretended to want her to leave?

The questions and doubts I didn't have before Cheyenne's appearance, spin faster and faster. I blink harder, willing myself not to cry.

Alexander gets into the driver's seat. "Pheebs—"

"Don't!" I warn.

He claims, "You're not being fair."

I huff. "I'm not being fair? Your girlfriend interrupts our date, sits across from you, and holds your hand. And you sit there and let her!"

"I was as shocked as you were. I told her to leave. And I pulled my hand away! You saw me!" he argues.

I scoff. "Yeah, once you knew I was behind you."

"I thought I made it perfectly clear I'm no longer interested in her, nor do I want anything to do with her. I told her multiple times. You heard me. So I'm not sure how much clearer you want me to be," he states.

I seethe, "She was pretty clear she wants to take another ride on your stallion!"

His face turns red.

I add, "I'm pretty sure if you go back inside, she'll kindly spread her legs for you right in the booth."

He groans. "Come on, Phoebe."

"Oh, don't you dare act like I'm exaggerating! She wasn't taking no for an answer!"

"Yes, but I was. I was nothing but adamant I wanted nothing to do with her. Or did you conveniently miss that part?" He raises his eyebrows.

I keep my glare on him, annoyed with the entire situation. And I can't help wondering how he could be into me if he found her attractive enough to do everything I'm assuming they've done.

Alexander reaches for my thigh.

I move closer to the door. "Don't touch me right now."

"Pheebs, come on. It's over with her, and I've been up front with her about it. And there's no reason to let her ruin our night."

I snap my head toward him. "No reason to let her ruin our night? She's in the bar, talking about your dick, Alexander."

He clenches his jaw, staring at me.

My insides quiver harder. I lower my voice, and it shakes as I say, "She seems to think you're still together too."

He claims, "I'm not with her. I've told you what our relationship was about and that it's done."

I boom, "Why does she think you're still together, then? Oh, wait, maybe because you're friends with benefits and haven't told her it's over. Or are you keeping her on the sideline for when I leave?"

His eyes turn to slits. "Leave? What are you talking about?"

I close my mouth, feeling sick from my insides shaking so hard. I stare out the window, clenching my hands together.

He softens his tone, asking, "Pheebs, are you leaving?"

"My employment's up after the two-month period, you know that."

Silence fills the cab. I wait for him to tell me I don't have to go after the two months are up, that this is real between us, and he wants me to stay, but the longer the silence goes on, the worse it gets. I blink hard, but my tears win.

And I fear it's true. What if I'm just another friend with benefits to Alexander, even if he claims we're more?

Maybe I'll be tossed aside just like Cheyenne was.

It serves that woman right.

How could he ever be with her?

"Pheebs." He reaches for my hand.

I close my eyes, take several deep breaths, and swipe some tears off my cheek.

He sternly orders, "Phoebe, look at me."

I slowly turn my head toward him, questioning, "What do you see in her anyway?"

He clenches his jaw.

I scoff. "What? I'm not supposed to ask? She's in the bar talking about your stallion, and I'm not supposed to ask?"

"Stop talking about my dick. And she shouldn't have said that," he adds.

More anger hits me. "You think? Or she just shouldn't have said it because now I'm pissed? Actually, how many other women in town know about your stallion?"

He stares at me for a few minutes, taking shallow breaths and gritting his teeth.

I wait him out.

He snarls, "I'm not fucking everybody in town, Phoebe."

I accuse, "No, you're fucking her!"

His voice rises. "I'm not fucking Cheyenne anymore. I told you it's over between us."

"Then why doesn't she think that?" I repeat.

He blows out a frustrated breath, offering, "Phoebe, if she wants to keep making herself look like a fool, I can't do anything about it. But I told her it was over."

"When did you tell her it was over?"

"The last time she texted me, after you and I decided we were going to see where this goes. And I, for one, want to see where this goes. But what about you? Do you no longer want to be with me because of Cheyenne acting like a child?" he questions.

My heart beats faster. My pulse bangs between my ears. My chest tightens to the point I can barely breathe. Everything inside me trembles harder. I turn toward the window and put my hand over my face, unable to stop the barrage of tears.

Alexander slides his arm around my shoulders. "Phoebe, come on, this isn't how tonight's supposed to go. I would never want to hurt you. I told you about the arrangement Cheyenne and I had, and there's nothing else to say about it. I made it clear to her our situation was over. I'll show you the text message I sent her the last time she contacted me."

I sniffle, trying to stop crying.

He turns my chin toward him and asks, "Do you want to see the messages? I reiterated it three times, and all I kept saying was, 'It's over. Stop contacting me.' Do you want to see them?"

My voice cracks. "I don't know what I want."

His face falls.

Tension mounts between us.

I can't stand his gaze on me anymore. I turn back toward the window and softly ask, "Can we go, please?"

"Pheebs..." he says with desperation in his voice.

"Please, I want to go," I say, hating myself for being so emotional, detesting how Cheyenne acted like I was nothing and dug up all my old ghosts, and loathing the way Alexander's looking at me.

All I want is him. But the thoughts of him with that woman, and especially when she so confidently claimed she knows what he needs, drives me insane. Add to it her adamant insinuations that I'm not good enough for Alexander, and it makes me wonder if I am enough for him.

What if she is better for him than I am?

He reaches for me, putting his hand on my thigh. "Pheebs, look at me."

I try to, but I can't. I look away with more tears rolling over my cheekbones.

"Please look at me," he begs.

I admit, "I can't right now. Please, let's just go."

Another moment passes. He slowly lifts his hand off my thigh and starts the truck. Country music blares into the cab, and he quickly shuts it off.

We drive in silence. I barely notice my surroundings. It's dark out, and I can't look away from the window. I try to calm myself the entire time, taking deep breaths and telling myself Cheyenne and what she said don't matter.

I attempt to convince myself he doesn't want anything to do with her, but it's hard. She didn't seem to think he didn't want anything to do with her. And I still can't fathom what kind of woman sits there continuing to hit on a man when they've already been told that person doesn't want to be with them.

The questions keep coming and coming, pummeling me until I feel semi-crazy. When Alexander stops the truck, I feel no better or calmer. I'm still silently crying.

He gets out, and I blink a few times, staring out into the darkness, unsure where we are. He comes around the truck and opens my door.

"Where are we?" I question, wiping the tears from my face.

He unbuckles my seat belt and turns me toward him. He puts

his hands on my cheeks, answering, "We're on one of our acres on the north side of the ranch."

"Is this where you bury my body?" I try to tease, but it's emotion filled.

His lips twitch. He answers, "I'm only burying your body if you're next to me."

"Don't say stuff like that," I blurt out.

He arches his eyebrow. "Pheebs—"

"Don't say stuff like that. You know you don't know what's between us. You're figuring this out. *I'm* figuring this out. Don't say long-term stuff like that," I reprimand.

He stares at me. The silence becomes too much. The tension thickens, and thoughts run through my head about how I don't know where this ends.

After my two-month contract is up, will he kick me out? Is it going to be over between us? Am I going to have to figure out where to move to and get new employment with a broken heart?

I scold myself, trying to convince my brain we haven't been together long enough for me to have a broken heart, yet I realize it's too late.

I'm in love with Alexander Cartwright, and even though he doesn't love me, I hope he will someday. But he might never because he's used to casual, and I don't even know how to do anything but serious.

He tugs me closer to him so my legs are between his hips. He puts his hand through my hair and leans closer, stopping inches from my face. His hot breath hits my lips. His challenging stare locks on my eyes. He orders, "Listen to me, Phoebe. There's nothing between Cheyenne and me. I told you we were just friends with benefits. I've never *had* deep feelings for her. I never *will have* deep feelings for her."

"What does that even mean?"

"What does what mean?" he questions.

"Deep feelings," I ask, scared I'll not get the answer I want.

He doesn't hesitate, declaring, "It means I care about you. It means when I think about the person I want to be with, it's you, not her or any other woman. *You*. Do you understand that?"

His words should make me feel better and heal anything between us, yet a small part of me isn't satisfied. I want him to tell me he loves me like I love him, but he doesn't, or he would tell me. And I wonder if he ever will.

Am I in another situation where I'll be left alone, wondering where I went wrong with the man in my life?

Alexander presses his lips to mine. As much as I want to fight him, I can't. His tongue urgently pushes against mine, and within seconds, I'm submitting to him, kissing him with the cold air circling our bodies.

He retreats. "Pheebs, I'm only going to say this one more time. I need you to listen and really hear me. Do you understand?"

I take a shaky breath and nod. "Okay."

He asserts, "You're the one I want, no one else. I don't care what Cheyenne says or how loud she screams it. There was never anything besides sex between us, and there never will be."

"Do you miss it?" I blurt out and then cringe. I hate that I'm expelling all my fears to him.

His face drops. "Besides Cheyenne interrupting our date with her false narrative, have I given you any reason to doubt how I feel about you?"

My insides quiver harder. I ask, "But what about the sex?"

He grunts, claiming, "I don't miss anything about Cheyenne, including the sex. I love everything you and I have together."

He loves everything between us.

Does he love me?

It's not the same thing as saying "I love you."

I just need to give him more time.

He continues, "I mean it, Phoebe. You're the one I want. Now, what do I have to do to make you believe it?"

I swallow hard and push away Cheyenne's voice in my head, along with the look she gave me, that screamed I was worthless and she was everything to him.

Alexander urges, "Tell me."

I softly answer, "Just kiss me again."

He grins, and within seconds, I'm back in my nirvana of Alexander's lips and tongue all over me. Before I know it, he's pulling off my pants, and a loud clang echoes in the darkness from his belt buckle hitting the metal sideboard.

I hold him tighter, drowning in him, desperately wanting all of him for only myself.

He lowers his face, pushing me back so my elbows rest on the console. Then his tongue swipes against my clit with ferocity.

He groans as I start quivering. Only this time, it's not from sadness. It's from adrenaline building up in every part of my body.

My fingers slide through his hair, clenching it, pushing him closer to me. My thighs squeeze against his cheeks, my body already trembling.

He flicks and sucks, and flicks and sucks, and I feel like I'm being swept up in a tornado that's destroying everything in its path.

Incoherent cries fly from my mouth. Adrenaline spins every- where as a high slams into all my cells, and the world turns fuzzy. Before I know it, he's inside of me.

His cock thrusts in and out. He slides his tongue back into my mouth with the taste of my orgasm all over it. He murmurs. "Fuck, you're the one I want, baby girl. Always you."

I moan, another wave of endorphins bursting in my veins.

He flicks his tongue on my ear, adding, "All day long, I sit and think about you and everything I want to do to you."

"Like what?" I breathe.

He murmurs, "How it feels to be inside your tight little pussy. The noises you make, like right now. Everything. How you touch me, how you kiss me. How you secretly gaze at me when no one else is looking. Everything, Pheebs. Do you understand?"

"Yes," I affirm in a ragged breath, blinking hard from the white light stealing my vision.

He thrusts harder, going deeper, stretching my walls to the point I feel like I might explode.

My arms circle around him. I lace my fingers in his thick locks, tugging on them. My body violently convulses against his.

He groans, declaring, "Fuck, my stallion only loves you. You understand me?" Then he releases everything he has inside of me, gritting out before I can answer, "Fucking greedy pussy. You want all of me, don't you, baby girl?"

"Yes, all of you."

His hot breaths pant against my neck. He thrusts harder and harder until I'm screaming in ecstasy.

Everything flashes from white to black and white again. Then the quivers simmer while his breathing slows.

I should let him go, but I can't. I never want to let him go. And I realize I'm utterly fucked.

If Alexander doesn't fall in love with me, I'll never love again. This isn't anywhere near what I experienced with anyone, including Lance.

He doesn't move for a while, and it's as if he can't let me go either. When he finally retreats, he looks deep into my eyes, holding me firmly. He adamantly asserts, "You're the one I want, Pheebs. Don't forget it. Do you understand?"

I nod. "Yes."

He slowly grins. "Good. Now, let's go back home. We're going to have a new bet tonight."

I giggle. "Oh?"

Mischief fills his expression. "Yep. We're going to play naked Christmas trivia. New stakes though."

I smile, feeling happy again. I ask, "What are we betting this time?"

"If I lose, I make you dinner, naked. Then I lick your pussy again."

I tilt my head. "What if you win?"

His smile intensifies. "You cook me dinner, naked. Then I lick your pussy again."

I laugh harder. "Deal."

He stares at me another moment, gives me another long kiss, then strokes my cheek. "I'm glad we worked this out." He winks.

"Me too," I confess.

He gives me another quick kiss and then helps me back into my pants. He pulls up his jeans, goes around the truck, and gets in the driver's seat.

I put on my seat belt.

He turns on the engine, puts on the music, and grabs my hand. He kisses it, and everything feels right again, except for one thing.

I do my best to push it away, but I'm in love with Alexander. The problem is I don't know if he'll ever be in love with me or if he'll break my heart into millions of pieces.

25

Alexander

A Week Before Christmas

"*L*ater!" Wilder shouts as the boys run out the door. My sisters volunteered to take them to town for a Christmas scavenger hunt, and they'll be gone most of the day.

I turn to Phoebe and stare at her.

She puts her hand on her hip. "Yes?"

"Why haven't we painted your room yet?"

She shrugs. "I don't know. We've been busy."

"Everyone else in the house has their room painted, but yours is still blah. You even painted the family room and kitchen," I point out.

Her lips twitch. "So you thought it was blah too?"

I admit, "Once you pointed it out."

She adds, "You really like it though, right? You're not just telling me you like it?"

I chuckle. "Yes. I wouldn't lie about liking something. And you were right. This place definitely needed some color."

She beams. "Good!"

"Don't you think it's time we paint your room though?"

"Today?" she questions.

"Yeah, today. There's no time like the present. Plus, the boys are gone. We can paint naked if we want."

She laughs. "You want to paint naked?"

I wiggle my eyebrows, confessing, "I like to do everything naked with you."

She wrinkles her nose. "We might want to keep our clothes on since your family's always coming in and out."

"I could lock the doors."

"Did you forget they have keys? If you tried that, they'd be coming in faster than we know."

I sigh. "Okay, we'll paint with clothes on. But seriously, we've got to get your room done. What color did you pick anyway?"

She reveals, "It's a pale yellow."

"And it's here? You bought it when you were in town, right?"

She nods. "Yes. It's in the pantry."

"Okay, go get your paint clothes on. We're going to get your room done today," I declare.

Her face lights up. She claps. "Yay!"

I groan, kicking myself for not insisting we paint her room sooner. She made it clear she wanted some color. I shouldn't have allowed her to do every room except hers, but I was too engrossed in getting the horses ready for the next race. "Phoebe, we should have done your room first."

She insists, "No, you needed your room done."

I step forward and put my hand on her cheek and wrap my other arm around her waist. I palm her ass and tug her into me. "I love what you did to my room. It was very sweet of you, but you have to stop putting yourself last."

"I don't."

I set my finger over her lips. "Shush. You do put yourself last. You're always putting us first."

She shrugs. "It's my job to put you first."

I shake my head. "No. That's not right, Pheebs."

"I'm not complaining. I like taking care of all of you."

My heart warms. I admit, "I love having you taking care of us."

Her lips curve up. "You do?"

"Mm-hmm. I love it when you take care of my boys. I love it when you take care of me." I kiss her jawbone, then over to her ear, and add, "I especially love it when you take care of my stallion."

She laughs and pushes my chest. "Keep your head straight if we're going to paint my room."

"Okay, let me go toss on some clothes I can destroy. Contrary to what you might believe, I'm a sloppy painter."

She feigns shock, gasping. "Are you?"

"Yup. You'll have to cut in the edges, or we'll have to get some tape."

"Nope, no tape needed. I'm good at cutting in," she declares.

"Why am I not surprised?" I question, grinning. I slap her on her ass. "Okay, get ready. I'll see you in your room."

"Okay."

I whistle and go into the bedroom, excited we get some alone time, even if it involves painting. I love every minute I spend with Phoebe, but we're usually surrounded by people and acting like there's nothing between us. And since it's a week before Christmas, it'll be busier than ever with festivities. My family will be everywhere, so this is the last day Phoebe and I might get a stretch of alone time.

As tempted as I am to drag her to bed and play all day, it's bugging me her room's not painted. And I love everything she's done with the rest of the house. The boys' rooms are just what they wanted, and they're always raving about them. She patiently waited to do hers last, and I scold myself again that I wasn't more insistent she paint hers after she surprised me.

I put on a pair of shorts and an old T-shirt that I no longer care about. Then I go into her bedroom.

She's tugging her T-shirt over her chest when I enter.

I tease, "Do you have to put that on?"

She bats her eyelashes. In a horrible Texas drawl, she chirps, "Why, Alexander Cartwright, how very inappropriate of you."

"That was a pretty good accent," I fib.

"You think? Can I convince people I'm from Texas?" she questions.

I don't have the heart to tell her no, so I encourage her. "If you keep working on it, you'll fool everyone."

She beams. "Really? I always thought my accents were bad."

"I don't know. I'm biased," I say, then glance over at the heap of tarps. I ask, "Should we move everything to the center of the room and cover the floor?"

"Wow! My man's smart too!" She bats her lashes.

"Every now and then," I claim.

We spend an hour moving the bed, dressers, and desk. We put tarps on the floor and then I declare, "Time for the paint."

"It's still in the pantry."

"Okay, I'll go get it." I go into the kitchen and find the paint. Then, I pull a screwdriver from the junk drawer and return to her room.

Her expression lights up every one of my cells. She chirps, "I'm so excited."

I chuckle. "I can see that, which is why you should have been first."

She shakes her head. "Nope! That's not the way the cookie crumbles."

"Hmm. Well, maybe I'll have to give you an extra gift since you were so patient."

She grins. "Is this another bet?"

I give her a lewd glance from head to toe, then lock eyes with her. "Quite possibly."

Her face flushes, but her smile widens, and my heart almost leaps out of my chest.

My new daily goal is to make Phoebe happy. I literally wake up and think about what I can do that day to make her smile more. And every time she does, I feel giddy.

"Oh, I have to go get the paintbrushes. Hold on." She disappears and returns with a handful of supplies and a stir stick.

I open the can and stir the pale yellow until it looks consistent. Then I pour some into a tray.

She hands me a roller. "You roll, I'll cut in."

"Deal, but we're going to need a ladder."

"Oh, duh," she says.

I chuckle again. "I'll go get it." I leave and go to the garage. I grab a stepladder and bring it into the bedroom.

She's already painting the bottom of the wall. I study her for a minute, impressed, muttering, "That's crazy."

She stops and turns her head. "What is?"

I point at the wall, stating, "I don't understand how you can do that without tape. That's a perfectly straight line. You don't have any on the trim."

"Yep, I know," she perkily singsongs.

"Crazy," I repeat, then grab the roller. I coat it with yellow paint and then apply it on the wall. After half the wall is painted, I step back, asking, "Do you like the color now that it's actually in your room?"

"I love it. It's super cheerful."

I agree. "It is. Just like you."

She bats her lashes. "Why, Alexander Cartwright, I feel like you're trying to make me blush."

"Oh, no. I'd make you do that naked if I wanted you to blush," I tease, continuing to roll the wall. By the time I finish all four, she's completed the bottom part. I put the roller down and pat the step of the ladder, grinning. "Time to get your booty up."

"Yes, dear," she coos, strutting over to me, her hips swaying.

I groan, warning, "Don't do that, or you won't finish the top."

She smirks. "Why is that?"

I reach around her waist and tug her into me. She sharply inhales. I lower my face to hers. "Because I'm going to do things to that booty of yours."

She giggles. "Don't tease me."

My erection hardens as I palm her ass.

She pushes me away and wiggles her finger between us. "Uh-uh-uh. We have to get the top done."

"Yes, ma'am," I state, redirecting her to the ladder.

She climbs up it, and I kiss her ass as she's cutting in.

She freezes, then pulls her arm down, scolding, "Don't do that. I'm going to hit the ceiling."

I gasp. "What? You're talented. Surely, you can handle it."

"Seriously, Alexander. I'm going to hit the ceiling, then we'll have to paint it. You have to behave!"

I groan. "Okay, I'll contain myself."

"Thank you!" She refocuses on the line near the ceiling, slowly moving the brush.

347

I stare again in awe. "I could never do that."

"Yeah, but you can do many other things I can't."

"Like what?"

"Manly things," she states.

I chuckle. "Manly things? You're going to have to be more specific."

She snickers. "Well, I've seen you smack your brothers around pretty good."

I grunt. "Yeah, they deserve it when I do that."

"I always wonder what they're saying whenever I glance across the yard and see you do that."

"Oh, so you stare at me all day?"

"No, I didn't say that," she proclaims.

I chuckle.

She adds, "You also do that thing with the rope."

"What thing with the rope?"

"You know. You whip it in the air in circles before you toss it."

I laugh so hard tears fall from my eyes.

She stares down at me from the top of the ladder. "Why are you laughing? What's so funny?"

I use the back of my wrist to wipe a tear off my cheek. "I've never heard anyone describe lassoing like that. It's cute."

"I can think of other cute things to do to you if you want," she teases.

My cock hardens again. "Really? Like what?"

She glances down with a smirk, revealing, "Like that thing I do to your stallion with my tongue."

My dick throbs. I groan, asserting, "You're not allowed to talk about that unless you're going to do it."

She gives me an innocent look and says, "Oh? Who said I wasn't going to do it later?"

I scream "yes!" inside my head. I love it when Phoebe gives me blow jobs. Everything about it is super intense. She always knows exactly how to lick and suck and tease me until I'm begging her and holding her head down over me.

I don't think I've ever been with a woman who makes me feel how she does when she sucks my dick. It only took her one time to learn how to take all of me in, which is another thing women normally struggle with, so I inform her, "You get extra stars for that trick."

"Okay, back to work! Get your head out of the gutter," she orders.

"Then you do your job," I retort, pointing to the ceiling.

"Yes, sir." She wiggles her ass in front of me, and I smack it. She yelps, then states, "I'm returning to the painting now. No funny business."

"I'll behave," I say, and watch her create another perfect line between the wall and the ceiling.

It takes us a half hour to make our way around the room. Then we go to the kitchen and eat a sandwich for lunch. We go back into the room and paint another coat. When we finish, we stand back, staring at the walls.

I take another glance around the room. "This looks great."

"Agreed," she chirps.

I snap my fingers. "Hold on, I have something for you."

"What do you mean?"

"I have something for you. Just wait," I insist and then go into my bedroom. I step into the closet and pull out a metal piece of art I found in town. It's an infinity sign with hearts threaded through it. I take it into the bedroom and hand it to her. "This is for you."

Her eyes widen. She holds it out in front of her. "How did you find this?"

"Ace told me it's something you love. I saw it in town, so I got it for you," I tell her, even though I searched online for days looking for it. I don't know why I don't want to tell her that, but I stick to my little fib.

"Alexander, this is... Wow," she says, staring at it again.

"So you like it?"

She scoffs. "Like it? Are you kidding me? This is my favorite metalsmith. I saw this piece online, and Ace asked me about it. But..." She stares at me.

"What?" I question.

"This was in town?"

I nod, lying again. "Yeah."

She peers at me closer. "Where?"

I chuckle. "None of your business. Do you like it?"

"No, I love it! But this is too much!" she declares.

I wave my hand in front of her. "No, it's not. Now, where should we put it?"

She glances at it again, then sets it on the bed. She tosses her arms around me, kisses me, then says, "I love it. Thank you."

I pull her closer, and we kiss for a long time until I murmur, "I'm going to have to get you more gifts."

She retreats from the kiss. "You don't have to buy me any gifts. You know that, right?"

"Of course. And I know you don't expect anything. But I like buying you stuff. Especially things you actually want."

She stares at me and bites her lip.

"Don't get all weird on me about me getting you a gift. You should change your viewpoint on money anyway," I add.

"What do you mean?"

"Well, you come from a scarcity mentality. You should come from a thriving mentality."

She scoffs. "It's not easy to come from an abundance mentality when you don't have much."

"I don't know. I bet we can change your mindset," I declare.

She laughs and gives me a little salute. "Aye, aye, sir."

"I'm glad you like it though."

"I do," she affirms.

"Good." I kiss her again, and within minutes, I'm tugging her shirt off and unhooking her bra.

Her phone blares with a new song she added to her ringer last week. She retreats from me a step.

"Do you have to get that?" I question, pulling her back to me.

"No." She kisses me again, and the song dies, but then it rings again. She pulls away and scrunches her forehead. "Maybe I should get that."

"Okay. Maybe you should."

She goes over to her desk, picks up her phone, then turns it off, groaning.

"Who is it?" I question.

"No one. Let's go back to what we were doing." She takes two steps toward me, and her phone rings again. Her face falls and then irritation blooms in her expression. She grabs her phone again and silences it.

I press, "Baby girl, who is it?"

She rolls her eyes. "It's Lance."

My gut drops and then anger fills it. "Lance? Why is he calling you?"

She shakes her head in annoyance. "To bug me, why else?"

My jealousy flares. "I didn't know you were still in contact with him."

"I'm not."

"Then why is he calling you?"

Her head jerks back. She holds her hands in the air. "I don't know. He likes to call and try to get me back. I don't take his calls though."

The jealousy explodes inside me. "You made a big stink about Cheyenne, who I've done nothing with since you got here, and you've still been in contact with Lance?"

"I didn't say I've been in contact with him."

"Then how do you know he's trying to get you back?"

She admits, "Because he texts me and calls me all the time, leaving me messages in my voicemail."

My heart pounds harder. "Why haven't you blocked him if he's harassing you?"

She shrugs. "I don't know. I ignore it."

"Why are you keeping him in your life?"

"I'm not keeping him in my life."

"Sounds to me like you are," I hurl out as the phone blares again.

She glances at it and then at me, pushes a button, and it stops. She proclaims, "I'm not keeping him in my life. I told you—"

The phone rings again.

I order, "Answer it."

"No, I'm not answering it."

"Why not?"

She pushes the button again and turns her phone off. She tosses it on the bed. "There. He's not going to bother us anymore."

"Why aren't you answering it, Phoebe?"

"I don't want to talk to him. There's nothing for me to say."

My hatred for him overpowers my better judgment. I blurt out, "But you haven't blocked him. Do you like the attention? Is that it?"

Hurt fills her expression. "What? Why would you say that?"

"You're still engaging with him. You're keeping the door open between you," I accuse, afraid he'll come back into her life and take her away from me.

She cries out, "I am not! I don't want anything to do with him."

"Are you sure about that?" I boom, my jealousy flaring. I hated that guy from the moment I heard about him. I couldn't stand him even more when I met him. But to know he's still contacting her? Why hasn't she blocked him?

She firmly asserts, "Alexander, nothing is going on between Lance and me."

"Really?"

My phone rings. She glances at her desk and reaches for it, snipping, "Maybe it's Cheyenne." She hands it to me with a glare.

"Don't you dare," I warn and then answer the phone. "Hello?"

Mason's voice comes through the line. "Bro, Phoebe's boyfriend's in town. He's drunk off his ass. I think you better get down here."

The blood drains from my face to my toes. The hairs on my neck rise.

She demands, "Alexander, what's wrong?"

Mason questions, "Alexander, did you hear me?"

I snarl, "Yeah. Stay right there. I'm on my way."

26

Phoebe

lexander's face reddens with anger. He hangs up the phone, then points at me, ordering, "Call him."

"I'm not calling him," I repeat.

His eyelids lower into slits, and he accuses, "I told Cheyenne it was over. It seems like you haven't told Lance anything."

I put my hand on my hip, insisting, "That's not true. I told you I broke up with him."

He tosses his arms wide to the sides. "Then why is he still calling you? You don't see Cheyenne blowing up my phone, do you?"

"No, she just tells you to your face. In front of me, I'll add. Real classy woman you picked to hook up with!"

"That's rich coming from the woman who dated Mr. Douchebag for four years! And that was a week ago we ran into her. I also made it perfectly clear I wanted only you! Not once did I back-track in front of her about my intentions," he shouts.

"I've told Lance several times I don't want to be with him anymore and to stop contacting me!"

He points at my phone again. "Call him." He gives me a challenging stare.

I meet it, not flinching, but then I finally cave. I say, "You're being ridiculous," and pick up the phone.

"Humor me," he mutters.

"Fine!" I pick up my phone and turn it on. Then I swipe the screen, and hit the call button. I put it to my ear, and it rings. My stomach flips.

Loud noises fill the background. Lance slurs, "Phoebe, why haven't you been answering my calls?"

Rage fills me. It wasn't a big deal for Lance to ignore my calls when we were dating, but now that we aren't together, he thinks I owe him expediency. I spout, "Lance, you need to stop calling me. Don't contact me again. I've told you it's over."

The music gets louder, and I'm about to hang up, then I freeze. Goose bumps erupt on my skin.

Since when does Lance listen to country music?

He barks, "Phoebe, this game you're playing is over. You're coming back with me."

Panic hits me.

What does he mean by coming back? As in, he's in Texas?

The last thing I want is Lance on the ranch. I don't want him anywhere near me; Alexander will go nuts if he comes close.

Please, please, please don't be in town, I repeat over and over in my head.

Alexander's eyes narrow further.

I lift my chin, repeating, "Lance, it's over between us. You need to let this go. Don't call me again."

"Phoebe, I'm not joking. You're returning to California with me, and we're getting married. This nanny business is over," he states.

I close my eyes. "Lance, you're not listening to me." I exhale deeply, then open my eyes and see that Alexander's expression is even more pissed off. My insides shake harder. I assert, "Lance, it's over. Don't call me again." I hang up.

Alexander stares at me.

I ask, "Are you happy now?"

He doesn't say anything. He just continues staring at me.

I swipe on my phone and pull up Lance's contact info. I hit the block button, then turn the phone to show Alexander. "I've blocked him. And it's not my fault if he kept trying to contact me. I've told him before, and you just heard me tell him again," I babble, as if I've done something wrong and need to convince him.

I do. He doesn't believe me.

I don't understand how Alexander can think I want to keep things going with Lance. And why is he so upset he called me? It's not like I gave him any attention.

Lance is in Texas, I remind myself, panicking again.

He needs to go back to California.

Lights flash in the window, and I turn my head. The SUV parks near the house.

Alexander moves into his room.

I follow him, asking, "What are you doing?"

He quickly puts on his jeans and his boots. He tosses the T-shirt over his head, tugging it down, and goes toward the front door.

"Where are you going?" I ask.

He grabs his cowboy hat off the hook, puts it on his head, and slides into his jacket. "I'm going to take care of what I should have a long time ago."

The hairs on my arms rise. "What does that mean?"

"I'll see you later, Phoebe. Please take care of the kids while I'm gone." He opens the door and steps out onto the porch.

"Alexander!" I call out, then grab my coat off the hook and step in to my slippers, following him outside.

It's a bad mistake. It's muddy, and my slippers sink into the muck. I try to raise my foot out of the mud, shouting, "Alexander!"

He charges toward his car, ignoring me.

Ace shouts, "Dad! We had the best day!"

Alexander pauses as Ace hurls himself against him. They hug and he tousles his hair, stating, "Boys, I have to run into town for business. Stay with Phoebe and your aunts, okay?"

"You're not going to hang out with us? You said you weren't going to work this week," Wilder whines.

"I'll be quick, don't worry," he says, adding, "I've got to pick up Mason and Jagger. They drank too much and need a ride home."

"I thought you said it was for work," Ace points out.

Alexander replies, "Your uncles are work. I'll be back soon, okay?"

"Okay," Wilder says to him, then yells to Ace, "Race you," before he turns and runs toward the main house.

Ace follows him, quick on his heels.

"Alexander!" I call out again, but he ignores me and gets in his truck.

He starts the engine and peels out.

I watch him zoom past the gate, then freeze.

Willow and Paisley stare at me. Willow's eyes narrow, and she orders, "Paisley, go with the boys and start the crafts. Phoebe and I will join you in a minute."

Paisley doesn't argue. She tears her questioning gaze off me and heads toward the main house.

Willow grabs my forearm, pulling me toward Alexander's house.

I leave my slippers on the porch. We step inside, and as soon as the door shuts, I fret, "Am I in trouble?" I try to turn it into a joke, but it doesn't come out like one.

She tilts her head, asking, "I don't know, are you?"

I blink hard and look away. I hate lying to Willow. I detest that Alexander's mad at me. I don't know where he's going, and I can't stand Lance interfering in my life when he shouldn't be.

Willow's face falls. She pulls me into a hug. "Hey, everything's going to be fine. I don't know what's happening, but trust me, everything will be fine."

I mutter, "I don't know if it will."

She pulls back and adds, "I think it's time you tell me what's going on in this house."

My lips quiver. "I don't know what you're talking about."

She smirks, puts her hand on her hip, and tilts her head. "Do you think I was born yesterday?"

I don't say anything, shaking harder.

"Come on." She pulls me into the kitchen, then slides the chair away from the table, ordering, "Sit."

I don't move.

"Phoebe, sit down."

Not knowing what else to do, I sit.

She opens the fridge, grabs two bottles of beer, then pops the caps. She sets one in front of me and then sits beside me. She takes a long sip and then nods her head toward my bottle. "Go on, have a drink."

At a loss, I follow her lead.

We sit there, drinking beer until half of our bottles are gone, and she sets hers down. She smiles, asking, "Are you ready to tell me what's going on?"

"With what?" I question, trying to play dumb but doing a horrible job.

She tilts her head again, giving me a knowing look. "Phoebe, I know my brothers well. Something's going on between you and Alexander, so tell me what it is. Spill it, let's go."

"I don't know what you're talking about," I fib, but she can tell I'm lying.

She drinks another sip of beer, tapping her fingers on the table. She asks, "How many beers will it take before you tell me?"

I put my bottle down and stare out the window.

She grabs my hand. "Phoebe, it's okay, just tell me what's going on. I know you and Alexander are romantically involved."

My mouth turns dry. I swallow the lump in my throat, my heart pounding harder. I turn to her, and my eyes well with tears.

She scoots closer and puts her hand on my back. "Babe, everything's okay. Just tell me what's happening."

I can't help myself. I hate secrets. I loathe lies, and lying is all I've been doing. Willow's my friend, and I'm ashamed I've been covering things up. So it all comes pouring out.

"Alexander and I have... Well, I mean... We can't say anything because of the boys."

She arches her eyebrows. "What about the boys?"

"He doesn't want to hurt them."

She nods. "Okay. And why would the boys be hurt?"

I blurt out, "Because I'll be leaving soon."

Her expression hardens. "Phoebe, do you really think you're leaving?"

"Yeah. Your parents will be done with their mission trip. I-I don't know." Tears fall faster at the thought of leaving the ranch and the Cartwrights, but especially the boys and Alexander.

Willow rubs my back. "Babe, I can tell you one thing. I know my family. There's no way you're going anywhere unless you escape us." She wiggles her eyebrows.

I laugh through my tears, but it's short-lived. I admit, "Alexander would have to want me to stay."

She insists, "He does."

"How can you say that? You didn't even know what was going on between us."

She smirks. "You two were under the staircase, and both of your shirts were untucked. Your hair was a mess, and there was lipstick on Alexander's cheek. Do you think I don't know what all that means?"

More goose bumps pop out on my skin. I gape at her, and embarrassment floods me.

She takes another sip of beer and then gets up and grabs two more. She sits back down.

She leans closer. "It's okay, you can confide in me. I won't tell anybody else."

"So you knew but you didn't tell anyone?"

She scoffs. "No. Do you think I'm like Jagger and Mason? You obviously didn't want anyone to know, and Alexander went in the bathroom and cleaned off the lipstick before he got in front of others, so"—she takes a sip of beer—"your secret's still safe."

"Mason and Jagger know," I blurt out, my pulse skyrocketing.

She arches her eyebrows. "Those two know, and they kept it a secret? How did that happen?"

"I don't know. They saw Alexander kiss me the night we went to the racetrack. He made them promise not to say anything," I confide.

She snorts. "I'm shocked they kept a secret. They always spill the beans somehow."

"But they didn't?" I fret, once more worried about others knowing. Alexander is going to kill me when he finds out Willow knows.

She shakes her head. "No, not that I'm aware of. Nobody has said anything to me. I just knew because I saw you two. Plus, I see the way my brother looks at you. He's in love with you."

"He's not," I insist.

She scoffs again. "Like hell he's not. I've never seen him so happy."

"You haven't?"

"No. Plus, he's daydreaming half the day."

"What are you talking about? He never daydreams."

"Sure he is. I see him glancing across the corral instead of yelling at Mason and Jagger. Trust me, he's in love with you," she declares, as if it's a sure thing.

My heart swoons, but then I remember our situation. I shake my head, asserting, "No. He thinks things are still going on between Lance and me. And it's not my fault. I told Lance it was over, but he keeps calling, and your brother just got mad at me about it. Oh, and I'm pretty sure Lance is in town, and I'm scared he might come here. Alexander will go nuts if he does!"

She tenses. "Where was my brother going?"

I shake my head. "I don't know, he wouldn't tell me. He got a phone call. I don't know who it was, but I think it was one of your brothers because I heard, 'Bro.' But that's all I heard."

She reaches for her purse. "Well, let's find out."

"He won't tell you if you call him. And if he knows you know about us, he'll be mad at me."

She waves her hand. "Oh, shush. I'm not saying a word to him, nor am I calling him."

She gives me a mischievous grin that reminds me of Alexander's.

"Then how will you find out where he's at?"

Her lips twitch. "Since I know your secret, you can know mine."

"Which is?"

"I put a tracker on all of my brothers' phones."

I jerk my head back. "Why would you do that?"

She laughs. "Ava and Paisley have it on theirs as well."

"Why?"

"Do you know what it's like being a girl in this family and trying to go on dates? Sure enough, my brothers will show up anywhere I am, and this town is small. The last thing I want to do is run into them when I'm on a hot date. If I do, it's because I want to run into them. So I have a tracker on their phones, and it alerts me if they move. So if I'm out and they're going somewhere else, I'll get a notification. I can usually figure out where they'll be, so I can either move my date to a different location or deal with them. It depends on my mood or how much alcohol I've drunk or how hot my date is." She winks.

I laugh. "You're crazy."

"No, I'm a Cartwright woman with four older brothers. Trust me, it's survival mode. Otherwise, I'll be single the rest of my life," she claims.

"No way. You're a hot catch," I tell her.

She smiles. "Thanks. But they still make my life miserable. Now, let's see…" She refocuses on her phone and taps the screen. She wiggles her eyebrows at me. "I know where he's going. And hold on…" She swipes her screen a few times, announcing, "Yep, Mason and Jagger are there too."

I question, "Where's Alexander going?"

"To Booth's."

"He's going to the bar?" The pit of my stomach drops, and a fresh sense of panic hits me.

"Yeah. Why do you look sick?" she asks.

I remember the country music in the background of Lance's phone call. "When Lance called me, it was really loud. I heard country music, and he never listens to that genre. He kept saying I was coming home with him. You don't think…" My insides quiver harder.

Amusement fills her expression. She declares, "We definitely cannot stay here right now."

"What do you mean?"

"Go get dressed."

"For what?" I question, glancing at my shorts.

"Put on jeans and a T-shirt. Let's go."

"Where are we going?"

"Booth's. Duh!"

"But we've been drinking. We can't drive."

"Paisley will drive."

"Who's going to watch the boys?"

"My mom, silly. Evelyn and Ava are at the main house too."

"But Alexander said—"

"I don't care what Alexander said. Come on, we're not missing this. Let's go."

"But, Willow—"

"Get dressed, Phoebe," she demands.

Sighing, I go get dressed, and Paisley's already in the driver's seat by the time we get to the SUV. She suspiciously glances at me, asking, "Why are we going to Booth's?"

"You'll see," Willow answers.

"Willow, I don't know if we should be doing this," I say, wanting to know what's going on in town but also scared about it.

What if Alexander thinks I showed up because of Lance?

Plus, he'll know Willow knows, and now Paisley will too.

"Stop worrying," Willow advises as Paisley takes off down the driveway.

I barely hear anything in the car the whole way there. My insides are a mess.

We pull up to Booth's, and Paisley finds a parking spot down the street. We walk toward the bar, and I pray Lance isn't there. I hope it's a stupid situation with Mason and Jagger that Alexander has to get them out of. But my gut knows it's nothing of the sort. And when I step inside, it's worse than I thought.

Lance is on top of the bar. He's holding up a photo of me, slurring loudly, "This is my woman. My fiancée. Texas, you can't have her."

"Get the fuck off my bar," the bartender shouts.

Alexander grabs Lance's pant leg. He pulls him off the bar and onto his feet.

Lance slurs, "You can't have her. You want her, but you can't have her."

Alexander curls his fist. "Don't!" I cry out, just wanting this entire situation to end.

He doesn't even pause. He slams his fist into Lance's face.

Blood spurts everywhere. Lance goes down and the crowd cheers.

Mason and Jagger clink mugs of ale in the seats next to the scene.

Jagger praises, "Nice one, bro."

Mason gets off his barstool and grabs the photo. He holds it up, asking Alexander, "Do you want me to do something with this?"

Alexander doesn't take his eyes off Lance.

His blood-covered face begins to swell. He spits, "She's mine."

"The hell she is. You better get the fuck out of town and never come back. And if you contact her again, I will kill you," Alexander threatens.

I grab the chair, shaking harder.

Willow puts her arm around my waist. She murmurs in my ear, "See? You're not going anywhere. You're one of us now."

27

Alexander

lood covers Lance's face, but it doesn't make me want to let him off the hook with just one punch. I pull my hand back again.

"Alexander, stop!" Phoebe cries out.

I freeze, then curl my fists tightly at my side and turn my head.

Shit. What are they doing here?

Phoebe's standing near the door with Willow, her eyes wide in horror, her face pale. Willow has her arm around her waist. Paisley's standing on the other side of her.

Great, now my sisters know about us.

"Don't. Please stop," Phoebe begs again.

Mason steps beside me, suggesting, "I think that's enough now."

"I've got the rest of this," Jagger claims, and grabs Lance's arms.

"She's mine," Lance mutters, his cheek swelling so badly his right eye's shut.

I squeeze my fists again.

Mason grabs my arm, murmuring, "Enough. Easy, bro," as he nods at the women. Then to Jagger he orders, "Get him out of here."

Jagger drags Lance toward the back exit.

The patrons step aside, making an aisleway. They cheer as Jagger and Lance pass them.

I don't move.

"Alexander, go take care of business," Mason commands.

I glance over at Phoebe. The blood's drained from her cheeks. Worry fills her expression.

I need to get her out of here.

I take a deep breath before I make my way across the bar to her.

"Let's go," I say to Phoebe.

She doesn't move.

My sisters stay planted as well.

"Willow, step aside," I demand.

She shakes her head at me but steps back.

I put my arm around Phoebe's waist, leading her out of the bar and to my truck.

"Alexander," she says, but I don't answer.

I open the passenger door, commanding, "Get in."

She obeys.

I shut the door and go to the driver's side, sliding inside and trying to calm my anger. I start the truck and veer onto the road, gripping the steering wheel so hard my knuckles turn white.

"Alexander—"

"I'm not ready to talk yet," I tell her, trying to calm down. I'm still pissed Lance is in town, waving her photo around the place as if he somehow has a claim to her. He acted like she was his and not mine. And I heard her tell him to leave her alone, so he's got a lot of balls doing that in my town.

I'm not mad at Phoebe. Well, I tell myself I'm not, but part of me is upset with her.

How could she get so pissed at me about Cheyenne when he was still contacting her and she never even told me?

Neither of us speaks the entire way home. I drive past the ranch.

Phoebe questions, "Where are we going?"

"Away from everyone," I say, turning down a dirt road.

I go into the field we stopped at the night of Christmas trivia, park the truck, and turn off the engine. I sit back, taking deep breaths, staring out the window.

She breaks the silence, asking, "Are you going to say anything?"

I slowly turn to look at her. "Why didn't you tell me he was calling you?"

"Why would I tell you?" she questions.

"*Why?* You want to make a big stink about Cheyenne and then you keep that from me?" I spout.

Her eyes narrow. "What was the point? I wasn't taking his calls. I told him it was over. Why would I tell you when I assumed I'd never see him again?"

"You should have told me."

"Why, so you could get angry like you are right now?"

I don't reply, staring at her, wanting to reach out and kiss her, but I'm too mad. I can't let it go.

"Why exactly are you mad at me? Is it because my ex-boyfriend's calling me or because something's still happening with you and Cheyenne, and it's your way of covering your guilt?"

I sarcastically laugh. "You've got to be kidding me."

"It's a fair question. You're acting like a lunatic when I've done nothing wrong," she asserts.

"A lunatic? Because I beat up your boyfriend for being a douchebag?"

She glares harder at me. "He's not my boyfriend."

"Yeah? Then don't make accusations about Cheyenne and me when you know damn well the only person I'm into is you."

She glares daggers at me. "That goes both ways, Alexander. Nothing is going on between Lance and me either. So why am I supposed to believe you, but you don't have to believe me?"

I blurt out, "I didn't say I didn't believe you."

She scoffs. "You just accused me of still being with him."

I try to take deep breaths, but the capacity in my lungs seems to have shrunk. The air turns stale. She's right, but I'm also a proud man. So I hurl out, "I told you to watch the boys."

Her eyes widen, then her cheeks turn red. She points at me. "Don't even act like you're upset because I'm not watching the boys right now."

"I am. I told you to watch the boys. You weren't supposed to be in town."

She huffs. "Why? So I couldn't see you create a bloody mess in a bar with my ex-boyfriend's face?"

My heart beats faster. I grip the wheel so tight my knuckles turn white. I question, "Why does that bother you so much?"

"I'm not a big proponent of violence," she declares.

All the stress makes me chuckle until my eyes water.

"Why are you laughing?"

"You're in Texas now, not California. This is how we do things here. You man up or you don't survive."

"So you would've killed him if I hadn't come into the bar and Mason made you stop?" she questions.

"Don't be ridiculous."

"Well, then maybe you should stop being ridiculous." She crosses her arms and locks her challenging gaze on mine.

I don't flinch. "This isn't about me being violent. You're upset I hurt your little boyfriend."

"Don't you dare twist this, Alexander. And stop calling him my boyfriend!"

"I'm not twisting anything. He stood on the bar with your photo in his hand, claiming you were his!" I cry out, more anger and jealousy flaring within me.

She shakes her head. "Are you listening to yourself right now?"

"Yeah, I'm hearing this whole conversation loud and clear," I reply, even though I wish I could stop being angry and make things right between us.

But I can't.

The rage swirls inside me, mixing with jealousy, until I feel like I'm going to explode.

I hate the thought of her with him. I've loathed it ever since I heard about him when she first told me they were on a break. But the minute he stepped on the ranch with his cocky grin and his arrogant ego, a new level of hate took over.

She lowers her voice. "I don't control other people, especially Lance. I told him we were done. I broke up with him. It's not my fault he showed up."

"He claimed you were his fiancée!"

"You know I never was, so why are you letting that bother you?"

I take another deep breath, then slowly release it. I admit, "I thought he was out of our lives."

"So did I."

"But he's not, is he?" I accuse.

"He is," she insists.

Tense silence grows between us. I can't get the vision of her with him out of my head. I toss out, "How could you even have been with him? He's a loser."

Her head jerks back. "Don't you dare question who I dated in the past while you've tramped all over town with your 'friend with benefits.'"

I seethe, "There you go again. Judging me like you're a perfect saint."

She blinks hard and turns away. "You're out of line, Alexander."

I start the engine. "This conversation isn't going anywhere."

She turns back toward me, asserting, "No, it's not. Take me home."

"Gladly." I drive down a few more dirt roads and then go through our back gate. I pull through it and make my way toward the house.

As soon as I park, Phoebe jumps out of the truck and stomps into the house.

I sit in the cab, lean against the headrest, and close my eyes.

I need to fix this.

She should have made it clear to him she's not his anymore.

She did. It's not her fault.

He was showing her picture all over town.

It's still not her fault.

I don't know how much time passes before I finally go inside the house and into the kitchen.

Phoebe sits at the table with a first aid kit, bowl of water, and towel.

She softly states, "You're bleeding. Sit down."

My fist throbs in pain, and it's covered in blood. So I sit down but stay quiet.

She takes a washcloth, dips it in the water, and carefully cleans my knuckles. Then she puts ointment on my broken skin and wraps gauze around my hand. She asks, "What are you telling the boys?"

"About what?"

She motions toward my hand. "About why you have gauze around your fist."

"I'm going to tell them I pummeled your ex-boyfriend," I state.

Anger flashes in her eyes. "You're going to tell them you pummeled my ex-boyfriend, but you won't even tell them about us?"

"I was being sarcastic," I admit.

"Yeah, of course you were."

"Don't start with me about the boys, Phoebe. You know the deal."

She scoffs.

"Want to explain that reaction of yours?" I demand.

She glares at me. "The deal. The deal for what purpose?"

I groan. "You know what the deal is. I don't want my boys hurt."

She challenges, with disgust in her tone, "Right, so you can toss me aside when my employment is up, correct?"

"I didn't say that."

"No? Are you sure about that? Because from where I'm sitting, that's what it feels like," she claims.

"So, that's all you're thinking about every day?" I question.

She stays quiet.

"You really don't know anything about me, do you?"

She glances out the window, answering, "I guess not."

I add, "Well, that's too bad. I thought I've been trying to show you who I am."

"Yeah, well, who *I* am must not be good enough for you," she replies.

Frustrated, I rub my hands over my face. "Why would you say that?"

Her voice grows louder. "Really, Alexander? Do I have to spell everything out for you?"

"Apparently, you do, because you're talking in some poetic language that I can't understand," I insult.

She glares at me. "Don't act dumb."

"Then speak English," I snap, harsher than I should.

Hurt fills her expression. She blinks again, and her eyes turn watery.

"Don't cry," I say, meaning it sincerely, but it sounds nasty.

She rises and picks up the bowl and rag. She goes to the sink, tosses the water down the drain, then steps into the laundry room. She reappears without the rag and then leans against the wall, crossing her arms.

I don't say anything.

She continues to glare at me, which angers me further.

"I'm still waiting for you to tell me what you're so mad at me about besides hitting your boyfriend."

"Stop it! He's not my boyfriend," she claims.

"He seems to think he is," I repeat, knowing I'm digging myself deeper in the hole, but I can't stop. All I can see is that bastard waving her photo in front of everyone.

"This isn't going anywhere," she states.

I think she's talking about the conversation, so I reply, "I totally agree."

Sadness washes over her face. She swallows hard, then blinks and turns toward the window again, muttering, "Good to know."

"Exactly," I say, still thinking we're talking about our fight and not realizing she means something else.

More time passes. All I hear is the ticking of the clock.

I break the silence, upset with myself she saw me hit Lance. I know Phoebe hates violence. She's a teacher, after all. Plus, I'm frustrated we're fighting. I soften my tone, repeating, "You shouldn't have left when I told you to watch the boys."

She snaps, "Your mom was watching the boys. They're perfectly fine. You can dock me some pay if you want."

I shake my head. "Don't make this about money."

"I'm not making anything about money. Isn't that what you're insinuating, that I'm not doing my job?"

"I didn't say anything of the sort."

She huffs. "But didn't you? Is there anything else you want to get off your chest about how I perform my duties?"

I grind my molars.

She takes deep breaths, her chest rising and falling faster, not looking at me, continuing to stare out across the yard.

I don't know what to do. I want to turn back the clock to when we were painting and having fun—before she got those phone calls. Now that we're in this argument, I can't seem to find my way out of it.

I've never felt so helpless. I need to make this right, yet right now, I can't see straight.

She walks toward the door, announcing, "I'm going to go see how the boys are doing. You can punch me back on the clock."

"I didn't mean that, Phoebe."

She spins to face me. "Yeah, you did. In fact, I think you meant a lot of things that you said."

Tense silence builds between us once again.

She shakes her head. "I'm going to go now." She opens the kitchen door.

"Wait," I call out.

She stops, then slowly turns. I can see the hope on her face, and it's the moment I should seize to make everything better.

But instead, I say, "What did you tell my sisters about us?"

28

Phoebe

*D*isgust fills me. He threw insult after insult at me, and now he's back to worrying that others know about us.

I'm his secret. His mistress living in his house.

He says it's about the kids, but it's not. He wouldn't care if his siblings knew about us if it were only about protecting the boys.

"Phoebe, what did you tell my sisters?"

My insides shake harder. "I didn't tell them anything. Willow already knew."

"Don't lie to me. Out of all the people, I would hope you wouldn't lie to me," he accuses.

"I'm not lying! Willow knew."

He grunts. "So she just figured out we were sleeping together?"

I put my hand on my hip. "No, she saw lipstick all over your neck and face the night we were under the stairway. And don't act stupid. She told me you went into the bathroom and came out, and it was gone, so you wiped it away. Plus, my shirt wasn't tucked in. I looked a little disheveled after our tryst in there. Put two and two together, Alexander!" I hurl.

He shakes his head, clenching his jaw.

"You have no right to be mad at me about this. You're as much at fault as I am for Willow knowing."

He mutters, "I don't need my sisters knowing about us."

"Why? Because my time here is almost up?" I cry out.

His eyes narrow. "You know what the deal is, Phoebe."

I laugh. "The deal! I'm so sick of you talking about the deal. I am not a deal, Alexander. I'm not something you can go and negotiate."

"We discussed this. You know how I feel about my boys. I'm not looking to hurt them," he claims.

I sarcastically laugh. A few tears fall, and I swipe at them. I confess, "I'm so tired of hearing that excuse."

"It's not an excuse. I don't have the luxury of being reckless." He clenches his jaw.

I glare at him.

"Don't look at me like that," he orders.

"How am I supposed to look at you? You just stated you don't have the luxury of being reckless. And it really sucks since I'm in love with you, so thank you for clearing up what you think I am to you!"

His eyes widen.

Oh shit! What did I say?

I turn and stare out the window, grabbing the door to steady myself.

He quietly says, "I didn't say that's what you are to me. Please don't put words in my mouth."

Still embarrassed I blurted out I love him, and hurt he's avoiding it, I snarl, "I'm not putting any words in your mouth. That's what you just said."

"I'm a single parent. Their mother is dead. All they have is me. That's all I meant," he claims.

I cross my arms over my chest and fight my emotions. I point at him, declaring, "They don't just have you. They have a whole family who loves them. They're surrounded by more love than most people will ever know."

He sighs. "Phoebe, you know I'm their only parent. I can't be reckless."

My insides shake harder. I toss my hands in the air and shout, "Stop referring to me as something you're acting reckless over!"

Tense silence invades the room. Neither of us moves.

Hurt floods me to the point I feel like I can barely breathe. I lower my voice. "So that's what you see us as? Just a reckless adventure?"

He puts his hands over his face, scrubbing it, then looks back at me, dismissing my statement. "Phoebe, don't create things that aren't there."

"I'm using your words, Alexander. These are things you're

saying right here, right now. So don't act like I'm a crazy woman making stuff up," I retort.

He shakes his head, staring at the table, tapping his fingers against the wood. More time passes, and he meets my glare again, repeating, "You knew what the deal was when we got together."

Pain digs deeper into my soul, and another tear runs down my cheek. I swipe at it.

He says, "I'm not trying to make you cry."

I don't answer.

He adds, "We have to remember the kids. We have parameters in place, and we created those when we made our deal."

I feel sick. I put my hand over my stomach, hating how the truth is so harsh and staring me right in the face. I swallow the lump in my throat and lift my chin. "Don't worry, Alexander. And you're right. I knew the deal. So, I guess I've overstepped. I'll start looking for my next employer. I would appreciate it if you give me a good reference."

"Phoebe, don't be crazy."

"Don't call me crazy."

He puts his hands in the air. "Okay, that's a bad word, but you don't have to quit."

My voice shakes. "I'm not quitting, but in a few weeks, my employment's over, so I need to make sure I have work. Are you going to give me a good reference or not?"

"Of course I would give you a good reference," he insists.

"Great. Thank you."

"Pheebs..."

I stare at him, waiting with hope in my heart, but he never says anything else.

He's never going to love me.

I'm his reckless adventure, and now it's over.

I finally force myself to say, "Thank you. I appreciate the reference. Let's return to the normal employer-employee mode. This deal is only hurting us."

"Pheebs..." he starts, but once again, no other words come out of his mouth. He just stares at me with a mix of anger and helplessness in his eyes, and I can't take it anymore.

I add, "It's the best thing, and you know it."

He continues to stay silent.

The entire time I'm staring at him, all I want him to do is tell me not to go, that he wants me forever.

He never does. He just sits there, saying nothing and staring at me.

I can't take it anymore. I wipe the tears off my face and silently exit the kitchen. I grab my coat and put it on, stepping out of the house and rushing through the cold to the main house.

When I get inside, I step into the bathroom, splash some water on my face, and make sure I look okay.

Ten minutes pass before I think it's safe to go do my job. I force a smile and find the kids in the family room. Tables fill the space, and they're all making Christmas crafts. Alexander's sisters, Georgia, and his mom are in the room too.

Willow and Paisley look at me, and I want to crumble inside. They keep glancing over with questions in their eyes, but I try to avoid them.

I work on making a wreath with Isabella. We finish, and Willow pulls me aside. She drags me out into the hallway, and lowers her voice, asking, "Babe, what's going on?"

"Nothing," I lie.

"You don't have to hide anymore, Phoebe. Just tell me what's happening," she pushes.

I lift my chin and straighten my shoulders, my voice shaking when I say, "Nothing is wrong. Alexander and I are finished. I'm going to finish my term here and then I'll move on to my next employer. Please keep everything we discussed between us."

Her eyes widen, and her head jerks back. "Don't be silly. You two are just fighting. Every couple fights."

"We aren't a couple."

"You are!"

I shake my head. "No, we're not. It's over," I repeat, my insides shaking harder and trying to convince myself everything will be okay.

"Phoebe—"

"I don't want to talk about this, Willow. Promise me you'll keep things between us. And please make Paisley stay quiet too," I sternly say.

She studies me.

"Please," I beg.

She nods. "Sure. You have my word."

"Thanks." I brush past her and return to the bathroom. I lock the door and lean against it.

Tears slide down my face and I cover my mouth, trying to stay quiet. I don't know how long I'm in here. All I want to do is run back to the house and beg Alexander to make things right between us—whatever that looks like—but I know it won't happen.

He's made it clear.

I'm just a deal to him.

I'm his reckless adventure.

I'm his current friend with benefits, and I should have known better.

And I saw it in his face when I accidentally admitted I love him. He doesn't love me, and he's never going to. I was fooling myself, thinking I was any more than Cheyenne was to him. I was just more convenient.

I keep my eyes closed, and the thought of him running back to her makes me feel sick.

Then I think about leaving the boys and all the Cartwrights. It tears me apart, and I don't know how long I keep crying.

I finally force myself to clean up, but my swollen eyes can't be hidden.

I exit the bathroom and run into Ruby. "Oh! I'm sorry!"

Concern fills her expression. She grabs my arm. "Dear, are you okay?"

"I may have eaten something bad. I just got sick. I'm going to go to bed for the rest of the day if that's okay?" I lie, although I've never felt more ill.

She puts her hand on my forehead. "You don't feel very hot. Do you have food poisoning?"

I nod. "I think so."

"You just got sick?"

I hate myself for lying to her. Ruby's another person who's been nothing but good to me. She's treated me like I'm one of her own kids, and it chokes me up.

I've missed having a mom, and as much as I try not to think about it, Ruby's been like one to me. It's been a long time since my own mother was mentally capable of being a mom, and I didn't realize how much I missed our relationship.

New tears roll down my cheeks. I swipe at them, but there are too many.

"Phoebe, tell me what's wrong," Ruby demands, putting her hand on my cheek.

"I'm just sick. I have to go," I say, brushing past her, unable to take it anymore.

I grab my coat when I reach the front door. I step outside, barreling across the yard, the chilly wind beating against my face.

Alexander steps onto the porch the minute I get to the door.

I freeze, unable to stop the tears.

"Phoebe, what's wrong?" he asks in alarm.

What's wrong? How can he even ask me that question?

Because I've meant nothing to him.

I was just a deal.

"I don't feel well. I'm going to bed for the rest of the night," I say, and push past him. I rush into my bedroom and lock the door.

He knocks. "Phoebe?"

"I don't feel good. Can you please just leave me alone?"

"Phoebe, let me in," he says, turning the doorknob, but it's securely locked.

"I just need to sleep," I call out, not wanting to discuss anything.

There's no point.

I'm in love with Alexander Cartwright, but he's not in love with me. I'm just fun and games for him, a reckless relationship that will end up doing nothing but hurting his kids. And I curse myself for ever thinking we could be anything more.

Maybe it's not in his genes to love anyone except his dead wife.

Perhaps I'm just not good enough, and he's looking for a woman who can offer more. What that is, I'm unsure.

Whatever the reasons, Alexander will never truly be mine. I can't continue doing the things we're doing, knowing this is going nowhere.

He says through the door, "Okay. I'll check on you later tonight and make sure you're okay."

I warn, "Don't. I'm going to sleep. Let me be." I put on my headphones to drown out any further attempts from him to talk to me.

I put on sad music, silently crying into my pillow, wishing things could go back to earlier today when we were painting my room. I glance at the beautiful yellow color that gave me so much joy, and now represents my numbered days in this house.

I barely sleep throughout the night. I finally can't handle any more music and have to take off my headphones.

When the rooster crows, I hear Alexander get up. He knocks on the door softly, but I don't answer.

I wait until I hear the front door shut and then I glance out the window.

He walks across the yard to the corral. Mason and Jagger are already guiding two horses inside it.

I get out of bed and go into the bathroom. I take a shower, try to get rid of my puffy eyes, and get dressed. I do my hair and makeup, forcing myself to look as nice as possible for the boys' sake.

Over and over, I tell myself that no matter what, I need to stay away from Alexander. The communication I do have to have with him needs to be strictly professional.

All day, I dive into doing all the holiday things with the Cartwrights, faking a cheerful attitude the whole time. I avoid any moments where I might be alone with Willow, not wanting to answer any of her questions. Anytime she looks at me, it's all over her face. Ruby is just as concerned, but I assure her I was only sick with food poisoning, and today, I'm fine.

Every moment I spend with the boys makes my heart ache. I didn't think I could love two kids so much, but I do. I love them like they're my own. Soon, I'm going to be leaving them. It's just as painful as Alexander not loving me.

The excruciating agony digs into my soul, mixing with the ache I can't shake off. At the end of the day, I go back to my room, avoiding Alexander again, and I pull out my laptop.

I search for employment but don't know where to look. I debate about whether to stay in Texas or find something in another state, but I decide it's best if I can get as far away from Alexander as possible.

A position for an art teacher pops up. I click on it, and my heart races. It's in Alaska—a place I've never been. The frozen state seems like a good place for me to disappear. So, I apply for several nanny positions and a few teaching jobs.

Before I know it, people are responding to me, even though it's the week of Christmas. There's a shortage of teachers, and they're desperate to fill positions for the start of the new year.

I don't really want to return to the classroom. In a perfect world, I'd stay here or find another family to nanny for, but I need to be smart. I'm not independently wealthy, and I have no one to depend on but myself. I can't afford to be choosy right now.

One of the charter schools is offering not only employment but a subsidy for an apartment and food. It's a good deal on paper. I apply for it.

I pace my room for five minutes, then my computer dings. I check my laptop, and my stomach quivers. There's a response from one of the school principals.

*D**ear Miss Love,*

Are you free to have a video chat? I'd love to discuss all our school can offer someone with your qualifications. Plus, Alaska has so much to offer its residents.

Sincerely,

Mrs. Corrine Dillard

. . .

*M*y heart pounds hard against my chest. My fingers shake as I reply.

*D*ear Mrs. Dillard,

Yes, I can make a video chat happen. And I'd love to come to Alaska. When is a good time for us to speak?

Thank you for your consideration,

Phoebe Love

29

Alexander

Two Days Before Christmas

The last few days have been horrible. I can't eat or sleep. Anytime I try to talk to Phoebe, she avoids me. But even if she would talk to me, I'm unsure what I'd say.

I don't want her to leave, but I also can't risk my boys getting hurt. She means more to me than Cheyenne ever did, but I don't know how to mesh my dating life with my kids. They got handed the short stick when their mom died. I don't want to mess things up with Phoebe and then they get screwed again.

I've already destroyed us.

No, she just needs some time to cool off. Once she's ready to talk, we'll work through this.

I'm dying to pull her into my arms and try to make everything right, but we're past that point. This won't get worked out without a calm conversation.

She said she loved me.

I cringe, thinking about how I avoided acknowledging her admission.

I love her too. But what if we tell my sons about us and then things go wrong? Not only will I be devastated, but they'll be crushed. And I can't stand the thought of hurting them.

Yet I hate seeing Phoebe's expression every time she looks at me.

Several times, I've almost grabbed her and held her until she hugged me back. But the warning in her eyes stopped me.

I need to stop being such a pussy and figure this out.

I put Calypso back into his stall and latch the door. He nuzzles into my chest just as my phone rings.

I pull it out of my pocket and glance at the screen.

It's a number with an area code I don't recognize. I normally send unknown calls to voicemail, but something tells me to pick it up. So I answer, "Hello?"

A woman's voice comes through the phone. "Is this Mr. Alexander Cartwright?"

I sigh, stating, "It is, but I'm not interested."

"Wait! I'm not a telemarketer," the lady cries out.

"Alright. Can I ask who this is?"

"Sure. My name is Corrine Dillard. I'm calling on behalf of Alaskan Higher Hopes Charter School."

The hairs on my arms rise. I cautiously ask, "Okay, and why are you calling me?"

She chirps, "I've been told that you're Phoebe Love's current employer, is that correct?"

My gut drops and my pulse skyrockets. The air turns thick. I reach for the post and reply, "Yes, I am."

"Great," she says.

I stare at Calypso, feeling like my world's falling apart under my feet. I didn't think things could get worse after the last few days, but I was wrong.

She continues, "I've interviewed Ms. Love for a teaching position at our school. She's highly qualified and sounds like a delightful young woman."

I have to force myself to agree, not because it isn't the truth but because I don't want Phoebe to leave, much less go to Alaska. My voice cracks when I answer, "Yes, she is."

"She told me she's been taking care of your sons, Ace and Wilder?"

"That's correct," I affirm, closing my eyes.

She adds, "It sounds like you're raising two wonderful young gentlemen."

I clear my throat. "Thank you."

"On a scale of one to ten, what would you rate Ms. Love's work performance with your children?"

I grind my molars, not answering.

"Sir, are you still there?" Corrine inquires.

"Yes."

Another moment passes.

She asks, "Do you need me to repeat the question?"

"No, ma'am. I would give her a ten. Actually, no, I wouldn't. Scratch that. I'd give her a hundred. She's amazing with my children and my nieces and nephews. She's super talented at art. Plus, she understands everything to do with school that most adults these days don't understand, like TEKS math. But she also makes it fun for my kids to do their homework. So she doesn't just tutor and help them learn, they actually enjoy it," I babble, releasing a winded breath.

I can picture this woman beaming with her chipper voice as she replies, "Great. Well, thank you so much, Mr. Cartwright."

"Are you hiring her?" I blurt out, feeling sick.

"Well, I'm not supposed to tell you anything before I tell her."

"I won't say anything," I state, feeling more loss burning through my veins.

Corrine lowers her voice. "Okay, Mr. Cartwright. It'll be our little secret. But please don't ever tell her I told you, but yes. I'm thrilled to offer her the position. I'm ecstatic to welcome her to Alaska."

Phoebe's going to Alaska.

My stomach flips, and bile rises up my throat. I swallow it down, squeezing my eyes tighter. Dizziness hits me, and I hold the post tighter.

"Thank you so much for your time, Mr. Cartwright. Have a great day."

"Thank you. You too," I say and hang up. I stare at Calypso, feeling like the entire world just shifted.

Dad's voice tears me out of my ill thoughts. "When are you going to get that stick out of your ass, son?"

I spin toward him, snarling, "Meaning?"

He shakes his head, shuts the barn door, and steps closer. "I think it's time we had a talk."

"I'm not into being lectured, Dad."

He crosses his arms. "Put on your big boy pants, son."

"What?" I question, not into dealing with anything right now, especially taking shit from my old man.

He grunts. "From where I'm standing, you need to get hit over your head."

"Don't start with me," I say, still unsure what he's even talking about, but not caring anyway.

Phoebe's going to Alaska.

He crosses his arms. "Are you going to let that girl walk out of here and go to Alaska?"

My chest tightens.

He chuckles. "Do you really think everyone around here doesn't know what's going on between you two?"

Shock fills me. How would my parents know? They were gone most of the time Phoebe's been here.

He waves his hand in front of him. "Come on, son. Your mother and I weren't born yesterday. It's clear as day you two have gotten a little cozy while we've been gone. Hell, you were cozy while we were here for Thanksgiving."

My stomach flips, my thoughts running a mile a minute.

He steps closer. "What exactly is the problem here? You have a woman who's amazing with your kids and is crazy for you. And that's a hard thing to find, by the way. You're no peach pie on a daily basis."

"Gee, thanks, Dad," I mutter.

He grins, then continues, "Everyone in the family loves her. Why on Earth would you ever give her a reference to go to Alaska when she belongs right here?"

The thought of Phoebe bundled up, standing in snow, freezing her ass off in Alaska with some other man trying to warm her up is a new nightmare to haunt me.

He declares, "I'm not going to live forever, son. You want to spit out an answer to my question?"

"It's complicated," I claim.

He snorts. "It's only complicated if you make it complicated."

"It's not. I have two kids who lost their mother. I don't have the luxuries that other men have. I don't get to make mistakes."

He shakes his head. "Son, you're giving yourself way too much credit."

"What does that mean?" I snap.

He steps even closer and jabs me in the chest. "Do I have to spell everything out for you?"

"Apparently, you do," I retort.

"Your kids are fine. They love Phoebe. She would never hurt them."

"I didn't say she would hurt them. But if they find out we're together and then it doesn't work out between us, they're going to be crushed," I proclaim.

Dad shrugs his shoulders. "Yeah, they would. But they'll also be crushed if she leaves, and you'll be crushed for the rest of your life if you don't stop it."

I stay silent, my pulse shooting even higher.

Dad continues, "Wilder and Ace are fine. They'll be okay either way. But you're in a pickle, son. You can either crush them now and let her leave, or you can take a chance and follow your heart for once in your life."

"For once in my life? I've done that before," I remind him.

He softens his tone. "Alexander, we all lost when Clara died. But you can't keep yourself from loving someone else just because of one tragedy. And I've seen you two together. You and Phoebe are like peanut butter and jelly. You just go together. So stop being a fool and do something about it. Because if that girl leaves, you're not finding another one like her."

I stare at him with my heart hurting at the thought of Phoebe flying off to Alaska and never seeing her again. Then it finally sinks in.

I can't let her go.

"You're right," I say, and brush past Dad, yanking open the barn door.

"Good, but she's not here. She took the kids over to Evelyn's. You might want to go over there," he informs me.

"It's okay. I have somewhere I need to go first," I claim, going right to the truck. I slide onto the driver's seat, turn on the engine, and peel out the driveway, passing the gate quickly.

I go into town, park in front of the jeweler's shop, and take a deep breath. My heart beats faster.

What if she says no?

Don't be a fucking pussy, I tell myself and get out of the truck.

I go into the jeweler's, my stomach flipping with nerves, but knowing this is what I want.

Old man Denny looks up. He smiles, and his wrinkles expand. He booms, "Alexander, good to see you. Looking for some last-minute Christmas gifts?"

I announce, "It's not a Christmas gift. I need an engagement ring."

His eyes widen. He chuckles. "Who's the lucky girl? Is it that nanny you've been seen around town with?"

I groan and shake my head. "Does anything in this town stay quiet?"

"Nope. You know how it is around here," he states and then opens a glass case. He pulls out a box that has a dozen rings in it, asking, "What kind of ring does your girl like?"

I step closer and admit, "I don't know. She's never told me."

He chuckles. "Well, that's a keeper. How many women don't tell their man what kind of ring they want?"

"She doesn't exactly know I'm here."

"That's good. She's not supposed to know you're here," he assures me.

My palms sweat as I stare at the rings.

Denny says, "Let me help you out, son. Tell me about her."

"She's beautiful. She's great with my kids. They love her and she loves them. She takes care of us. She's a super-talented artist, fun, and always happy. Well, except for when I'm pissing her off. But she's the most amazing person I've ever met." I stop and realize how I probably sound. I look away, taking a couple of deep breaths.

Denny taps the glass. "Sounds like you've got a keeper. Now, I think this is a ring you should take a look at." He holds up a gold band with a flower pattern made of diamonds.

I take it from him and study it, admitting, "It's beautiful."

He asks, "Can you see it on her finger?"

I imagine it. "Yeah, I can."

"Can you see her face lighting up when she sees it?"

I think about how Phoebe's face would light up when I present her with the ring, making me feel good for the first time in days. So I nod. "Yeah, I think she will."

He picks up another ring. It has one large stone and is flashier. He asks, "And what about this?"

I try to imagine it on Phoebe's finger. I shake my head. "No, that's not her."

He goes through the rings one by one until the only ring left is the one he originally picked out.

I question, "How did you know this was the ring?"

He chuckles. "Son, I've been doing this for nearly forty years now. You think you're the first man to come in here not knowing what kind of ring their woman wants?"

"Point taken," I say.

"Great. Do you want me to wrap this up nice and pretty? Make it look like a Christmas gift?"

I shake my head. "No. I already got her a different gift for Christmas. This is just from me."

He grins. "Good call." He puts it in a black box and hands it to me. "Take good care of that. That's the only one of its kind."

"I will, sir."

I pay for the ring and leave. I put the ring in the console of my truck and then drive to Evelyn's.

"Dad, what are you doing here?" Ace says as I walk in.

I answer, "I need to steal you and your brother for a little bit."

"Where are we going?" Wilder questions.

"It's a surprise. Come on."

Phoebe looks at me in question, and my sister does too.

Evelyn demands, "Where are you taking them?"

"None of your business. Take some time off, Phoebe," I say, barely refraining from reaching out, grabbing her, and kissing her.

She gives me another confused look, and I take the boys to the truck.

We drive to my house, and they get out of the cab. I grab the ring and go inside. I sit them down at the kitchen table.

Wilder asks, "Dad, you took us away from the fun to lecture us?"

I chuckle. "No, I took you away to talk about something serious."

Ace leans closer. "Did you find a stallion for Phoebe?"

I chuckle again. "No. Not yet, son."

"Aw, man. That's what we need to get her for Christmas. Everything else we got her doesn't seem cool enough," he claims.

"Well, I know she'll love the presents you got her. And I have another gift for her. But it's not for Christmas."

"What is it?" Wilder questions.

I reach into my pocket and put the box on the table.

The boys glance at it, then at each other. I open the box and wait, trying to gauge their reactions.

Ace grabs it first. "This is what you're giving Phoebe?"

"Yes."

"Are you going to ask her to marry you, Dad?" Wilder questions.

"I am. How do you boys feel about that?"

"Yes!" Ace exclaims. He jumps up and pumps his hand in the air.

"So she's not going to leave?" Wilder asks.

I hold my hands up. "I'm not sure. Don't get too excited yet."

Wilder's eyes narrow. "Why?"

"Sit back down," I say to Ace.

He obeys, and the boys' expressions turn serious.

I admit, "I might've screwed up a little bit with Phoebe."

"Like you took her on a bad date or something?" Ace questions.

I nod. "Yeah, something like that."

"What did you do, Dad?" Wilder demands, disapproval on his expression.

"That's between Phoebe and me. So I'm not sure if she's going to accept my proposal. I don't want you guys to be disappointed if she doesn't. And if she doesn't want to marry me, that's on me, not her. But I thought you should know. I don't want to hide the fact that I love her from you anymore."

Ace grins. "Well then, make her stay, Dad."

"Yeah, all women love diamonds. Just give her the ring. She'll be fine," Wilder states.

I chuckle and tousle his hair. "You have a lot to learn about women, son."

"Dad, go ask her now," Ace orders.

I shake my head. "These things have to be done in the right way."

They stare at me.

"So you boys will keep this a secret, right?" I ask.

They both nod their agreement.

Ace says, "Your secret's safe with us."

"I'll make sure he doesn't spill it," Wilder adds.

Ace smacks him across the shoulder. "I wouldn't spill the beans."

Wilder gives him his cocky Jagger grin. "Yeah, yeah, yeah."

"Okay, so the secret's just between the three of us," I tell them.

Ace asks, "Who else knows?"

"No one. Well, the jeweler knows. That's it. So it's just the three of us. No other Cartwright knows," I repeat.

Wilder grins, as does Ace.

"But, Dad, ask her soon," Ace orders.

"Yeah, before Christmas, so it's not cheesy. Because you got her a different gift, right? That shouldn't be her Christmas gift too," Wilder declares.

"Why does that matter?" Ace questions.

"Duh. Because then she gets more gifts and will want to stay," Wilder claims.

"Mmm, I don't think Phoebe's going to decide to stay or go based on the number of gifts she receives," I assert.

"I would," Wilder says.

I shake my head and sigh. "That's not right, and someday when you grow up, you'll realize that."

He shrugs.

"Alright. I'm taking you back to Evelyn's, but mum's the word. Okay?"

They agree, and I drop them back off. I don't go inside. The rest of the day, I try to figure out when I'll ask Phoebe. I think about all the special things I could do and try to make happen, but I can't do most of them before Christmas.

Also, I know my time is running out. The clock is ticking. I don't know when Phoebe will leave for Alaska. But if she accepts a teaching job, my guess is she'll have to be there come the new year.

All day, I stress over how to ask her. When dinnertime comes, everyone is in the dining room.

The entire meal, I stare at Phoebe, but she continues to avoid me, blinking hard several times.

I know she's hurting, and it kills me. When the table is cleared and dessert is brought out, I rise and clear my throat. "Can everyone take a break for a minute?"

Everyone stares at me.

I move over so I'm in front of Phoebe, and hold out my hand. "Stand up for a minute, Pheebs."

She pins her eyebrows together with fear on her face. She utters, "What are you doing?"

"Just stand up. Please?" I beg.

She cautiously takes my hand and rises.

My stomach flips, and I announce, "There's something I need to tell you, and I should have told you this a while ago. And I definitely should have told you this the other day."

Confusion replaces the fear as she glances at my family and then back at me.

I put my hand on her cheek. "I love you. My family loves you. The boys love you. But most of all, *I* love you. And I'm not good with words. Everybody knows that." I pull the box out of my pocket and flip the lid off. I get down on my knee.

She puts her hand over her mouth, gaping at me.

I keep my hand in hers. "Pheebs, the moment you walked in here, my life got better. All of our lives got better. And I know I screwed up last week. Trust me, I know. But I love you, and you're more than any woman I could have imagined."

A tear slips down her cheek and her lips tremble.

I continue, "I want you to forgive me and be my wife. Please, forgive me. Will you marry me?"

She stares at me, shaking, glancing between the ring and me.

"If you don't like the ring, I can get a different one," I blurt out.

"No! I love the ring," she replies.

My chest tightens. "Then, will you marry me?"

"Yes, I'll marry you," she says, and more tears slide down her cheek.

My family erupts in cheers.

I get off my knee and pull her into my arms, kissing her until Wilder shouts, "Dad, gross. Come on."

I retreat.

She beams at me, laughing.

The rest of the night is spent partying with my family and my soon-to-be wife staring at me with love and happiness in her eyes. And everything I've ever wanted is finally in front of me.

30

Phoebe

Christmas Eve

*A*lexander sneaks up behind me, sliding his arm around my waist. He murmurs in my ear, "What are you doing?"

I turn my head and look up, smiling, feeling so much joy and happiness. I'm still unable to believe he asked me to marry him. I answer, "I have to get changed."

"Phoebe, I have a serious question to ask you."

"Why does that make me nervous?"

He grins. "Why are your clothes still in this room?"

I glance at the closet, then back at him, "I don't know. Are they not supposed to be?"

He shakes his head. "No, they're supposed to be in my room. Don't worry, I've made plenty of room in my closet."

"You have?" I ask, grinning like a fool.

"Yep, the boys helped me all morning."

"They did?"

"Sure did. Now, let's get this stuff moved over." He releases me and steps in front of my closet, grabbing a big armful of clothes on hangers.

"I'll get her shoes," Ace states, running into the room.

"Should I go through your dresser?" Wilder questions.

"No, I'll do the dresser," I say, not wanting him to go through my panties.

Alexander reprimands, "Yeah, don't go through her dresser. That's private stuff."

Wilder holds his hands up. "Sorry, just trying to help."

I tousle his hair. "It's okay. I appreciate it. If you don't mind, please help your dad with my clothes in the closet."

"Okay." He goes over and pulls a pile of shirts off the shelf.

Alexander steps in front of me. He kisses me on the lips. Then, he grins at me mischievously. He teases, "Do you want *me* to go through your dresser?"

I laugh. "No, I got it."

"Okay. I made room in my dresser too." He wiggles his eyebrows.

I laugh, and more joy fills me. It's like I'm living a fairy tale. I have two boys I love and a man who's way more than I ever could have expected.

It only takes a little time before all my stuff is neatly organized in Alexander's closet and dresser.

Wilder asks, "What will we do with your bedroom now?"

"It's going back to the guest room, duh," Ace states.

"Maybe it could be my man cave," Wilder declares.

Alexander arches his eyebrows. "You need a man cave?"

"Yeah, every man needs a man cave."

"According to whom?" Alexander asks.

"TikTok, duh."

Alexander groans. "I told you not to be on that app. There's craziness on there."

Wilder shrugs.

Alexander crosses his arms. "I mean it. I told you you're not allowed to use social media until you're older. How did you get on there anyway?"

"Ah, Dad, everybody at school is on it," Wilder whines.

"I don't care. How did you get on it?" Alexander repeats.

Wilder doesn't answer.

Alexander warns, "I'm waiting for an answer."

He finally admits, "Uncle Jagger and I were looking up stuff when I stayed at his house."

Alexander sighs. "You're not staying at his place again."

"Aw, Dad, come on!"

I stifle a giggle.

Alexander turns to me. "You find this funny? There's inappropriate stuff on that site eleven-year-olds shouldn't see."

I try to keep a straight face and shake my head. "No."

"I'm almost twelve!" Wilder claims.

Alexander narrows his eyes further. "It'll still be inappropriate."

"Ugh. It's so unfair. The other kids in my class—"

"I suggest you change the subject," Alexander threatens.

Wilder huffs. "Fine. But can I turn the room into my man cave?"

Alexander shakes his head. "No. Now, it's time to tend to the horses. Boys, you want to come?"

They practically run out the door.

Alexander pulls me to him and slides his hand in my hair, giving me another long kiss until I'm breathless. "Don't forget you're mine, Phoebe," he says and squeezes my ass.

I giggle, shoving his chest. "I won't. Now, go."

He grabs my hand and stares at the ring. "It looks good on you. It's just how I imagined."

I bite on my smile. It really is the perfect ring. I never imagined what my ring would look like, but Alexander nailed it.

"Admit it. I did good," he teases.

I rise on my tiptoes and give him another peck. "You did more than good. It's perfect," I praise.

He grins, gives me another kiss, and pats my ass. "I'll see you at breakfast."

"Sounds good."

I stroll over to the main house and go into the kitchen. Georgia's been baking all week, and this morning she's making sugar-free muffins for Sebastian.

"Hey," she says, beaming at me.

"Hi. Where's everyone else?"

"Paisley and Willow went out last night. They didn't get in until late." Georgia's lips twitch. She adds, "Ruby went to give them some headache medication and get them out of bed. Evelyn called to say she's struggling a bit too. She'll be over later."

I admit, "It's strange only seeing one person in this kitchen."

She nods. "Yeah, I know. I don't think I've ever been in it alone before."

"Really?"

She shakes her head. "No, not that I can recall. By the way, I'm happy you're joining the family."

"Thanks, so am I."

She chirps, "It's a great family."

"Yeah."

She softly adds, "We're lucky," and a little sadness crosses her expression.

I cautiously agree. "We are. Are you okay?"

She forces a smile, answering, "Yes. I just get a little nostalgic sometimes around the holidays, thinking about my parents and grandparents."

A wave of sadness hits me too. "I can understand that."

She tilts her head. "Sebastian said Alexander told him your mom and sister are in different places?"

I take a deep breath and release it, admitting, "Yeah. I wish they were closer. They were far away from me when I lived in Pismo Beach as well, but I could at least drive to see them. I was kind of in the middle of where they both were."

"Oh, I'm sorry to hear that," she says, offering me a sympathetic look.

I force a smile, stating, "It's okay. I've gotten used to it."

"Well, I'm glad you're joining the family." She hugs me, and I squeeze her back.

"Thank you. I heard your cupcake business is doing well. That must've been scary starting a business all on your own."

"It was, but I had Sebastian by my side. He's a business whiz."

"He says you are too," I tell her.

She laughs. "I'm learning a lot, but I couldn't have done all I've done without him."

"It's nice that you two work together so well."

"Yeah, it is." She turns on the mixer.

I open the fridge and take out the bacon, eggs, and other ingredients to start breakfast.

The other women arrive to help, and we spend the morning cooking and laughing. Around ten o'clock, I ring the bell and shout, "Breakfast!"

The men slowly filter in, and soon enough, we're all around the big dining room table, including the kids. The usual joyful presence of the Cartwrights fills the room, and

I soak every detail in, still not believing this will now be my family. I get to stay here with Alexander and the boys and everyone else, and nothing has ever made me so happy.

After breakfast, Alexander pulls me aside, declaring, "Hey, I have a surprise for you."

"You do?"

"I do. We have to go somewhere though."

"On Christmas Eve?" I ask.

He glances at his watch. "Yeah. Don't worry. We won't miss anything, and you'll be happy, I think."

"You think?" I ask, my stomach filling with nerves.

His expression turns anxious. "Yeah, I'm pretty sure."

"Why am I nervous all of a sudden?" I ask.

He chuckles. "No reason to be. Come on." He kisses my hand and leads me to the front door. He helps me into my coat, and we go outside and get in his truck.

He turns on country music, and we sing on the way into town. Then he pulls into the lot of a facility called Crossroads and parks near a building decorated for Christmas.

"Where are we?" I question.

He glances at me, again looking nervous.

"You're making me feel like I'm in a mystery movie," I tease, but my anxiety grows.

He smiles, then it falls, his expression turning serious. He strokes my cheek. "You know how you said your mom and sister are far away?"

"Yes," I say, unsure where he's going with this, and finding it odd I'm talking about them twice in one day when I don't talk about them very often.

He studies me.

My pulse shoots through the roof. "Alexander, what's going on?"

He releases a breath. "I arranged for a tour of this facility. It's a long-term home. They have different solutions for different needs. And it's the best in the county."

I break out in goose bumps. I glance at the building again, then at him. Still confused, I cautiously say, "Okay?"

He announces, "I thought we could move your mom and sister here."

I gape at him, the blood draining from my face.

"Would you like that?"

"Are you being serious?" I manage to get out, my voice shaking with emotion, my eyes tearing up.

"Yes. I wouldn't joke about this."

"But I can't pay for this place. This looks really nice," I fret.

He grunts. "Don't worry about the money, Pheebs. We have plenty."

I look at him as if he's crazy.

He declares, "You're going to be my wife. Your family should be near us just like mine."

Tears spill down my cheeks. "Alexander, are you being serious right now? I swear to God, this is a really cruel joke if you're not being serious."

He shakes his head. "No, baby girl. This is real. As long as you approve. But let's go tour it, okay?"

I can't say anything. I'm too caught up in emotions and speechless. He gets out of the truck and comes around to open my door. He helps me out, then pulls me into him and quickly kisses me. "Are you okay?"

"I just can't believe you're serious about moving them here."

"I am."

"And we can afford this for the long term, not just for a week or something?"

Amusement lights his features. "Yes. And we haven't gone through finances yet, but we should do that soon. Why don't we do it after the holidays though? I don't like mixing business with Christmas fun."

I stare at him like he's crazy. I start adding up what a facility like this might cost for just a day, much less a month, a year, or several, and times it by two.

"Come on, baby girl," he says, tearing me out of the spreadsheet forming in my head. He slides his arm around my waist and leads me into the facility.

Shawna, the director, has me sign documentation to transfer my mother's and sister's records so we can discuss their needs in more detail. We spend several hours on a tour, then return to her office.

Her assistant hands her two folders. "Here's the information you requested on the basic medical needs."

I gape.

Shawna takes them. "Thank you."

Her assistant leaves and shuts the door.

I blurt out, "How did you get these so quickly?"

"We know how to do things pretty thoroughly around here," she says with a wink.

I stare at her, still unable to believe I'm having this conversation and that my mom and sister might be right down the road from me.

She takes a while reviewing their charts.

I sit on pins and needles, hoping nothing will prevent my mom and sister from moving to this facility. It's beyond nice, and there's no doubt in my mind they would get better care here.

Alexander holds my hand. His other arm is firm around my shoulders. He kisses the top of my head.

I glance at him.

He orders, "Stop worrying."

Shawna glances at us and puts the file folder down. She declares, "It doesn't seem like there's anything here that we wouldn't be able to handle."

"Really?" I question.

"Yes. Would you like your mom and your sister to live here? Mr. Cartwright has assured me that you can pay for an expedited transfer."

I glance over at him once again, gaping. It's like he's thought of everything.

He chuckles. "Pheebs, you have to answer."

I ask him, "Are you sure about this? Because once we do this, I don't know if I'll be able to get them back into the facility they're in."

His face turns serious. "Yes. As long as your mom and sister need medical care, we will take care of it. They will be here near us if that's what you want. They will have the best care available. Now, is this what you want?"

Tears escape and roll down my face. I can barely answer. I'm overcome with emotions—mostly gratitude and shock.

"You just have to say yes, baby girl."

"Y-yes. Please," I choke out, crying harder.

He pulls me into him and holds me, telling Shawna, "Please start the process."

Shawna smiles. "Great. I'm going to give you two a moment." She rises and leaves her office, shutting the door behind her.

I'm hit with a wave of relief. I sob against his chest, wondering how I got so lucky. Years of guilt and frustration swirl inside me.

He lets me cry for a while, and I finally retreat from his hold. He grabs tissues off the director's desk, dabs my cheeks, then teases, "Don't worry. This isn't your Christmas present." He winks, and mischief lights up his expression.

"Don't be crazy. This is more than a Christmas gift. You never have to get me another gift again," I quickly proclaim, meaning it.

He laughs. "Don't be silly."

"Alexander, I don't know how I'll ever repay you for this. This is beyond generous," I declare.

"Pheebs, you're going to be my wife. There's no paying me back. Our families are each other's, and we're going to take care of our families. Understand?"

More emotions hit me. He swipes a fresh tear that escapes my eye. "No more tears. Come on. I didn't mean to make you cry. I'm sorry."

"You're not doing a good job not making me cry," I tease, then wipe another one. I blink hard until they stop, then I take a deep breath.

He rises and reaches for me. I take his hand and stand next to him. He says, "Let's go home, baby girl. After all..."

I arch my eyebrows.

"It's Christmas!" he shouts gleefully.

I laugh, wondering how this man, who loves me so hard, could ever have been put in front of me.

EPILOGUE

Alexander

Early June

"$\mathcal{B}$y the power vested in me by the great state of Texas, I now declare you Mr. and Mrs. Alexander Cartwright. Sir, you may kiss your bride," Santiago, the wedding officiant, declares.

I'm overflowing with happiness. I stare at my beaming wife, who's made a more beautiful bride than I could have ever imagined.

Her hair is in a French twist, curling around her face. Her fitted, white lace dress has a low back and a small train, perfect for the June weather. The sun shines over the lake, and our family surrounds us.

I reach for her and kiss her until her knees weaken, holding her close to me, and the others cheer loudly.

I pull back and realize I've never seen her look so happy. She lights up my life like she has since the first moment I saw her, even when I didn't realize it.

We walk down the pink carpet until we reach the end. The guests all take their turns giving us their congratulations and then we go into the tent.

The interior is dotted with regular tables and several tall cocktail tables. Music plays softly in the background, and my bride continues to beam as she talks to her mom.

A caregiver is with her, making sure she's okay. But since she got to Texas, the home we chose for her has provided better medical care. She's been allowed to leave more often with a caregiver, and it was a big deal to Phoebe that she was here.

The boys run up to us, each grabbing Phoebe's hands.

Ace exclaims, "We have a surprise for you!"

"Yeah, you're going to love it," Wilder adds.

Phoebe's eyes widen. "Oh, what is it?"

"You have to come with us," Wilder insists.

She looks at me. I hold my hands in the air, fibbing, "I don't know anything about this."

Her eyes narrow. "Why do I feel like you're lying?"

I wiggle my eyebrows.

She laughs. "Okay, where are we going?"

"Actually, you have to close your eyes," I say.

I take out a white scarf and tie it around her head, covering her eyes.

"Wow. I don't know if I should be nervous or excited."

"Be excited! Be really, really excited!" Ace answers.

"Yeah. You're not going to find this anywhere in the world. Well, very few places," Wilder adds.

She laughs again. It's both anxious and animated, and I love everything about it.

The photographer steps in front of us. "Can I take a picture?"

"You sure can," I say, and stand behind Phoebe. The boys step closer to her.

She asks, "Am I getting my picture taken right now?"

"Yep. Smile, baby girl."

The photographer snaps several shots. He says, "Oh, those turned out great. You're going to love them, Mrs. Cartwright."

Her grin grows. "Thank you."

I pat her ass, and she jumps slightly.

I say, "I think it's time we get this surprise revealed."

"Come on, Phoebe. Don't worry. We'll make sure you don't fall or anything," Ace assures.

"Why, thank you."

"Yeah, we don't want a bloody bride," Wilder declares.

I groan. "Way to go to the worst scenario possible."

He grins, giving me his cocky Jagger look again.

The boys lead her to the golf cart.

Ace orders, "Time to get in."

She reaches in front of her.

I inform her, "You're at the golf cart. Just sit down carefully." I help her into the seat.

The boys and I get in the cart as well. They hop on the back, and I take the driver's spot. I maneuver the cart through the trees and toward the barn. I pull out of the woods and park, telling her, "Wait for me to get out. I don't want you hurting yourself."

"Okay," she agrees.

I get out, quickly move to her side, and carefully help her to her feet.

Ace and Wilder have excited expressions on their faces, and I can't help but grin. They've been dying to reveal their surprise. I've called them Mason and Jagger more than once, telling them they'll be just like their uncles if they can't keep their mouths shut. But they have.

The boys step back next to Phoebe, and each takes one of her hands again. I lead the way, opening the barn door.

She steps closer and wrinkles her nose. She asks, "Why do I smell hay and manure?"

"We're not telling," Wilder answers.

"Be careful with your heels," I advise, then say, "Hold on a minute." I realize her fancy white shoes aren't meant for a barn. So I scoop her up in my arms.

She yelps, laughing.

"I got you, baby girl."

"Whoa, thanks," she says with a giggle.

"Those stilettos are going to sink if you attempt to walk."

"Okay. Why are we in the barn?"

"You'll see. Be patient like you always tell us," Ace scolds.

She puts her hands in the air. "Okay, okay."

I kiss her on the lips, and I can't wait to pick her up and take her to the cabin where we decided to spend the first night. All I want to do is make love to my wife, but I know I'll have to wait all day for that.

We finally step inside the barn, and I ask the boys, "Are you ready?"

One of the horses lets out a loud neigh, and Phoebe jumps in my arms.

I laugh. "Don't worry. You're not going to get bitten by any horses."

She tilts her head, smirking.

She's actually become quite the rider. We go on rides almost daily. Sometimes I can't go, but she'll go with the boys after school. But more often than not, she's on a horse.

Wilder instructs, "Okay, take the blindfold off."

I release it.

Phoebe blinks a few times.

Ace orders, "Look! He's yours!"

She gapes at the white horse.

Wilder announces, "It's not just any stallion. It's a rare one! Look at how white he is."

She gazes at the huge animal.

My stomach flips. "Do you like him?" I've scoured everywhere, looking for the stallion, and I'll be just as crushed as the boys if she doesn't like him.

She continues to gape.

"Aren't you excited? You have a stallion," Ace asks.

She stares a little longer, then looks back at me. "Are you serious?"

"Yeah, I thought you needed a stallion," I cockily state and then wink.

She laughs and looks back at the horse.

Wilder suggests, "You should get on him...feel him out."

I grunt. "Phoebe's not getting on the horse in her wedding dress."

She looks at the stallion again.

He steps forward.

She reaches out and pats him, then says, "Wow. You guys really got him for me?"

Ace answers, "Yes! But Dad wouldn't let us name him. He said you have to name him."

"I get to name him?"

"Yeah, it's your horse," Wilder says.

She stares at her gift, petting it.

He tries to nuzzle her, but I move her backward.

"Don't want you smelling like a horse on your wedding day."

"What are you going to name him?" Wilder questions.

"I don't know. Can I think about it? It's a big decision," Phoebe says.

"Okay. Do you love him?" Ace asks.

She nods. "Absolutely. I can't believe you guys did this for me."

"Yes! We knew you'd love him," Wilder says, and Ace gives him a high five.

She leans back to whisper in my ear, "I'm so excited. Now I have two stallions." She bats her eyelashes, smirking.

I grin. "Yeah, and the most important one is waiting for you. He's been waiting for you for a long time."

She beams at me, and my heart swells.

Everything in my life is perfect. I have my kids, my family, and now, I have my wife. She's a woman I never knew existed until my family forced me to hire her, but I discovered I need her more than I could ever have imagined.

* * *

Quick note from Maggie:

Thank you so much for reading Holiday Hire! I really hope it brought you all of the holiday feels! Alexander and Phoebe were a blast to write and I really hope you enjoyed reading their story.

You don't have to say goodbye to Alexander and Phoebe just yet, you can read about them and the rest of the Cartwright family in Willow's Book - Holiday Rider - which will release on November 1, 2025.

But before you go, have you read Georgia and Sebastian's story in Holiday Hoax? If not, read it now!

And did you know that you can grab your paperbacks, ebooks, and audio at a deep discount by visiting Maggie's personal bookstore?
https://maggiecolebookstore.com/

HOLIDAY RIDER

Ready for Willow Cartwright's story?

Get ready because this holiday romance is going to be hot, hot, hot!

You probably got the notion Willow's obsessed with bull riders.

She IS.

Pre-order your copy now and don't miss out when this bad boy goes live!

CAN I ASK YOU A HUGE FAVOR?

Would you be willing to leave me a review?

I would be forever grateful as one positive review on Amazon is like buying the book a hundred times! Reader support is the lifeblood for Indie authors and provides us the feedback we need to give readers what they want in future stories!

Your positive review means the world to me! So thank you from the bottom of my heart!

CLICK TO REVIEW

MORE BY MAGGIE COLE

Grab e-books, paperbacks, special editions, and audio at discounted prices!
Visit https://maggiecolebookstore.com/

Holiday Novels

Holiday Hoax - A Fake Marriage Billionaire Romance

Holiday Hire - A Billionaire Single Dad Nanny Romance

Holiday Rider - Coming November 1, 2025

Wilted Kingdom Duet- (*A Dark College Billionaire Romance*)

Seeds of Malice-Book One

Thorns of Malice-Book Two

Club Indulgence Duet (*A Dark Billionaire Romance*)

The Auction (Book One)

The Vow (Book Two)

Mafia Wars Ireland

Illicit King (Brody)-Book One

Illicit Captor (Aidan)-Book Two

Illicit Heir (Devin)-Book Three

Illicit Monster (Tynan)-Book Four

Mafia Wars New York - A Dark Mafia Series

Toxic (Dante's Story) - Book One

Immoral (Gianni's Story) - Book Two

Crazed (Massimo's Story) - Book Three

Carnal (Tristano's Story) - Book Four

Flawed (Luca's Story) - Book Five

Mafia Wars - A Dark Mafia Series

Ruthless Stranger (Maksim's Story) - Book One

Broken Fighter (Boris's Story) - Book Two

Cruel Enforcer (Sergey's Story) - Book Three

Vicious Protector (Adrian's Story) - Book Four

Savage Tracker (Obrecht's Story) - Book Five

Unchosen Ruler (Liam's Story) - Book Six

Perfect Sinner (Nolan's Story) - Book Seven

Brutal Defender (Killian's Story) - Book Eight

Deviant Hacker (Declan's Story) - Book Nine

Relentless Hunter (Finn's Story) - Book Ten

Behind Closed Doors (Former Military Now International Rescue)

Depths of Destruction - Book One

Marks of Rebellion - Book Two

Haze of Obedience - Book Three

Cavern of Silence - Book Four

Stains of Desire - Book Five

Risks of Temptation - Book Six

Brooks Family Saga

Kiss of Redemption- Book One

Sins of Justice - Book Two

Acts of Manipulation - Book Three

Web of Betrayal - Book Four

Masks of Devotion - Book Five

Roots of Vengeance - Book Six

It's Complicated Series (Chicago Billionaires)

My Boss the Billionaire- Book One

Forgotten by the Billionaire - Book Two

My Friend the Billionaire - Book Three

Forbidden Billionaire - Book Four

The Groomsman Billionaire - Book Five

Secret Mafia Billionaire - Book Six

ALL IN BILLIONAIRES

The Rule - Book One

The Secret - Book Two

The Crime - Book Three

The Lie - Book Four

The Trap - Book Five

The Gamble - Book Six

STAND ALONE NOVELLA

JUDGE ME NOT - A Billionaire Single Mom Christmas Novella

ABOUT THE AUTHOR

Amazon Bestselling Author

Maggie Cole is committed to bringing her readers alphalicious book boyfriends and fiercely strong heroines.

She's been called the literary master of steamy romance. Her books are full of raw emotion, suspense, and will always keep you wanting more. She is a masterful storyteller of contemporary romance and loves writing about broken people who rise above the ashes. Her books can often be found hanging out in the top 100, even years after publication.

Maggie lives in Florida with her son. She loves tennis, yoga, paddleboarding, boating, other water activities, and everything naughty.

Her current series were written in the order below:

- All In (Stand Alone Billionaire Novels with Entwined Characters)
- It's Complicated (Stand Alone Billionaire Novels with Entwined Characters)
- Brooks Family Saga- A Dark Family Saga – Read In Order (Each book has different couples)
- Behind Closed Doors-A Dark Military Protector Romance – Read in Order (Each book has different couples))
- Mafia Wars (Stand Alone Novels with Interconnecting Plot and Entwined Characters)
- Mafia Wars New York (Stand Alone Novels with Interconnecting Plot and Entwined Characters)
- Club Indulgence Duet A Dark Billionaire Duet – Read in Order (Same Couple)
- Mafia Wars Ireland (Stand Alone Novels with Interconnecting Plot and Entwined Characters)
- Wilted Kingdom Duet-A Dark Bully Billionaire Duet

Maggie Cole's Newsletter
Sign up here!

Maggie Cole's Website
authormaggiecole.com

Get your copies of Maggie Cole signed paperbacks!
maggiecolebookstore.com

Pickup your Maggie Cole Merch!
Click here!

Made in United States
Orlando, FL
04 December 2024

54988847R00268